HOW BLUEGRASS MUSIC DESTROYED MY LIFE

HOW BLUEGRASS MUSIC DESTROYED MY LIFE

STORIES BY JOHN FAHEY

Chicago: DRAG CITY INCORPORATED
2000

Drag City Web Address: www.dragcity.com

Printed in the United States of America

Library of Congress Catalog Card Number: 99-75130
ISBN 0-9656183-2-3

Third Edition

Editor's Note

John Fahey writes like no one else in the world. Or at least no one else in *this* world. You don't have to get far into one of John's stories before you realize that he travels between worlds with the same nonchalance most of us feel catching a bus to work. There is an alien energy that courses through his language—if John needs a word that doesn't exist, he makes one up. Ordinary rules do not apply here. For this reason, editorial changes to the original text were kept to a minimum.

This project started with a box of sticky and suspiciously stained papers, covered edge to edge with the intense and feverish prose you will find in these pages. It's all kind of a blur now, but it seems as though it must have taken an act of some wild brand of voodoo witchcraft to transform that box into the finished book you are now holding. Admittedly, it was a slow-moving and temperamental magic that would not be rushed. I am deeply indebted to the following people for helping to push the whole thing along: Dean Blackwood, Gene Booth, Byron Coley, Melissa Stephenson, David Grubbs, Dan Koretzky, Jim O'Rourke, Dan Osborn, Jeremy Pickett, Philip Smith, and Mary Lass Stewart.

John's work resists categorization—it is part memoir, part personal essay, part fiction, part manifesto. His worlds have their own logic, religious dogma, and mythological history. He succeeds in creating a surreal landscape that is as hilarious as it is frightening. Transcribing these stories was a bit like following John through some of the dodgiest parts of town. Still, I learned that he always knows where he's going. And he's a wonderful tour guide. But be prepared: John talks to demons. They call him up on the telephone. Lucky for us, he likes to talk back.

Damian Rogers, December 1999

Introduction

One origin of this book (and in true Fahey fashion, there are many!) could be found on my phone line in '96 as I was talking to Fahey about various bits of music, film, and their combinations, when we came upon the subject of *Zabriskie Point*. I'd always found it an amusing, and misguided, attempt to "critique" materialistic and hedonistic America. John had a different angle. "Antonioni? Aw, I punched that guy out." I couldn't believe my ears. *What?* He proceeded to tell me a version of the story you'll find in this very book, of how he flew to Rome, was subjected to long dailies of the desert "orgy" scene, his attempts at recording music for it, and his subsequent argument with Antonioni that left him reeling to the floor. I was impressed. "That's incredible John." "Aw, yeah, I wrote it down, I got it around here somewhere. I got a bunch of stuff." I knew his liner notes of course—incredible free-thinking rants and dissections—so I expressed my interest in seeing them, and he said he'd get some to me. Great. Wait. Another phone call. "Aw, I threw a bunch of them out, but I went down to the garbage and got you some. I'll send them." I laughed, thinking it was John's self-deprecating humor. A week later I got a Fed Ex package from John. I ripped it open to find a mass of pages: bent, torn, and, not so oddly, stained with garbage. *Oh, man....* I sat down immediately, and poured through them. I couldn't believe what I was reading. They were brilliant—more direct than anything in his liner notes, but more expansive, and definitely more, for lack of a better word, revealing.

Page forward a few months, and we're in Southern California doing some shows. After a San Diego show, I went back with Fahey to his hotel to do a little taping of him talking, and get some more info about these stories, but instead I learned how they could come to be in the first place. The hotel used those credit card-like keys, and John's was severely lacking in room-number-info, so he proceeded to do what any sensible person would do: he started trying every door. After a few futile attempts, we heard a bustle from inside one of the rooms. "Who's out there?" Wide-eyed, John bolted. Halfway down the hall he turned around, and called to no one in particular, "Isn't there any elves around here that can help us?" He turned a corner and was gone. In what seemed like seconds I heard a distant call from behind me, "Jim, over heeeeere." I turned to see that John had somehow reached the other end of the building in seconds flat. It took me a few minutes to reach him, and he was already thumbing through the bulging wad of papers jutting from his T-shirt pocket, like someone looking to a daisy for a confirmation of love. "No… no…no…." Each "no" punctuated with John dropping the receipt/number/advertisement/random scribble to the floor. Occasionally something seemed worth keeping and he returned it to his pocket. Without a word, he turned and walked on, leaving Mount Papyrus behind. This was getting strange. Again I heard a call from behind me, "Jim, over heeeeeeere." He had found his room, so I rambled over with the two show promoters (who came for the "ride") in tow. Once in John's room he announced he was going to order room service. He picked up the phone, and spoke as he circled the three of us with his eyes, "Hmmm, I'll have two hamburgers, two BLTs, three fries," he gave us another summing glance, "and a pitcher of iced tea." He lowered the phone and turned to us again, "Do you guys want anything??"

Since then I've had the honor of being around John enough to witness countless evidence of the other dimension which is Fahey's realm. It's here. It's not a fluke, nor a fake, nor a phantom. These stories may seem fantastical; there are cat people who dance suspended in air, aliens who live among us, country musicians with illegitimate (only in the journalistic sense) children who have powers we don't (think we) have. Sound like fiction? Not to me....

Jim O'Rourke, September 1999

CONTENTS

Neighborhood

I. Jews

My family and I moved to the Washington, D.C., suburbs in 1945. Right after we dropped the big ones on Japan. We had been living in the exact center of the Washington, D.C., ghetto where all of our neighbors and all of the kids down at school were Jews. Since my father had a Lower East Side accent, and perhaps for other reasons, everybody thought we were Jewish. I was too young to know the difference. And I was too young to know that my great-great-grandmother on my mother's side was a Jew by the name of Weil. My mother was not dumb. Had a very high IQ. This seems odd to me now because most of her women friends then, and later, too, after we moved to the suburbs, were Jews. I guess none of these friends of hers ever told her she was Jewish.

And I knew nothing about it until I saw my great-grandmother's birth-*Segen*, a very colorful, decorated document from Pennsylvania written long ago in High German script.

I didn't see this certificate until I was in my early forties. I prefer hanging out with Jews because Jews are much more direct with their emotions than goys. And I was quite insecure in my feelings and found it hard to trust goys. I never could figure out what they were thinking about or planning behind those steely, opaque, impenetrable eyes.

And I still can't.

Know what I mean?

Jews are different than every other ethnic group. If you are not a Jew and you want to hang out with them, they will accept you. You don't need to say anything about it. You simply do it and soon you will find yourself accepted as part of the crowd, and, to some extent, unofficially, they will think of you as "Jewish."

Jewish in that you are part of a Jewish group of friends.

Goys say lots of things about Jews which are anti-Semitic. Jews are said to be clannish by goys. I have never found this to be true of Jews. But I have found it to be quite true of goys.

So, there I am growing up among Jews and considered a Jew in Northwest D.C. Nobody ever said anything about it. And I was too young to understand that there was any difference between my friends and I.

In fact, there wasn't any difference in real life. In
EXISTENZ.

Maybe on paper there was. Maybe in the minds of rabbis and priests there was.

But in everyday life I was treated very nicely by everybody in the ghetto. This was a time of great peace and happiness in my life. It was soon to change, but I look back on that period with warm emotions.

I remember the night we moved into the new house in the suburbs. I was sleepy and didn't like what was going on. I remember the following morning, feeling afraid and shy, but preparing myself to go across the street where I saw the local kids hanging out. My mother was encouraging me. She gave me a lot of support.

That day, for some reason, I thought I should dress up in some kind of costume. So I wore a pith helmet, and changed my habit in other ways I can't remember.

I was nervous and afraid because I was so shy, but I went nevertheless and found the kids playing in the basement of Denny Briss's house which was a few houses west of my new house, on the other side of the street.

II. **Eddie**

There were about fifteen kids, mostly boys but a few girls were there too, ranging in age from seven to twelve. I was younger than any of them. Five years I had.

A twelve-year-old boy named Eddie came over to me and said, "Well, what have we here? You going on a safari or something?"

Suddenly I was terrified because I didn't understand him.

"What's a safari?" I asked Eddie.

All the kids were listening silently. A new kid on the block was a big event.

Eddie: "A safari is when you go hunting in the jungle for lions and tigers and things. The sun is so hot that everybody wears pith helmets like you have on your head. It protects you from the sun's rays which are really hot around the equator."

"Equator?" I asked. "What's an equator? I never heard of that."

"You never heard of the equator?" he asked, quite surprised. "We need a globe to show you what the equator is. We have one at my house. I'll show it to you later today when we go over there."

"What's a globe?" I asked. "I never heard of that either."

"My, my," Eddie said. "You don't know very much for somebody who is eight or nine years old. How old are you?"

"Five," I said. "How old are you?"

"Twelve. I'm twelve years old and my name is Eddie. What's your name?" he asked.

"Johnny Fahey," I said. "I came over to see if you guys would let me play with you. We just moved in last night."

"Johnny Fay," he said, pronouncing my last name incorrectly. But I didn't correct him because I didn't care. I just wanted to be there and play with the other kids.

But that is the reason why Eddie and his brother Larry made fun of me for a few years. They thought I was a Jew. There are Jewish names like "Fay" and "Faye" and others which are similar to Fahey. I've seen these names listed in various synagogues and in the YMHA I went to when I was older.

"Oh, I see," said Eddie. "You're very big for your age. I thought you were older. But now I understand why you don't know what those words mean. They haven't taught them to you yet in school. But I'll show you what they mean anyway."

"Thanks," I said, not really caring about the meanings of various words which were new to me. All I cared about was being with these kids and playing with them. I didn't care what it was we played. I didn't care about words. I just wanted to be with them.

"Well," Eddie said, "of course you can play with us. You live in the neighborhood. You're one of us."

"Gosh," I said. "Thanks. I was worried you might not let me play with you because I saw you were all older than me. I was afraid."

"Oh, no Johnny," he said. "There's nothing to be afraid of here. We wouldn't exclude you because of your age. We'll let you play with us any time you want. There's nothing to worry about here. Nothing to be afraid of. And if there is, you come right over and tell me or my brother and we'll fix things up for you. This is a nice, wonderful neighborhood, and we want to keep it that way. So we all help each other out whenever we can. We stick together and support each other. There aren't any kids in this neighborhood who are lonely. That wouldn't be right."

"Who is your brother, Eddie? I don't know who he is because I just got here."

Eddie took me by the hand over to his younger brother Larry and introduced us, quite formally. Just like adults would do.

Larry had fair hair, while Eddie had dark hair—wiry and black. They didn't look like each other, but that didn't matter.

Larry was almost as tall as Eddie, even though he was two years younger.

Eddie never did get very tall. But he was strong and had a lot of muscles and could run faster than anybody else. And he was very smart.

A lot of times Eddie *had* to run faster than anyone else.

Eddie was the leader of the neighborhood gang. In those days, gangs were quite different than they are now. Too bad. Sometimes

Eddie called us a club. And when he got older he and his brother created a special club so they could put on socials once a month. Dances.

They called it the Echo Club. Eddie was always an organizer. A leader. And a politician.

"You moved into five-ten, didn't you?" Eddie asked me.

"Huh? What's that?"

"Oh," he said, once again explaining things to me as he often would in the future, "that's the number of that bungalow across the street, two doors down. Houses all have numbers. Didn't you know that, Johnny?"

"No. I didn't know that. But I know how to count. Let me show you."

"OK," said Eddie. "Can you count to ten?"

"Sure," I said, and showed him.

Then he wanted to see if I could count to a hundred, and I did, but it was a little hard, so Eddie coached me a little bit.

The reason why I told him I could count was because I hardly understood anything he had said previously, and I didn't want him or the other kids to think I was dumb. If they thought I was dumb, they might not like me. They might not let me play with them. Once again I felt scared and insecure.

But it gradually went away as I played with these new kids every day.

Eddie and Larry were the best friends I ever had. I didn't know it at the time, but I was pretty dumb and backwards. In fact, I was slightly retarded intellectually and socially.

And this amazing thing happened. They, Eddie and Larry, decided to help me catch up in my learning and reading and speaking skills. Every day, starting from the day after I met them, until sometime in 1948, they came over to my house and got me and took me around with them everywhere they went. Every day. Everywhere. And they taught me. They cared about me. For some reason they loved me and felt sorry for me, and instead of simply snubbing me like most kids would do, they took on the responsibility of rearing me and educating me.

They helped me enormously. Eventually I did catch up with the other kids. And it was all due to the help these brothers gave me for hours and hours and years and years.

They were the best friends I ever had. They treated me like—and I felt like—I was their brother. Nobody in my whole life ever did so much for me as Eddie and Larry did. I never loved anybody as much as I loved Eddie and Larry. I would still be stupid and backwards if they hadn't helped me.

After lunch, Eddie and Larry came over to my house and spent the entire afternoon helping my mother and me unpack all the stuff. And there was a lot of it, too.

But they wanted to help us. We were neighbors. And that was very important to them. And they helped us in many ways, many times in the future.

You don't meet people like that anymore. You really don't.

I'll never forget them as long as I live, and I hope if there is a heaven and I go there—I hope I'll see them again. I hardly care about anybody else. I mean I hardly care about seeing anyone else again. Just to be with Eddie and Larry again like we were together when we were kids—that is my idea of paradise. That, just that, would suffice to keep me eternally happy. I wouldn't need anything else. Just being close with them again—that's all.

There was something about this Eddie that made everybody trust him right away, all the time. He had a very deep voice and pronounced words very clearly and distinctly like he studied hard and got good grades. And, in fact, he did study hard and get good grades.

And considering the fact that he had an early-morning paper route—*The Washington Post*—I guess that he didn't sleep very much.

But he never looked or acted sleepy. He was always full of energy. He was a year or two older than any of the other kids. Something about his dark black hair and eyebrows and his face and his voice made you know you could trust him.

And you really could trust him if you were in the neighborhood gang. And the adults could trust him too.

But you had to be from the neighborhood. If you lived outside it....

Eddie glorified the neighborhood and the people who lived there. He told us all that it was a special place like Valhalla or paradise. The very soil was sacred. The water in the creeks and springs was holy water. The oak trees were the highest in the world. And these oak trees weren't like regular oak trees. They were sacred oak trees planted by the Great Koonaklaster himself while he was creating the world.

Eddie taught us that it was the same with the grass and the flower bushes and the azaleas and the water and the fish and the birds and the turtles. Turtles were sacred to Big K. The common box turtle (*Terrapene carolina carolina*) was Big K's totem.

So, of course, whenever we found a turtle, and there were lots of them around, we made sure that they had been eating properly, and if they hadn't we fed them ourselves in temporary turtle healing and improving pens. If we found a turtle who came out of hibernation too early and had contracted the deadly turtle *icth* disease, we fed and kept it inside until it was warm enough for it to be outside. And when we let it go we took it to the safest forest land there was. Far, far from any streets or highways because cars are the turtle's natural enemy, despite their similar morphology. And when we did find a turtle that had been run over we exacted revenge on the outlanders by throwing the squashed turtle at the windshield of a fast passing car on Piney Branch Road or Philadelphia Avenue. This started us on an anti-car campaign and Eddie said that Big K was all for it. We found places to throw rocks at cars, and later when we could get cherry bombs and other explosives we threw them at cars, too. Who the hell did all these people think they were driving their cars so fast right through our sacred

NEIGHBORHOOD

our

UHRHEIMAT.

???

I REPEAT WHO? WHO? WHO?

without even asking our permission and killing Big K's totem animals.

It was a magic land. Anything could happen there. Anything was possible for the people who lived there. He nagged various people from time to time to clean up their yards, mow their grass, weed their gardens, and things like that.

He found it odd that some people didn't recognize the royalty and divinity of the land they lived on. It was a sacrilege not to concern yourself—not only with the true nature of the soil we lived on, but also the appearance of the houses and yards.

He called our neighborhood the *Uhrheimat*. I'll explain about his knowledge of German later. He told us that all *Kultur* had started right there where we lived. That was where people had first learned to talk and invented the first alphabet. Where architecture, religion— not the Christian religion, of course, but true religion—and art and music and everything had started, right there where we lived.

And we believed him. He was a great orator. A great rhetorician. He could get us to do virtually anything. Like if somebody didn't clean up their yard, we went and cleaned it up. And he always protected the other gang members from getting in trouble. We needed that because we were always playing pranks on people.

III. Plank Prank

I am out with the gang on my first Beggar's Night. In those days, in the Sligo River basin *Kultur*, Halloween was two nights. The first night was Beggar's Night. On Beggar's Night we went around the neighborhood and canvassed every house for goodies. Candy and apples, Tootsie Rolls, spices from the Far East, gold and silver coins, valuable gemstones, artifacts, and pickled foreskins. On Halloween proper, the next night, we played pranks on people who didn't give us any goodies.

I am only five years old. I don't understand what in the world is going on as we canvass each house for candy and stuff.

We come to Blood Guilt Avenue. 7500 Blood Guilt Avenue. Right next to the Azalea City insane asylum.

We were milling around across the street from the nut factory in the now-vacant, ancient horse pasture. Across the street from where the Kasancevers, Mr. and Mrs., live. We can see clearly through their gigantic, stupid picture window. They are facing us, but can't see us as they watch their stupid television set.

I could not see that any purposeful activity was going on. I was still quite dumb and backwards. It looked to me like everything looked to me. People were just wandering around talking about things I couldn't understand and doing things I couldn't understand. I had no understanding of "purpose" yet. Or "sequence." The way I saw things, it seemed that everything happened at random. And you could never tell what was going to happen next. I had a very primitive understanding of cause and effect.

But I felt things. Why in the world, I wondered, do these useless, old people with all their white hairs and dressing gowns and ugly bodies—why do these parasites want us to *see* them? We don't want to see them. If we look at them long enough, it might happen to us. *We* might get old. Anyway, we are standing next to a big twelve-foot-long wooden plank laying innocently on the ground. I do not wonder at the time how or why the plank arrived at its present location. I am still too backwards and stupid to look for teleology in events. Still too retarded even to look for, much less comprehend, intelligibility. The universe and all that is in it, including the people, including myself, still appears to me to be randomly placed, and the actions of any agent to be causeless and incoherent. I wander around in a nightmarishly cubist-expressionistic habitat. I am a savant.

What actually did happen that night, I only put together many years after the fact:

At some point we all begin to pick up the heavy plank of wood.

"Careful, Berg," says great Eddie, my leader and protector. "Watch out for splinters."

Eddie. Always on hand at the right time with the right help and advice. Later, his brother Larry did the same.

Eddie and Larry called me "Berg" because they thought that I was Jewish. But that was the extent of the venom they used on me. Both Eddie and Larry were also very patriotic. And to be a patriot you had to be anti-Semitic in those days of yore. Those golden days I remember so fondly, when, ah. . . .

Anyway, having elevated the huge plank from the ground of the horse pasture, in such a manner that we held it firmly, Eddie—speaking to everybody, quietly, almost whispering—ordered: "Now remember, it's very important to do this in slow-motion until I count to three. As soon as I say 'three,' throw it as fast and as hard as you can. But until then, don't go any faster than I do. Remember, slow motion until I say 'three.' OK, here we go," and we all started moving the great plank upward and forward and into visibility due to the streetlights, so that the useless old parasites could see us and we could watch, yes, their suddenly terrified, terrified faces as they saw us moving—ever so slowly but forcefully—the plank towards the stupid, giant picture window and the old lady, yes, pointing at us and trying to say or, yes, *yell* something at the old fat fart, her husband, yes, and suddenly I see the flash of someone's camera going off, over and over again, yes, getting a very clear record of the whole, yes, thing, yes, yes, yes, and the Kasaneevers, frozen in their geriatric, unable to speak or move or scream, only the, yes, dread and the, yes, awe frozen on their terrified, frightful, fartful faces as they, yes, spy the edge of the encompassing (Jaspers), yes, as they fall off the side of the earth in their fear and terror which is the whole point of the operation, as the uncanny, unknown, underground monster that we are and the plank which is our extension, approach the soon-dead through the void, yes, of this little bedroom community, safe and secure, har, har, har, yes, that's what they thought, har, har, yes, safe and secure from the groids and splibs and cans, white trash, har, har, but they didn't know, and nobody told them about us, har, har, har, nobody knew about us, the monster and our great creative potential, nobody, as

One, two,

THREE.

And we run, yes, as we hear the shatterproof glass shattering and tinkling and the old fart and fartress finally screaming, yes, that was the whole point, as we run down Baltimore Avenue towards Lower Portal Park, whatever in hell that means, yes this, our very first

KRISTALLNACHT.

Our very first. There would be others in the future, but that one, our very first, was the best.

And as uncomprehending as I was, for years and years I loved looking at the photographs of the terrorized ancients. The best shots were the ones taken before the plank hit the glass, the expressions on the Kasaneevers's faces. That was best. The most fun. We kept them in the clubhouse altar, which was our ark of the convenant of sacred land, soil, blood, freedom, forever-youth.

The covenant we made with The Great Koonaklaster. He was not only the autochthonous god of our local sanctity and the land and soil, but, as it turned out, was a king above all the gods of the universe. And he was our friend. Our best friend.

Eddie was the first person to make contact with Great K. And Great K was the source of his power and leadership. And as time went on, Great K became the source of our strength, too.

I wish I could see those photographs now. They gave us a sense of identity.

Know what I mean?

IV. **Explore**

I will never understand why Eddie and Larry befriended me so much. Decided to take me under their wings and teach me how to grow up without losing the fun of being a kid.

Teaching me how to talk and pretend polite and how to fight and not be polite and teaching me who the enemy was and on and on.

After dinner, that very first day, Eddie and Larry came back over and asked my parents if I could go out with them. They wanted to show me around the neighborhood.

"Well," my mother said, "alright, but you gotta promise to keep an eye on him every minute. He's kinda wild."

I was wild? I didn't know I was wild. Nobody ever told me I was wild. Did they mean I was wild like a wild animal?

Why hadn't they told me before they spoke about me that way to other people, right in front of me? It made me mad as hell. The least they could have done was talk about me behind my back!

"Oh, we won't let him get in any trouble, Mrs. Fay. Don't worry," answered Eddie.

"Well. OK, but don't you dare let him go far enough that you can't see him."

"No problem."

My parents had been overprotective of me for years. They wouldn't even let me cross the street. They made me go to bed at 7:00 while all the other kids were still outside playing. There was nothing I could do at that age to fight back. So I didn't. Not then. Not yet. So I bided my time.

But once I went outside with Eddie and Larry I was free. I could do practically anything that I wanted to do. Eddie and Larry were no squares. They weren't nebbishes or flakes or wingnuts. We did lots of dangerous, fun things.

I remember that first night they took me up in back of Bliss Cathexis school. I saw that all the ground was black and made out of some strange, grainy soil. That was because the Baltimore and Ohio main line went by there. All that land beside the railroad was covered with black cinders. And the only plant that grew in that awful stuff was ivy. And the ivy had free reign of the area next to the railroad for about twenty feet. There were great tentacles reaching, reaching, reaching....

It was like a different planet.

And they took me over to the asphalt park where there were swings and giant machines I didn't understand—all for the use of us kids.

So, over the following months, they taught me how to use all those machines.

And it was fun.

You got a good workout that way, too.

And there was a seesaw.

And a maypole.

And other machines I don't know the name of.

With all the other kids around, the three of us got separated for awhile. But that was OK because all the other kids treated me so nicely because I was a new member of the neighborhood.

The gang had an official meeting once a week.

The name of the gang was the Azalea City Penis Club.

We had a flag. Painted on the flag was a giant penis and balls flying through the sky on white-colored wings. The penis was red and the sky was the color of blue that is on the Flag of Israel. It was a beautiful flag. Many people laughed at it. But it was beautiful.

I was the youngest kid out there in the suburban paradise.

The other kids all told me it was paradise.

In a few ways it was.

I mean it was clean and pretty and there were lots of woods to play in.

And lots of turtles and rabbits and 'possums and raccoons and trees and flowers and stuff.

They made me a member of the Penis Club.

I attended a few meetings. They were pretty boring. Nothing happened. Nobody had anything to say. All we did was take the minutes.

What the hell fun is that?

Finally, one day, things got pretty exciting.

President Eddie, twelve years old, brought up the subject of churches:

"Churches are just like all the other institutions—the schools, the police, the Lions Club, etc. Churches are repressive organizations. The members want children to be seen and not heard. They don't like kids. They would be happier if we were not even seen, or better still, if we did not even exist. The only reason they let us live is to keep up property values. Adults want their stupid, sylvan community to look like Happy Land. Lots of nice, innocent kids running around, playing innocent, stupid games. The truth is that the people driving by on, say, Hell Avenue, see us running around and, at a distance, we look good. We look innocent. But the truth is when they come closer to look at a house, or check out the neighborhood, or whatever, they get nervous around us. They get nervous around all us kids because the sight of kids reminds them of their youth, before they were socialized—before they were taught to not like certain bodily smells, to not like the sight of dirt on somebody, to not get turned on by children openly and naturally engaging in foreplay (or even the real thing). And they get turned on. But they don't want to get turned on, do they?"

"NO!" everybody shouted.

"They want to stay in their shells and think about things like making money, selling stocks, painting the goddamn living room over the weekend. ('Say, wouldn't you like to come over and help us paint? It's so much fun. Oh yes it is. YES YES YES YES YES.')"

Eddie painted a living room in pantomime as he spoke to us, bedazzling us with every word, every motion.

"('And say, next Tuesday is little Elmer's birthday party. Don't you want to come? Oh yes. YES YES YES.') Adults do not like children. They hate children because children are weak, children are not religious, children like to have fun and be sadistic.

"All week long we have to go to school. On Saturdays we have to help our parents clean things up. And on Sundays, it's church. We don't have one single day when we can play and just be kids. What in the hell is wrong with being a kid? You tell me."

Everybody: "Nothing. Nothing is wrong with being a kid."

"If church is so important, why don't our parents go, too? All they do is drop us off there."

Everybody: "Yeah, that's right. *Sieg Heil.*"

"Church is the same as the Lions Club, the schools, the PTA, the police, the YMCA, the Masons, the Jews, the VFW, the Post Office, and on and on and on. There is a gigantic conspiracy against kids. Churches are no different. They are repressive organizations just like the others. And who is it they want to repress, I ask you?"

The club members: "Yeaaahhhhh, booooooooooooo, yeah, whoooooo, screeeaaammm, yelllll."

"It's us kids they want to hold down. Us. And what in the world did we ever do to them, I ask you?"

The club members: "Yeaaaahhhh. What *did* we ever do? Scream, yell, boooooo."

"Nothing," said Eddie, his voice gradually rising as the excitement increased. "*We* never asked to be born did we?"

The club members: "No never, yes, booo, scream, yell, down with schools and churches."

"It is certainly not our responsibility that we were born and that we started to grow up and be natural and have a lot of energy and like to play games a lot and rape and pillage and break and destroy and crash and smash."

It was common knowledge Eddie listened to many recordings of his idol, Adolf Hitler, and learned how to get everybody all excited and yelling and screaming, even though half the time the kids didn't understand what he was talking about. Eddie had even studied and learned German and he could speak it and understand it. He had done this simply so that he could understand Hitler's speeches. Hitler, whom Eddie admired greatly, was nothing but a great and effective gang leader. The Nazis were just another gang. Bigger and more powerful than most gangs. But just another gang.

And Eddie was right.

"But that's besides the subject," he hurled at us, voice growing louder and boomier with each utterance.

"Yeaaahhhh, yell, screeaaaammm, besides the point, kill, murder, hate!"

"They hate us and yet it was those very same people who brought us forth and threw us into existence, as Martin Heidegger said."

The Club: "Hoorraaayyy, Martin Heidegger, oooo, scream, yell."

"Oh yes," Eddie went on, "we look good and innocent from a distance. Oh, yes. They have no idea whatsoever about the games we really are playing, like Multiple Sclerosis, or Incantation or Mutilation or Program or Amputation or any of the other games we kids invented ourselves. Uh, uh. Uh, uh. They don't know anything about what we're really doing down here, and we don't want them to know, do we?"

The Club: "No, yes, never, it's our business, down with the proletariat, yell, scream."

"We got a right to make up our own games and sing our own songs and chant our own chants. They want us to play their games and sing their songs so they can get control of us like they do of all the other kids on this planet. *Don't they!*"

The Club: "Yeah, yes, no, boo, kill, down with the grownups, they oughta leave us alone."

"And they've got all kinds of Communists and 'philes they pay to write songs and make up games for us like Pete Seeger and Leadbelly and the Brothers Grimm and Mother Goose and all that deprecation. But we know better. Whenever they send some 'phile around here to try and

SUPERVISE

us, we know what these creeps are really up to. They all want to

PLAY WITH US

because they're all pedophiles, aren't they!"

The Club: "Damned right. They're all a bunch of creepy 'philes. Down with 'philes. Kill their games and songs, down with everything, hooray for Eddie, he's the only gang leader who knows what's going on, hooray for Eddie, hooray for the Azalea City Penis Club!"

"You show me a child supervisor and I'll show you a child molester. Am I right?"

The Club: Unanimity. Things were really getting exciting now. I had never seen or heard anything like this before. It was really exciting. I didn't understand a lot of what they were talking about but it didn't matter to me because everybody was yelling and screaming and making lots of noise. And that's what I liked. Noise. I loved noise and excitement and emotions and yelling and screaming.

I loved Eddie and all the kids and the gang and the warmth and even the heat of belonging with some other kids who treated me with respect. Nobody had ever done that before.

And now, Eddie leaned on another rhetorical trick:

"OK," he said, somewhat quietly and getting quieter as he went on, "let's all calm down now so the grownups don't hear us and come over and start bugging us."

But the only reason he said and did this was so he could start over again, louder and faster, so that he could whip us up to an even higher fever pitch.

At the time, of course, I didn't understand all this, at least in words. But even though I was pretty aphasiastic and backwards and could hardly talk, I was putting it all together conceptually.

Like Hitler, his speech mentor, Eddie started over again, pausing and then speaking quietly, accelerating and accelerating.

"*We* never did anything wrong," he said, quietly and apologetically. "We're just a bunch of kids with a lot of energy and high IQs. We never asked for much," he said in a leading manner, ever so humbly. "Never. We just wanted to have the right to expend all this energy we kids have. That's all we really ever wanted. Isn't it?" He was almost begging now.

Club: "Sure Eddie, that's all we ever wanted. That isn't too much to ask. Why don't our parents understand us? What's wrong with them? There's nothing wrong with us."

"No," Eddie went on quietly, "there's nothing wrong with us. But they treat us like—oh, they treat us like...." And then louder and faster, "they treat us like we are monsters. Yes," he said reflectively and pausing for a moment, "that's what it is. They treat us like we are

MONSTERS."

And now, Eddie rapidly accelerating, "And so monsters we shall be!!! They think we're monsters, they'll get what they want. They treat us like monsters, we'll be monsters, WON'T WE?"

The Club: "Hell yes. We are monsters. That's what they did to us. They made us into monsters. *We* didn't want to be monsters. But we are monsters. And it's all their fault."

Club: Unanimity.

"All they care about is keeping up with the Joneses, whoever in hell the Joneses are. It's just status, that's all. All they care about is status.

"Am I right?"

"Yeaaahhhh, hooray, scream, yell."

Eddie was really accelerating now. And the cusswords....

"Adults do not like children," Eddie kept repeating himself, driving his point home. "They hate children because children are weak, children are not religious, children like to have fun and be sadistic.

DON'T WE!"

Club: "Yeaaaaaahhhhhhhh, YES, You're right as rain Eddie, SPEAK."

And now he quieted down again, so that there would be an increasingly fast accelerating rhythm—quiet slow easy reflecting thoughtful responsible to raving insane mania screaming hate hate hate hate.

But we did hate. And for exactly the reasons that Eddie gave us.

Now, quietly: "Let me ask you a very simple question. An easy question. Not that any of you is dumb, but just to show you what's going on. A question everybody knows the answer to but none of the adults want us to know. What, I'd like to know, is so great about getting good grades and not having any fun? Why in the world does the enemy want us to do the one and not the other? I don't understand. Do you? What's so great about getting good grades and not having any fun?"

Club: "Nuthin'. Nuthin' at all. Boo. Hiss. Down with everything."

"And what's so great about sittin' in church while the big preach tells us how bad we kids are—just us kids—we're the evil ones. Not the adults. Just us kids with our early, young, strong, 'drives' har har, and our energy and all. We're supposed to be evil because we have those attributes. But we were born with those qualities. We didn't make them. They are hereditary. If our parents didn't want those qualities to exist because they're evil, then they shouldn't have had us.

"They're the ones responsible. Not us. There's nothing we can do about those instincts we have. We just have 'em that's all.

"What's so great about
                    READIN'?"
"Nuthin'!"
                    "WRITIN'?"
"Nuthin'!"
                    "ARITHMETIC?"
"Nuthin'! Down with everything!"
"What's so good about
                    BEING NICE?"
"Nuthin'!"
             "DON'T ROCK THE BOAT?
             DON'T FIGHT CITY HALL?
             DOWN WITH EVERYTHING!"

Club: "Yeah. That's right. *Sieg Heil.*"

"We need to form our own church. A church where we can have fun. We need to have our own gods."

Club: "Yeah. Right. *Sieg Heil!*"

Of course, we already worshipped the Great Koonaklaster pantheon, but for the present, under Eddie's spell, we forgot.

"Do I have any nominations?"

"Thor," somebody shouted.

But nobody knew who Thor was.

"Jupiter," somebody shouted.

But nobody knew anything about Jupiter.

"Thomas Dewey."

"Maybe, maybe. I'll get some information from the Republican Committee in Silver Spring."

"Hitler," somebody yelled.

"Now we're getting somewhere," said Eddie. "Better than Dewey. Those guys in the *Bund* sure have a lot of fun."

And then somebody made a most interesting nomination.

"Let's have Satan. The Devil."

"Who's he?" some of the kids asked.

"He's in Captain Marvel comics sometimes," said some kid.

"That's who Dracula really is," said another kid.

"It is?"

"Yes, it is," said Eddie. "Are there any more nominations?"

Temporary silence.

"We have to research the guy," said Eddie. "We don't wanna take any chances and get the wrong god for the club."

"How could that happen?" some kid asked.

"Well," said Eddie, surprising everybody just like he frequently did, "the problem is

MONOTHEISM.

Some people say there's only one god."

"How boring," said one of the kids.

"Yeah, that's not any fun," said another.

"If there's only one god then they can't get in any fights and wars and stuff like that," said another kid.

"Yeah," said Brain, the club brain, speaking for the first time. He never spoke until the discussion was way over everybody's head. Only then did he get interested in things. Everybody suddenly got absolutely silent. When Brain said something, it never made any sense, but it always sounded great, and was usually funny as hell.

"Yes," said the Brain. His real name was Agony Flea. "Ontological monism. Everything is one thing. If, in fact, there is ontological monism, then there is no motion, no arguing, and everything we are doing here today is an illusion. Therefore, I recommend ontological dualism. It's much more fun."

Club: "Hooray for ontological dualism. Down with ontological monism. Boo. Hiss."

"We have to have ontological dualism," said the Brain. "That means polytheism. As long as we have that, we're safe from some god who turns out to be the same old god, Yahweh, the God of

MAKE NICE

with a different name. Yahweh in a costume. Some people think that all the gods are one, but they have different names."

"How horrible," said Eddie's brother Larry.

"Right," said Eddie, "we've had enough of the god of the adults, the one who takes orders from our parents and school teachers. We don't want the god who reigns in the churches and supports the unbearable *status quo*. And we don't want some other god who turns out to be a pain in the ass, another superego."

Club: "Down with Yahweh. Down with the superego. Down with the status quo!"

"We want some god who's strong and likes kids. Some god who will side with us kids and help us."

Club: "Yeah. Hooray. Yell. Scream."

Club Meeting One Week Later:

"The meeting will now come to order," Eddie, our gang leader, announced. "Does anyone want to have the minutes of the last meeting read?"

"No, boo," the kids shouted.

"OK, then, let's have a report from the executive committee for the investigation of Satan."

"Hooraaay, yell, scream."

"I call upon the club brain, Agony Flea, who did most of the investigatory work."

"Hooooraaaaaaayyyyyyy."

Agony Flea approached the leader's podium. As he did so, everybody held their noses. The Brain never took baths.

"Good afternoon club members."

"Hooray, yell, scream."

It was hard to understand the Brain because he really was a brain. He knew all kinds of big scientific words. He read *Scientific American* magazine, and had a small chemistry laboratory. The reason we called him Agony Flea was that he always seemed depressed about something, we never knew what. He was always moping around like a sad sack, and when he talked he always whined. He put on an English accent, too. A whiny English accent. But he *was* very smart. He showed us lots of chemistry tricks and made small bombs for us. Some chemical that when you spilled it somewhere it didn't go off for about fifteen minutes. It just sat there like some water or something. It didn't do anything. But after some time went by it exploded into flames and set everything around it on fire. We had a lot of fun with that chemical.

Brain also insisted that he could make an atomic bomb if he had enough money to get the parts. We believed him and planned some-day to raise the money for him so he could build the big one.

Brain spoke: "Here is our report. The first thing we did was assemble all the old Captain Marvel comics we could find. A consid-erable quantity, I must say. Fifty-five editions, covering most of the period between 1940 and 1948. The significant issues all came out during that period. C. C. Beck maintained control of the operation until the PTA got after Fawcett Publications."

"Yeaahhh, scream, yell."

"There is no better source, as I am sure you are all aware, than Captain Marvel comics for matters, uh, occult, shall we call them? OK, now, Captain Marvel comics did have several stories about Satan in them. I place them here as exhibit A for your inspection."

"Hooray, scream, yell."

"We also went to the library and found numerous entries under 'Satan'. . . ."

"Oh yeah," some kid yelled. "Who is this 'we' you're talking about?"

We all loved to tease the Brain. And he enjoyed it.

"Oh, alright," the Brain answered, "if you insist then, it was I, just I. Nobody would go with me and help me. Honestly, I don't know why I come to these club meetings."

"Neither do we, Brain. Why do you come?" some kid yelled.

"Oh, very well," the Brain said, "let's get on with it. *I* also found numerous citations in the library card file under 'Satan.' Let me summarize my findings."

Club: "Hooorrraaaay, summarize."

"Well, actually," the Brain went on, "there isn't really very much to tell you. This is a rather obscure matter, you see."

"Boo, hiss, stop holding out on us Brain, tell us the truth or we'll make you imprecise."

"But, honestly," he tried to go on, "there really isn't . . . ."

"Ah shut up and talk," everybody jumped on the bandwagon.

Then we all ran up to the stage of our clubhouse. First we ripped up all the Captain Marvel comics. Then we all started yelling at the Brain.

We had it all planned. We had several bars of soap and some wash rags. We picked the Brain up and carried him down to the creek. But before we took all his clothes off and scrubbed him so hard his skin almost fell off, President Eddie gave him a lecture.

"Look, Brain, the club already has a god. The Great Koonaklaster. If you'll only take baths and stop smelling so bad I will reveal unto you the secrets of the Great Koonaklaster. But first you have to be worthy. And who in the hell is worthy who never takes baths and smells like you do?"

The Brain was screaming incoherent algebraic formulas and secret Hindu mantras.

But I think he was actually enjoying himself. We gave him the only attention he ever got.

Then we stripped him and threw him in the creek. And this creek was full of all kinds of bad stuff. It smelled worse than the Brain did.

But the whole thing was a joke. In addition to smelling, the Brain was not a good sport. When we played tricks on him he actually got mad and started screaming and yelling.

The Brain was actually an atheist.

He didn't *believe*.

And so he had to be punished frequently.

So the whole thing about church and Satan and all those speeches that Eddie gave us the previous week were just a setup for the Brain. And the whole point was to punish him because he was an atheist.

What else could we do?

V. **CHANT**

One of the strange things the kids did out there in the suburbs was to

CHANT.

They taught me how to chant and we spent a lot of our time chanting. I didn't realize at first that chanting was a religious practice. Nobody told me.

At first.

So while all the kids in the outlying lands were playing baseball and football and other obnoxious and stupid games, we were busy chanting, alone or together:

KANTALEVER, KANTALEVER.
KOONAKLASTER, KOONAKLASTER.
KANTABRIGIEN, KANTABRIGIEN.
HUMILATOR, HUMILATOR.
WEST VIRGINIA, WEST VIRGINIA.
KANCELATOR, KANCELATOR.
HEMAGLOBIN, HEMAGLOBIN.
TEUFELKINDER, TEUFELKINDER.
KINDERTOASTER, KINDERTOASTER.

And the most important conjure-word,

KELVINATOR, KELVINATOR, KELVINATOR.

Eddie said that that was the most important word you could know, except for Koonaklaster. And not only to chant. But to use any time I got in trouble or needed help bad. And also

SATANAMA SATANAMA SATANAMA
SATANAMA SATANAMA SATANAMA.

It was fun. It seemed harmless enough. I did it myself all the time. I didn't know what the German and Sanskrit words meant. I didn't even know they were German and Sanskrit.

I tried to teach them a chant that I had learned downtown in the Ghetto:

ASHKENAZY ASHKENAZY
ASHKENAZY ASHKENAZY.

But they didn't like it because they said there was something Jewish about it.

And that was no good.

That's what they said.

It was 1945 and all that summer long we chanted in small groups or by ourselves. It wasn't good to be alone. In fact it was dangerous. Mostly because of the 'philes. But if we chanted, Eddie told us, the 'philes wouldn't bother us.

And they didn't.

It was also important while we were alone to know that all the other kids were chanting. And that way, when we were alone doing something we had to do alone, we didn't feel so lonely. And, in fact, we were not alone. We were all united in the great all-together when we chanted. We were always united in Great K. In reality, we were all together someplace else, and where that place was was a secret. We would learn about that someplace else someday when we got older and grew up and would be initiated into the Hindu Dharma and get real *bija* mantras and deity mantras and learn what sex we each were.

So we chanted all the time. It made the time go by faster. It always made me feel good when I did it or when we did it together.

I asked Eddie about the origin of chant. He knew all the answers to all the important questions. Even the really hard ones like only the questions that the Satmar Rabbi was supposed to be able to answer. Eddie said that all Aryans had chanted since the beginning of time and that Great K had taught it to the people of the Sligo River Valley—*Uhrheimat*. Later he taught it to other people who wanted to learn. People, that is. There were lots of impostors around. Krell-like beings from other planets who masqueraded as human beings. Evil, Krell-like beings who, if you could see them the way they really were, were green and had scales and were reptilian and had tails and gills and tentacles and stuff like that. And someday when Great K finally came in his entirety, he would rescue us from these evil Krell-like beings. He would conjure up a double-whammy and immediately everybody who was really green would look green and not white. And then we would have a "program." That's what it was called. It would make all the evil beings go away or die or something.

But one hot, sunny day, while the Negroes were chopping their cotton to be sold in the fleshpots of Upper Marlboro, while us white kids scrubbed down the great pyramids along the sacred river, chanting, suddenly

THE SUN WENT OUT.

I looked up and there was a great black cloud hanging not far up above my head.

It was blotting out the sun. Like a shroud would do.

And all of a sudden the temperature shot up fifteen or twenty degrees and a kind of ecstasy came over me. And not just me. I looked up at the other workers on my pyramid. The same. They were all standing immobile, looking up with their mouths open and their eyes wide. We, all of us, black and white, were in some kind of trance. And everybody seemed to like it. Except me. I didn't like it because I couldn't move.

It was very frightening.

And then all the kids around me started chanting a new chant, without coaching or anything. A brand new chant. Very quietly at first. And very slowly.

ADOLF HITLER, ADOLF HITLER.
HERMANN GÖRING, HERMANN GÖRING.
JOSEPH GOEBBELS, JOSEPH GOEBBELS.
ADOLF HITLER, ADOLF HITLER.

Then the chant changed a bit. Everybody started chanting Jewish names with Nazi names.

FINKELSTEIN, FINKELSTEIN.
KALTENBRUNNER, KALTENBRUNNER.

Etc.

And at exactly 12:00 noon, while everybody was chanting, they all turned suddenly, raised their right hands, and pointed straight at me, chanting and chanting in this same manner, Jewish names alternating with Nazi names. And a new word I heard that day:

RASSENKRANKHEIT RASSENKRANKHEIT.

And finally the magic words:

KELVINATOR KELVINATOR.
KELVINATOR KELVINATOR.
KOONAKLASTER KOONAKLASTER.
KOONAKLASTER KOONAKLASTER.
OM SRI ADOLF HITLERAYA NAMAH.

Finally, I found that I could *move*. Even though all the other kids were still frozen in their chanting. I was scared so I ran and hid in the great Black Forest on the other side of the great Sligo River where the very secretive cat people lived.

I didn't like all those kids suddenly turning and pointing and chanting at me. And I didn't know what it meant. So I stayed in the woods for about an hour praying to the Great Koonaklaster to make the scary chanting go away and never come back.

When finally I did come out of the forest, the shroud cloud was gone and the chanting had reverted to the usual Deutsch-English gobbledygook:

EVINRUDER, EVINRUDER.
KATMANDU, KATMANDU.
MENTHOLATUM, MENTHOLATUM.
COMMUNISM, COMMUNISM.
WASHINGTON POST, WASHINGTON POST.
PEOPLE'S DRUGSTORE, PEOPLE'S DRUGSTORE.
DINNERTIME, DINNERTIME.
DINNERTIME, DINNERTIME.

Yes, the cloud was gone, and the evil chanting. And the fear. Everything looked the same. But it didn't feel the same. And it wasn't the same. Something *was* different.

I was determined to ask Eddie what was going on the next day.

"Ah, yes, Berg," he said, "I'm glad you came over. I've been expecting you."

"You have?" I asked. "Why?"

"Because I want to talk to you."

"You do?" I asked.

"Yes, Berg," he answered. "I heard that you got freaked out during the group possession the other day. Is that true?"

"You mean when the great big shroud cloud came and everybody started chanting and pointing at me?"

"Yes, Berg," he said. "That's just exactly what I wanted to talk to you about. Now listen to me. This is all very important."

"OK, Eddie," I said.

"Listen, Berg. Those group possessions are very important. There will be lots more of them, now that the war is over and Hitler blew it—I mean he didn't win the external war.

"Yes," he went on, "now *we* can proceed over here and finish His great work."

"Huh?"

"Oh, don't worry about it, Berg. You're still too young to understand a lot of these things. I'm sure we can get a Goswami to change your caste before the next 'caust."

"I'm sorry Eddie," I said, "but I don't understand what you're talking about."

"Oh, don't let it worry you. You're still too young to understand. You flunked the shroud cloud visitation test, but that's because you're still a little too young. Next time the shroud cloud shows up, try to control your fear. And for heaven's sake, don't run away and hide in the woods again. Today, if you had stood where you were and didn't run, you would have passed your first test and you'd be on your way to

INITIATION.

"We all get a little scared when the shroud cloud comes around. Don't feel bad. Eventually you get used to it and it doesn't scare you anymore. It's just a test."

"A test, huh," I countered. "What does it test?"

"Well, Berg, I can't tell you right now. I will, but not right now. But let me say this: The shroud cloud does more than test. It also teaches."

"OK, Eddie," I said, "but what does it teach?"

"Everything you will ever need to know. Everything. Not the stuff they teach us at school, but things that are much more important. And you can't feel it when it teaches. It doesn't use words. No.

It transmutes the GNOSIS into the real you, which is way down deep inside. You're probably not even aware of it, but that's where *you* really are. Way back inside yourself. That's the real you, Berg. Someday you'll get in touch with it. But you have to be a little older."

"Uh...."

"It's called the

ATMAN.
The Aryan
ATMAN."

"What's the Aryan Atman, Eddie?" I asked.

"It's your true inner self."

"Oh," I said. "I know what you mean. You mean *The Watcher.*"

"Yes, that's the way the late Upanishads put it. *The Watcher's there when there is none other.* The schoolteachers don't want us to know about it because they are nonbelievers, infidels, atheists, perverts, Communists, schoolteachers, parents, PTA members—and those adults, these atheists, who were born in this magic valley have all betrayed the true faith."

"Yeah?"

"Absolutely. And in doing so they have betrayed their own selves, because their true selves or Aryan Atmans are identical in essence with the Great Koonaklaster who created us all—who created this sacred valley—and created his own, sacred people. Us."

"Wow." I didn't know what else to say.

"You see, Berg," Eddie went on, "the adults, especially the schoolteachers, don't want us to know the truth. And they don't believe it themselves. They don't want you to know who you really are. They want you to be somebody else. A construction."

"Why?" I asked.

"The Great Koonaklaster created all the demigods."

"What's a demigod?" I asked.

"Oh, all the other gods you hear about. Jaina, god of the Jaina religion. Buddha, god of the Buddhist religion. Mohammed, the god of the Moslem religion. Brahmin, the god of the Hindu religion."

"Wow. I see. I didn't know that."

"Yes," Eddie said, "the Great Koonaklaster created everything. He created our valley. He created us. He created the earth, the universe, and everything in it. He created you and I and he created Valhalla."

"What's Valhalla?" I asked.

"Valhalla is Heaven on Earth, Berg," he said. "After the great battle of Armageddon, the Great Koonaklaster will live and reign with us here forever and ever. Isn't that wonderful?"

Then we started dancing around his office in ecstasy.

"Someday, Berg, someday, Eddie, hooray, yell, scream, clap, chant, whistle, someday, some happy day, we'll all be together in Valhalla, where the fish and game never run out and where we can finally be ourselves and rape and pillage and kill and disembowel and castrate and electrocute and torture and murder and amputate and have sex and all the ice-cream sodas and hamburgers, any kind of food we want, and only true human beings will be there, real people like us, and no more reptiles disguised as Aryans and other disguised Krell-like monsters from outer space and from hell."

Then we started singing our favorite club songs like the
HORSTWESSELLIED
and
DEUTSCHLAND, DEUTSCHLAND
ÜBER ALLES.

Then Eddie sat down at his desk and said:

"Let me read you a little from this book."

"OK," I said.

Eddie picked up a great big, thick tome: "This is what the book says, Berg. It's not something we made up, it's true. 'This race of people that came from the Sligo River Valley called themselves Aryans and their religion the Aryan Way (Aryan Dharma).' That's Sanskrit, Berg. I've already taught you some Sanskrit, now haven't I, Berg?"

"Yes, Eddie," I answered. "It's a neat language."

"Yes, Berg, it sure is. It is the only language that is pure and 100-percent correct as far as descriptions and ideas go. There is no clearer language. And Sanskrit is the language the Aryans spoke."

Me: "Uh...."

Eddie: "They had the first and only true religion in the world. They practiced the Aryan Way of Life, or Aryan Dharma, like I told you before. Gautama Buddha, who lived here in the sixth century B.C., called the truths he taught the Aryan Truths."

"Wow," I said. They sure give us a different picture of the Buddha in school and at ashram."

"Yes, Berg," Eddie said, "they certainly do. You see, Berg, schoolteachers don't want us to know the truth."

"Why not?" I asked.

"You'll know in good time, Berg. Everything in its proper season. You'll have to learn these things I'm teaching you now, or you won't be able to understand racism. Just be patient, OK Berg?"

"OK," I said.

"Now, Berg," he said, "I'm going to tell you why I asked you to come here today.

"Nothing to be afraid of. Don't worry."

"OK," I said.

"Now I want you to remember these things, so listen very carefully," Eddie said.

"OK."

"Now listen, when the shroud cloud comes, there's another thing it does. It cleanses you."

"You mean like a bath?" I asked.

"Good thinking, Berg," he said. "It's kinda like a bath. And you're not afraid of baths are you?"

"No," I said. "I'm not afraid of them."

"Then there's no reason you should be afraid of the shroud cloud and the enchantment. It's just like a bath. It gets all the Jewishness out of you so you won't be caught in the next 'caust."

"What's a 'caust, Eddie?" I asked.

"Oh, you'll find out soon about the last 'caust. The one that is just getting over. You'll see some nice pictures of it soon. Don't worry. I'll show them to you when they get printed. We're going to have a 'caust museum in our new clubhouse when we build it. And a 'caust altar too. You'll love it, Berg. Lots of fun."

"Really?" I asked.

"Yes, Berg, for real," Eddie said. "It's all going to happen, the Great Koonaklaster came a while back and told me all about it. He gave me instructions and everything. And someday when he finally appears to us in his true form, with all his strength and might and *Einheit* in the Great Altogether, there won't be any people except people like you and I. Good people. This is what they called Persian Dualism, or polarity. But those are just bad words for good things. And on that day when he comes we'll all finally be WITH each other; I taught you about WITHNESS—didn't I, Berg?—and *Gemütlichkeit*."

"Oh, yes," I answered. "You sure did."

"Well, on that great day, when we come together in our *Einheit*, we will know true happiness and freedom. And it will last forever and ever."

"Gosh," I said, amazed.

"And that's not all, Berg," he said. "That's not the end of it at all."

"No?" I asked.

"Oh, no," Eddie said. "That's not the end. That's just the beginning. When he finally comes, he's going to change everything into Koonaklaster Land so that everybody will be happy. Happy forever and ever. Because Great K is going to purify that land and everything therein. There won't be any more suffering. Believers will find nothing but peace and happiness and unto the ages and ages and ages world without end amen."

"No kidding?" I asked.

"No kidding," Eddie said. "Everything will be free. You need some clothes? They will simply appear right there in front of you in the air. Even before *you* know you need them. You get hungry? A plate will just suddenly appear right there in front of you with your favorite food. And you can eat and eat all you want. You'll never get fat.

Because this food, the true food that the Great Koonaklaster gives you, is true food. The only real food. Food that, if you didn't *want* to ever eat again, would feed you and keep you nourished forever and ever and ever, world without end amen. You like steak, Berg? These will be the true, real steaks made from the sacred fatted-calf herds of Brahmin cattle in Hinduland."

"Will they have french fries, too?" I asked.

"Yes, Berg," Eddie answered. "They will indeed have french fries. All you want. Only these french fries will taste like no other french fries you or I or anybody ever had. They will be Platonic french fries. And you can eat all you want, forever and ever and ever and ever until the Escutcheon."

"Really, Eddie," I asked, "is this really true? It sounds too good to be true, I mean...."

"Oh, it's true, Berg," he said. "Don't ever doubt. You believe me, don't you? You trust me, don't you?" he asked.

"Of course I do," I said. "But it sounds so fantastic and...."

"But Berg," he said, "I met the Great Koonaklaster myself and he made me a soda and it was the best cherry soda with vanilla ice cream I ever had. And he promised me that always in the future and for-everandeverandeverandever all the sodas I had would taste like the one he made for me, Berg, and he was telling the truth. Every time now I order a soda at Shepherd Park or wherever they all taste like the one he made for me. I could live on just those sodas alone, Berg, without anything else. Honest I could, Berg. Why would I go to all this trouble and tell you about Koonaklasterland and Koonaklaster ice-cream sodas and everything if it wasn't true, Berg? Why on earth would I do that? I'd have to be crazy, wouldn't I, Berg?"

"Yes," I agreed. "You would have to be crazy."

"And, Berg, tell me if I'm crazy or not. Come on Berg, tell me."

I sensed, but did not know yet, the demonic side of Eddie. To a great extent I did believe him, and of course eventually I found out that he was telling me the truth. But then—way back then—I wasn't completely sure.

"No, Eddie," I said, "I know you're not crazy."

"So I must be telling the truth. Right, Berg?"

"Right," I said, loudly and affirmatively. And now he came to the naked girls.

"All day long, Berg, gentle breezes will blow through Koonaklasterland smelling of wonderful perfume and incense and myrrh. And naked girls, Berg. Naked girls all over the place."

"Naked girls?"

"Yes, Berg," he said, "the most beautiful naked girls you ever saw."

"I never saw any naked girls Eddie. Honest."

"But you'd like to, wouldn't you, Berg?" he said conspiratorially.

"Well," I said, "I wouldn't just wanna see them. If I saw them I would wanna, uh, touch them and play with them and, uh, and...."

"Ah yes, Berg," he said, "I know. I know what you wanna do. I know all about it. Believe me I do. We all wanna do the same things."

"We do?"

"Oh, yes, Berg," he said. "That's just normal. All boys wanna play around with girls. All."

"That isn't what they told me at church. They told me that only bad boys wanted to uh...."

"Sure, Berg," he said. "I know about church. I know what they tell you there. That's why Larry and I never go there. They tell us nothing but lies. Lies, Berg. Those are all lies. There's nothing wrong with you because you like girls, Berg. That's normal, Berg. Normal."

"It is, Eddie?" I asked. "That's hard to believe the way they make you feel at church."

"That's the way they make you feel, Berg," he said, "and it's a dirty trick, but it isn't true—what they are teaching you. Honest, Berg, it isn't true. There's nothing at all wrong with you. You didn't do anything bad or wrong. Everybody's got those attractions."

"Then why do they lie to us, Eddie?" I asked. "They make you feel terrible."

"Churches are built on lies, made out of lies, and all they do is tell lies. They want to make everybody feel bad and not have any fun. And the reason they want to do those awful things, I can't really tell you, Berg. Either they're crazy, or they're just mean—I'm not sure why, but I do know one thing. They hate kids."

"They hate kids, Eddie? Why do they hate kids?"

"Because they're afraid of their own feelings and impulses. And when they see them in kids they want to stamp them out and kill them—and the kids, too."

"Gosh, Eddie," I said, "that's pretty complicated. I'll think about it, but I'm not sure I understand it all."

"I'm not sure I do either, Berg. It takes a long time to figure out why crazy people are mean and crazy, and sometimes you can't do it at all."

"What a drag," I said, using a word Eddie had taught me.

"It is a drag, Berg. A terrible drag. But don't let it get you down. Big K doesn't look at things that way."

"He doesn't?" I replied.

"No," he said, "Big K likes kids to have fun. He's no Churchman. Didn't I tell you about the naked girls in K-land? You can do anything with them you want. Just think of that, Berg, when churches and things get you down."

This picture of doing things with naked girls was a very strong attraction to me. I liked it a lot. I liked ice cream, too. But I liked this idea a lot better.

That day, without knowing it, I permanently set my mind against churches. And the idea of Koonaklasterland became highly charged in me. It began to appeal to me more and more. Naked girls? I'd do anything to get my hands on some naked girls. Anything.

"Yes, Berg," he went on, "it will be wonderful in K-land. The trees will be diamond and jewel trees. You want a diamond, you just reach up and take one. Or two or three.

"And there's gonna be lotus blossoms everywhere. And they will shine forth in an effulgence of uncanny brilliant blue-green light of ineffable beauty. And the radiance of those blossoms is the light of K-land. There's never any night or winter. All the light comes from those emeralds and jewels, twenty-four hours a day. And the roads and the streets will all be paved with pure gold. And the light will shine forth unto all mankind foreverandeverandever.

"Won't that be wonderful, Berg?"

"Oh, yes, Eddie," I shouted, excited. "That'll be too much."

The gold and the diamonds and all that stuff was fine. But I was thinking about naked girls. That's what I was thinking about. I don't know what everybody else was thinking about, but that's what I was thinking about.

"So when you think of the Great Koonaklaster, or chant his great name, you will have the Great Koonaklaster's mind in all its pure and happy and peaceful perfection. In other words, Berg, that person's mind is a Koonaklaster-mind. Isn't that wonderful, Berg?"

And it all had this snakelike sexuality about it. Maybe Eddie and the others were thinking about ice-cream sodas, but I wasn't.

"You, Berg," he went on, "will always know these words and the truth about things, I mean the way they really are. These words'll come back to you when you need them. Don't worry, Berg. You've got them in you forever."

"Gosh, Eddie," I said, "I don't know how to thank you. It's really nice of you to do all this for me."

"The only thing I want you to do for me and for yourself and for all other Aryans is to keep chanting, Berg. No matter what happens, keep chanting. Will you promise me that, Berg?"

"OK, Eddie," I said. "I promise I'll keep chanting."

"No matter what happens, Berg?" he added.

"No matter what happens, I'll keep on chanting."

"Forever and ever, Berg?"

"I'll keep on chanting forever and ever no matter what happens, Eddie. I promise."

"OK, Berg," he told me. "Don't ever forget. Please don't ever forget because I want you to be with me and *all* the gang in the great altogether, someday when he finally comes. I want to be in the pure land with *all* the gang, when the Great Koonaklaster finally comes and establishes his Kingdom and changes things all around so that everything is right the way it's supposed to be and nothing is wrong anymore."

"Gosh, that's really neat, Eddie," I said. "I wish something like that would happen to me sometime. I'd like to meet him like you did."

"Oh it *will*, Berg, it will. Just keep chanting and sooner or later he'll come and talk to you, too."

"What does he look like, Eddie?" I asked, wondering.

"Well, Berg, it's not like a he or a she or a person," he said.

"No?" I asked. "Well tell me what he does look like."

"Well," he said, "like I told you it's a whole lot more than a he. And it's not just a visual, or even like a visual-talkie, like a movie. It's like if they had movies where you felt things too, ahhhh," he started trying to think how to tell me. For a long time he was silent. Then, finally, he said:

"Well, I'll try and tell you but I don't know if I can. But here it is. It's a symbolic allegory—at least to some extent. Suppose one hot summer day, you took your bike—I know you don't have a bike, but one day you will—and you pedaled and pedaled—or walked and walked—it doesn't matter, and the sun was real hot but you kept on walking in the heat way out in the country, and there were fewer and fewer houses and roads and people and the roads weren't made out of concrete or asphalt anymore, and slowly they turned into gravel roads and then dirt and finally sand. Yeah, sand. And so you took this sandy road and you were riding down it slowly, or walking, and there were great big leafy trees on both sides of the road, so it kind of looked like a tunnel, but it was nice and cool. And so finally *you* began to cool off and everything was fine except you were very thirsty. Very thirsty.

"But you didn't know how or where to find a drink of water or a coke or anything and so you were just standing still thinking about how to find some water, and you were standing beside an old broken- down barn, with holes in it and the roof obviously leaked, and it hadn't been used in years, and in a way it was kind of sad, you know, because nobody cared about this old barn anymore. Don't you think that's kinda sad, Berg?"

"Yeah," I said. "Real sad. It almost makes me wanna cry."

"Yeah, right," Eddie said in approval, "nobody cared about it anymore, or even thought about it, and it just sat there all alone, like if maybe it was alive it would be feeling real sad because nobody even knew it existed anymore."

"That's really sad, Eddie," I said. "It's a good thing it wasn't alive because if it was alive it would have to feel bad. It could never feel good again."

"Right," said Eddie, "but now let's suppose that it is alive and, even though nobody even thinks about it or cares about it anymore, it isn't sad, it's happy."

"How could that be?" I asked.

"There's a secret, you see, that nobody else knows about," he said.

"What's the secret?" I asked.

"On the side of the barn where you are resting and thinking about water, there's an old faded hex sign. In all kinds of colors even though it's all faded."

"Yeah, so what?" I asked.

"That old hex sign is the Great Koonaklaster," Eddie continued. "This is no story. This is what happened to me. I was thinking about water and the hex sign spoke to me."

"Huh?" I asked.

"Yes, Berg, it spoke to me. It said, *You wanna drink, kid?*

"And I looked at it and it was smiling. And you know all those circles and curlicues and dots and teardrops and spikes on hex signs?"

"Yeah?" I said.

"Well I got drawn into the hex sign. I mean, first I got kinda hypnotized, like I was in a trance—like the day the shroud cloud came—you were in a trance for a little while, right?"

"Yeah," I said, "but then I got scared."

"I was too tired and thirsty to get scared. And when I heard the word 'drink' I just gave in and I said, *Yeah, I sure would like a drink*, before I could even think about it. See, Berg, I didn't have time to get scared."

"Yeah, I see, Eddie," I said. "So what happened then?"

"Suddenly I was inside the hex sign, going down and down and around and around, but I wasn't scared because the Great Koonaklaster kept talking to me and saying, *Don't be scared kid, nobody's gonna hurt you, I'm just gonna take you inside here for a little while so you can have an ice-cream soda. Wouldn't that be nice?* he asked me."

"Wow." If I didn't know Eddie better I would have thought he was telling me a story.

Eddie: "And he had a nice warm voice that made me know he was friendly and wouldn't hurt me. And then suddenly I was inside of some great big, cool, air-conditioned drugstore, sitting at a soda fountain, and a man with the voice of the Great Koonaklaster came up to me—he was wearing a soda jerk's white uniform—and he said to me, *Now what kind of soda would you like, Eddie?*

"See, Berg, he knew my name. And that was a surprise.

"So I asked him, *How come you know my name and who are you and where am I?*

"Then he says, *One thing at a time, kid. first tell me what kind of soda you want.*

"And I told him my favorite kind of soda, you know what it is, Berg!"

"Sure, Eddie," I answered, "you always get cherry sodas with vanilla ice cream."

"Right, Berg," he said, "and so that's what I asked for.

"And he made one for me. Real fast. And let me tell you," and here Eddie got pretty serious, and spoke heavy and loud, "that was the best soda I ever had in my life. It didn't taste just like cherry and vanilla ice cream, Berg. It tasted like everything good in the world. Some of it even tasted like T-bone steak and popcorn and all the other flavors I had ever tasted and a whole lot I hadn't ever had before. It was like eating all the good things in the world in one soda.

"And I sure wasn't thirsty anymore after I drank it. And I didn't want anything else to drink or eat. In fact, I never felt so good in my life."

"Wow," I was beginning to think maybe Eddie was telling me a story. But things happened later so that I knew he was telling the truth.

"And then the nice man in the soda jerk uniform says to me, *That soda OK Eddie?*

"*Gosh*, I said, *it sure was. Best one I ever had.*

"And then he said, *Nothing but the best for you, Eddie. You're a great gang leader. You never let any of the gang members get in any trouble. I wish all the gang leaders were like you.*

"*How come you know about that?* I asked the nice man behind the soda counter. And you know what he said?"

"No, what did he say?" I asked Eddie.

"He said, *I am the Great Koonaklaster. I live inside that old hex sign in the barn upstairs. You've heard of God, and gods?*

"And I answered, *Sure, but what are you?*

"He said to me, *Listen kid, I was around before there were any God or gods. I know all about that stuff. Because I am*

THE GREAT KOONAKLASTER.

And I've heard you chanting my name. Oh yes. You're a really good kid.

"*Well, uh, yeah,* I said to him. *I don't know exactly why I feel so strongly about chanting, but I do it all the time, and I teach all the other kids in the neighborhood to do it and we all do it every day.*

"Then he asked me, *You know why you feel that way, kid?*

"*No, I don't. Do you?*

"And he said, *Suuuuuurrrrrrreeeeee I do, kid,* stretching out that 'sure.' *I sent you my name and that desire to chant while you were asleep. And you did it.*

"*Is that why I do it?* I asked him.

"And he told me, *It sure is kid, but let me tell you, I send that same message to a lotta kids all over creation, but you're the only one who ever did anything about it. You're a really good kid, Eddie, and that soda I gave you is just one little thing I'm gonna give you. You're gonna get all kinds of presents from me. And they're all gonna be first-rate like that soda you just drank. Isn't that the best soda you ever had?*

"*Yeah, it sure is. I really appreciate it. Can I ever get another one like that?*

"And he said, *You sure can, kid. From now on, whenever you have a soda anywhere it's gonna taste just like that one. A gift from me. As long as you keep chanting.*

"*Wow*, I said. *Really, can you do that?*

"He says to me, *Kid, you wouldn't believe somma the things I can do. But you'll find out as time goes on. We'll meet again lots of times and I'll give you nice things. As long as you keep chanting. Just keep chanting Eddie, and you'll have a great life.*

"But before I could say anything, Berg, I was back on my bicycle. And I wasn't absolutely certain that what happened was real. But then I looked over at the hex sign, and it smiled again, and it said, *Don't lose faith Eddie. That soda you had was as real as the nose on your face.*"

"Gosh," I said. And this is what I was thinking: It must be true what Eddie is telling me because nobody could make up a lie like that.

"Of course, Berg," he told me, "we do lose faith from time to time. It is simply impossible for a human being to be absolutely consistent one hundred percent of the time. Or eighty or seventy even. Because we live in time and we have scrawny bodies and appetites. There's nothing we can do about that.

"So, from time to time, the strength of our faith wavers.

"But, if we don't worry about it or fall into despair, and above all if we keep chanting, our faith will stay stronger.

"So keep chanting, Berg, keep chanting and don't ever give up. And someday, Berg, the Great Koonaklaster, Berg, the Great Koonaklaster," Eddie yelled triumphantly.

And I echoed his affirmations and echoed what he said, "Hooray, hooray, someday the Great Koonaklaster."

"Someday the all-in-all, the one in one, the altogether in the all-in-one. Hooray!" we both chanted.

I had this beautiful picture in my head of what the altogether would look like when the Great Koonaklaster finally came. There were rainbows all over the land going up into the sky, and there were fireworks going off and a gold, heavenly city up in the sky where everybody lived and was forever happy.

I told Eddie about it.

"That's wonderful, Berg," he said. "Because that picture in your head is no myth. I've actually *been* there. It's something else, let me tell you.

"And, from the fact that you are having pictures of it in your head now, I know that someday, Berg, someday, you will live and reign with me and the others in Valhalla, with the Great Koonaklaster."

"Hooray."

"Hooray."

"First the Koonaklaster-Armageddon, when we kill all the Krell. But don't worry. We'll have the Great Koonaklaster with us. We'll have a good fighting chance."

Then we went outside where lots of the other gang members were waiting for us.

"And Great K will lead us and not only him but the former chief of the Hitler *Jugend* in the USA,

ADMIRAL KELVINATOR.

Yes,

ADMIRAL KELVINATOR,

the inventor of the refrigerator and of Kelvin degrees will be there to fight with us and advise us."

At the mention of our two great leaders many of the club members started up in excitement and started cheering and clapping and dancing up and down while they chanted:

OM SRI, JAI SRI, ADOLF HITLERANANDAYA.

ADOLF HITLER ADOLF HITLER.

HITLER HITLER HITLER.

HITLER ADOLF, HITLER ADOLF.

ADOLF ADOLF.

Etc. Then one of the kids yelled:

"Hey, let's go out back and use the

GAMELAN.

And we did. We chanted while we played the

GAMELAN.

I don't know exactly where it came from or how it got to Azalea City, but out back of Denny Briss's place there was a complete Javanese Gamelan (orchestra). Gamelans are large ensembles of idiophones and metalophones. Instruments which you hit. There are also flutes and at least one fiddle and a Javanese guitar or *chelumpung*. And there is a small *mrdungan* or South Indian drum. It has two heads on the same body and is much more fun to play than a stupid fucking tabla. The drummer leads the ensemble and, as far as I am concerned, there is no music more beautiful than Gamelan music.

The Briss's house was full of strange things like giant shark's teeth and shrunken heads and fetishes and black magic stuff. Mr. Briss traveled all over the world doing something, but I can't remember what it was.

I could tell you lots of things about gamelans. But I don't want to waste time. One thing, though. Gamelans are not tuned the way Western instruments are tuned. If you have a pair of *gangsas*, they are not built so that they are exactly in tune. Rather if, say, you have four gongaphones, only one of them is built so that it plays a 440-cycle A note. The other three are tuned slightly sharp and flat. And so when you hear a gamelan, all the 'phones give off a shimmering effect which you never hear in Western orchestras or bands. The tonality is strange but quite beautiful and very soon you find yourself seduced by the tones.

So there we all sat the rest of the day, playing and singing our favorite club songs like the "Horstwessellied."

And then one day it was time for me to take the practical joke. I didn't know it of course, and it scared the hell out of me.

One morning that summer, I got up and ate breakfast, and then I went across the street to Eddie and Larry's house so I could chant and play with the gang.

So I see Eddie and right away he says to me:

"Oh, hi, Berg. How ya doin?"

"Oh, fine," I said, "fine. What are we gonna do today, Eddie?"

"Well, I don't know yet," he said, "but you know something very interesting is gonna happen to Georgie today."

Georgie was one of the diminutive members of the gang. Older than me, he was nevertheless even stupider than me.

"Yes," said Eddie, "it's been decided that Georgie doesn't make too good of a boy. So today he's going over to the Sanitarium and they're going to have to

CUT IT OFF

and make Georgie into a girl. We hope he'll make a better girl than he did a boy."

Then Larry came out on the front porch and said:

"Yes, Berg, what's gonna happen to Georgie today, or maybe Georgiana, is very important and we want you to pay very close attention to everything, because we think that, in time, you'll make a pretty good boy. But we want to educate you about the sex-change process, so you won't be scared."

"Yes, Berg," said Eddie, "it's not such a big deal as it may seem. I mean anything you can take off you can sew back on. If Georgie doesn't make a good girl, they can always change him back. You can buy penises in lots of places."

"Yes," Larry continued the thought, "you can get them at Youngblood's Hardware Store and at People's Drugstore. It's no big deal."

"Yes, Berg," said Eddie, "we're just trying to teach you about life."

"Oh, OK," I said. "fine. I'll pay close attention, but what game are we gonna play today?"

Nobody had anything planned for that day, or any particularly good ideas, so we decided to walk up to Silver Spring and see what was going on up there.

It was pretty hot that day, and we didn't find anything of particular distinction to do, but that was OK. I just wanted to be with my friends.

Eventually we walked the long way back home at dinnertime.

After dinner the sun was still high. It was deep summer. And it was still hot out. Very hot and humid.

I walked across the street to Eddie and Larry's. They were sitting in the cool shade of their front porch.

Nobody said anything about Georgie. Nobody said anything about Georgie's penis. Or sex or anything.

These guys were really good. When they played a trick on somebody, they really played a trick.

We talked about everything else under the sun except Georgie.

Finally, I asked, "Gosh, I wonder how Georgie's doing."

I was really very curious because we, or at least I, was terribly confused about who had penises and who didn't and how many and what they were for and why.

"Oh, ah yes, Berg," Eddie said to me, pretending he had forgotten about Georgie. "I wonder how Georgie is doing."

"Yes," chimed in Larry, "maybe we ought to go up and see if everything, uh, turned out OK."

"Yes," I continued, "I wonder what Georgie looks like now if he's a girl."

"Well," said Eddie, in a concerned fashion, "we ought to go up anyway and make sure he's OK. Sometimes things go wrong in operations like that."

"Yes, they do," said Larry. "We should always visit anybody when they're sick or have an operation, anyway, so let's go up and see."

So we started walking up Buffalo Avenue.

"I wonder if they let Georgie keep his penis?" asked Larry.

"I dunno," said Eddie. "But there he is out back. Let's go see."

"Hi Georgie," we said. "How ya feelin'?"

"Oh, fine," he said. "Just fine."

Eddie: "Did they let you keep it, Georgie?"

Georgie: "Oh sure. It's in the fridge."

Eddie: "Can we see it, Georgie?"

Georgie: "Sure. Let's go in the kitchen."

So we went up the back stairs and through the screen door and into the kitchen. Eddie opened the inferior GE electric refrigerator and started poking around: "Hmmm. I wonder where it is. Let's see."

I was standing right behind him straining my neck out of curiosity and amazement.

"Let's see," said Eddie, "I wonder if THIS is it."

And as he said "this" he turned around very quickly facing me and started shaking this thing in my face. I couldn't really see what it was because he kept shaking it.

"Here it is. Here it is. Here it is," he started yelling at me.

Suddenly I got scared as hell and started screaming and crying, "NO NO NO."

I tried to bolt, but everybody was standing all around me and I couldn't move. But then Eddie saw that I was really scared—more scared then he had expected me to be—and started yelling, "It's only a chicken neck, you ninny. It's only a chicken neck. They cut his head off."

But then things got out of hand. Something nobody expected. I thought they had cut the head off of their rooster. So I started screaming louder and louder until Eddie said, "It's only a joke, Berg. Calm down."

"No, it isn't," I screamed. "You cut off your rooster's head. You cut his head off you cut his head off you cut his head off how could you do that I hate you I hate you I hate you."

"No, we didn't," he shouted at me, trying to calm me down by shaking me. "This thing came from the Safeway. It's only a joke, Berg. Only a joke."

But I was folded up on the floor crying. I couldn't believe them.

"Oh, come on, Berg," Eddie said. "We'll show you our rooster. He's OK. Nobody cut his head off," he went on in a condescending manner.

So I got up and we went down to the chicken yard in back of their house and they showed me their rooster. He was OK. I would still hear him first thing every morning.

Gradually I calmed down and everything was OK again. But for a while there....

VI. My Secret Life

Of course, I didn't tell Eddie or Larry or any of the other kids that I lived a dual life. That I was a citizen of two different countries, regions, customs, talk, ideologies, and other things. The reason I didn't tell them that was because I didn't know it myself. I was not yet capable of conceptualizing the fact that I had two different sets of friends, antithetical friends, friends who hated each other—that I was two people, one guy for while I was at school in the D.C. school system, and another when I was at home, or in the vicinity of home, in Azalea City.

I was only aware in an aphasiastic manner that I was a green card.

And I was repressing a lot in re the two groups. While I was with one, I denied the existence of the other.

You see, when my family and I moved to the Maryland suburbs of Washington, D.C., the elders of the family decided that I would not go to the Maryland grade school, but would attend the nearby D.C. grade school.

For some mysterious reason there was no tuition for Maryland kids to go to D.C. schools.

For a while.

And my parents thought that the D.C. schools were better than the Maryland public schools.

There were a few other kids in my vicinity that commuted to the D.C. school. But nobody in the gang.

One Jew, Judy Levine, and one *Mischling*, David Bittle, crossed the boundary to receive the supposedly better education.

And so I entered school in D.C.

I didn't know many of the kids there. I went to church across the street from the school. Trinity Episcopal Church.

PROTESTANT.

Even though I had been baptized without my knowledge as a Roman Catholic, which church I have always had a great love and esteem for, even though I was a Jew, not knowing.

Now, Bittle had an identity problem from his earliest conceptualizing days. His father, you see, was a Jew, and his mother a Catholic.

Was Bittle a Jew or a goy, Bittle wondered, and obsessed, and took long walks trying to figure it out, trying from his earliest days until his last to figure out who and what he was. It was an obsession with him.

Not only that, but there were competing teams of Jews and

Roman Catholics out to rush him, include him, devour him, enmesh him in their own concerns and *Weltanschauungen*.

The Hawn family had the same problem but fought it out not in the breast of one person, but in two: Patti and Goldie Hawn. *The* Goldie Hawn.

Mr. Hawn was the Jew and the mother was of the goyim.

Patti decided she was a shiksa and Goldie decided she was a *Mädala*.

Me? I didn't even know that I existed yet as an independent entity, capable of being isolated, or located, epistemologically apart from whatever group I was with.

Without conceptualization—I was too young for that yet—I was a chameleon fading into and indistinguishable, and not knowing about separation, about discrimination, but just changing color and shape and accent between the

BIG THREE POWER.

I was an appendage of the Fahey family, I was a member of the neighborhood goy gang, and, at school, I had a secret love who nobody else knew about and, without knowing I was being secretive, never told anybody about, never, not for thirty or forty years.

At the D.C. school, I started playing with this little girl in the first grade—or she started playing with me—say 60/40 on her side. And she taught me new games. Language games. She did not teach me to conceptualize. Not her. Maybe her father in years to come, but not really her.

She taught me of a strange and alien and wonderful, un-Krell-like people who ate strange but wonderful tasting food—for she took me to her home near the D.C. school. Then she told me about this strange music. She said, "Johnny, I've got to tell you about this

FUNNY MUSIC

they play when we have parties. There's lots of funny sounding clarinets, and drums, and sometimes the music's real fast and people dance to it, but I don't know what it's called."

"Well, sing me one of the songs," I told my wonderful, close, first-grade girlfriend. "Then maybe I can understand what you're talking about."

So she sang me "Tzena, Tzena, Tzena" and "Oyfn Weg Shtet A Baum" and "Die Zilberne Kasene" and "Frölekes" and "Fidel Tanz" and the "Hatvikeh," and others. And, once again, just as I had been enchanted by the *Mädala* herself and her deep black eyes and hair and her most understated figure, and her clean clothes, and her smells, and the food at her house, and her alien, wonderful new world, funny with its many names and characterizations of various kinds of screwed-up people and situations, I found myself captured by the strange Armenian-sounding new mode of these songs. They had minors where there should be majors and majors where there should be minors, and I was where I shouldn't be: "never, never, never hang out with Jews, they'll screw you, they're cheap and rich, and...." This is what I had been taught by Eddie.

But here, manifestly, these things were not true, not with

NATALIE FELDMAN

and her family, who I dearly loved then in the first, second, and third grades, as much or more than I have ever loved any one of my adult wives or girlfriends, much, much more in fact, perhaps, only perhaps, because I wasn't supposed to according to Eddie and Larry and the Azalea City Penis Club, no, no, no, I shouldn't even talk to the evil seductress, because not only would it all come to naught, I was in for a big hurt.

I should have listened to the anti-Semites, because that is exactly what did happen.

It didn't happen until the third grade, and for a long time we bonded, secured with shackles made of laughter and joy and jokes and songs we made up for ourselves, safe away from the adults, who would soon wound us and wound us deep...without even thinking, deeper by far than all the pains and shame and sads forced on us by all other people and institutions of people, deeper by far than all the pains that would come to us in the future, and the adult life.

VII. **The Story of Natalie Feldman**

Femme fatale in grade school.

No joke.

Of course, she was smarter than all the other kids. And she liked to play word games.

Show me some American goyim that play word games.

And song games. Fantasy games.

They were different fantasies from the games we played in the suburban gang.

The Azalea City Penis Club.

Much more cerebral. Violence and sex and kill and maim and all that too. But all verbal.

She, already at that age, saw and understood the hypocrisy and the Great Beast that had been loosed, and the everydayness, the boredom, the sameness, the rage and hatred and aggressive desire hidden in the receding consciousness of the surrounding middle-class goy culture. She could see it in her own culture. And not only that, she could describe it. She could teach it. She could explain it all to me and make it comprehensible to me, even though in and of itself this stuff was all irrational.

Oh, I was aware of the irrational. All of us were. But only Natalie could explain it.

And so I walked her home from school every day. And I spent every minute I could "playing" with her.

But we weren't playing the games the other kids played.

We weren't running around and playing tag and other stupidities involving bodily motion.

We were stimulating each other's brains.

We were playing expose the hypocrisy, the craziness, and the sickness of the adults who ruled us.

And although at first I was only her student, I got sharp real fast and started making discoveries about the "society" we lived in. Discoveries about the things we were not supposed to discover.

That's why she took me on as a student. That's why she was my guru. That's why she was my friend. That's why we were inseparable.

Natalie was the real school I went to every day.

Nobody could laugh like Natalie Feldman. Loud, deep, guttural, completely abandoned.

Sexy.

Also, she was teaching me Yiddish.

She was teaching me words like

FARPOTCHKET

and

TSISMUS.

They were all part of a different and fascinating paradigm, a paradigm which lived right next to and inside of the dominant WASP paradigm, that was not even known to exist, a paradigm in the dark, in another world, another time, another place, another *Weltanschauung*.

A completely new world. And to explain what these Yiddish words meant, she made up such far-blown (FARBLONDJET) examples that frequently, on any given school day, the first time we saw each other before we even spoke we broke out in hysterical laughter— which was very hard to stop as long as we could see and hear each other.

My favorite word:

ONGEPATCHKET.

And we made up endless songs, I mean songs to which there could be no end as long as there was

EXISTENZ.

Songs like,

> *Oh, where have you been, Billy Boy, Billy Boy?*
> *Oh, where have you been, charming Billy?*
> *I have been to buy a bagel,*
> *I've been reading too much Hegel,*
> *He's a young thing and cannot leave his mother.*
> Or
> *I have been unto the Ghetto,*
> *For to purchase a stiletto.*

Or

> *I have been to see Pope Pius,*
> *I'm afraid that he might fry us.*

Or

> *I have been to see Pope Urban,*
> *Just to give him a turban.*

Or

> *I am going to buy a Menorah,*
> *Just to go with my fedora.*

Or

> *I am going to buy a rosary,*
> *Just to match my hosiery.*

Or

> *Oh, I have to go to Schul,*
> *I don't wanna be a fool.*

And

> *I have been unto the mohl,*
> *To have him make for me a goil.*

Yes, a very fascinating new world she was teaching me.

We were the closest of friends. Lovers at a very young age.

Bonded.

And then one morning she came to school and told me her father had told her that she couldn't marry me because I was a goy.

"A goy?" I asked.

"Yes, and goys make terrible husbands. Daddy said so and Daddy knows the Satmar Rabbi."

"Marriage, goys, husbands—what the hell are you talking about, Natalie?"

"Well, Sheygetzes beat their wives, they don't take care of their children, they don't like to work because they're lazy.... They're never as nice to their wives as Jewish husbands. Goy men just lie around and drink all the time. So I'm sorry, Johnny, but I can't marry you."

"Marry me?" I asked. "Aren't we a little too young to get married?

What the hell are you talking about?"

I thought she might be sick or something but she was spouting tears like a *Mädala* sperm whale.

"Oh well," I said, "I don't care about any of that stuff. I just like to play with you like we always do."

And then she said the fatal words:

"But we can't play with each other anymore."

"Can't play anymore? Why in the hell not?"

"Daddy said we might get ideas."

"Ideas?" I said. "Ideas?! What in the hell...."

And then I saw red. The whole earth turned red. And then it stayed red all day.

And I had to play with the goys or with nobody. So I played with nobody. I just watched shades of red pass over everything.

This went on for some time. Until the red went away and the black came.

The black did come and then it too went away.

And so did the memories.

It took a while, but the red, the black, and the memories all went away.

For thirty years they went away and only came out in psychoanalysis.

This is what happened.

Being phony liberals, when Natalie's birthday rolled around her family invited the entire class over to her house. Even me.

Equality.

Ha!

It was then that I finally met face to face with my nemesis, Mr. Feldman, with his shiny, polished bald head, his roundish body, his Brooks Brothers suit, and his phony smile.

I acted innocent. I acted stupid. I acted like I wasn't even there as I accepted the paper plate full of birthday cake and Neopolitan ice cream.

Of course, I didn't eat any of it.

I stored it under my chair.

Then I went back and got another.

And another.

I was so obsequious that I got five platefuls and the creep never noticed.

Then, when his back was turned from me, I started sailing the paper plates of goo at him.

ONE, TWO, THREE, FOUR, FIVE.

Oh joy, oh delight, oh triumph of the will. He was covered with ice cream and cake. My ship was sinking, indeed it had already sunk, but I was going down fighting. Nobody should ever treat a kid—or anybody else—like he treated me and his daughter. But when this birthday tree came towards me, the menace visible in his frosting-smeared eyes, I didn't wait for him to catch me or tell me to leave or kick me out or 86 me or....

No, I just ran.

Once I was outside I was safe.

He couldn't get me out there.

I thought I was safe.

I was safe from others.

But not from myself.

As I approached the overhead railroad viaduct, that's when things started to turn black.

BLACK, BLACK, BLACK, BLACK, BLACK.

Black days, black nights, there is black on everything.

But within a few weeks, I had completely repressed the incident.

Along with the shame and self-disgust and anti-Semitism.

And I didn't think about it again.

Except for once.

I saw Natalie at the Fourth of July celebration that year after school was out. I hadn't seen her in two months.

"Hi, Johnny."

"Hi, Natalie."

She looked grief-stricken and I knew she was going to cry. I knew I was also going to cry.

"Do you still love me? I still love you."

We had never spoken of love before.

She didn't give me a chance to answer.

She knew my answer by the way I looked at her.

"I'm sorry for what my goy-fearing father did to you. I know he made you feel terrible. I'm really sorry."

Once again, there was salt water all over both of us.

"You and I," she said, "we both used to be so happy until...."

She couldn't finish the sentence.

Oh, I still loved her.

Yes.

And she still loved me. But we were all victims of our parents in one way or another.

Later that day, we managed to forget our pain and agony by singing our song again.

Our song.

> *Oh, where have you been, Billy Boy, Billy Boy?*
> *Oh, where have you been, charming Billy?*
> *I have been unto a briss,*
> *Come let me give you a kiss,*
> *He's a young thing and cannot leave his mother.*

And we laughed and laughed and laughed.

Happy Fourth of July.

Shortly thereafter, her family moved unto the suburbs and I never saw them again.

She didn't even mention the cake and ice cream.

Nice of her.

I suppose.

And then I forgot.

My first two wives were Jewish, of course. Take that, Mr. Feldman.

Gang Leader

Eddie was about fifteen when he decided that he wanted to go away to college.

He was patriotic and a born leader, but he really couldn't be himself in our little town—except on Halloween when he could dress up like a girl. He would put a mop over his head from behind so it looked like hair and swish around just a bit—he didn't have to swish much because he was very beautiful anyway. He couldn't be himself in our little town and also go around and destroy things, smash things, break things, ruin things, trash things, abbreviate things, fracture things, crack things, slash things, separate things, disunite things, tear apart things, disassemble things, partition things....

You know.

I mean how could he do both things? Go around thinking and pretending that he was a girl and still break things up all over the place. How could he do that in the same town at the same time? And then go around and be a Republican, lead the local teen-age social club, have a paper route and....

So Eddie worked for two or three years at a supermarket and he eventually went to Texas A&M and lived in a frat house. His great secret predilection remained unknown both at home and in the Lone Star State. He would study economics during the day and then sneak over to gaytown and do the hoobala-boobala all night long until the sun came up.

Years later I visited him in Houston where he had moved. He had just come down with AIDS which at that time everybody called
GAY CANCER.

He didn't want me to know. Didn't want to hurt me. He was still the same old protective gang leader. Same old Eddie.

And we spoke of old times and it was very sad. He told me that he had moved to Houston in 1980-something.

"That was a very rebellious year."

He had always spoken in that manner—speaking actually of himself but putting everything in vague and general terms.

So the exact reason that that was a rebellious year I never gleaned.

Now he worked as a child advisor in the Houston school system.

In other words, he was still a good gang leader.

He had never changed.

He never would change.

Good.

I admired him for his guts.

"You'll be surprised to learn that I work with black children," he said as he led me into his antique-infested living room.

"Ironic," I said. "Considering your club's ideology. And I saw your brother, Larry the Diminutive. He's teaching black pre-teens, too."

"Yeah. I mean, what else can you do?" he asked.

"Not much," I replied.

I looked around the duplex at all the bric-a-brac. He had an incurably beautiful six-foot-tall Tiffany-like art nouveau lamp. I can't remember anything else—except the Depression glass which I could hardly stand, but I didn't say so.

But that lamp....

He was still looking healthy. He hadn't started to lose weight, yet.

"You've led a much more exciting life than I have," he said.

"Big deal," I said. "That is a curse among the Chinese. *May you have an exciting year.*"

"I didn't know that."

"I'll tell you," I said, "it's just a lot of hard work, what I do. If you're going to enjoy all that excitement, you have to be in top-notch physical condition. And I don't like lifting weights. Boring. You know what I mean?"

"Yeah," he said. "I know what you mean."

We discussed his deteriorating condition. Told me all the symptoms he was suffering from—especially the mucus in his bowels.

He called it cancer.

"Gay cancer," I said.

"How did—?" An unfinished sentence.

"I get around a lot, you know. I know about gay cancer. I have other friends who have it."

"You didn't—?"

"No, no, don't worry about that. It's not in my itinerary. I wouldn't even know how to."

"Oh well, that's a relief. I never wanted to be the cause of any trouble in the neighborhood. Not to you—especially not to you, because you were so young—or really to anyone."

"I know. You're a real friend. Best friend I ever had. You're a great gang leader."

"Thank you," he replied. "I did my best."

He remained silent. I did, too. Hoped he would restart the conversation.

"Bobbie Seeman jacked me off in the seventh grade. That's what started it."

"I know."

"How do you know?"

"You told us all back then. It was never a secret."

"Oh well, I guess I forgot."

"That's cool," I said.

And this was the Eddie who even taught me the word "cool."

"You know," I said, "Seeman's father was a vampire—I mean a pedophile—you remember the code. I bet Mr. Seeman played around with Bobby a lot when he was a baby. Maybe that's when it started."

"Maybe so," he said, looking at me with curiosity and amazement because I knew so much.

Our conversation trailed off into nothingness. From time to time we had both tried to produce some effect. Laugh or something. But we had both miserably failed. We were talking like two members of some stupid board of directors.

The mood was low gray. Maybe off-white or even puce.

It was a J. E. Powers afternoon. There was nothing you could do about it.

He spoke as if he were in a dream from very far away.

"That was a long time ago, so long ago, so...."

And he started crying. It was a sudden burst. An explosion.

And then I exploded in tears, too.

So we just sat there awhile crying. Like we did when we were kids.

Eddie was going to die.

We both knew it.

But we weren't crying just about Eddie's Death. We were crying about all the pain in the world.

There's a lot of pain in the world.

And also we were crying about all the hopes and failures in the world. Especially *our* hopes and failures.

How in the hell could we have ended up like this? So far away from home. So far from our real selves and lives which we had when we were young and everything was out there in front of us.

Now all our hopes were down. Out.

We had dreamed such big dreams about the way things were going to be someday.

But now someday was here and things weren't like that.

Failure. Failure. Nothing but a failure.

"I wanted to own a big Southern mansion," he cried.

"I remember," I said. "You wanted to be a big politician, too. I mean, that's what we played at all the time. Politics. Remember all those games we had."

"I sure do," he said sadly.

"Those were all your games. You were the one who invented them. You were a great gang leader."

"You really think I was a great gang leader, Berg?"

He was still calling me Berg but that was OK. He was my friend and a person I admired very much. And he was going to die soon. What did I care if he still called me Berg?

"You were a great gang leader, Eddie. You kept us all out of trouble. Most gang leaders don't bother with all that. But you did."

"I tried. I really tried hard."

"And you succeeded," I went on. "None of us ever got in any trouble. And that was because of you. You cared about us. And so later, when I became a gang leader, I made sure nobody ever got in trouble. And nobody ever did.

"And you know what?" I asked him.

"What?"

"I couldn't have done that if you hadn't done it first. I really have always admired and respected you."

"You have?" he asked.

"Yes, and why don't you try and look at it this way. Even if you never did anything else that was great—and frankly, I kinda doubt that—you were a great gang leader and the influence you had on us went on and on and it will never stop.

"I mean, like, I influence people and then they influence other people and so on and so on. It never stops. What you did never stops."

"I never thought of it that way, Berg. Never."

"See and what you did, Eddie, was you changed a lot of other people's lives for the better. And doing that is more important than anything else. More important than making a lot of money in banking or whatever it was you tried to do. All of that stuff doesn't matter so much.

"You gotta try and look at it that way, Eddie, because that's the way it is, that's the way it was, and it will always be that way. You will live on and on and on in other people's lives forever and ever.

"Now that may sound corny but it's true. So you can take it or leave it. But don't leave it, because if you take it you can check out with a better feeling. You can know that you were a victor, a conqueror, a hero. You did have an effect on OPs and on the world.

"So, now you're gonna die soon. So what? You can't beat them forever. Sooner or later your gonna have to cash in your chips. You taught me that and that's the way it is.

"You did the best you could and a hell of a lot more than anybody else I know. I'm not joking. Really," I said.

"How many people were in your gang, Berg?"

"Oh not many, maybe 19 or 20 at the most. Nothing like your gang. But I kept them all out of trouble. Just like you did, Eddie."

"Did you want to become a guitar player, Berg?"

"Hell no. It just fell into my lap. I had to make some money."

I was trying to turn it into other than a J. E. Powers afternoon.

I was trying to make Eddie feel better.

And I was succeeding to some extent.

There was nothing that I could do about it except try. And I was trying.

"I'm not at all sure I even wanted to leave home. No I just wanted to settle down with some girl, say over in Hyattsville or Riverdale. Raise kids, maybe at most gain a little wisdom at the end. Keep up with old friends. Stuff like that," I confessed to him.

"But," I went on, "they wouldn't even let me have that. It's all been a big mistake and a misunderstanding. I had no control over it. I mean, absolutely no control. Things are a hell of a lot bigger and stronger than I thought they were. Did you have any control over it?"

Eddie: "I thought that I did, but I didn't. Not really."

Me: "Yeah, I know what you mean. I sure do."

We sat there in the dark of his living room for some time without speaking.

Finally I said, "I'll come by tomorrow afternoon. It's the least I can do."

"Good," he said, "I'd like to see you again before you leave and before it gets worse."

"Right," I said. "I'll be here."

"One more thing," he said, "Are you still fighting? Fighting them and their machines and their values and their goals and their thought control and psychic vampires and...." he trailed off.

"You mean their rigmarole, their shallowness, their religion, their vacuousness, and their sadism, and how they were always taking it all out on us kids? Yeah, I am. You know, when the battle started I didn't even hardly notice it. They dazzled me and I lost my sight. They dangled me. For years and years I didn't know what the hell was going on. But later I gained it back. What you taught me. And, yeah, I still fight. And I'll never give up."

"Then all is well," he intoned. The Azalea City Penis Club Gang chant.

Now he was himself again. I had brought him back to it.

And I was glad.

I was very happy.

It was time to leave and so when I went out the door I chanted the same thing.

And this time I meant it.

Because all was well.

There were a few more times I saw him. He got sicker and sicker there in Houston.

Then he went to die at his sister's place on the East Coast.

He got so weak that he couldn't take care of himself. So he went to live and die with his sister.

Now his sister had been my baby sitter years before and I had to some extent stayed in touch with her. So when it got near the end she called me up and told me to come soon because he was dying.

So I went.

I was with Eddie as he started to go. Sitting beside his bed.

"It's been dark out there all these days, Berg. I'm glad you came. And now I see some light out there. It isn't so dark, anymore."

"Right," I said, "do you see anything else?"

"Yes," he said, "I think I do. Yes. There's more light now. I'm coming into a beautiful green land. It's beautiful. And I can hear music and people laughing."

"Wonderful," I said. "Maybe it's Valhalla."

He was silent for awhile.

Then he came back: "It's the Fourth of July town picnic and parade. Oh, it's wonderful. Better than I've ever seen it before."

"What do you see?" I asked him. I suspected he was on his way out, his last go around.

I wanted to know what it was like where he was going because I wanted to go to the same place someday myself and see him again.

I loved him very much.

And I always will.

"Oh I wish you could see it, Berg. I've never seen anything so wonderful."

"Tell me what you see," I said. "I want to know."

"Well, Berg," he said, "there are giant bleeding penises hanging all around the park dripping blood."

"Beautiful," I said. "What else?"

"There's Thomas E. Dewey giving a speech from the killing-floor stage. Body parts hanging all around the stage and hanging from the trees."

"Fantastic," I said.

"Oh he's giving a lecture with illustrations on sex and amputation. Mutilation and exotic incurable diseases. He's just wonderful. There, somebody in the audience just cut off the arm and tossed it up to him. Everyone is clapping their hands. There goes a foot. A head."

"You are in Valhalla, Eddie. You've finally made it. I wish I was there with you."

"Someday you will, Berg. Someday. You know why I can tell?" he asked.

"Why?"

"I can see your name on the Legion of Honor building."

"Wow," I said. "You mean now I can *know* that I am going to Valhalla too, Eddie?"

"Yes, Berg. I'm there and I can only talk to you a little while longer but everything is really clear now and I can see your name on the roster. And so that means there isn't any doubt or dialectic around. Someday you too will go to Valhalla just like me. And you too will be happy.

"Yes," he went on, "and now I am happy. So, don't worry, Berg. Everything's alright now. I feel fine. The fight, the struggle, the pain, the humiliation, the suffering—it was all worth it. Don't ever give up fighting."

"I won't," I promised him. "Tell me what you see, Eddie. I want to know."

"Oh, OK, Berg. Things are really exciting now. They're going to have a mass lynching. Beautiful. Just beautiful.

"Now," he went on, "they're playing the Horstwessellied. Oh it's beautiful. And now I can see somebody coming up on the stage and it's—ohmygod—it's Gerald L. K. Smith and—oh I can't believe it, but it's true—it's Father Coughlin."

"Too much," I said.

"And now the band is playing and everybody is singing the National Anthem."

"The real one," I said.

"Yes," he said, "*Deutschland, Deutschland, Über Alles*, and now, oh this is too much, but it's real and it's true, oh it really is, and he is still alive and always will be and he never really left us alone, no, it's

ADOLF HITLER.

"Oh it's wonderful, Berg. It's wonderful. And I'll be gone completely in a few seconds, Berg, over to the other side, Valhalla, but I want you to know you'll love it when you get here, too, you'll just love it. It's wonderful. It's wonderful. I'm going, Berg, I'm going, here I go, I'm...."

And he went. He had a beatific smile on his face. He was in ecstasy. There was no pain in the end. He was happy. He was triumphant. He went to Valhalla and he knew it. It was OK. Everything was OK.

A quiet kind of peace.

I left the room and told his sister he had gone to Valhalla.

"Oh, praise Great K," she whispered. "Thank you for coming, Johnny. I know he was happy to see you."

"Right?" I said and I went back to his room to keep watch until the others came for the grand finale.

After about an hour the others came in: his sister and Larry, his brother, and some of his old friends and gang members—and the ochre-robed Swami whose name I never learned. But he was really good at the chanting. A truly good chanter.

We all kneeled on the floor and got out rosaries as the Swami began the chanting:

OM SRI, JAI SRI, ADOLFAYA SHIVANANDAYA NAMAH
OM SRI, JAI SRI, HOETLERANANDA RAKSHOMON
OM NAMAH SHIVAYA GURUWEG
OM GOOOOOOM GURUWEG NAMAH
OM GOOOOOM GURUWEG NAMAH
OMMMMMMMMMMMMMMMMMMMMM

Two

I was about 8 or 9.

This guy used to come by all the time and grab me and make me walk up the street with him.

He made me walk all the way to Chicago Avenue.

And all the way he talked about a little black dog.

A dead little black dog.

A dead one.

Obviously, he was crazy.

He wasn't in the club.

Nobody knew who he was.

Or cared.

I never thought I'd miss him.

But you don't run into people like that anymore.

Do you?

See, the first time he came by, he said,

"Ah, Johnny, there you are. I want you to come and take a walk with me. Just a little walk. It won't take long."

I didn't know how this guy knew my name. I still don't.

"Where you wanna go?" I asked.

"Ah, Johnny, I'm going over to where my friend the little black dog used to live. Did you know him, my friend? The little black dog?"

His voice faltered whenever he said "friend." He almost started crying every time he said that word.

"Gee, I don't know," I said. "There's a lotta dogs around here."

"Yes, Johnny," he agreed, "there *are* a lotta dogs around here. You're absolutely right. But this dog was different. He was special. I used to come see him every day. Every day. Yes, Johnny, every day."

"Every single day?" I asked him.

"Yes, Johnny, absolutely every single day," he said.

"Gosh," I said, "that's an awful lotta days."

"Yes, Johnny," he went on, "that is very many days, Johnny. Very many. But, you see, I didn't mind. No, Johnny, I didn't mind. Not one little bit, Johnny. Not one little bit."

"Why not?" I asked.

"Well, you see, Johnny, he was my friend. He was my friend."

"How can a dog be your friend?" I asked.

"Oh, Johnny, don't ask such a silly question. All those turtles you got. Aren't they all your friends?"

I wondered how in the world this guy knew I had turtles. I had never seen him before.

"Yes, they are," I said, "but let's keep it a secret, OK?"

"OK, Johnny, we'll keep it a secret. Just between the two of us. I won't tell anybody. I promise. OK?"

"OK," I answered.

"But right now, Johnny, the important thing is for you to come along with me and visit the shrine of the little black dog, Johnny. It's very important for you to see."

"Why is it so important?" I asked.

"Because, you see, Johnny, it's a ritual. Yes, Johnny, it's a ritual. And all rituals must be observed. Mustn't they Johnny?"

"What's a ritual?" I asked.

"I'll show you one right now, Johnny," and he grabbed my arm and started twisting it. "I'll show you one right now. Now let's get going. To the shrine of the little black dog. The little black dog is gone now Johnny. Gone, forever-and-ever-and-ever-and-ever. And nobody noticed, Johnny. Nobody noticed. Not even you, Johnny. Not even you. Not one single person missed the little black dog. Except me, Johnny. Oh, yes, Johnny, I noticed.

"You see, Johnny, he was my friend. He knew too, Johnny, yes, he knew just as well as I did and he didn't care. He knew that one day they would come and catch him and take him away and then he wouldn't be seen anymore. Never again, Johnny. Never again."

I got mixed up because this guy was talking so fast.

"Never again what?" I asked him.

"Never again would anybody see him, Johnny. Never again. Because, you see, Johnny, he knew that someone would come by and take him away—take him away. Take him away, Johnny, take him away and never bring him back, Johnny. Never."

"Gosh," I said. I didn't understand what the guy was talking about but I decided to wait until the end of the story and then try to figure it out myself.

"But, Johnny, he knew. Yes, he knew that someday, yes, Johnny, yes someday, they would come, Johnny, they would come, Johnny, someday, they would come and take him away. But you see, Johnny, he didn't care. *Let them come*, he thought, *let them come*. Oh, yes, Johnny, I could tell that he knew, Johnny. I could tell. See, we had this secret language between us, Johnny, but I won't tell you about that right now. Not right now, Johnny. Not right now."

"Oh, OK," I said.

"*Let them come. It won't make any difference.* And I thought the same thing, Johnny. Let them come, it doesn't matter, because you see, Johnny, the important thing was that he was my friend."

Again, when he said "friend" his voice went way down real sad-like.

"What's true now," he went on, "is true forever and will always be true, always and always, and for all ages and ages and ages to come amen, what's true now will always be true, Johnny. Always, always, always. Nobody can change the truth, Johnny. Nobody. Not for me or for

THE LITTLE BLACK DOG.

"And you see, Johnny, it's OK. See, it's all OK, because he's my friend and nobody, I mean nobody, I mean noooooooooobooooooody can change that. Never."

"Sure," I said, "I understand."

Whoops, I was beginning to talk like him so I cut it.

So then we walked all the way up to Chicago Avenue and took a left and went to this kinda small stupid house and we stopped at the back door.

"There, Johnny, that is where the little black dog used to live. Right there, Johnny. Right there."

And indeed we did not see any little black dog.

No dogs of any description at all.

So, what was the big deal all about?

So I asked him: "What's the big deal all about? There isn't any little black dog here. There isn't any dog here at all. OK, why's you make me come all the way up here when there wasn't any dog here all the time? What's a matter with you? You spun or something?"

The guy looked horrified.

As if I had said exactly the wrong words.

And he looked very sad.

Very sad, and then he started to cry a little bit.

And he said quietly, almost in a whisper:

"Don't you understand, Johnny. My friend (gulp), he's
DEAD.

"No, Johnny, and that's why we came up here. To pay our respects to my little friend. Just to remember him if only for a second. That's all, Johnny. Was that too much to ask?"

And as he said the last few words, he was whispering. And he was looking so pained and grief-stricken that I had to answer him this way. I said:

"Well, no, it's OK, I guess. It's OK."

You know, I kinda felt sorry for the guy.

"Thank you, Johnny," he said solemnly, "thank you." And he turned and walked on up the bridge to Silver Spring.

I never thought I'd see the guy again. And, in a way, I didn't mind. The guy was kind of scary, you know?

But before long he came by again and caught me by the arm again and twisted it behind my back and made me walk all the way up to Chicago Avenue where the little black dog wasn't.

"Yes, Johnny, he knew and I knew that someday they would come and take him away. It was very sad but it was really OK because what's true once is true for ever and ever and ever. Isn't that right, Johnny?"

"Gee, I guess so," I answered.

"And another thing, Johnny, you've got to understand is this, Johnny, that not only did he know, and I know, but now you know, Johnny. You know about the little black dog, don't you, Johnny?"

And he twisted my arm a little harder.

"Yes," I shouted because he was twisting my arm so hard. "Yes, now I know, too. Right. Leggo of my arm, will ya?"

"Why sure, Johnny," he said, "I was just making sure that you were awake, Johnny. That's all. Don't get upset."

"OK, OK," I said, "but you don't have to twist my arm so much, I always do what you say anyway even if it doesn't make any sense."

And then he looked very, very angry, and I got afraid, and he yelled at me:

"What's that you say, Johnny, *doesn't make any sense?* Did you say that, Johnny? Did you say it doesn't make any sense?" And he twisted my arm harder and harder.

"No, no, I didn't say that, I'm sorry," I said.

"OK, Johnny," and he stopped hurting my arm so much. "Don't ever let anybody say that it doesn't make any sense. Because it does, Johnny, it does make perfectly good sense."

"OK, OK," I said. "Maybe it makes sense, but what is it that I'm supposed to know? I don't get it."

"Why, Johnny, that's really very simple," he said.

"What is it, then?" I asked.

"Why, Johnny, now you and I and the little black dog all know the same thing. *We* all know about the little black dog. See, it's very simple."

"WHAT do we know about the little black dog?" I shouted.

Once again he started twisting my arm.

"Don't ever shout like that, Johnny, not in the presence of the little black dog. He can hear everything you say, Johnny, no matter where you are, Johnny, because you see, Johnny, the little black dog isn't really dead. For saints like you and I and the little black dog, Johnny, there is no death. It just looks that way. Johnny, in reality, the little black dog is up in heaven with God and Jesus and the angels and the Blessed Virgin Mary. And although we can't see him, he can see us all the time no matter where we are or what we do. So, Johnny, you've got to be real careful what you do because if you do something wrong the little black dog will hear you and then he'll tell God and God will punish you.

"UNDERSTAND?" he asked, shouting, as he twisted my arm farther back than ever before.

"Yeah, I got it. I understand. Leggo my arm, I understand."

And so then we walked on up the hill and turned right at Chicago Avenue and walked down to the stupid little house where maybe the little black dog used to live.

And he said some prayers.

"Heavenly Father, Heavenly Mother, Heavenly Sister, Heavenly Brother, Heavenly Little Black Dog, we pray that you will look down upon your unrightful servants and bless us because of the fact that we and only we have remained faithful to you and the little black dog all these days and we will do so unto the end of our days we will always remain faithful to the observance of the death of the little black dog for always and unto ages and ages and ages world without end,

AMEN."

So this guy came by again and again and he always grabbed me and made me go up there with him and the whole time he always talked about his friend and about how it did and how it didn't matter what had happened to the little black dog.

Again and again.

And we always said our prayers, too.

Christ!

And then one day he came by and he told me that he had to go away to some military program at school for three years and that he wouldn't be able to observe the celebration of the death of the little black dog.

"So, now that you know," he said as we walked up the hill once again once again once again, "Johnny, now that you know, you will have to carry on the ceremonies while I'm gone, won't you, Johnny?"

"Ah, yeah, sure, I'll go up there every day and say some prayers to the little black dog. Sure, no problem."

"Good, Johnny, and now that you know all about it," and he started twisting my arm again,

"DON'T LIE TO ME JOHNNY DON'T LIE TO ME OR I'M AFRAID WE'RE GONNA HAVE TO CUT IT OFF!

"You get your ass up there every day I'm gone and say those god-damn prayers or I'll have the little black dog kill you—you understand that, Johnny? I'll have the little black dog kill you, so don't you dare forget."

"No problem," I lied, "I'll go up there every day and say prayers for the little black dog. No problem. I'll do it. Leggo my arm. I'll do it do it do it."

So he let go of my arm.

And once again we walked up the hill towards the house where the little black dog had lived supposedly and said our prayers to the little black dog but this time together was the last time the last time the last time.

And as we walked away and up the hill, he said:

"Don't ever forget, Johnny," shaking his finger at me. "Don't you ever forget."

Well, once the dead dog guy had gone away to the military programmatic school, I was thinking to myself one day, well maybe I oughta go up there to Chicago Avenue and ask around and see if there ever had been a little black dog.

Suppose I found out that there had never been a little black dog?

How would I appraise the dead dog guy then?

What would I do?

How crazy was this guy?

So I walked up to Chicago Avenue and I saw a bunch of kids playing on the Baltimore and Ohio Railroad tracks.

I walked over to them and asked them if they had ever known of a little black dog that lived on Chicago Avenue.

But all of them, without exception, said that there had never been a little black dog that lived on Chicago Avenue.

Or anywhere near there.

So I concluded from what these kids had told me that there never had been a little black dog on the block or on the scene or on the anywhere.

But, in that case, I wondered, why did the dead dog guy....

Why did he do what he did?

I didn't know what to call it then and I still don't.

Three years later, the dead dog guy shows up at my front door.

"Oh, no," I thought to myself. "He's back."

Now he was all grown up and he wore a suit and tie.

"You thought I'd forget about you didn't you, Johnny?"

Of course, by this time I had grown up quite a bit, too. No longer could this weirdo twist my arm behind my back to worship some stupid dog that never existed in the first place or anything else for that matter.

"No," I said, "I never thought that. Maybe I hoped you'd forget about me but I never thought you would. Main thing was I hoped I'd forget about you."

"Oh, no, Johnny, you don't really mean that. I know you, Johnny, and I know that you never forgot the little black dog or about me. No, Johnny, I fixed things in your mind before I left so you could never forget about me."

"Gee, thanks a lot," I said maliciously. "Thanks a lot."

"That's OK, Johnny. That's OK. When I first saw you, Johnny, you didn't have any religion so I thought I would help you, you poor kid. You didn't even know about the little black dog."

"No, I sure didn't know about the little black dog. I used to be happy before I met you."

"Now, Johnny," and for the first time the guy started laughing. He never had done that before.

"Now, Johnny, come on. Tell the truth. We did have some good times going up there and saying prayers to and for the little black dog. Come on, tell me the truth. It was different than anything else you ever did, wasn't it?"

"Yeah, I suppose so. Yeah. But what in the hell were we doing? See, I went up there to Chicago Avenue while you were gone and I asked around and everybody told me there was never any little black dog lived around there.

"So," I went on, "would you please explain to me what in the world we were doing? What were you trying to pull on me?"

"Oh, Johnny, I wasn't trying to pull anything on you. And I don't care what those people told you up there. There really was a little black dog. There really was, Johnny, and he was my friend (gulp). Oh, Johnny, how can you talk that way about (gulp, gulp) my friend, my dear little old friend, the little black dog?"

"There wasn't any dog, you creep. There never was any goddamn dog. What the hell were you trying to pull on me? Come on, you pervert, tell me tell me tell me tell me."

"Oh, Johnny," he said, "please don't say things like that to me. I was the only friend the little black dog ever had. Ya see, Johnny, he was (gulp) my friend, my only friend, and I was his only friend, Johnny, nobody paid any attention to him except me, and I did that, Johnny, I did that because I loved I loved him I loved him and he loved me and he loved me and he loved me, and he knew, Johnny, he knew and I knew that someday...."

And so we were off again. Same old thing.

Only this time it got worse.

But I have to admit, after all this time has gone by, yes, I have to admit that it was kind of fun. And you know what? You don't meet people like that anymore.

No, you don't.

Think about it.

But, like I said, it got worse.

"Did you keep your promise, Johnny?" he wanted to know. "Did you go up there and say the little black dog prayers every day like you promised me you would, Johnny? Did you do that?"

"No, you slimebag. I never once even went up there and said any stupid dog prayers to anybody or anyone. You think I'm crazy like you are?"

I thought I had him there. I thought I was big enough now, tough enough, world-wise enough to defeat this lunatic.

But I was wrong.

He was way ahead of me.

I mean way ahead.

You know what he did?

This is what he did. He fell down on the floor and started crying.

"BOOOOOOOO HOOOOOOOOO WAAAAAAA WAAAAA, how could you be so heartless, Johnny? How could you? Not one prayer, Johnny? Didn't you even go up there once and say a prayer?"

"No, not once. You think I'm crazy like you are?"

"Oh, Johnny, you're just like the rest of them. You're just the same. You didn't care about the little black dog either. You're just like the people who killed (gulp) my friend the little black dog in fact Johnny it was you the whole time yes it was you. You killed the little black dog didn't you come on now you little rat

BOOOOOOOOO HOOOOOOO HOOOOOOO
You killed the little black dog."

But this made me feel bad. I didn't kill any dog.

"No, I never killed any dogs or cats or turtles or anything."

"Yes you did I know you did you're a snake in the grass I never did trust you, you little barf-bag it was you the whole time you killed (gulp) my friend the little black dog you you you you you—"

"I did not. I did not." He had me. "I did not kill your dog or anybody else's. Damnit there never was any little black dog. You're crazy. Leemealoneferchristsakes. Quit."

He slowly sat up, drying his tears. He dusted himself off and slowly rose to his feet, saying:

"Call me crazy now, Johnny. Go ahead. It doesn't matter. Go ahead. But I'm on my way to Nashville now. I'm on my way to the airport." He said it quietly, self-righteously, all composed and collected.

"But I'll be back, Johnny. Don't think I won't be back. And when I come back I'm gonna show you all my royalty checks for these songs I've written about, oh, uh, (gulp) friends of mine. Singing waterfalls. Train whistles blowing in the night, mansions just over the hilltops, all kinds of

DEATH, DESOLATION, DESPAIR.

"But most of all, Johnny, I'm going down there with songs about dead dogs, all kinds of dead dogs, not just little black ones, Johnny, no, not just little black ones, but all kindsa dead dogs and I don't care what you think I'll show you I'm not crazy because I'm gonna make all kindsa money. And anybody who makes all kindsa money isn't crazy and I'm not crazy, I just love dead dogs, I just love dead dogs because when they're dead—

"THEY CAN'T BARK ANYMORE! HA! HA! HA! HA! HA! HA! THEY CAN'T BARK!"

"Wow."

And he was out the door.

And you know what?

He was right. He sure as hell was crazy but he did make all kindsa money off songs about dead dogs.

His name was Fred Rose and he wrote "Old Shep" and "Little Buddy" and "The Dead Horse's Prayer" and all kindsa songs about dead animals and the public loved it.

Wow.

That's all I can say. You know?

Wow.

That was a very strange neighborhood I grew up in.

Yes.

There were all kinds of very strange characters around and they were all over the place.

And it seemed like they all came to pick on me.

Just me.

Why?

I never could tell.

And I can't tell you now.

But I would like to say that most of the people I meet these days are pretty boring compared to these kind of people from this strange neighborhood I grew up in.

And I kind of miss them.

They were pretty crazy, I guess, but they were never boring like most people are now.

No, never.

Anyway, there was another obnoxious character in the neighborhood named Donald Cadillac.

He was never boring. Never. He was crazy but never boring.

And this was his number.

This is what he was always doing to me.

In the end I got even with him.

And that was funny, and I'll tell you about it.

But, anyway, this is what he was always doing to me.

He came up behind me and put his arm around my shoulders with a great big warm smile on his kisser and in a warm, firm voice, he said:

"Ah, Johnny, there you are. I have been looking for you. I have something wonderful to show you Johnny. Something marvelous. Just come with me and I'll show it to you."

And he dragged me off just like Fred Rose to the site. We walked and walked and walked until we found it, and then he pointed at it and said, warmly and confidentially, "Look, Johnny. Dog poop."

It was always the same thing. It was never cat poop or bird poop or horse poop or cow poop, no, it was never anything exciting or different, it was always the same thing. Always.

"Look, Johnny," he said, every single time, caressing me with one hand and pointing with the other.

"There, Johnny, dog poop."

And that was it.

Now, you try and find a guy like that today. There aren't any around anymore. I don't understand where they all went but there just aren't any around anymore.

Donald Cadillac did this to me at least once a week.

I always went with him so I could try and figure out what his game was.

What the purpose of it was.

But I never found out.

Never.

Probably he was searching for the missing female penis like everybody else was.

Well, anyway, we started to grow up.

And at some point he stopped taking me places and showing me dog poop.

With a warm voice and a warm smile and a warm arm around my back.

But I never forgot.

Never.

Who could forget something like that?

Not me.

Anyway, like I said, I got him back.

I really did.

Listen.

Here is what happened.

They started building a Methodist church across from the swimming pool in the same block where my grandparents lived, at the corner of Fourth Street and Van Buren Street.

But while they were building it they had to stop for awhile because there came a series of very bad rainstorms.

It might have been a hurricane, but I forget.

So most of the thing was erected. But for awhile they left the basement unfinished.

And you could walk in there and there was lots of sand and water—very clean sand and water.

And, you know what else I found in there?

Foreskins. Hundreds of foreskins.

These are called

RELICS.

Whenever they build a new church or ashram or synagogue or Parthenon or temple or convent or monastery or whatever they place lots of relics underneath the Oedipus.

And among the relics, and almost exclusively under churches and synagogues, they place foreskins and larger pieces because of their belief in circumcision.

The swamis come at night and place them there and have a

RELIQUARY PUJA.

And so that is what churches and synagogues are built on top of.

I knew that.

But Donald Cadillac did not know that.

Donald Cadillac did not know that because he didn't study yoga like I did.

I studied yoga from a swami from India and he taught me all about that sort of thing.

Yes, I got him back.

This is what I did.

See, by this time I was as big as Donald Cadillac.

So I wasn't afraid to do it.

Now because I was living at my grandparents' house it was a very long walk to Donald Cadillac's location.

Four or five miles.

But that very hot and rainy day I said the hell with my gang-member friends at the playground and the swimming pool and I started walking over all the way to Donald Cadillac's house.

And when I got there I found him.

And this is what I said to him when I saw him.

First I put my arm around his shoulders and smiled warmly and said in a very warm voice, I said:

"Donald, I have something to show you. Something very beautiful and wonderful. Come with me."

"Hey, Fahey, that was a game we played when we were kids. Lay off. Go back home and play with your turtles."

"I ain't got no turtles no more. My parents are playing that new game you know. The one they call divorce."

"Oh, gosh, John, I'm sorry to hear that."

"Come with me, Donald," I said speaking warmly, with a warm smile on my face and putting my arm around his shoulders warmly. "Come with me, I have something, wonderful to show you."

"Hey, come on, Fahey, lemme alone. I ain't no kid anymore and neither are you. You wanna do something, let's go shoot some pool."

"Come with me, Donald, I have something to show you."

"Oh Christ, Fahey, don't you ever forget anything? That was ten thousand years ago."

"NODONALDINEVERFORGETANYTHINGYOUKNOW THAT. Now, Donald, come with me, I have something to show you," I said warmly, "something wonderful."

"Cut it out, Fahey, or I'll—"

"You won't do anything to me, Donald, because now I am taller and stronger than you. Come with me, Donald, I have something wonderfultoshowyousomethingwonderfultoshowyousomething wonderfultoshowyou," and on and on and on.

"Goddamn, Fahey, this is a dirty trick. Lay offa me will you?"

"Never, Donald, never. I'm gonna stay here and keep talking to you until you COME WITH ME DONALD I HAVE SOMETHING TO SHOW YOU SOMETHING WONDERFUL."

And again and again and again.

So, finally he said:

"OK, OK, let's go see it, whatever in hell it is. What is it, by the way?"

But I just kept repeating

"COME WITH ME DONALD I HAVE SOMETHING TO SHOW YOU SOMETHING WONDERFUL."

So he came and we went.

And it was a very long walk.

A very long walk.

And when we finally got there I walked over to the pile of fore-skins and I pointed down at them, and I put my other arm warmly around his shoulders and said warmly and with a big warm smile, I said:

"Look, Donald,

FORESKINS."

And you know what he did?

He looked down at the

FORESKINS

and he said,

"Goddamn, Fahey,

FORESKINS.

I don't believe it. What the hell are all those

FORESKINS

doing here? I don't get it. I don't get it. I don't get it."

But I didn't tell him about it, I mean, what the swami told me. So, instead, we went and shot some pool.

COMMUNISM

It is 1951.

A long time ago.

I am in the seventh grade.

Only the seventh grade.

But the torture has started.

Oh, yes. The torture had started.

And not only had it started but it was in full swing.

Everyday the torture was in full swing against us kids.

And who was doing the torture?

You know who.

If you don't know who it was then there is something wrong with you.

You should go and get psychoanalyzed.

I'm not joking.

You won't be able to understand what I'm writing about here.

You have some kind of terrible impairment.

I am telling you this for your own good.

I'm not out to hurt anybody other than the enemy.

And if you don't understand what I am talking about here then it is a certainty that the enemy has deranged you seriously.

And you should very quickly go and get that fixed.

Because if you don't very quickly go and get that fixed you will never know who the enemy is.

And you will never know who the friend is.

You will never know who *you* are.

So please go and get yourself fixed.

It's never too late to try.

Anyway, it's 1951. A long time ago. And I am in the seventh grade. And it is very cold out.

Very cold.

And I am out with some adults who were visiting each other.

They knew nothing about me.

I was a nothing.

Even in my own sight, I was a nothing.

I was not recognized as being sentient.

I did not even think of myself as being sentient.

Because I had been taught by thought, word, and deed that I was not sentient.

I was at most a toy. Maybe a robot. Maybe a house pet.

I was merely an appendage of the two adults with whom I had arrived at the meeting in the car.

These two adults, the ones with whom I had arrived, these two were called my

PARENTS.

One of the other two officially recognized sentient beings was my fourth grade teacher who was known as Mrs. Anis.

She was the female.

The male was called Mr. Anis.

"Anis" was actually the name that these two beings who resided in the same domicile together were known by.

I'm not joking.

Those of my classmates who were from the South pronounced it "anus," of course.

Har, har.

Nobody spoke to *me*. Nobody suspected the unseen transformation that was taking place right before their eyes, right in front of *them*. Had they known about it, "God" only knows what they might have done to me.

And I? I was busy daydreaming of other places; things; colors; smells; tastes; tones; music; other people; other planets; planetoids; other subjective, invisible domains. Something had happened and, as a result, *I* was no longer a pure spirit wandering around in the ether. No, *I* had, by virtue of testosterone, become grounded in the earth by newly grown, but invisible, roots and sap. I was intoxicated by strange, new alien secretions from recently matured glands.

I was incarnation.

But nobody knew about it.

Good.

I was much safer that way.

Unknown to them, I was a secret monster. And, like all monsters, I waited.

I was not yet a threat.

But, like all monsters, I would be. Oh, yes. Just give me time.

A threat.

Yes.

And I knew I was.

Oh, yes.

I knew now that I was an earthling. What these other beings around me were—I did not know. And frankly I did not care. Now I understood that I was not the same species that They were. Even though They told me we were all the same species.

Sure! Har, har, har.

The other inhabitants of this dismal, pastel, Ethan Allen furniture–filled dwelling place sat around and spoke of polite, civil matters. They smiled at each other nefariously, hiding their teeth as well as their genitals, waiting until they could politely consume each other and "me" in some mysterious and unseen monster-manner. By some occult, covert process, probably psychic absorption or something of the sort.

These "folks" pursued a non-alcoholic WASP investiture of small talk; a polite parade of non sequiturs. The weather. "How" one was. The football game. Inflation.

You know.

Alcohol would have involved too much of a commitment for these Protestants. Too much trust in each other would have been involved. How could such an atmosphere exist in the presence of the knowledge that each one of them was potential food for the other, sooner or later?

Yes, sooner or later.

These marauders and impostors had become "friends" four or five years previously at a meeting of similar, other humanoids called the "PTA." The PTA is an organization of gourmets primarily concerned with the best methods of preparing and seasoning their favorite dish—children. I had wondered why I was allowed to be present at a strategy meeting in which they planned direct warfare against children.

Could they not tell, foresee that some of us might, though barely awake yet, recall in the future their sadistic battle plans? Did they never suspect that some of us future "lost children" might rise up against them?

Virtually omnipotent, many of these creatures, "teachers," "advisors," "principals," "guidance counselors"—can you believe in the existence of such salutary, grandiose titles they gave themselves?—were not too bright, despite their pretensions of being, har, har, har, "educators."

But now I understood. Time had come. *Khairos* was here.

BONG BONG BONG BONG BONG BONG BONG BONG BONG BONG BONG

They sat around politely using parliamentary procedure such that they would not all try to consume each other at the same time, then and there, plotting how to drive us kids slowly and painfully mad, discussing the methods they would use in this endeavor and what methods they would use to keep themselves absolutely in power. And they assumed that I, whatever it was that I was, could not comprehend their campaign.

When, finally, the meeting at the domicile of the Anises was over, we left and entered the "family" car.

I sat alone in the back seat, safe, warm, and secure. Ah, with the heater on everything was okay for now. I still loved my parents very much.

It was true that every night I had strange dreams in which I found the dead bodies of both my mother and daddy under the back porch. But I had not yet learned to discern the meaning of dreams.

My "father" had to drive very slowly because there were very few street lights in Azalea City back then. And that night there was no moon. And no stars. None at all.

As we were driving, we turned a corner and all of a sudden we saw a great, red glow in the sky—a veritable pillar of fire—up in the heavens above the New Hampshire Avenue valley far, far down below.

This was the section known locally as

THE EDGE.

"Maybe it's a fire," I suggested.

"Let's go and see," Daddy said conspiratorially.

We drove further down and came around the corner of New Hampshire Avenue and there it was, what looked like an enormous art deco TV set covered with innumerable red neon pastel electric lights. And in the middle of all this visual chaos, in twenty-foot-high glittering letters, it said

ALLEN.

I soon found myself completely enchanted. Not only by the

ALLEN

Theater, but by all these teen-aged boys and girls wearing jackets striped with school colors—maroon and yellow—walking in and out of the theater.

And in the parking lots all these kids were shaking each other's hands. They were smiling and talking to each other and treating each other with respect and love and caring.

It was really quite beautiful.

These kids were not like the kids in my school in Montgomery County.

Not at all.

These kids didn't all hate each other. Instead they were being quite polite to each other. They were smiling and happy.

This was Prince Georges County. Paradise.

Montgomery County, where I lived, was Hell.

It was the richest county in the entire USA. It boasted the highest living standard of any county in the USA. The highest educational rating in the USA. It was the healthiest county. Had the lowest incidence of venereal disease.

But also: Montgomery County had the lowest birthrate of any county in the USA. Highest per capita insane rate of any county in the USA.

Largest per capita suicide rate of any county in the USA.

Yes.

"But," I thought to myself, "eventually. Yes, eventually."

I knew what these kids were doing there. *Now* I knew.

You see, the Christian ministers had made a mistake with me and given me my puberty injection in the sixth grade. At least a year too early. And then, too, I had never really had a latency period because of what my father had done to me when I was three and four years old.

I knew what was going on, man.

"It's a new movie theater," said my father. "And look at all those kids. My, my."

Daddy knew what was going on, too, man.

"It is?" I replied, pretending innocence and stupidity so that nobody would suspect that I was a real monster and getting larger and more powerful every day.

Secretly I was determining to myself that someday soon I was going there myself and if I did not go in the theater with some chick then I'd find one inside.

Someday. Someday, and not too long.

Making a right on Eastern Avenue, going up into the darkness, I still felt safe and snug in the back seat. But also I began to feel something nauseating and frightening.

I had the continuous feeling that I was being forced to eat garbage. I had that constant fantasy in my head.

Was it really a fantasy?

You see, in the seventh grade, I was being slowly driven crazy by being forced to be in close proximity to all these sexy girls in open, tight-fitting clothes all day long and not getting any relief.

Masturbation? You call that a relief? You're crazy as hell.

Because of the blockage of relief, all kinds of infantile things had suddenly become interesting. Smells of sweat. Even my own sweat. And other smells I frequently found myself contemplating. This was driving me crazy, too. Along with the visuals. I wanted to kill my parents and then myself.

That's what the strange dreams meant. I wanted to kill us because there was something wrong with us. And everybody knew it, too.

It was probably the incest garden.

Yes, I'm sure that's what it was.

And everybody knew.

Except, of course, my mother.

You know what I did? I started reading a magazine called *Fur, Fish, Game*. Stories about killing animals. I mean wild animals. Animals that lived in the woods.

Substitution. You know.

And the world-system school. A system within a system. Systems measureless to man.

They all wanted to make us celibate at the age when we had the highest testosterone count.

That is what the official way or
                    TAO
                    was.

How I hated the Montgomery County
                    TAO.

No relief from the testosterone. Nobody wanted to help me. Nobody even wanted to know about the blockade. All the institutions were conspirators in this melee. Especially the churches and synagogues and temples and pagodas and pyramid clubs and sisterns and septic tanks where everybody went to worship.

Things have changed in schools now. And what was previously hidden has been made manifest. Gangs and drugs and guns and knives and murders and rapes and on and on.

Now the kids in schools are acting normally. The adult leaders of the world-system school systems assumed grievous errors. There was, they thought, such a thing in the real world as "adaption." There was in the real world, they thought, such a thing as "sublimation."

HAR HAR HAR HAR HAR HAR HAR HAR HAR HAR HAR HAR HAR HAR HAR

"SUBLIMATION."

But these assumptions are and were wishful fantasies and aspirations. They were airheaded and idealistic assumptions about real people, live people who had very high testosterone counts. And they were completely fallacious assumptions. Any scientist could have told them that.

But they didn't want to know. And even now, nobody wants to know the truth.

This system was not made for man. It was made to destroy man.

And that is what it was doing to me.

Now, as a matter of course, children kill their parents and teachers. This is real progress.

At the same time as the testosterone flood, something else started happening at school.

I was taught in university that this thing is called socialization.

Har, har, har.

What happened was this. All my friends at school started disassociating themselves from me. Nobody liked me anymore. They were all starting to wear strange, slick clothes and combing their hair and taking two baths a day. Really loony stuff. They were splitting up into couples and cliques and things. They were organizing the new

WASP IN-GROUP.

And I was on the outside with a few other unwanted, oddball

rejects, mostly Jews and transfer students who nobody cared about. Nobody wanted us around.

There was something else that the adults were trying to teach us that was more malevolent in the long run than anything I have already described.

Yes.

They were trying to teach us that we should compete with each other for position so that in the future we could cancel everybody else out and be at the top of the pecking order.

And they were teaching us that this was perfectly ethical. Hell, it was good Christian behavior. It was good practice. And one day we would be able to consume large quantities of our fellow beings on this planet. Male and female.

But in order to make this grade we had to give up sex for years and years and years and years. Eventually we would be able to stand victorious at the site of a pile of corpses of our fellow students, our fellow conspirators against each other.

Hell, that is what a good parent did. That is what a good school did. That is what a good teacher did. That is what a good counselor did. That is what a good principal did. That is what a good minister of the church did. That is what a good priest did. That is what a good rabbi taught. That is what a good swami taught. That is what a good roshi taught.

Bite grab snatch kill outdo overdo murder your friends. All of them. And while you're at it, dispose of any older competitors who might be around. Kill them all as quickly as you can. Get rid of all of them. Don't let any of them live. Even the pathetic ones. You never know. They might get stronger and rise up. Kill them. Do them in. Murder them. *Schnell*. Fast. Quick. Move. Destroy. Murder. Rape. Hate. Kill. Love.

Yes, love.

See, they taught us to love each other at the same time they taught us to kill one another.

But it wouldn't work with me. It just wouldn't work. I tried. I really tried. But I couldn't make it work. And then I felt guilty. I hated myself. I really did. I hated myself because I couldn't make these two things work together. I couldn't. You don't know how hard I tried to follow these crazy-making instructions, mores, assumptions, actions.

Even today, when I think about it, I almost start crying.

Sometimes, in fact, I do start crying.

It was very sad.

Very sad.

But, anyway, when I got hormones of testosterone, see, I gave up trying to do both things and make them fit together because the testosterone also affected my brain, I guess. Because all of a sudden it was like I woke up.

And when I woke up I saw that these two things could not, could never fit together. And mean as I was in other respects I did not want to kill my fellow students. Except for one set of them. The cooperators.

I grouped together all adults. Because all adults I knew taught that this horrible dichotomy was a unity.

And with all the adults I grouped together all the kids who played by these blood bath rules. They were the enemy, too.

Now, I want to say that I never bothered the dumb kids. The ones they segregated us from. Beginning in junior high school. With IQ tests.

Oh, yes. We all noticed it. Us smart kids. We noticed it.

But so did the dumb kids. They noticed it, too. You couldn't fool them that much.

I never bothered these kids.

They were not the cooperators anyway.

Whenever I could, I helped them out.

I identified with them, anyway. And with poor people.

I did not like these rich, spoiled, carnivorous, cooperating kids. I wanted nothing to do with them.

But I did the best that I could.

Honest.

And meanwhile, unknown to everyone else, the monster was growing.

And so there I sat, day after day, in a pile of dandruff and pimples....

And I knew that there was only one thing that could explain all this torture and insanity.

It was the knowledge that adults enjoyed hurting children more, much more, than they enjoyed hurting and hating each other.

Child torture was more fun.

The true goal toward which everybody worked so hard accumulating wealth was child torture. The more money you had, the more pain you could dole out to the kids. And clearly society was organized to promote the wishes of these adults and to insure the preservation of their power and authority and legitimate-appearing reasons for child-bashing, and child-fucking, and endless sadistic mind games designed to drive me insane.

And not just me.

All kids.

For what those adults did to us kids they all deserve a slow, painful death. Nothing less. The majority of the kids in my class thought all this sadism was normal and it was the way that things not only were but the way things ought to be.

Denial of reality.

The seventh grade dragged on and on.

The twenty-year-old teacher was a beige-dress, no-make-up, and very plain, 100-IQ monotone. It would have helped us if we actually had some good teachers once in a while. Then we could get our minds off of girls at least once in a while.

But no.

Gradually I did learn some of this new social stuff from the Jews and goy transfers.

But above all I learned a lot of this stuff from this tall guy, D. D., who came from Minnesota.

Because he was a transfer student he was considered and treated as an outcast, just like I was.

And he was after girls just as much as me. We became fast friends and plotted to meet some girls even though nobody wanted us to.

For a girl is a man's salvation. True then, true now.

Or his hell.

You know what I mean?

Probably not.

Being in the out-group was pretty bad. Because all of us in the out-group hated each other. The gruesome thing was that we accepted the values and the aesthetics and standards and morals and goals of the in-group even though we hated their guts.

Because we also loved them and looked up to them.

But they wouldn't have us.

Now, you see, this was just another way the adults got us. They wanted to drive us crazy so they could lock us up in concentration camps. Then, as in the Holocaust, they could do anything. Svengali-type experiments, mass graves, ovens, electric fences and

ARBEIT MACHT FREI

just like in Auschwitz.

Yes, the ultimate trip for any intelligent adult sadist who really wants to make it to the top and have more power, and therefore more child torture, is the concentration camp. Student government, taxes, churches, politics, schools, governments, PTAs, Boy Scouts—all institutions existed so that someday *they* could start building the furnaces. It would begin when they put the razor-wire electric fences up around the schools, giant smokestacks going up. Teachers would be issued guns and whips and stuff.

By Halloween of the eighth grade, I had learned how to look and how to dress so that I looked handsome, tough, and a little sadistic.

A dermatologist had cured my acne and dandruff.

And things were looking up a bit. Kids were forming gangs in the Langley Park Shopping Center and the Green Meadows Shopping Center. At Eastern High School, there was a gang called "The Lords." The Langley Dukes and The Green Meadows Guys at their highest number and greatest power probably numbered, maybe, four hundred per gang.

At Mount Rainier Junior High School, in the same town where William Peter Blatty's exorcism actually took place, the kids took one of the teachers up on the roof and threw him off, killing him.

Maybe the revolution was beginning.

I listened to WGMS, then called WQQW. They played a lot of Shostakovitch and Prokofiev—Russian, Communist composers. The music was so angry that I believed that the revolution was going to come.

And it did!

Now, this guy D. D. had a girlfriend out in Georges County somewhere. She was just a washed-out blond, wore paste-colored glasses and shoes. She wore a lot of beige-colored clothes. She was dumb and umpy-frumpy. Just like her clothes.

I don't know why D. D. liked her.

But he did.

One day when Prince Georges County schools had a day off but Montgomery County schools didn't, D. D.'s girlfriend and her girlfriend Dorothy came over to see us at D. D.'s instigation. It was a very cold, windy, sunless October day, just before Halloween. No one in his right mind was outside.

But these girls walked two or three miles through the wind and gloom just to see D. D. and I. The girls had put on all their coats and sweaters and extra socks and boots but they were still cold. So what they did was this. They tied remnants all over themselves. D. D. and I were sick and tired of girls from the middle class and up. All they thought about was money, power, position, prestige, privilege, and money, money, and money.

I could hardly see Dorothy she was so wrapped up in remnants. I took her mittened hand and said:

"Come here. Don't be afraid. I won't hurt you. I know how to warm you up and keep us both warm. I can't hear you or see you because of the wind and the earmuffs and the remnants but you seem to be an awful cute little girl."

"Not a little girl," I heard her say even though I could hardly hear it because of all the remnants covering her mouth and her whole head.

"No, no, I didn't mean that. I meant that I like you."

Maybe she said, "Oh." I'm not sure what she said but she did say something.

I found a tree and put my back to it. I said, "Now, here's a way we can both be warm."

I took off my leather jacket and put it around her back. I leaned my back against the friendly tree. I put my arms around her inside the jacket.

We got warm pretty quickly.

"Feel better now?" I asked.

She took one of her remnants off of her mouth and put her face against the side of my neck.

"Yeah," she said, "now I'm finally warm. I've been freezing all day long."

"I hate weather like this," I said. "It was really nice of you to walk all the way over here in this wind. I really appreciate it."

She was too shy to say anything so she just hugged me closer and harder.

That was sufficient.

And even though I couldn't see very much of her, I could feel that she had a nice shape.

And a pretty face.

We made a date.

Eventually she and the beige girl went off into the cold and wind to try and get home without freezing to death.

I was sorry to see her go. I already liked her.

And when I did see her I was pleasantly surprised to find out that she was skinny and virtually beautiful. She wore dark-framed glasses. She was intelligent even though she was only in the seventh grade.

And she was a Catholic. That was obvious.

She had a quiet, pleasant voice and beautiful black hair. I like the way she smelled. And there was something elegant about her. I can't really tell you how. It was partly in the way she held herself and looked at things and partly in her quietness and partly in her body. But it was no pose. It was inbred. She couldn't hide it if she tried.

She lived in a bungalow on Prince Georges Avenue.

Once when I went over there to see her, I met her father. He was sitting out in front of the house reading a Bible. He had a strange, deep, ancient voice like the actor Walter Pidgeon in the film *Forbidden Planet*. He asked me what my name was and then repeated it over and over again, as though it was something that was very important. As though it were a word he'd never heard before. He was trying to hypnotize me by repeating my name over and over again. He was caressing my name like you would pet a cat. He was trying to charm me and get me under his power.

There was definitely something wrong, definitely wrong, with the father. He had been at Dorothy—but then most of our fathers got to us first.

Mine, too.

I didn't care about her father at the time because I was so enchanted by Dorothy.

And Dorothy really took to me.

She was wonderful. Warm, pretty, sexy.

But now, looking back, I can tell you without any doubt at all that her father was a pedophile and that he had been at her before me.

Very sad.

But I didn't care about that back then.

Anyway, D. D. and I walked over to her house for our date and after we picked the girls up we strolled down Ethan Allen Avenue, on our first date, and went around the corner and up the hill through the Allen Shopping Center. And we felt like we were in paradise.

We felt the wonderful touch of freedom.

Maybe just a little bit of freedom but enough to make us glad.

We bought tickets and then went in the Allen Theater. And there in the safe dark we did things. And it was wonderful. And we became Communists. All four of us. And after the movie was over we went and did more things in Spring Park.

It was paradise. Victory. We were a Communist cell of four. And all the adults in the world couldn't keep us apart.

And we fought the adults. We started a reign of terror.

The newspapers called what we did "senseless, random acts of violence."

And random they sometimes were.

But not senseless.

We collected dynamite torpedoes off the B and O Railroad tracks and we sent away for cherry bombs. And aerial bombs. And we went out at night with slingshots and shot these bombs at passing cars on New Hampshire Avenue and from the top of the Allen Theater. Nobody ever caught us. Here's how we did it. Since the cherry bombs had real dynamite fuses and since these fuses always burned at a constant rate of speed, it was perfectly safe to do what we did. And this is what we did. I held out the slingshot and the bomb while Dorothy lit the fuse. And I held onto the cherry bomb until the very last minute when it would explode. And then I let go of it so it would explode at the place I aimed at.

We usually shot it at cars or at groups of adults.

That was really fun.

But what was even more fun was this. We bought a pack of Pall Mall cigarettes and went down a dark street late at night. We stuck cigarettes on the end of the dynamite fuses and lit the cigarettes and left and did it to the next house and the next and so on.

That way we could be well away from the explosions when they came marching down the rows of houses and all the people came running out to see what in the hell was going on.

Now that was really fun. Maybe even more fun than the things we did in Spring Park. And maybe the danger enhanced the sex we had there. Sometimes, we deliberately picked places to make love so that it was very possible that other people walking by would see us. There was nothing like it. We took a stand against all the adults and the cooperator kids.

We were on top of the world and on top of its reptilian mesh of systems. And we never got caught or got in trouble. And everybody in town was trying to figure out who it was that was terrorizing the place. And why.

Sometimes we picked out a teacher or a principal and aimed a nine-shot aerial bomb at his or her house and put a cigarette on the end of the fuse and left and went to one of the houses we lived in when the parents were out for the evening.

I called up the teacher and started raving at her: "All the students have started a rebellion against all the teachers and we are going to kill them all."

And while I did this, D. D. and the girls sang the Communist "Internationale." And each time I waited for the culmination when I finally heard the bombs exploding on the other line.

I passed the telephone around so we could all hear the teacher freaking out.

Picture that, will you? It was a riot.

High point of my life. The absolute highest.

But the ultimate trip was to try to shoot a cherry bomb so that it went into a passing car through an open window and exploded in the car.

But we never accomplished this noble but technically difficult feat.

On the other hand, you'd be surprised what you can do with rotten apples. Mrs. Briss on Philadelphia Avenue had an apple tree in her backyard.

Wow. Those were the days.

And that was not all that we did to the adults. Not by a long shot.

But I can't tell you everything.

By accident we set a place on fire and there was considerable amount of damage done.

Not part of our schedule.

But now the cops were looking for us. They had a description of us.

We found this out because we had a friend in the police department and he told us it was time to cool it. We were going to get caught if we kept it up.

I was the leader and educator and theoretician of our cell. And so one night I had to tell the others that we had to disband. We had had three great years of terror but I could not continue to be their leader because I was sure we were going to get caught and get in trouble.

So I told them that what we should do was to disperse ourselves among the Langley Dukes.

We still wanted the benefits of gang membership.

But we couldn't simply have our own gang anymore.

So we all joined the Langley Dukes.

And we never got into any trouble.

So finally the adults won. We always knew they'd win in the end.

But for three whole years we kept them at bay. We were just kids and we beat them through and through, time after time.

And we had a lot of fun doing it.

And we were fiercely loyal to each other.

The adults hate fraternal loyalty among kids.

They hate it more than anything else.

Because it is a threat to their hegemony.

And because they do not have any loyalty themselves.

And nobody knew anything about it.

And nobody did anything about it.

And I want to tell you that this being a gang member and directing and protecting the others was very important in my character development.

Actually, I had learned to be this way from my neighborhood gang leader, a guy named Eddie.

And what I did was to pass on Eddie's legacy.

And, you know, I still have Eddie's legacy.

I really haven't changed at all.

And that's alright with me.

I never wanted to change anyway.

So, what the hell?

Henry Vestine and the Allure of La Plastique

Let me tell you about Henry Vestine.

This is very interesting.

I was there when he met his Muse.

Now, let us consider something that is inevitable despite appearances to the contrary.

Someday the Canned Heat Blues Band will die. When that happens some people are going to wax nostalgic and sort through their memories.

Let us consider. Who will they remember the most? Will it be a giant, crude, gross, fat guy?

I doubt it. Will they recall a virtually blind, shy endomorph? A guy who was always squinting and trying to smile, tears in his eyes—Al Wilson? Frito, the Mexican drummer?

I will remember Wilson, of course, because he was my roommate for about half a year. How could I forget his odor?

And how could I ever forget the wonderful music he played and sang?

And how could I ever forget all the things he taught me about music?

That would be impossible.

But I think a great many people will remember Henry Vestine. He has a very long track record. He's been on the scene much longer than the other guys in the band. Also he is still alive.

And that helps.

Henry was born on Christmas Day in the same town I was born in. We went to the same junior high school.

I forget exactly when we met, but when we did meet we both had guitars. Henry had an electric guitar and I had an acoustic guitar. We were both slow learners. We didn't play together. The fact that we were pursuing different musical paths didn't even show for a long time. Henry and I were not aware of the difference ourselves. But gradually I did notice that Henry really went for long, sustained electric runs. He liked arpeggios, the way B. B. King played them. He was listening to postwar blues records by people like Hound Dog Taylor, T-Bone Walker, Lowell Fulson, and John Lee Hooker.

I liked Hooker. But I was listening to John Hurt, Charley Patton, Blind Willie Johnson, Sam McGhee. These guys played acoustic music and they were fingerpickers.

No, Henry and I got along fine. We both respected each other a lot. We still do. Once we went way up north on Route 1 where this guy played in a shack that served Gunther beer. His name was Roy Buchanan. He was really good and we both admired him.

We still didn't notice much that we were headed in different musical directions. We didn't even care. It was just fun to be friends and do things.

Henry eventually got so good that he could play long, long wailing improvisations that sounded just like he was John Lee Hooker. That was great. I couldn't do it too well because I had an acoustic guitar. And you needed an electric guitar to sound like John Lee Hooker.

Henry played this Hookeresque stuff at high-school and Catholic Youth Organization dances.

Even though Henry was still only in junior high school.

He looked much older than he was.

So did I.

Everything was going along fine.

I liked Henry's music and he liked mine.

But then Henry heard something strange and alien.

Maybe it was B. B. King or Albert King.

Somebody like that.

Who didn't really play jazz and didn't really play blues.

It was light jump music. Nothing too hot. Nothing too invigorating. Slightly lewd. But only slightly. Eclectic and suggestive at most. Not really one thing or another.

But always synthetic.

And Henry started playing this lightweight, cheap, and thus perverse middlebrow black rhythm and blues music.

Now, most people think that Henry started playing this music because he heard it on some old records.

And this is true.

But only to a certain extent.

The plastic music Henry plays is much more chromatic than the music on those old records.

It is much less emotional.

One could call it "cool."

I remember the night when Henry first discovered the pastel allure of plastic.

I was there when Henry made the great change.

We had chanced to meet at the Coelecanth store in the Allen Shopping Center. We were both admirers of this well-known, popular aquarium fish.

"Someday, I'm gonna get rich and have a Coelecanth aquarium all to myself," he vowed.

"Yeah, I know what you mean, Henry," I said emphatically, there in the midst of time.

We walked on down into the newly opened co-op and passed into the giant syntho-products room.

Suddenly Henry froze in his tracks, his mouth hanging open.

"John," he said, "what is that?"

"That's a mannequin, Henry."

It was a female mannequin, only partially dressed.

"But, John," he went on, "she doesn't have most of her clothes on."

"She's not real, Henry," I told him. "She's not real. Made out of plastic."

"All the better," he said. "I've never seen anything so...."

But he didn't finish the sentence. He saw something else.

"Well, what's that?" he asked even more excitedly, pointing at another object.

"That's a plastic art deco lamp," I told him.

"That?" he pointed.

"A small, cheap, kitsch statue of a horse," I said.

"Wow," he said. "Where am I?"

"But, John," he shouted even more excitedly, "What's that?"

"It's a plastic vacuum cleaner."

"My god," he said, "look at the electric cord. I've never seen anything like that in my life. It's so absolutely...."

But Henry was so excited that he couldn't finish the sentence.

"John," he said finally, and very quietly, his eyes transfixed. "You go on ahead. I think I'll just stay here a while."

"OK, Hank," I said. "I'll see ya later."

So I left him there.

But I know for a fact that he spent many, many days there. He kept going back to that roomful of plastics. He spent a great deal of time in there.

I know this because I kept running into mutual friends and they told me that he wouldn't leave the place. They were worried about him.

They told me he started taking his guitar in there.

So I went over to see him one day.

There he was, in the same room, with a very expensive, plastic Stratocaster guitar. No amp.

Just guitar.

He was in some kind of mystical trance.

"Oh, hi, John," he said, in a hardly audible voice which seemed to come from far away.

"You know what I'm trying to do, John?" he asked.

"No, Henry, I'm sorry but I don't. Why don't you tell me."

"Well, see, John, it's like this. I've got to do this thing or I'll never be happy."

"What's that, Hank?" I asked.

"I've got to make a commensuration, a musical analogue, a congruence or translation of this washing machine. I've got to do it and I will do it somehow. I can't give up. It's the most important thing that I've ever tried to do."

"Right on, Henry," I said. "Don't give up. You can do it."

I knew that Henry was very intelligent and that he probably would succeed in making a segue.

I smiled at him, reassuring him that I had faith and trust in him.

"Thanks, John," he uttered from far off. "Thanks."

Now, I should like to say that although I have never tried to make a concordance between music and plastic, I am not entirely unaware of fascination by and love of the synthetic.

But my specialty has always been interpretation in the fields of reptiles and mud.

That's my thing.

But I understand Henry's thing.

So let me say a few words in this connection.

The love of the cheap—bric-a-brac, art deco, modern kitsch—originated with an imagined imperative insistence upon identification with the poor, the downtrodden, etc., by a group of misinformed but well-intentioned idealists in Berkeley, California.

This group founded the co-op department store and grocery store movement in the late '40s.

They were trying to spread the wisdom they thought they had learned at California.

They were, in Walker Percy's words, "Trying to help Niggers ...."

And they were also trying to help themselves.

And they did help themselves.

This making solidarity with the poor is a bygone obfuscation and I'll tell you why.

Never, not once in the entire creation, did a poor person go to some store like the co-op in order to purchase some eating utensil, a dish, a spoon, what have you, or a chartreuse ashtray, or a chair, or some article of wearing apparel or anything while thinking about the material the object was made of. Never. Nor did any poor person ever concern himself with the price.

Either you had the money and bought the items—or perhaps you stole them.

But the reason you found them so desirable had nothing to do with the appearance (*Erscheinung*) nor the efficiency of the object. Nothing to do with the utility and never mind the *need* for God's sakes.

NEED?

Oh, yes. I've heard this kind of talk.

Sometimes I really wonder where in the world some of these crazy ideas come from.

Maybe they came from the other world.

I don't know.

But no one wanted these items for any of these reasons, least of all the price. No, it was never the price, or the need, or the appearance, it was always the *odor!*

And nothing else.

You see, the true lover of plasticity, rich or poor, sooner or later will find a place and a large container such as a dumpster. And in that dumpster he will place used vacuum cleaner cords, nylon garments and hose, sections of cut-up mannequins, rags of slashed men's polyester shirts—especially shirts with palm trees painted on them, women's blouses of rayon, children's apparel made of Dacron and Rayethon television tubes, shredded plastic chairs, and other similar items.

Early in the morning the lover will rise and immerse himself in the confabulation and remain there for about half and hour while breathing in and out very deeply.

And after doing this he will emerge, take up his instrument, whatever it is, and wail.

And he will also do this before lunch, before dinner, and before retiring in the evening.

Only in this manner may one be said to translate fakement into music and art.

This is plastic twice!

But why, you ask.

It is really very simple.

Synthetics are not entirely real. They are not entirely authentic. How can they be? But on the other hand, they are not entirely falsifications. They have some integrity.

Not much, but some.

And so a person with very refined tastes, who does not wish to be either too positive or too negative but has a sensitive love for the "in-between" condition—a person who does not wish to be gross about anything, perhaps "timid" is a good word—finds his or her refuge in this synthetic *ambience*, this tender, difficult-to-define or point-out plastic condition.

Plastic has an ethics, an aesthetic, and an ontology.

Oh, yes.

Plastic may never be heroic. But it is nevertheless self-identical. It may be difficult to prove this but philosophy tells us a priori that everything, including plastic, is itself. If nothing else it is at least that.

There may be a sense in which the itself may not be itself. This is quite true.

But nevertheless and at the same time the itself must also and always be itself.

And this is true of plastics as it is true of anything else.

Plastic asks nothing else of you except pretense. It is what all true art is—pure surface.

It has no depths and it wants none. Nor is it pretentious in any manner.

It never asks for sacrifice.

In fact, it never asks for anything.

Thus, it has integrity.

And I want you to know that I was with Henry Vestine in the co-op department store plastics salon when Henry Vestine first became aware of the charm of these phony materials, especially plastics, because I was with him when it happened.

And still, to this very day, when Henry plays in deepest, darkest Eugene, Oregon, Earth City, his solos are essentially long, discursive lectures on plasticity.

I was there, Charley.

In 1965 I moved to LA, where Henry had previously moved himself. He was very nice and helped me find a place to stay and a girlfriend. Things like that. Many times I went with him to a little bar beside the San Diego Freeway.

Vestine was the head of a trio. Himself on guitar, drum, and bass.

The highlight of the evening was when the group played a very long plastic, halfway Dionysiac but not too explicit piece called "The Boogie."

It went on and on just like the dancing did. What triggered the ending I never could figure out.

Perhaps the dancers, by sweating, were becoming too definite. Too precise.

Henry had three friends and I always sat with them while Henry was playing.

One of the guys was a young black who I noticed was studying Henry's guitar playing very closely. He was a pleasant fellow and seemed well-educated.

The first time I sat with these guys, the black fellow introduced himself to me:

"Hi, man," he said, "my name's Jimi Hendrix. What's yours?"
1965.

Postscript:
Henry Vestine died in Paris on October 21, 1997.

APRIL IN THE ORANGE

"But then, everything must seem upside down and backwards," she said.

"How so?" I asked.

"Well, when I go to school in the morning, you're just coming home from work and going to bed. You must feel the opposite of the way I feel. You're tired when I'm just getting going."

This conversation happened late one April day. There had come a three-day Indian summer which didn't end but ushered in the spring.

I worked the night shift at an Esso gas station from 10:00 PM until 8:00 AM. The previous night the weather was warm and balmy. There was a great smell in the air. A gentle breeze brought pollen and promises.

After work I had returned to my rooming house and my landlady had made me a great breakfast. That was all I ate back then. Breakfasts. For dinner, for lunch, and in the morning I ate breakfasts. Nothing else. Lots of bacon, eggs, and pancakes. These were my favorite dishes. Breakfast was my favorite meal.

Usually I'd go right to bed after breakfast. But the weather called me to take a walk. Aimlessly I went, absorbing the first day of non-calendrical spring.

Soon I found myself in the park along Second Street, NW—the Coolidge High School football field. I was intoxicated by the vernal soaked salad afternoon. I felt at one with everything. Like I was in a slight trance.

I walked up to the swimming pool. It didn't have any water in it, yet. Officially it was still winter. The lifeguards and administrators didn't fill it up with water until they were certain that there would be no more frozen weather. If the water froze it would crack the cement of the swimming pool. So it lay empty all winter.

At the southeast corner of the pool there was a wooden bench which remained outside all year. As I approached it I saw a careening tassel of orange hair hanging over the back of the chair. I wondered who this hair belonged to. I advanced tentatively so as not to frighten the owner of this cascade.

Softly, almost in a whisper, I said, "Hello?"

A young girl, maybe thirteen or fourteen, turned around from her waist up.

She looked up at me for a long time staring into my eyes intently. Like she could see inside me but also through me.

And then in a soft, noncommittal voice, after quite a while she finally said something.

She said, "Hello."

"Hello," period. That was everything she had to say.

Nothing more.

She spoke as if she didn't expect a reply.

It didn't matter to her, you see.

That was the way she said hello.

But it left everything up in the air. I didn't know if I should speak or not. So I said:

"I thought I'd take a walk because of the balmy weather. Am I disturbing you?"

"No." That was all. Just "no." And a thick silence out there all alone.

"Do you live near here?" she finally asked. "I've never seen you around here before."

"Yes," I said. "I live two blocks up on Whittier. The reason you never see me is because I work the night shift at the Esso station out at Langley Park."

"Way out in Maryland?"

"Right."

That was when we discussed our topsy-turvy lives. How and if we differed because of our different schedules.

"You're varsity," she said.

I was wearing my high school sports letter jacket.

"Do you like the Coolidge colors?" she asked me.

"Yes I do," I said, "but, you know, I would never have thought up gray and orange."

"Neither would I," she said. "I still go to Paul Junior High. But I'm a senior."

I wondered why she had added the "but." Maybe she was trying to say that she wasn't a kid. Or maybe she was trying to say something like, "but I'll go to the same school that you went to soon."

I didn't know. Maybe it didn't matter. I went on:

"I really like your school colors. Maroon and white."

Another awkward pause.

"What's your name?" she asked.

"John. John Fahey. What's yours?"

"Dianne Kelley."

"You're Irish, too," I said. "Beautiful orange hair you have there, my girl."

"It's red," she said, slightly miffed.

"Yes," I said. "You're quite right, Miss Kelley. Red it shall be. As you wish."

I bowed, playacting.

She did not react, but continued staring into my eyes—far, very far deep into me.

"When did you graduate?" she asked.

"Just last June," I told her.

"And now you work all night while everybody else is asleep," she went on. "And you sleep while everybody else is working. Doesn't it make you feel strange?"

For some reason, with this girl, I had to be absolutely straight.

"Well, yes," I said. "It makes me feel different from everybody else. And I don't like that."

"Uh huh," she agreed. "But you're not."

"Not what?" I asked.

"You're not different from everybody else."

"Good," I said. "If you think I'm OK, then I'll think so, too. You seem like a girl who knows what she is talking about."

"I do?" she answered.

Well, I thought for that reply I'll give you the same. So I just stared at her and slowly moved my head up and down and tried to look very old and wise.

But it was just a joke. I didn't do it very long. So I went on:

"There's other people I meet that work at night. I do get lonely but not too lonely. The *Washington Post* route manager comes by about 2:00 AM and takes a break with me. There's an old guy, Pop Dirken, who cleans up the parking lots. The night shift cops rendezvous there. That's great. I can't get robbed while they're there."

"Have you ever been robbed?" she asked.

"No, knock on wood. I tell the cops stay as long as you want. They always need batteries for their flashlights. I let them take all they want."

"Isn't that stealing?" she asked.

"No, the boss told me it was OK to do that. It's OK."

"I'd be scared out there," she said. "Especially at night."

"I am scared out there and especially at night. That's the only time I'm there."

We both started laughing.

"A late-night waitress brings me coffee and doughnuts every night about three. She's a lot older than me and she likes to wind down there in the gas station. She likes me to sit in her car with her and talk."

"What do you two talk about way out there in the middle of the night?" the girl asked.

"Well, she likes to talk about, uh, strange things like reincarnation, the Loch Ness Monster, and things like that. She brought me a book about Nessie."

"Who's Nessie?"

"Loch Nessie. Over in Scotland," I said.

"Oh."

"You know," I went on, "you don't have to go all the way to Scotland to see a water monster. There's one in the Chesapeake Bay, called Chessie. And I saw it once."

"Oh, come on," she challenged.

"No, listen," I replied. "I saw it with my whole family. We all saw it one day when we were fishing at Cove Point, Maryland."

"Oh, sure," she said derisively. "What did it look like?"

"OK, I'll tell you. Do you know what 'bilaterally symmetrical' means?"

"No," she laughed.

"It means that one side of an animal is just like the other side. *You* are bilaterally symmetrical. So are cats and dogs."

"I'm not a dog," she shouted at me.

"I didn't mean that and you know it," I said.

"OK, OK. I was just joking. But what's it got to do with this monster, Chessie?"

"Well, Chessie is *not* bilaterally symmetrical. This monster was about twenty feet long and ten feet wide. But its fins stuck up out of the water. And there were lots of them. And they were all different sizes and they didn't have any pattern. It was like they were all there at random. It didn't make any sense at all."

"What was it doing?" Dianne asked.

"It was just cruising parallel to the shore about thirty feet out. I don't know what it was doing," I said.

"Anyway," I went on, "we're pretty good friends."

"Who?" asked Dianne. "You and Chessie?"

"No, me and Wanda, the lady who brings me the food and likes to talk about strange things. The one I sit in the car with. She's always telling me about Hinduism and astrology and ghosts and things. She's the one who told me about Nessie. Do you understand what I'm talking about, Dianne? Am I talking too much?" I asked.

"No and, yes, I understand. But you're not in love with her."

"No, I'm not. She's a good friend but—hey, wait a minute. How would you know that?"

"By the way you talk about her. And you didn't get that faraway look in your eyes."

"What faraway look?" I asked her.

"The one you didn't get," and we both started laughing.

"OK, OK. Good joke. Thanks."

"You're welcome," she said straightforwardly. "Are you going to work all your life at night when the whole world's asleep and eerie and talk to people about strange, obscure, occult, and maybe obnoxious things when you know you should be warm in bed in a home somewhere?"

She was lightly laughing and chuckling.

And taunting.

"Oh no," I said, "I've got a full, four-year scholarship at Tulane University in New Orleans. It starts in September."

"How did you get that?"

"Well," I said, "most guys apply to one school only. But I applied to twenty-two colleges. I had several offers. I took the best one. It even pays for room and board."

"What are you going to study?"

"Psychology," I said.

"You want to be a counselor?"

"No," I said, "I want to get an MSW degree. Master of Social Work. I'm going to specialize in psychiatric social work."

"What does a psychiatric worker—did I say it right?—do?" she asked.

"You said it right," I said. "People with neuroses, unhappy people come to me and they talk to me about their troubles."

"And what do you do?" she asked.

"I listen to them."

"You listen to them and they pay you for that?"

"That's right," I said and we both burst out laughing again.

And we kept laughing for a long time. We couldn't stop.

"I don't understand why they pay you just to listen to them, but if that's what they want to do I guess it's alright," she replied.

"Yes," I said, "it's just like you talking to me right now. And I'm listening."

"Because I'm crazy," she insisted.

"Right," I said, playing along with her. "You're crazy and I'm listening to you. Problem is, I feel crazy, too. Maybe it's this great weather?"

"Maybe we're both crazy," she said, "and we don't know it."

We both started laughing again. But right in the middle of all this laughter, she was staring into my eyes once again very deeply and with a serious expression on her face. And she said:

"So. I see. You think you're going to New Orleans in September. But you know what?" she asked.

"No," I answered, "what?"

"You'll never go to New Orleans. Never," she abruptly exclaimed, much to my surprise.

"What?" I asked. This was a strange thing for her to say. Predicting my future when she hardly knew me.

I told her so.

"New Orleans," she answered. "Some Coolidge grads go away to college, I know, but not you. Never!"

"Whaddaya mean, Dianne?" I asked her. "I meet a pretty girl in the park and she tells me my future. Are you a female prophet sitting out here in the park with orange hair? You think you're an oracle?"

"I don't know what an oracle is," she said, "but you'll never go to New Orleans. Never."

Then she changed the subject.

"And you think I'm pretty, huh?" she asked.

"Yes. You are certainly a very pretty girl. But why do you say I'm never going to go to New Orleans?" I asked.

"Suppose I said I didn't want you to go. Would you go, then?" she asked.

I found myself staggered by this question. Who in the hell did this girl think she was? I wanted to say something like, "But I hardly know you, how can you know so much?"

Or: "How can you be so sure right now?" But I got tongue-tied because even though what she said didn't make any sense, something she said scared me and there was a bit of doubt in my mind about what I would do if she said....

But I didn't even know her.

And before I could say anything she said:

"Do you think I'll like high school?" Changing the subject.

"Huh?" I muttered, still pondering her previous statement. But I couldn't do that forever.

"It's a good school, Dianne. I'm sure you'll like it."

"I hope so," she said.

"Oh, you will. It's one of the best high schools in the country," I said.

"Johnny?" she asked. So, now I was "Johnny." Only my mother called me that. What the hell?

"Yes," I answered.

"Guess what you just did?"

"What do ya mean?" I asked her.

"You just told my future. Why can't I tell yours?"

"It isn't the same thing," I insisted.

"Yes, it is," she said. "Look!"

She was pointing at the middle of the football field.

"The grass is moving," she said.

"That's just the vapor coming out of the ground. It's been trapped there all winter," I said. "The grass has been dormant, I mean asleep, all winter."

"I know what 'dormant' means. It means the same thing as 'hibernate.' Do you know what 'aestivate' means?"

"Uh, well, no," I answered.

"It means to hibernate in the summer."

And as she said this she looked me square in the eyes again. Our vision locked and she would not let me go for a long time.

After about five minutes of this I felt something break in me. And it felt good. Then she relaxed her deep blue eyes and smiled, releasing me from her eyehold.

Suddenly I got mad.

"Now look...."

"Yes, I know," she said, "you don't like being toyed with. I'm not toying or playing with you."

"You're not?" I asked.

"No, I'm not. Honest.

"Will you be here tomorrow night?" she asked, without taunting or teasing me. My emotions went askew. This little girl was confusing me.

But whatever it was that she was doing, it was quite pleasant. So I said:

"I'll come if you come."

"Oh, I'll be here," she said. "I promise I'll be here. Please don't worry about it, I'll be here."

How did she know I needed that promise? She knew it before I knew it.

I suppose that she walked off while I was thinking and meditating on this situation with my new acquaintance, Dianne.

In any case, she was now gone.

Other than orange—I mean, red—hair, what did she look like? I couldn't remember. I sat there without moving for at least twenty minutes, but now that she had gone all that I could remember about her was what we had talked about. And her red hair.

She was quite beautiful, I knew that. She was intelligent and perceptive. I knew that. But as to the specifics, I had no recollection.

It was time to go to work. I hurried up Aspen Street, feeling thoroughly confused.

She had given me a promise and that felt good. But how did she know that I needed a promise?

Her promise gave me a slight feeling of certitude. Just a little certitude. But that was better than nothing. And how did she know I needed a promise? How did she know that I needed one? How did she know all that stuff?

How did she know I would be thinking about her?

It was a good thing that I could do my work at the gas station automatically, not needing to think about it. Because all I could think about was Dianne.

Wanda Russell drove in at 2:00 AM in a '56 Ford Fairlane.

There were no customers, so at her invitation I got in her car. The doughnuts and coffee were great.

"Wanda," I asked, "Could we skip Hindu philosophy tonight? Please?"

Actually, Wanda was an aging stripper who used fans and lights and things like Gypsy Rose Lee did. The day shift and swing shift men had all told me about her.

They all had gone and seen her show. They were all trying to get into her pants. But they couldn't. They didn't know anything about reincarnation, or meditation, or sea monsters, or flying saucers, or pyramids, or ancient philosophy, or yoga, or demons, or the like. And Wanda wanted to talk about these things with other people who knew something about them, too. I knew a lot.

Wanda was my pal. She had a great shape. She had invited me to come over to her apartment any afternoon. She said she had a lot to teach me about sex. Things other people didn't know. But I never went. I liked her. Very much. But like a sister.

She was so much older than me. It wasn't the thing I should do. I wasn't sure why. I wasn't afraid of her. I would have done anything else for her.

But I was waiting. I didn't know I was waiting but looking back on it now I can see that I was waiting.

Waiting.

We were pretty good friends and conversationalists. We were both interested in obscure, occult things. And we read lots of books about strange things and told each other about what we had read. And it was quite fascinating. There was so *much*.

And we did love each other. But it was purely Platonic. And that really was OK with us both.

And we confided in each other and kept each other's secrets. We were great friends.

But not lovers.

"Wanda," I said, "I met a girl today."

"Ah," she said. "Tell me more."

"She's very pretty. She's only about thirteen or fourteen. Her name is Dianne Kelley. She has orange hair. Great shape. Highly intelligent. Not shy or neurotic. I don't think she knows anything about sphinxes or phoenixes or ESP or *pranayama*. But that's OK. She's very nice. I like her a lot."

"Wow," said Wanda, "she must be a real something. In all the time I've known you, you never brought up the subject of girls once."

"This isn't girls, Wanda," I said. "This girl is very unusual. I've never met anyone like her."

"Oh, I see," said Wanda. "Sounds serious. What's so special about this Dianne? Tell me, I wanna know."

"Well, Wanda," I said, "she did this really strange thing. I don't understand. I, uh...."

"Come on now, Fahey," she said with a laugh in her voice, "you can trust Aunt Wanda. I'm really very interested. Tell me what she did that was so strange."

"Well, OK, Wanda," I said. "We were just talking casually, you know, about this and that, about schools and school colors and the weather. Just a perfectly normal conversation like I could have with anybody. Ya know?"

"Yes," Wanda said. "Go on."

"Well, when I got to the part about my scholarship—I told you all about it, right?"

"Right," she said.

"Well, when I got to that part and told her about Tulane and about going away to New Orleans, ya know...."

"Yes?"

"Well, Wanda, all of a sudden she blurts out, but quietly and with certitude,

'YOU'LL NEVER GO TO NEW ORLEANS.'"

Wanda knew about my scholarship. She thought I was very lucky to get it. And she was right. I was very lucky to get it. And I would be a fool not to accept it and go down there and study. All my friends thought it was a really good deal and that I should go. *I* thought it was a good deal. It was definitely in my plans. I had talked to the president of the Psychology department over the phone, and then I had taken the train to New Orleans so Mr. Briggs, that was his name, could show me around, and we could talk more about my thesis, etc. We got along great. He was very interested in a paper I had done on Martin Heidegger and Karl Jaspers and psychology.

And not only did Mr. Briggs show me around the campus, he took me all over the place and showed me where everything was in New Orleans. He took me to the French Quarter and everything.

So I was just waiting to go and everybody was in favor of my intentions, everything was just fine and seemed in place and then this little girl with orange hair comes along and says, "No. You won't do it,

YOU'LL NEVER GO TO NEW ORLEANS."

And for some reason, I found this fact very disturbing. But I didn't know why.

"So, this girl you met with orange hair told you you weren't going to go to New Orleans. And it seems to have upset you. Am I right?"

"Yes, Wanda," I said. "It is disturbing me and I can't figure out why."

"Maybe she's crazy," said Wanda.

"Oh no," I said. "If she was crazy it wouldn't bother me what she said. But she's not crazy. Not at all. And that's part of the problem. Why did she tell me that? It's like I have this feeling that she knows things about me. Not just surface things but deep things. And quite frankly, Wanda, I'm afraid that she does know things about me that even I don't know. Isn't that crazy?"

"I don't know," Wanda said. "Tell me some more about your reaction to this girl and what she said. Tell me more about how you feel."

"OK," I said. "She tells me this loony thing that nobody could know about, one way or the other, and I can't forget it. I keep thinking about it. I can't stop thinking about her. I keep seeing her face in my head. I'm doing my work like a robot. I'm not really paying much attention to it. You know, I'm on automatic. I keep...."

"I think I see some light at the end of the tunnel, Fahey," she said. "Tell me just a little bit more. When you say you're upset, do you mean you're really upset? A lot?"

"I don't know what more to say. I can't get her out of my head. I can't think of anything else. Never go to New Orleans. I keep seeing orange all over the place—the color of her hair. She calls it red. But, see, once I had a tomcat. I was crazy about that cat, and he had the same color hair Dianne has. All the streetlights and car lights—same thing. All I see is orange."

Wanda: "That I understand, Fahey."

Me: "Well, what does it mean, Wanda?"

Wanda: "Oh, I think you'll know soon enough, Fahey. You'll understand soon. And don't worry. There's nothing wrong. Everything's going to turn out all right."

Me: "What things are you talking about, Wanda?"

Wanda: "Fahey," she said very dramatically, "you wouldn't believe me if I told you. So I'm not going to tell you. You're not so dumb. Be a little braver, Fahey. Just be a little braver."

"What the hell do you mean *brave?* I *am* brave. Remember the night that drunk attacked the...."

"Yes, Fahey, you're ferocious when it comes to fights, but you are afraid of girls."

"I am not. Gosh," I said sarcastically, "thanks a lot, Wanda. Thanks a hell of a lot. Uh huh, well, there's more but I'm not going to tell you now."

Wanda: "I want to help you, Fahey, and I would if I could. But in this situation only you and the girl can help. You and the girl. Not me...."

Me: "What in the world are you talking about, Wanda?"

Wanda: "I mean, it's a kind of situation that is developing, coming to be, and interfering in any manner—well, I just can't and I won't. And if I did you'd get mad at me. Please believe me, Fahey. And this, too. You can handle all this by yourself. You don't need me or anybody else except the girl. And it looks like you won't be suffering for very long. Honest, Fahey, if our roles were reversed, you'd do the same thing I'm doing. And I'll tell you this, too. If anything bad starts to happen, then I'll warn you. I promise. But please don't stop confiding in me. When you figure it all out, you'll see that I did the right thing.

"But look, Fahey," she went on, "if you want me to watch out for you, you've gotta tell me the rest. So spill it. What else happened?"

"Well, I trust you, Wanda. You know that. I don't know what in hell you're doing, but—well, see, she did this other weird thing."

Wanda: "What weird thing?"

Me: "Well, what she did was this. She asked me if I'd meet her tomorrow night. And I said I would. And then she took my hand in hers, squeezed it, and she told me that she *promised* she would meet me. She promised."

Wanda: "Yes, and so...."

Me: "Well, the funny thing is that at the time I didn't feel like I needed a promise. It wasn't a big deal *then*. But later on in the day, after I woke up, I was worried about meeting her. I *was* worried I might not see her again. And then I remembered her promise. And it helped a lot. I guess I really like the girl a lot. Sure. But how did she know I needed that promise before I knew it myself?"

Wanda: "Well, Fahey, you met a really smart girl. I'll tell you that. And she cares about you a lot."

Me: "She does?"

Wanda: "Oh yes, Fahey. And I mean a whole lot."

Me: "How can you tell? You don't even know her."

Wanda: "Look, Fahey, let Aunt Wanda interpret these events for you. It's all going so fast you can't keep up with it. But I can. I'm not involved personally so I can be more objective. Now here's what's going on."

Me: "Yeah?"

Wanda: "Here's the way I figure it. *She* knew that you would be thinking about her. You didn't know that but she did. And she knew that you would worry. And she didn't want to hurt you or cause you pain. She thinks that you, my boy, fell in love today. With her. But you're the only one who can answer that question. Only you."

Me: "Uh...."

Wanda: "So, she gave you this cushion, this pain pill like she was a female bodhisattva who came and incarnated again, refusing *Moksha*, just so that she could help you and stop you from suffering. And maybe help some other people, too. You ought to ask her if she's a buddha," she said, chuckling.

Me: "Uhhhhhh...well, I don't know if I fell in love, yet. Maybe I did. But what about the other thing? Telling me I wouldn't go to New Orleans."

Wanda: "OK, Fahey. I can see that you're beginning to figure it out. So I'll tell you what I think now. I think you are in love with her but you're not aware of it yet because you don't want to be in love. But you'll give that up as time goes on. And when you realize that you are in love, you won't want to go to New Orleans, and you won't go to New Orleans. But that's just what I think. You gotta find out for yourself."

Me: "Uhhhh...."

Wanda: "And you will, my boy, you will."

Me: "I got nothing against being in love but...."

Wanda: "You sure of that, Fahey? You sure?"

Me: "Well, uh, give me some time, Wanda. Give me some time. But tell me one thing, Wanda. Just one thing. Let's suppose that I am in love with her. Let's suppose that. How come she knows it before I know it?"

Wanda: "You are dealing with a very sharp girl, my boy. Very, very sharp. And quick."

* * *

Sometime before the sun came up, I was sitting outside the gas station office in the dark open and I fell asleep. I had a dream.

I was at Union Station, in downtown Washington, D.C., suitcase in hand. I was waiting for the Southern Railroad's "Crescent," the famous passenger train that went all the way from D.C. to New

Orleans. I was on my way to New Orleans to go to school at Tulane. The great green diesel pulled in. I got in my sleeping car and found my room. Then I heard all the porters shouting

BOARD.

The train began to move. But it wasn't going forwards. It was going backwards and it was heading north. Out to Northwest D.C., where I lived. Where Dianne lived.

I rang for the porter to ask him why the train was going backwards. But nobody came. The train started going faster and faster. Still none of the porters came. And this was "The Crescent" for Christ's sakes. It was famous for its service and cuisine. But I couldn't rouse even one porter.

I started to get up and go out in the hall and find somebody to ask why we were going backward. But just as I stood up an aged Hindu swami in an ochre-colored robe stuck his head in the door.

"Don't do it, my son," he cried, oh-so-mournfully. "Don't do it. Do the other.

"Oh," he said, "I almost forgot. The *Shankaracharya* changed your mantra. I brought you your new mantra, guaranteed to be the most powerful mantra in the entire universe—but only for you. Only for you. Only for you. Only for you...."

He kept repeating "only for you" over and over and over while he held a silver hand tray in front of me, like a waiter would do.

There was a small, orange-colored, square envelope sitting in it. Small. The size of an invitation envelope.

The *Shankaracharya* of India is the head of all the orthodox swami orders in India. Most people don't know this, but swamis all regard themselves as incarnations of god. They are priests of the Hindu religion. They don't usually tell you that either.

"Why did Sri Shankaracharya change my mantra? I've been doing fine with an occasional rosary."

"I don't know, *sahib*," he said, "I only work here. I just do my dharma. I don't make waves or ask questions. I follow the *Bhakti* path."

"Well, great," I said. "If you don't know why the big S changed my mantra, do you know what it is?"

"No, Captain," he said. "I have no knowledge of such matters. I am but a humble servant, lowest of the low, weakest of the weak, smallest of the...."

"Oh, come off it," I shouted, cutting him off. "Cut the humility routine. I can see your aura. You aren't an ordinary swami. *You* are the *Shankaracharya*, and if this note is from the *Shankaracharya*, then it's from you. You can't fool me. I've been around, buddy. So tell me the truth, Big S. What is my new mantra and why have you changed it on me?"

"Oh, my dear *Chela*," he answered, "I had to change it because a new element is entering your life, and you need some different transcendental *rasas* to deal with it. Please try to remember, the only reason I exist is to serve you. I am your very own. It is my dharma to change your mantra. What the hell kind of a guru would I be if I didn't watch out for things like this? Huh?

"Look, *Janakan*, the, uh, new factor in your life, uh, you know what I'm talking about," he said.

"Which new factor?" I asked him. "You mean my new gig at Tulane?"

"Oh no," he mourned, "not that. Not that. The other one. The other one."

"*What* other one?" I asked him. "What are you talking about?"

But then he began to dematerialize. Right there in front of me he was turning invisible.

"You fool," he said, as he became more and more imprecise, "if you can't figure it out any other way, look at your new mantra. The answer is there, my *Chela*. The answer is there."

And he was completely gone.

I was alone in a train going backwards. Without knowing why. Alone with the square, orange, invitation-type envelope which was supposed to contain my new mantra.

I was afraid to open it. I don't know why but I didn't have the courage to open it.

So I rang for the porter. This time a real porter showed up.

"Yassuh? Something ah kin do fo ya, suh?" he asked.

"Yes, porter. Would you be so kind as to fetch me a pint of Old Grand-dad? I'm coming down with something and I don't want to be unarmed."

"Yassuh," the old black man answered. "Comin' right up." And he was gone.

But he didn't take long before he returned and gave me the bottle. I took my first gulp and waited for the warm ambiance to take over my system. I took another and another and finally I felt strong enough to open the Gnostic epistle.

And I did open it. There was my "new" mantra,

OM MA

written in Sanskrit and English.

So I pulled the bell cord again. I needed some correct answers but quick.

The *Shankaracharya* of India stuck his head in my door again and asked:

"Yes, my dear *Chela*, is there something swami can do for you?"

"What's with this mantra?"

"Ah, yes," he said, entering my room and sitting in "easy pose" on the floor of my room.

"I understand. And I sympathize with your confusion. I really do. And I shall try to explain so that you will understand. It is a very heavy matter."

"You better explain things real good or I'll call the guru union as soon as I get offa this train."

"You might think you will but you won't. You see my po' *Chela*, this train is but a representation of your new mantra, OM MA. And so am I. And so are you. The mantra is all. Everything else is but illusion, *maya*.

"Ah," said the swami, with a beaming smile. "I see the problem. I understand. Please let me explain, my little *Chela*."

"Shoot," I said.

"The problem is, my dear *Chela*, that there is no problem. It only looks that way. You must disregard your Western training, vis-à-vis Aristotle and the Roman Catholic Church. In Hinduism we do not acknowledge the principle of non-contradiction. It is perfectly orthodox to disregard that silly, narrow philosopher Aristotle. Forget, my dear *Chela*, forget the principle of the excluded middle. And so I tell you my dear *Chela*, in your present existential condition your new mantra is and is not the same mantra, in the same respect and at the same time. You must forget all the Western mumbo jumbo. Just keep saying your mantra as often as you can, and soon you will understand everything."

And I felt very good, even though the train was still rushing backwards, faster and faster.

"I have to go now," said the *Shankaracharya*, "but before I go, let me give you a morsel to chew on. MA is waiting for you at the end of the train ride. At the end of this train ride and every train ride. MA will always be there. So do not ever fall into despair or confusion. MA is with you always.

"And this new girl you met—if I were you, my dear *Chela*, I would treat her exactly like you treat your mantra. And I would regard this girl exactly as you regard the Blessed Virgin Mary.

"You never know," he said, as he started to disappear again, "that girl might be MA in disguise.

"You never know," he said, just barely visible now.

"And furthermore, if you don't know it already, you will know it soon. One of the advanced principles of *Advaita Vedanta* is that one must treat EVERYONE EXACTLY AS ONE WOULD TREAT THE GURU. EXACTLY AS ONE WOULD TREAT GOD. EXACTLY AS...."

Once again he was gone. And as soon as he was gone, the train stopped. And the porters all started shouting, "AZALEA CITY, AZALEA CITY. NEXT STOP SILVER SPRING."

And I knew this was my destination. I opened the door to my sleeping room and walked down the hall towards the exit. And as I did so, I kept seeing MA and Dianne in my head, and I was hoping they would be there waiting for me. Just like the *Shankaracharya* had told me they would, but....

And then I woke up, feeling rested and quite happy.

And I knew what that dream meant. For a while. I knew.

Soon it was time to quit work and I walked towards the cheapo greasy spoon next door. The warm, balmy weather kept up. Strange vapors, odors, pollens, and just-melted humidity came awake invisible and slowly rose out of the ground. Thus liberated, these essences came to us humans and gave us strange and unnamable notions which we filed away without distinction under the category SPRING FEVER.

And I thought, yes, I have spring fever. That's all it is. Glands. Pollen. Nothing else. The girl, Dianne, probably had it, too.

The fever was probably responsible for my dreams, too.

Yes. That's what was going on in my life. Spring fever. And it made all this new stuff, this girl, the emotions, the dreams, exaggerated. Made these things too big. Out of proportion. Sure, that was the problem. Nothing to worry about.

I ordered breakfast from Hy, the owner of the little "eats" place. While I was eating it, he blurted out:

"Hey Fahey, where are you? Come back to earth. This is your home planet, you know."

"Huh?" I came out of it. But I couldn't remember where I had been. I guess I was thinking about my dream. I had been staring into space.

I guess part of me didn't want to go to New Orleans. OK. Fine. But I wondered how did this girl, Dianne, know that? Was she psychic or something?

"Hey Fahey," Hy called to me again, "you know what the weatherman says?"

"No," I replied.

"It isn't going to get cold again. Spring is really here."

"Great," I said, "I never talk much about it but I hate winter and fall. It feels like everything is dying to me. Those damned leaves all colored yellow, and then later they dry up and they're black and gray and ugly and dead. I hate it."

"Yeah," said Hy, "a lotta people feel that way."

That kind of weather was great to sleep or be dead in. *This* kind of weather was great to sleep in, too. But it was a peaceful sleep, brought on by the discharged pollens and stuff. The big thaw. I loved it. I looked forward to a great sleep all day.

And I did fall asleep when I got home. I fell into sleep quickly. But I only stayed asleep for about two hours. And then I woke up. What in the world did I have to wake up for?

Angry, I fell back asleep. But then I started having more crazy dreams.

Dreams I didn't want to have.

Well, the first one wasn't so bad. I dreamed I was in a dark room trying to turn the lights on. I knew what that meant. I'm sure you do, too.

But then I dreamt that I was way out in space somewhere on a planet where there was nothing but very dark green grass. It was freshly mowed and smelled real good. There was nothing else as far as I could see but this grass. I walked and walked all the way around the planet. Nothing but grass. No lawnmowers. No people. No houses. Just green everywhere.

I had the feeling that I had been exiled to this place because I had been dabbling in the occult like Wanda.

Suddenly I saw a black storm on the horizon, headed straight towards me.

Faster and faster it rushed towards me.

Then a twister caught me and I was spinning and flying around like Dorothy in *The Wizard of Oz*. Except that I wasn't in a house.

A bunch of slimy yellow leaves started attacking me, biting me, sucking my blood out, and sticking to me. More and more of them. I got so heavy and lost so much blood that I could hardly stand up, much less walk. I was getting weaker and weaker as the leaves got heavier and heavier. And then just before I fell out of the cloud, I saw a giant face. It was Wanda Russell driving a brown and white, broom-shaped Montgomery County police car. She was laughing and laughing and pointing her finger at me. Then she screamed: "New Orleans? Ha! Ha! Ha! Never. Not in New Orleans, not you, ha-ha, never. I know that orange-haired girl. She's my daughter. HA! HA! HA!"

And I kept falling until finally I landed gently on the Coolidge football field. Except it wasn't really the same field. Something was different about it. Now again I was surrounded by grass as far as I could see.

Over towards the railroad tracks I saw a very long train with endless red streamlined diesel engines and flat cars, all going north, all carrying gigantic clocks, all of which said

12:00 PM

HIGH NOON.

The engine bell had turned into giant clock chimes. They ran continuously, over and over.

BONG BONG BONG BONG BONG BONG BONG BONG.

And the name of the railroad was printed on each car:

THE BLACK DIAMOND EXPRESS TO HELL.

The flatcars carried nothing but tombstones and giant clocks. And the tombstones all had my initials on them. With my date of birth and the date of that very day I was having the dream.

Walking across the field was a little girl—not Dianne—coming closer and closer and closer and closer to me. In her hand she held a long-stemmed red rose. When she got to me she held it out in front of herself and stared into my eyes. She didn't move for a long time. She just stood there with her rose and stared at me.

All of her features—eyes, nose, mouth, and hair—were blank. Like Little Orphan Annie's eyes in the newspaper. Blank. Nothing. Death.

"Hello there," I said, with a warm, lilting inflection.

"Hello," she said. Then she handed me the rose. And then *she* started laughing at me.

"Hey," I yelled at her, "cut it out. This is only a movie. You don't have to try to scare me. It's not real. It's just a movie."

"You wanna bet?" she said in a teasing voice. "Think it's only a movie, huh? Then how come I'm scaring you if it's just a movie? How come, how come how come?"

"You can't scare me, I read Freud's dreams book. I know what everything in this movie means. I know who you are, too. Why do you want to scare me? Why don't we just sit and talk?" I asked.

"We can't talk because we're in the movies and the other people will get mad at us," she said.

"But I'll tell you this," she said, whispering in my ear so that the other people wouldn't get mad at us. "You *are* very intelligent. Very. But you don't know everything. Like, for example, this flower. You don't know what this flower means, do you?" she taunted me and started laughing louder and louder.

I looked at the flower and I knew fear. I did not know what the flower meant. I looked at the rose again and then I screamed in terror.

Then I woke up.

I knew what the rose meant. And the tombstones and the clocks. I knew.

I was *there* at 7:05 PM and she—I first saw her walking towards me and the eternal wooden bench a few minutes later.

My elbows were on my knees and my head hung down and it stayed up only enough so my eyes could see her.

Her manner was quite different this muggy evening.

She marched up to me, grabbed my right hand in both of hers, and put her left arm around me possessively and said:

"Oh, Johnny, this is really tough on you, isn't it?"

"What is really tough on me?"

"You know what," she said a bit roughly.

"Yes, I know. I'm sorry. I'm sure as hell not used to this. But it's OK. And I know it, too."

"It won't hurt very long," she said.

She had her head on my shoulder already. Then she reached up and fell on my neck and gave me three quick, moist kisses. Then she blew on them. This sent chills up and down my spine and made goose bumps all over my back.

"Oh, God, that felt good." I started crying a swamp of tears.

"Please, do it again," I heard myself say. "Please!"

Then she put both arms around my neck and kissed me all over my head and my face, again and again, holding my head by my hair.

Once again, I felt something break inside of me. But this time it broke all the way. I simply came apart at the seams and I threw my arms around her, still crying. I kissed her a bit roughly because I wanted to show her that I considered her my property.

She, by not drawing away—by going limp, by leaning against me—indicated acquiescence, agreement to the extent—without one word—that she, in fact, granted me those rights and much more, a great deal more, than I had asked for. Exclusive rights. She was all mine.

Forever, no matter what.

I began to feel better very quickly, and I held her and kissed her and she started breathing heavy and fast.

That made me feel good, too.

I was being resurrected in more ways than one. Then we had an "I love you" contest. Who could say the ultimate words the most quickest, the longest, the shortest, the most flippant, the most serious, the most everything.

* * *

After I had finally gone from misery to that warm, peaceful glow and we were both relaxed—a condition I had previously had not the slightest hope for—and we were just sitting there staring into space, listening to each other breathe and smelling each other and the water weather, I asked her, "You know all about this, don't you?"

"I don't know anything about it, but you do!"

"Hey, no kidding," I told her. "I don't know anything about all this. I have no experience at all. I don't know what to expect next."

"Johnny, you're the one who walked up here and said 'hello' to me."

"Yes, but I had no expectations. I never expected anything like this to happen."

"Are you sorry it happened?"

"No," I said introspectively. "No, not at all. But it is a bit over-whelming."

"Yes, it is," she said. "You wanna get out?"

"Oh, come on, Dianne," I said, "you know what's going on. No, I don't wanna get out even if it kills me—and it may, but that's OK."

"You don't look like you're gonna die very soon, Johnny," she said.

"No," I said, "the gods want me to stick this out for the duration. It's OK."

"Ya sure?" she asked.

"Yes, I'm sure," I said, "and you know it, dontcha?"

"Yes, I know it," she said. "I know it but I wasn't sure you knew it. Especially in your head. I wasn't sure. I'm sorry."

"Nothing to worry about, Dianne. Everything's gonna be alright. I can feel it."

So, we dabbled in this kind of babble for another half hour or so. Babble it may be, but it's an essential part of life and there's no way to get out of it. So you don't even try to get out of it.

Finally it was time to go, so I walked Dianne home. She thought I should meet her parents so they wouldn't worry when she was out and so they would know who she was with.

It was a warm and encouraging meeting. They liked me.

* * *

"Well, sonny boy, you sure look different. If I didn't know you and your problem better, I'd say you look happy," Wanda said to me later that night.

"I am happy. I saw her again and she kissed me and we hugged each other and all that and now I feel wonderful. I never felt so good in my whole life," I told her.

"Already? This is certainly a fast-working girl," Wanda said.

"Yep."

"You really are happy, aren't you? I can tell by the way you act. The way you talk. All relaxed and peaceful. Content and immobile. I've never seen you like this before, Fahey. This must be some girl!"

"That's the way it is. I never met anybody like her. I'd do anything for her. And she'd do anything for me."

"This is disgusting, Fahey. You used to be a man. You were cynical like me. Wise and tough like me. Now you've turned into a mouse."

"Wanna bet?" I challenged her.

"What about college?" she asked. "What about New Orleans and Tulane?"

"You know," I went on, "I completely forgot to ask her why she told me I would never go to New Orleans."

"Oh great," Wanda said ironically.

"You know what?" I asked.

"What?"

"I don't really care very much about New Orleans anymore. I can get my education here. Anywhere. I feel free. I am free. I never felt so free in my life. She did all that."

"Oh Christ," Wanda said with disgust.

"If she says I'm not going to New Orleans, I guess I'm not going to New Orleans," I said.

I didn't know why Dianne had told me that I would never go to New Orleans. I didn't know that. And maybe I would find out why she had said it and maybe not. But one thing was certain. I was not going without Dianne. I was not going to leave her here while I went off someplace, anyplace. I had to have her with me. And if that meant staying in D.C., I really didn't care.

"I worry about you, Fahey. Sometimes I worry about you a lot. Like now, I am worried. Could you introduce this girl to me? I would feel a hell of a lot better if I met her."

"Sure. I'll put the two of you together. But not yet. She doesn't know about you. I told her that you exist but I also told her that you were a waitress. Give me some time. Then there's another problem, too. We work the night shift but she works the day shift. I'm sure there's some way to do it, but I can't think of it right now. Give me some time, Wanda, and I'll make it happen."

I slept all day long like a log. There were dreams. Yes.

One of the dreams went like this: I was in the park again, some old but indistinguishable little friend beside me. Perhaps he was the former me.

The railroad tracks ran right across the wet grass and into the swimming pool under water and then out again and headed west.

Along came three bright red, Lowery-influenced diesels. They had straight, parallel purple stripes along the sides except that the stripes kept turning into purple garter snakes and getting all twined up and wrapped around each other.

Then for a while there was silence on the land and nothing happened.

But in the distance, I heard a strange and wonderful noise. It was every pitch in all the modes and all the ones in between them. And the noise contained all of the timbres of people—young, old, tall, sick, well—singing one pitch each to a loony, asymmetrical rhythm. And it came closer and closer. The closer it got, the louder the noise became. But it was a beautiful noise. Not dissonant. Not chaotic.

I wondered what *this* train would look like.

Finally it came around the bend from the north on the Baltimore and Ohio tracks. It was like an apparition. It was the largest, greatest diesel/electric engine I ever saw. Driving smoothly, slowly down the decline with its twin V-16 engines roaring.

Somehow it was smiling at me through its maroon and white stripes.

For a minute or two the noise of the engines went away and the chorus sang, now in unison:

> *This train don't burn no coal at all,*
> *Oh, oh, don't burn no coal at all.*

Fare you well, Johnny, if I don't see you no more,
Oh, if I don't see you no more.

Lemme tell you something, Johnny, just before I go,
Oh, just before I go.

You're a motherless child, you ain't got nowhere to go,
Oh, you ain't got nowhere to go.

You are, she is, but I AM,
Oh, sure as you were born, it's me and I AM.

Then the train rode majestically over the pool, and picking up speed it disappeared down the tracks to the west.

But then another train, a train with no discernible markings, came from the west on these same tracks. It was a steam engine train and it blew black smoke all over the place. That was why you couldn't see any markings. The engine and coal car and all the box-cars and caboose were nothing but black.

This affectless, unidentifiable train had nothing to say to me. It didn't acknowledge my existence in any fashion at all.

Then a feeling of awe and fear came over me and swallowed me up.

Suddenly the tracks shot up straight over the empty swimming pool as though they were giant rubber bands and two giants, off-screen, had suddenly pulled them in opposite directions. For a while the tracks vibrated. Suddenly they stopped vibrating and when they stopped a rooster stood up on the roof of the administration building and issued the trumpet fanfare from *Le Coq d'Or* by Rimsky-Korsakov.

In the real world, this rooster was a clock.

Suddenly the beautiful train—the colorful one that smiled and sang to me—came charging back from the west where it had gone previously. And from the east, on the same tracks, the dirty coal train came charging towards the friendly train.

Closer and closer and faster and faster they headed towards each other. The noise got louder and louder until I had to put my hands over my ears. I was yelling:

"Stop, please stop, you'll get in a head-on collision!"

And I couldn't even hear myself because the trains were making so much noise. They were both blowing their whistles and chimes, too. Talk about noise.

I was even more scared.

Finally they ran into each other, and the noise was deafening. But neither train knocked the other train off the tracks.

Then both trains backed up like two bulls fighting and both trains reared up and shot towards each other again until BANG.

Then a stage curtain came down and covered the scene of the terrible train wreck.

Then I saw the curtains parting and a little girl walked out onto the stage.

This little girl—I really can't explain it too well—she looked like Dianne and she didn't look like Dianne.

And that was even more scary.

Suddenly she was right in front of me with today's rose. Beautiful red rose. But there was something odd about the petals. I looked more closely and saw that they were all shaped like adder heads.

And as I looked the little girl vanished into thin air.

This was a late afternoon REM dream. Very confusing. I didn't understand that dream at all.

* * *

We both arrived at 7:00 and discovered again why we have bodies. Bodies communicate in a manner comparable to speech but very much different than speech. Bodies enable us to know that we are grounded in the earth and held by gravity. But, in addition, when two people cling together thousands of words and hours of time can be saved. The communion of people is a most important, expedient exchange of quick and urgent necessities by which one compounds decades of words, one on top of the other but all adjusted by the clinging motions, each one fine-tuned, modified mostly to admit subtleties, some amended, some with subscripts, some underlined in red, adjusted slightly to the left or to the right, some with markings totally unique and unknown to any existent tongue outside of the intimacy, until the breathing slows and each returns to himself, but greatly changed. Transferred, moved, but the scatter stopped and the soul centered, cool and clear....

"I missed you terribly," she said. "It's getting bad now for me, too. How much did you miss me?"

She already knew the answer to that. What she wanted was some word—it had to be just the right word—that would give her the emotional experience she needed right then and there. A word that she would immediately recognize as stemming from the center-seminal-reason. The Truth. Precisely and all of it. Only that. Nothing else would do.

It had to be perfect as her "promise" had been for me.

Maybe there were better words, but the ones I used sufficed quite sufficiently:

"Wretched. I've been wretched without you. I can't think about anything else except you. So it's like you are with me all the time. But it's not good enough. Nothing but torment and pain without you."

"Yes, I know what you mean. It's been the same for me."

"Really?" I asked, feeling insecure in this world about all things in this world and never experiencing certainty. It's part of being alive, I think. Kind of thing philosophers like Sartre and Heidegger and others talk about. Being "thrown" into the world. That's the way they like to talk about man's wretchedness, weakness, inauthentic-ity, anxiety, ambivalence, fear, inconsequentialness at the mercy of strong, much stronger forces all the time—time, heredity, emotions, fragility, lack of permanence, epistemological confusion, self-decep-tion, suffering, old age, and death.

I was not particularly insecure with Dianne. To some extent I felt more secure in her presence.

But even with my head in her lap, or when we were entwined in each other's arms, underneath it all I felt insecurity.

And now that I knew her, being without her was almost unbearable. The previous night I had been happy and warm at first. But as the night wore on I felt empty and useless. I felt like a ghost. A wraith on the move.

Twelve hundred dollars worth of business—that is about two hundred customers, all of whom I spoke with—not one did I know or remember, wandering around the cars and trucks and gas pumps, suspended in

WAIT.

A kind of nothingness, emptiness without her.

And yet I had done my job as well as I always did, which was pretty good. I was on automatic. And I had thought to myself, I've misled Dianne in a couple of things. I'll have to tell her soon. I didn't want these things affecting us in anyway. I better come clean. I can't lie to Dianne. Not her. I felt guilty and wretched because I had misled her a little.

After we had communicated with our bodies and souls for a while and began to feel normal again, I said to her:

"Dianne, I have some confessions to make to you. A few things I gotta tell you."

"Oh?" she answered, looking slightly, but only slightly, worried. Only slightly.

"I don't think it's very important, but I want to and have to be absolutely honest with you," I said. "It's part of this deal. It's the way we are—I know you're that way, too. But when I met you I really got hit hard and...."

"I know. I know," she said soothingly. "Trying to make a good impression. Fudged on a couple of things, eh? I doubt if it's anything important, either. Tell me. Please, tell me."

"Well, first of all, that waitress I told you about, who brings me hot chocolate and doughnuts...."

"Yes?"

"Well, actually she's not a waitress. She's kind of old for it, but she's a chorus girl and a stripper."

"Oh, Johnny, I don't care about things like that. I know you don't love her. So why should I worry? I know who you love."

"Well, that's great," I said. And I meant it. "But I gotta get this stuff off my chest, ya know?"

"Yeah," she said. "Sure. I understand. What else is there?"

"Well, the other thing you gotta know is I read a lot about those obscure things me and Wanda talk about. I'm really interested in some of them."

"Like what?" she said, looking puzzled.

"Oh," I said, "I like to read books about reincarnation and Hinduism and meditation and sea monsters, myself. I've been studying those things for years. I told you that it was Wanda who is interested in things like that. Not me. See, I didn't want to scare you off. I didn't want you to think I was any kind of weirdo. But I guess maybe I am. I don't know what to do. I really like to learn about those things but I don't want you to think, uh, you know what I mean."

"Oh, Johnny," she said, "I do know what you mean. And you know what? I wondered about that because I couldn't see how it could be a one-way street with her doing all the reading and research and her doing all the talking. But it didn't feel important to me. I knew you'd tell me more about you and your friend sooner or later."

All I could say was "gosh."

"I'd like to meet your friend sometime. I think maybe it would be good for all three of us. Then there wouldn't be any mystery. Or suspicious thoughts and feelings. Or if there were I could call her up and talk to her."

"Gee, Dianne, that's great that you feel that way. You know what? She wants to meet you."

"Really? Maybe she wants to check me out. I'm sure she cares very much about you. Maybe she is worried I'm not good enough for you. Or, I'm a crook or—or *something*."

Then we both started laughing.

"I think you're right, Dianne."

"Yeah," she said, "I just couldn't see you being only a receiver, listening to her babble all night long. But that's OK, Johnny."

"Really?" I asked.

"Really, Johnny. And I thought about something else, too, Johnny. I'd really like to see a sea monster. No kidding. Could we go and try to find 'Chessie' one day?"

"Sure. If I ever get a day off. Or I quit or whatever. We could have a lot of fun on a sea-monster hunt. We might or might not find one but we'd have a lot of fun anyway."

"I'm sure we would, Johnny," she said.

"But wait a minute. I want to go back to those confessions I made to you. There's something there that's very important."

"What's that?" she asked.

"We should both watch out for telling lies—I know you wouldn't lie to me, Dianne, and maybe what I'm doing is mostly talking to myself, but look, we really shouldn't let anything get in between us. Nothing. Because what we have going here is sacred and I don't want to defile us in any way. You know what I mean?"

"Yes, I do, Johnny," she said. "I never thought about it that much, but you're absolutely right."

"Yeah, ya know," I went on, "we have to try very hard not to let anything—anything at all—come between us. There's a lot of stuff all over the world, and a lot of it wants to get in the middle—and it will sometimes, you can't help it once in a while—we just have to try real hard to not let anything—anything at all—come between us."

"You're absolutely right, Johnny. I'll try real hard."

"Well, ya know," I went on, "even when those things get between us and ruin our, uh, discourse, there's always coming-back-together again. There's always coming home."

"Yes, I see what you mean. Gosh, Johnny, you're really smart. I didn't know—but, you know what?" she asked.

"No."

"*We* are a home," she whispered.

"Right. You're absolutely right," I said quietly.

"We gotta try very hard and pray a lot that nothing will break up our home," she continued, following my thought.

"Yes. I wanna be as close to you as I can," I whispered.

"Me too," she said.

"Sometimes," she told me, "sometimes I wanna be you. Isn't that funny? And not only that but sometimes I think I am you. Isn't that crazy?"

"Gee, I don't think so, Dianne," I said. "It might sound strange to somebody else but I know exactly what you mean because I've felt some of that, too."

"Really?" she asked.

"Really," I said. "I want to be inside of each other."

"Wow," she said in a whisper. "Sometimes I feel the same way."

"You too, eh?" I asked.

"Yes. Really. Say, Johnny. . . ."

"Yes?" I answered.

"Why are we whispering?"

"I don't know," I said.

"I don't know either, but I don't want to stop it," she said.

"Neither do I. Maybe we should whisper even more quietly. We don't want anybody to hear us. They'll think we're crazy if they hear us talk like we have been talking."

Dianne: "Yes, definitely. We don't want anybody else comin' in here right now. The silence is a symbol or an emblem or something."

Chuckling and laughing quietly, tiptoeing, we crept across the green, green canopy.

The big bugaboo came. The fall. The cold. The wind. Sometimes snow and ice. But this year the season of the dead summer's soul, the big yellow leaves, didn't bother me. The September sun went out like a dying ember. It rained and snowed. But I didn't care about it anymore. I was deeply enmeshed in other matters, or rather another matter: Dianne Kelley.

September came and went but I was quite content. I didn't care. I stayed right there.

I called the Psychology department at Tulane University. I tried to explain. But how can you explain something to someone who doesn't know anything about what you're talking about? In past years, I wouldn't have been able to understand myself. I certainly couldn't have understood any of the language Dianne and I used when we were exploring our condition.

"I'm sorry," I said. "I can't come down there. I don't dare. Something happened. And I can't explain it. Nobody could understand it if I told them."

I was talking to the head of the Psychology department. He was pretty mad. He was awfully smart, too.

"Why didn't you tell us until this late date? I'll have to find a substitute."

"It didn't happen until a few weeks ago," I said. "There's nothing I can do."

"You meet a girl or something, Fahey?" he asked. "I'll bet that's what it is, eh?"

"Well, gosh," I stammered, "that is what happened. I met a girl and everything changed. I can't take her down there because we're not married yet and I don't have the money."

"I thought so," he said a bit sardonically. "It happens a lot to my students and my students-to-be. We really could have used you with that great grade point average and your undergraduate thesis on Heidegger. It sure woulda been nice. But look, John. I don't want you to feel bad. This girl you met, you gonna marry her?"

"Oh, yes. I don't know when but, yes, we'll get married and I don't think it'll be far away."

"You meet her parents?" he asked.

"Yes, I did, and I liked them very much. And they liked me, too," I answered.

"So it's the real thing, eh? OK, Fahey, I don't wantcha to be unhappy on your honeymoon. And I don't want to make your wife unhappy. So look. You just forget about any guilt you feel or anything like that. It really won't take me much time to find a replacement."

"Oh, I hope not. I don't want to cause you any trouble. I really don't. There was just no way for me to know what was going to happen. I mean, I've had a lot of girlfriends but this is something altogether different. And I can't turn it off. I don't even want to change things. That's the way it is. I can't change it."

"Oh, listen, John, I understand. I really do. So please forget about it altogether. OK?"

"OK," I said.

But he went on, "If you ever feel like going back to school, please call me and tell me. That was the best Heidegger knockdown I've ever seen. And I'm not the only one. I sent a copy to *Philosophy Journal* and they want to publish it."

"Really?" I asked.

"Yes, Fahey, they want it. And they should. You've seen through Heidegger's tricks more than anybody else ever has. Including me.

"You're good, Fahey," he went on. "I'd really like to have you in the department. Please remember that. And you'd like it here, too."

"Well," I said, "I wouldn't mind going back to school at all. But right now I . . . ."

"Oh, I understand, John," he said. "You're only human, just like me. Really, I do understand and I wish you well. Will you do one thing for me, though?"

"Sure," I said. "What do ya want me to do?"

"Send me a picture of the bride-to-be and yourself. That'll make me feel better. Like I'm part of the family or something. I'm not exactly sure why, but I would really appreciate it if you would send me some photographs of the two of you."

* * *

As the leaves of brown came tumbling down—and the yellow ones, too—a lot of my former high school mates came by in the early evenings to check up on me and see what I was going to do. I was already a year behind them, college-wise. They were worried about me. This guy named Buddy and some others came by. This is what I said:

"Look, Buddy, everything's OK. I had a full scholarship at Tulane. And I woulda gone but I couldn't leave. Not now. I called the chairman of the department and apologized. And you know what he said?"

There was no way they could have known.

"Well, this is what he told me. He wasn't mad at me. And not only that. He liked one of my papers so much that he told me that if I ever want to go back to school, call him first. He'd really like to have me in the department."

"Really?" my friends asked.

"Yeah," I said. "That's just what he said. And not only that, he is getting my paper published in *Philosophy Journal*. I'll even get paid some money. About two hundred and fifty dollars. He's a really nice guy."

"OK, Fahey," Buddy said, "but you gotta get outta this town. It's a hick town. You know, you gotta grow up and get outta here while you still can."

"This is my home. I was born here for Christ's sakes. I'm not like you guys. I can't just pick up anywhere and move any time. I got friends here. And I like my old friends. I like them a lot. I don't wanna go somewhere I don't know anybody and have to try and make new friends. Here, guys, I like it just fine here."

Then of course, this: "OK, Fahey, that's maybe cool but lemme ask you. You gonna stay here until *they* start moving out here and take over? It won't be so nice around here then."

"So *then* I'll move. Lemme tell you something, old boy. I got other more important things to do and I gotta do 'em right here."

"You talkin' about that redhead somebody told me about . . . ."

"Yeah," I said, "you got it. But don't you fear. She's kinda like a university herself. No joke. I like the way she looks at things. I'm learning a lot and changing."

"How's that?" he asked.

"Well, it may sound corny but now I'm getting more and more involved with other people. And I like it."

"You've always been a loner, Fahey. What's the matter with you?" Buddy asked.

"Yeah, a loner way out in space somewhere with no connections.

Just me and me and me. Dianne grounded me. I'm right here with my feet planted on the ground. And I like it. I like it. I was never happy being a loner. Not really."

"Dianne, eh?" he went on. "A university called Dianne. You're talking about Dianne Kelley, aren't you, Fahey? She's just a kid. You're crazy, Fahey. Just crazy."

"Yeah, but I'm happy," I said. "I got everything I want right here now. I love being grounded. It was awfully cold out there in space."

"Uh," he said. But he couldn't think of anything more to say.

"She's taught me things, Buddy. I'm not joking," I said.

"Like what did she teach you?" he asked.

"Oh, like you don't have to make a lotta money to be happy. Mosta the things you really need are usually close by. In your backyard. Or in the woods across the street. That's one thing she taught me. Oh, she didn't use those words. It's something I noticed. She and her family are all that way. They're really fun people."

"She's Irish, right?"

"Right," I said.

"Is she a Catholic?"

"Of course. I like that. I like the way Dianne looks at things. I even like her family. I'm a happy man. Can't you tell?"

"Oh, well," he said, "I guess if you're happy...."

"Oh," I said, "I'm happy alright. I'm just gonna stay right here. If I went to New Orleans I might not be able to sleep right. I dunno. Just a feeling I have."

Yes. I really am lucky. And happy. What would have become of me if that St. Martin's summer hadn't come when it did? That "fatal" meeting. I'm just joking. Not very fatal. Dianne the university. She knew—she knows—things that aren't in books but ought to be.

Yes, I wonder what would have happened if I hadn't gone for a walk that balmy day in April. Whatever would've happened, I'm glad it didn't. As far as I can see or feel, Dianne turned out to be my salvation.

The girl I met that solstice spring day when she utterly destroyed my unconscious vow to remain superficial, unconnected, cold—that's why I had been afraid of the winter. I had been afraid of myself.

But she wasn't afraid of me. Not my beloved tassel time girl.

I got Wanda interested in the Yoga Sutras of Pantajali. What else could I do when she developed an interest in witchcraft?

OM MA. Know what I mean?

HONEY

It is the Buffalo Folk Festival.

And it is very late at night.

Sometime in the late sixties or early seventies.

I cannot remember exactly what year it was.

But, nevertheless, it was.

Everybody is very tired and irritable.

By "everybody" I do not mean the audience.

They all seem pretty happy.

No, I mean all the people backstage. The entertainers, the festival staff, sound engineers, producers, promoters, managers, booking agents, newspaper reporters, prostitutes, drug pushers, cameramen from radio and TV stations, photographers, groupies, wives, girlfriends, boyfriends, catamites, gunsels, sycophants, bodyguards, pretenders, and many other people whose precise relationship to the festival and the entertainers is unknown.

Unknown to everybody else backstage.

And there are lots of these occult figures wandering around.

Taking up space.

And there is not very much space.

But we cannot get rid of them because somehow they all have backstage passes.

And so in addition to everybody being tired and irritable, everybody also has claustrophobia.

Many backstage are having anxiety attacks.

Fortunately, there is a doctor and some nurses backstage.

It is around 11:00 PM or midnight.

The last three acts to go are Roosevelt Sykes, me, and finally Steve Goodman.

That is the schedule.

And that is what everybody expects.

Except Steve Goodman.

A staff walks quickly into the room.

Goodman isn't there, however. Goodman is too important to be there. He is somewhere else where there is more status and he can relax and he can feel more important.

Staff addresses Roosevelt Sykes, the greatest piano-playing blues singer alive.

Staff: "Say, uh, Roosevelt, Steve Goodman's got an early show tomorrow night back in the City. He was wondering if you could trade him time slots so he can get out of here earlier."

Sykes: "Why, certainly. I'll play whenever you want me to. That's fine."

"Oh, OK, Roosevelt, great," says the staff and without thanking him walks out. Sykes stays cool. He doesn't seem to care.

But I care. And I'm mad.

I mean, Sykes was getting up there in years. He was probably more tired than I was. But I didn't say anything about it right then.

And I wondered what the story with this Goodman guy was. I had never heard of him before this festival. But then I never did pay much attention to phony folk musicians, anyway. I didn't consider myself to be a folk musician, phony or real. But that's what I got billed and booked as. So I didn't really care. Call me whatever you want. I just want some gigs now and then. That's what's important.

The previous day I had seen Goodman perform. To me, he was mediocre. So I asked around what the big deal was about him. And I was told he had written a very "important" song, "The City of New Orleans." Not only was it "important," it was also "relevant."

Har, har, har.

What the hell my informants meant by "relevant" I never did find out.

Goodman had sold the song to Arlo Guthrie, and Arlo Guthrie had recorded it, and so they had both made a lot of money from royalties.

I remembered the song. It is an aggressively bland and aggressively consonant song. It is too perfect for my blood. There are no rough edges. It is a smoothie. A song that a person would write exactly the way some stupid book about writing songs said that you should write songs. Inoffensive. Safe.

I mean, it is just the glorification of an Illinois-Central-Gulf passenger train that ran between Chicago and New Orleans. The train was very popular and aggressively picturesque. Everybody loved it. If it still exists, Amtrak runs it.

So Goodman wrote this one very safe and intensely agreeable song. He wrote a song about something commonplace, unremarkable, everyday, something known about by millions, habitual, conventional, truly prosaic, quotidian, workaday, pansophical, cogitative, easily seen, ordinary, down-to-earth, nontranscendent. He might as well have written a song about something else that everybody is in agreement about.

Like food. Water. Clothes. Water lilies. Pretty girls. Music. Air. "Home."

Too bad he didn't write a song about the virtue of something mysterious, ambiguous, little known, obscene, occult, new, transcendent, something that does not yet exist but is coming into being, something, oh well.

And, in the success lexicon, Goodman wrote that one song, "The City of New Orleans," and that's it. Goodman was an aggressively inoffensive, grievously suburban, vividly moderate, tame, and

"NICE"

entertainer.

There are lots and lots of things that were distinctive about the

City of New Orleans train. It had a very colorful history. But you do not hear about them in this song? No. According to the song, this great train had no particular history, no grounding, no roots, no redeeming value, no faults, nothing in particular. It was, according to Goodman, a generic passenger train. Nothing special about it. I doubt if Goodman ever rode it. I did.

Furthermore, there is nothing distinctive or admirable about the song "The City of New Orleans."

And the same is true about Steve Goodman.

Now that he is dead we can talk about him.

Har, har, har.

I've waited a long time.

Meanwhile, Goodman thinks that he is such a big deal that he can go around changing other people's schedules if he feels like it. He doesn't even bother to find out what *Roosevelt* must do tomorrow.

He thinks he's great. And relevant. And important. Significant.

RIP. Har, har, har. RIP.

Anyway, Sykes and I had been talking about his, Sykes's, recording career. It was extensive.

Roosevelt had made records under the following pseudonyms: Dobby Bragg, Willie Kelly, Easy Papa Johnson, and St. Louis Jimmy. He used these pseudonyms so that he could record for more than one company at a time while being under an exclusive contract with one of them.

Roosevelt was a very civilized and intelligent man. He always wore suits and ties, took baths, read the newspapers, always civil and polite.

He was an odd-looking person. Short and fat, he had an imposing, large jaw.

He was light-skinned enough to pass himself off as a white man. And sometimes he told me he did this when he couldn't find a room in a black hotel.

Sykes was not a dirty old man. He was sophisticated, genteel, intelligent, and gregarious. But since he had made a lot of double-entendre records some people thought he was a dirty old man. And that previously he had been a dirty young man.

Some people *thought* that I was important. But I never thought that. And nobody ever accused me of being relevant. And I certainly never thought or said that I was "relevant."

Thank God.

And so I didn't go around thinking I was a big deal and I was very important and treating other people like they were inferior to me and changing schedules around and stuff like that. And Roosevelt, who was important, but maybe not "relevant" (who cares about "relevant" anyway?) didn't do these things either. He didn't want to bother anybody or treat anybody like a second-class citizen.

He was a nice guy.

So we were sitting around waiting to play, and he said to me, "Jawn," he asked, "what are you so upset about?"

"Roosevelt," I said, "I don't care how late they put me on stage, but I think it's a dirty trick on you to put you on last and have this other guy who is much younger than you change the schedule so that you have to stay up so much later. They shouldn't treat you that way, it's not fair, and it's not right."

"Oh," he said, "I see what the problem is. Yes, I got it."

"Problem?" I asked. "What problem?"

"Well, I've been in this business a long time, as you know. And things like that don't bother me. You see, I've already been paid. My agent always insists that I get paid the remainder of the guarantee before I go on stage. If there is a percentage I have to wait for that. But there won't be any percentage here. This gig is flat rate. Not only that, but it's a very good flat rate job. I wish I got more gigs like this. I'm perfectly happy."

"Oh well," I said, "I didn't know that was how you look at it. But it still seems to me that they ought to treat you with more respect."

"Respect?" he went on. "See, Jawn, I don't care very much about how these people treat me. I know that there are many, many people who do respect me and have respected me for years and years and years. So if I run into somebody who doesn't treat me with respect, I just figure that he is ignorant and there's nothing much I can do about it and, furthermore, his ignorance is his own problem and not mine. See what I mean?"

"Yes," I said, "I see what you mean. Well, OK, Roosevelt, if it's OK with you, it's OK with me."

"Alright, Jawn," he said in his Southern, whiney kind of a drawl. "Good. But that isn't the point."

"What point?" I asked.

"Well, look, Jawn, we have plenty of time until you go on. I want to show you something. Teach you something that is very important. Especially in the music business. And you can use it too, and it will help you a lot. Would you like to learn it?" he asked. "It's very important. But then it's also very funny."

"Sure, Roosevelt," I answered. "I'm sure that if you have something you want to teach me, it's important so, fine, go ahead."

"OK, Jawn," he said, "I'll do just that. And someday, down the line, after you've learned how to do this thing and have used it a lot, I hope you'll remember that old Roosevelt taught it to you and think kindly of me."

"Oh sure. I'll do that. But what is it you want to teach me?" I asked.

"Well, Jawn, I think that it is time that you learned about
HONEY."

"Honey, what's
HONEY
got to do with show biz?" I asked.

"Honey's got a lot to do with everything that is important in life, Jawn. Not just show biz, but everything."

"Well," I said, "OK, Roosevelt. If you say so. So tell me about
HONEY
if you want to. I don't understand what you are talking about now, but I'm sure once you explain it to me I will understand it."

"Oh yes, Jawn," Roosevelt said, "you will understand. And it will help you all through life. Just ordinary, plain
HONEY.
From now on you've got to learn to think about
HONEY.

It's very important. If you're going to stay in show biz for a long time, you've got to learn about

HONEY.

"Now, Jawn," he went on, "as you know

HONEY

is sweet, right?"

"Oh yes," I replied.

"And, another thing," he said, "it makes everybody happy and makes everybody feel good when they swallow some

HONEY.

"Right?" he asked.

"Right," I answered, wondering what in the world he was getting around to.

But I knew he wasn't crazy, and I knew he knew a lot, so I didn't say anything.

No.

I just listened to him.

And also the way he was repeating the word honey so much was kind of hypnotic.

You know what I mean?

But I knew he was "alright," so I kept a passive attitude.

Anyway, he went on: "What you've got to learn, Jawn, is to think about

HONEY.

And think about how sweet it is, and how good for you it is, and how nice and smooth it is, and how wonderful it is, and how good it is to you, and how wonderful it is for anybody who eats any of it. It makes them happy and it makes you happy. It's wonderful stuff, Jawn, isn't it?"

"Well," I said, "now that you mention it, I guess it is, Roosevelt. I just never thought about

HONEY

before."

"That's OK, Jawn. You are beginning to learn the secret about

HONEY.

You are already doing it, so before long you'll know all about it and how great it is and how you can use it by just thinking about it."

"OK, fine," I said.

Sykes: "For a while, it's very important to practice thinking about honey. Set a little time aside every day and just sit somewhere quiet and think about

HONEY.

And before you go to bed at night always think about honey, at least for a few minutes. It will help you sleep."

Me: "Well, I'll try it, Roosevelt. But only because you said so and I trust you. Because, I still don't understand why

HONEY

is so important."

Sykes: "Oh, you'll understand it very soon. You'll see why it is so important. Don't worry. Now, listen very carefully, Jawn. Once you learn to think about honey and think about it very deeply then whenever somebody comes around and says something unpleasant, what you do is you start thinking about

HONEY.

If you do then you can turn the conversation around 180° and the painful person will be on the end of the stick and not you. And furthermore it's *your* stick and not his."

Me: "Yeah, I think I'm beginning to get you."

Sykes: "See, by thinking about honey rather than thinking about what a jerk the other guy is, or the situation is, or whatever, then you will find yourself treating him as if *he* was doing *you* a big favor. And once the guy starts thinking that you are grateful to him and that he is, in fact, doing you a favor, then you have got control of the situation. You are in power. You are in the driver's seat. Not him, but you. And *that* is the whole point, isn't it?"

Me: "Well, yes, Roosevelt, now that I think about it I guess that is the whole point. By thinking about

HONEY

and talking nice to the guy, you switch things around, and you're the real boss."

Sykes: "That's it, Jawn. You got it. But now don't get confused. We're talking about feelings mostly and how to keep feeling good and on top of things. The bad guy *can* make you do things. He can make you do things that you don't want to do. But if you turn it into a situation where it looks and feels to both of you like you are doing the guy a big favor—if he can't control the way you feel, but you can—then you are the one who really wins, Jawn. Even if the other guy doesn't know it. You see what I mean, Jawn?"

Me: "I think so. You're telling me that the really important thing is not what I do but what I feel. If I have possession over my feelings, that's the important thing. Is that what you mean, Roosevelt?"

Sykes: "Yes, Jawn, that's exactly what I mean. You see, Jawn, it doesn't really matter what somebody does to your body, or what they make you do with your body. That isn't really important because, Jawn, you aren't your body, are you?"

Me: "I'm not sure what you mean, Roosevelt."

Sykes: "I mean, there's something else over there, something else besides your body, and that's who answers when I call 'Jawn.' That body doesn't answer. It belongs to the real you. And the real you is not your body. See what I mean?"

Me: "I think so, Roosevelt. Yeah, I see. There's this body over here but the me, I am something else."

Sykes: "Right, Jawn. That's what I mean. And look. As long as you can prevent this bad guy who comes along, and believe me there's lots of bad guys gonna come along, right?"

Me: "Yeah, I gotcha."

Sykes: "As long as you remember that you are not the same thing as that body, and as long as you can think about honey, then you can always control how you feel. Not somebody else, but you. And that's how you win the game, Jawn. That's the only way. And the important thing about

HONEY

is that it enables you to keep feeling good regardless about what the other guy says or does. See—look, Jawn. Some badmouth comes up

to you and says something unpleasant so you start thinking about
HONEY.
So you go along with what he says, you agree with him and you thank him because the whole time you were thinking about the many, many good properties of
HONEY.
And that way you can change the balance of power . . . . Now, in an extreme situation, where this, what I told you, doesn't work, then what you do is you start *talking* about
HONEY.
Yes. Tell the guy all about
HONEY
and how much you like it, and about the many good qualities it has. Now, the guy may think you're crazy, but that's OK. You *still* got him under control."

Me: "Gosh, Roosevelt, I think what you're telling me will work. Next time something I don't like happens, why I'll just start thinking and maybe talking about
HONEY."
Sykes: "Yes, and Jawn there's more to it than what I told you so far. You've got to realize that by putting things back in natural order or harmony, that you are doing this other guy a big favor. Because you are making him feel good, too. That way you both win. So, you talk like this, Jawn: *Why, of course, I'll help you. How nice of you to ask me. How nice of you to think so highly of me that you ask me to help. Sure. I'd be delighted.*"
Me: "Gosh. I think you got something there, Roosevelt."
Sykes: "I sure do. And the whole time what you've got to do is imagine that you have a great big pot of
HONEY.
And what you are really saying is, *Here, have some*
HONEY.

I've got lots of it. There's plenty to go around. And another thing you do is you make yourself feel like you're made out of honey. And so is the other guy. In fact, everything is made out of honey."

At this point, Roosevelt started to laugh quite agreeably.

And so did I.

Me: "It seems like thinking about it is funny, too."

Sykes: "Right, Jawn. Thinking about

HONEY.

is funny. And not only that but it rhymes, you see,

HONEY IS FUNNY.

Get it?"

And then I started laughing because it was so funny to think about everything being made out of

HONEY.

Sykes: "Why, Jawn, when you get right down to it, there is

HONEY

everywhere. There is no place you can go where there isn't any

HONEY.

And not only that but there is

HONEY

in your voice. It's in your mind. Why it's everywhere. And isn't that funny?"

Now we were both laughing like two madmen but it didn't matter and neither one of us cared because, you see, it seemed like everything in the universe had turned into

HONEY.

And this seemed very, very funny, and we kept on laughing and laughing for maybe fifteen minutes, and then when we tried to stop laughing we couldn't stop laughing because everything seemed so funny.

And when the staff came and told me I had to get ready to go on and I had ten minutes I still couldn't stop laughing and neither could Roosevelt Sykes and I'm sure that the staff thought we were insane. And maybe we were.

I didn't care.

So then the staff came back and we walked towards the stage and for a little while I managed to stop giggling insanely and then suddenly I found myself on stage.

I was seated and trying to keep from laughing. And I was succeeding. So I started to play my first song but right in the middle of it I started laughing again and I couldn't play the guitar because I was thinking about honey and everything seemed very, very funny. And I thought the audience will get mad at me if I don't stop laughing and play them some music, but in fact they didn't get mad at me. Not at all. And see, what happened was they, the audience, all started laughing, especially when I tried to apologize and then I explained to the audience what Roosevelt had taught me about honey and why, but I still couldn't stop laughing and neither could the audience and it went on and on and on and on and we were all out of control because we couldn't stop laughing.

Finally after about fifteen minutes I did, somehow, manage to stop laughing and so did the audience and so I played a bunch of music and I couldn't believe how well I was playing.

It was really great. I don't play that well so often.

I guess the laughter helped.

And when I was through playing I got a huge ovation and people were screaming and yelling

MORE MORE MORE

And so I did several encores and I didn't have any more trouble with laughing and everything was OK.

So then after I played I listened to Roosevelt's set, and it was very good. But he didn't have any trouble with laughing.

When it was over, I went back to the tent and found Roosevelt and shook his hand and said,

"That was a really nice set, Roosevelt. It made me feel real good."

"Why, Jawn, I didn't expect you to stay up so late just to listen to me."

"Roosevelt," I said, "I enjoyed every minute of it. It was just like
HONEY.
Smooth and sweet."

"Why, thank you, Jawn. Thank you."

And then he changed the subject and he asked me:

"Say, Jawn, can you tell me how to get to the hotel?"

"Sure, Roosevelt, I got a car and I'll drive you over if you want."

Roosevelt didn't have any gear to carry so he picked up one of my guitars and carried it to my car and I drove him to the Delaware Street Holiday Inn where I was staying, too.

That was one of the most fun evenings I ever had in my entire life and I'll never forget it.

And I owe it all to Roosevelt Sykes and also to

HONEY.

Yes,

HONEY.

Antonioni

If I had to do it all over again, I honestly don't know whether I would do it or not.

I did make a lot of money.

But it wasn't any fun. I'll tell you that.

Really.

I walked into a difficult and unique situation knowingly, where I had no experience whatsoever. Where I found myself stuck to a power-mad egomaniac and an enormous and powerful organization.

What could have been an interesting and fulfilling experience turned out to be a nightmare.

I suppose the thing could have been a lot rougher. I had hoped to learn something valuable.

So anyway, one morning in 1969, the morning came but I remained asleep because I like to stay up late and sleep late.

I value my sleep very highly. I have great and wonderful dreams.

So it was late in the morning, but I was still lying in bed asleep.

My wife Jan comes into the bedroom and starts shaking me.

She wants me to wake up and get up.

Something is urgent.

URGENT URGENT URGENT URGENT URGENT

And she is very excited.

She is going to make me get up come hell or high water.

Because something is urgent.

Now if there is one thing that I have learned in life, even as far back as 1969, it is this: Whenever anybody says something is urgent, it almost never is.

But if it is urgent, look out. The situation is bound to be dangerous.

I have painstakingly tried to inculcate this belief into my wife's *cabeza*.

And she has tried very hard to learn this very important truth.

And, indeed, she respects me very much. And she listens to me and trusts me. She is a great wife. But because of the way she was brought up, she is a little slow about learning this lesson in re "urgent."

She is a very ambitious person.

Too ambitious.

When a person is that ambitious they will invariably become disappointed in life.

And they may hurt themselves and other people too with their ambition.

And it is hard not to take the bait when there is a lot of money involved.

But I was of the belief that everything usually comes to somebody who does very little or even nothing. All you have to do is not consider anything crucially important. Or Urgent.

It all comes down to he who waits.

I think that that is an old proverb or something.

Because everything that I have done, in re business, music, gigs, money, women, sex, food, clothing, shelter, etc., fell into my lap.

I never go out and pursue things a great deal or very hard. Most of the time if you do this you don't get anything, anyway.

But my wife hadn't learned this enough yet.

And she hadn't learned if you are seeking fame and fortune to any great extent the potential for disaster is very large.

I also believe in the principle of the conservation of energy.

Very much.

But at the time this stuff happened, I have to admit that I hadn't learned these lessons enough myself.

Yes, I have to admit that.

I'd rather blame it all on my wife.

But the truth is that I was sniffing the bait, too.

Finally my wife has me awake. And she is screaming in my ear: "John. MGM is on the telephone. Michelangelo Antonioni wants you to fly to Rome tomorrow and do some music for his new film."

"Ah look, dear," I say, trying very hard not to bust her in the kisser, "look, honey, it's," very hard I am trying not to emancipate her continuum—you know what I mean—"look, honey, it's just a joke. Try and calm down. Just a prank, see? I get a lot of crank calls." (We have only been married a short time so she does not know about the crank calls.)

"It's just a practical joke, so please don't get all upset. Just go and hang up the phone and let me go back to sleep. Everything is alright. Someday I will take you to Italy myself. Now please just relax, calm down, and hang up the phone."

"John," she says loudly—her name was Jan; a damn good wife, by the way—"John, it's real. I can tell. It really is MGM and they really do want you to fly to Rome tomorrow. You've got to wake up and talk to them."

Now this wife is Jewish, and so she is very intelligent and therefore difficult to put one over on, so I figure, Christ, it probably is MGM. What a drag.

"Jan, darling," I said, "please calm down. Even if it is MGM, I'm not going anywhere tomorrow. And I'm sure as hell not going to Rome. Now please just go and hang up the telephone."

But me? This is what I think: "Anybody who asks you to do a big thing like fly over the ocean, TOMORROW, is either crazy or dangerous or both."

"John," she says in a very caring way, almost in a condescending manner,

"John, remember when we saw *Blow Up*?"

"Sure," I said, "nice movie."

"Well, the director of that film was Michelangelo Antonioni. He is working on a new film and he wants you to go to Rome and help him and do part of the score for it. I know you like to do film scores, don't you honey?"

Har, har, har, she really has me there. This is my favorite kind of work. And I am very good at doing film scores. I had done several scores at this time and would do many in the future. I really enjoy getting inside the director's head and feelings and matching in music what he is telling me about, but mostly what he is feeling about while he is talking.

"John," she says, and really, you know, meaning well, "John, you're being lazy. I'm not going to let you pass up this opportunity. I'm not going to let you go back to sleep. So you might just as well get up and talk to the nice lady at MGM."

"Sure," I think, "nice lady at MGM."

By this time, I recognize that no matter what I do or say or feel, I am going to at least have to talk to the nice lady at MGM, who is probably in reality a power fiend.

And Jan is of course doing what she has been taught to do. She is looking out and helping me with my
CAREER.

There's that damned word again.

People other than myself do not understand that I do not have a "career," I have never had a "career," I do not want a "career," and so I probably never will have a "career." Fine. That is the way I want it.

If other guitar players want to have careers, OK. But not me. I don't want one. For what I do, to call it a career is a misnomer. An exaggeration. A preposterous conception. A gigantic pretension.

And I do not want to fool around with things like that because I really don't have all that much ambition anyway, and I don't need it because everything falls into my lap anyway, and I am not interested in Rome, or Romans, or MGM, or Michelangelo's present, past, or future.

It is pretentious and dangerous to want or to expect things like that.

What I have is this, and it is very important: I have a small little niche carved out here where I play guitar for people once in a great while.

I make just enough money to get by and have a little left over.

And that's all I want to do.

For me, to work any harder than that would be unethical and greedy.

"John, get up!"

On the other hand, I am only human. And therefore not continually consistent about things because I have a body and I am involved in time and change.

So I have to admit that, at least to some extent, despite my aversion to "big deals," I was tempted and was, in fact, seeing dollar signs in the air.

But of course I can't let anybody know that.

If anybody knows that they will take advantage of me.

And Jan keeps talking to me so long that now I am actually and fully awake.

"Oh," I say, "alright, Jan. I'll talk to them. But don't think I am stupid enough to not know who it really is who wants to go to Rome. Har, har, har. You can't fool me."

Wife laughs, pretending to look slightly guilty.

So I go into the next room and find the telephone, and I pick it up and say:

"Hello."

MGM: "Mr. Fahey, is that you?"

Me: "I dunno, sister. Maybe it is and maybe it isn't. What's on your mind, baby?"

MGM: "Good. I am calling you because Michelangelo Antonioni wants you to fly to come tomorrow and compose some music for his new film. Did you see his last film, *Blow Up*?"

Me: "Yes, I saw it. It was a pretty good movie."

MGM: "Good. You see, *Blow Up* was his statement to the world about Britain. And this new film he is making is his statement about the USA."

Me: "Wait a minute, baby. Hold on. *Blow Up* was a good movie. It was a good story. But what in the world do you mean when you say it is a statement?"

The voice does have me interested. I am already floundering in my resolve and in my mixed metaphor.

MGM: "You see, Mr. Fahey, I work with Mr. Antonioni and I really admire him so I really enjoy talking about his wonderful films. He explains to me what he is doing and let me tell you, Mr. Fahey, that he is a very interesting and intelligent and perceptive man."

Me: "I'm sure he's all that, kiddo, so shoot."

MGM: "Well, you see, Mr. Fahey, Michael Antonioni is a very committed person. Many people don't understand that. Especially here in the USA."

Me: "OK, toots, but what is it that he is committed to?"

MGM: "Oh, to the truth. What is really going on. In *Blow Up* he succeeded brilliantly, uh, in my opinion—and a lot of other people think the same thing—to portray the materialism and emptiness and insane drive for power and sex of the relevant people. He wasn't criticizing *all* British people. Just the relevant ones. The future movers and shakers. You see, Mr. Fahey, *Blow Up* was not just a story. It was an exposé."

Me: "Oh, I see what you mean. Yeah. I've been over there and I have to admit that in that regard he, Mr. Antonioni, did a very good job on that one. Yeah. I see what you mean. Neat. I never thought of it that way. But that's right. It is an exposé."

MGM: "Yes, Mr. Fahey. What Michelangelo does is try to get at the essence of a particular cultural scene and film it and show it to the world. *Blow Up* was about Britain and the new one is about the USA."

Me: "Sounds interesting, and I'm sure I would like to participate in it, but not tomorrow. You've got to give me a couple of days."

MGM: "But Mr. Fahey, when Mr. Antonioni says 'tomorrow' he means 'tomorrow.'"

Me: "Fine, toots. When I say 'tomorrow,' I mean 'tomorrow,' too. And when I say 'not tomorrow,' I mean 'not tomorrow.' Here's what you should do. You should call my manager. His name is Gene Schwindler. You call him, and I'll do what he says. See, I don't negotiate anyway. He does that. So you call him."

I give her Gene's number, say thank you, and hang up.

Whereupon and quite naturally I immediately call Gene and tell him what is coming down and that I don't particularly care about the whole deal, but if they really want me to go, I'll go, but they're going to have to pay through the nose for it. And if they really insist that I leave tomorrow—and Gene, I really don't want to do that—I've got to have a bonus for that. *Comprendez-vous?*

Gene: "Sure, John, gotcha. I'll get you a good deal. And I think they ought to pay you a bonus too, if they really want you to leave tomorrow. That's just not enough notice."

Now, you see, I really am a home boy. At that time I didn't really have any great interest in going anywhere that was not in the USA. I am very patriotic, and as far as I was concerned everything important is right here. Why take a horrible, long night air flight to Italy? I had not yet discovered how friendly and fun Italian people are.

And I didn't care much about it.

I went back to bed and fell asleep again.

OK, so maybe I am, or rather maybe I was too chauvinistic and lazy. But let me tell you how I saw the whole thing. I'll show you but let me tell you that I was right.

Here is what happens.

Some great big organization with all kinds of money and power exists somewhere. They think they can push people around because they have so much money and clout.

And they can push people around.

And they do push people around.

But they don't care about people. They don't care about you. They don't care if they kill you or drive you crazy. And they don't care how you feel and look at their megalomaniac loony project.

And so along comes some new *enfant terrible*, i.e., Michelangelo Antonioni for example, and having made several films which didn't make any money he finally hits the jackpot, probably quite by accident, with this film called *Blow Up*. So then, all of a sudden, he has all this clout because maybe he can do the same thing again.

Therefore MGM decides to pander to his every little whim or wish.

And if this jerk wants somebody on Mars tomorrow, they will get him there. Believe me, he doesn't have a chance.

They will use every trick in the book to accomplish whatever it is they are supposed to do.

So, of course, they first pave the way by telling Wife all about Italy and how beautiful it is there and how much money they will pay—and they will pay lots, believe me—and sure, of course, they will fly Wife over too, sure, why not, they want everybody to be happy, har, har, har, sure, and what this will mean to Wife's husband's

CAREER.

Ugh. There's that damn word again.

CAREER. CAREER. CAREER. CAREER.

Boy and do they use it while talking to Wife.

Wife's eyes get big, and Wife becomes covetous and greedy and ambitious and on and on.

These obnoxious things are taught to Wife by the big whatever it is. All they have to do is use the word, even in an off hand manner. And use it again and again. It will get in Wife's head and she won't even notice it and once they put it in there it will never go away.

Anyway, when finally I got up that afternoon, I see Wife is beaming from ear to ear.

I know what that means, baby.

It means that they have all conspired against me and against my wishes, and that they have delivered me over to mine enemies who oppresseth me on all sides, and they are studying and practicing war against me. And they have been shooting Evil Thought Rays at Wife and manager. They have also been shooting them at me but I am protected by organic and inorganic chemistry.

To some extent.

But not to every extent.

No. I have smelled the bait.

In fact, I am on the verge of biting it.

Well, anyway, the next day as it has all been prearranged by other people, not me, a limo comes and picks me up. And it is driven by a chauffeur.

I have never once in my life been in a limo with a chauffeur. See, they are trying to make me feel important. And despite all that I have learned and despite all my reservations and all my existential resolutions and religion, these guys are winning and I am beginning to feel like everything is

IMPORTANT.

And I hate it but I can't completely stop it.

I didn't ask for a limo and a chauffeur. What do I want with a limo and a chauffeur?

Nothing. I like to keep a low profile. I can drive better than most chauffeurs, anyway. See how they insinuate themselves into your life and get you to think like they think?

Everything is important. I am important.

I hate it.

But I am on my way to LAX in a limo, and there is nothing I can do about it. Nothing. I have sold out. Given in. Surrendered. Not stood up for myself.

I am being bullied about by hundreds and hundreds of people.

When this sort of thing happens to you there are only two things you can do.

The first thing that you can do is to buy an uzi and mow them all down. Then they will leave you alone and people will understand you because what you have done is overt.

And I am in favor of overtness. I don't like covert people myself because I never know what they are planning on doing to me.

And the fact is that they usually are planning on doing something to you.

Now, the covert method of disengaging the enemy is for you to go underground and use the methodology taught everywhere by psychiatrists and psychologists and shrinks and advisors and counselors and alienists and doctors and mental health professionals and group therapists and hypnotists and people like that who really know what they are talking about. The best thing to do in a situation like this is to become

PASSIVE AGGRESSIVE.

Because once you have been become passive aggressive they can't find your ego to push against and threaten and intimidate and force and coerce you into doing this stupid thing, whatever it is that they want you to do but that you do not want to do.

In this manner they cannot dangle you.

But you can dangle them.

And that is the whole point.

Who's on first is the whole point.

So how do you become very passively aggressive quickly when you run up against a very difficult situation that you are not equal to? This is what you do. You get

DRUNK.

I mean only as a last resort do you do this.

But it works. It really works.

I remember.

I don't drink anymore. I have health problems.

But also I don't want to drink anymore. I don't like what drinking does to my consciousness.

And I have been psychoanalyzed and now I know how to stand up for myself.

And I am much quicker at identifying the enemy.

I have developed much more sophisticated techniques for dealing with crazy, power-mad loonies.

But this is happening back then.

So I got drunk and stayed drunk all the way to Rome.

I don't even remember arriving in Rome, getting off the airplane, or anything.

I do remember arriving at some studio somewhere in Rome and going inside and meeting this guy with all the power and fame, Michelangelo Antonioni.

He seemed civilized and erudite and intelligent and polite and suave and sophisticated.

Of course, now I know that those are the most dangerous kind of people that exist.

But I didn't know it back then.

So I let him put the make on me, so to speak. I allow him to ingratiate himself to me and show me and tell me what it is that he wants to do. I allow him to impress me by various methods as to how perceptive, quick, wise, significant, and relevant he is. With all guys like him, the thing they want most in life—even more than money, even more than sex—is they want other people to say "Look at him. You know who he is? He is

RELEVANT."

So then, after he has supposedly made me think that he is relevant, he takes me into this little theater inside the studio.

I expect to see something intellectual and *avant-garde*, because he has this big reputation for that kind of thing.

But that isn't what he shows me.

Not by a long shot.

No, you know what he shows me?

A really terrible and long skin flick.

Of some twenty or so "couples," har, har, har, out in the desert doing the hoobala boobala in all sorts of positions and combinations and it scares the holy hell out of me.

So I don't actually watch it.

I pretend to but I don't actually watch it because I am afraid it will make me horny.

And if I get too horny I will go insane.

And I don't want to do that.

So I face my head in the right direction and watch just enough to know what this section of the film is about and to see if it changes dramatically, but actually my eyes are turned down at the floor.

But I do see just enough to notice that there is no change in anything.

Just the same stuff keeps happening for fifteen or twenty minutes.

I have to watch for a dramatic change so that if there is one I can change the mood of the music.

But there isn't one.

So he makes me watch it once.

But that's not enough.

He makes me watch it three times.

And then the lights come on.

And of course I say,

"Gosh, that's a really beautiful film, Mr. Antonioni."

I mean, you know the guy is obviously completely insane and probably dangerous.

He must have paid all those people to do that.

And now he wants to pay me to write some music for this skin flick in the desert.

And he wants to pay me a lot of money to do it.

Nuts, completely nuts.

So I am very nice and polite to him because I don't want him to fly off the handle and kill me or something like that.

I mean, you never know what nutty fruitcakes like that are gonna do.

In reply to my assertion that this skin flick I just saw was

BEAUTIFUL,

Mr. Antonioni answers back,

"Yes, John, it *is* beautiful. Very beautiful.

"Very

BEAUTIFUL."

The way he says this sentence is like the way Bela Lugosi would say it looking down at an about-to-be-vampirized virgin.

So not only is this guy nuts, he is a creep.

What I should have done was to simply stand up during the first few frames and yell

MR. ANTONIONI I DON'T MAKE NO STINKING SKIN FLICKS PLEASE TAKE ME HOME IMMEDIATELY.

But of course I am still young and impressionable and there are so many psychic vampires and thought control police everywhere, and they are all shooting Evil Thought Rays at me and trying to control my mind, that I coalesce.

I am also under attack by Wife, family, relatives, MGM, value systems, the art-fart system, the world system, and culture vultures, so I acquiesce.

These people have played a really dirty trick on me. I am old-fashioned and I have a lot of inhibitions. And scruples. And I never go to strip shows, or read magazines with naked women in them, or anything like that because, although I do enjoy sex very much, I want sex to adhere to Aristotle's principles of unity and I don't want to go around being made horny all the time by skin-flicks and porno movies and magazines.

And furthermore this isn't just normal sex.

And furthermore the people engaging in these very strange, exotic, non-Euclidian sex positions are all kids.

Kids. Yes. Very young kids.

And it is a long scene, maybe twenty minutes long.

And later I learn that this footage had to be smuggled out of the USA so that the state DA could not arrest and incarcerate Michelangelo Antonioni and anybody else who had anything to do with it, because he had paid these kids to do this thing and most of them were underage. And that footage is needed to convict Antonioni.

Without it, the state doesn't have a case.

So there I am in Italy, and this jerk shows me an illegally made skin flick when I was expecting to do something exciting but not illegal, immoral, base, gross, and (to me)

VERY FRIGHTENING.

And in order for me to be over there in Italy working for this jerk—and he really is a super jerk the more I think about it—he, Antonioni, had to make assumptions about me. He had to assume that I was a sex maniac. He had to assume that I was a voyeur. He had to assume that I didn't have any hangups or scruples or morals or religion, etc. In fact, he had to assume that I was something like the people in the skin flick.

And I am not at all like the people in the skin flick.

Furthermore, he did not check to see if I would be interested in this sort of thing. He simply assumed it. Furthermore, he doesn't let me know anything about it until I am all the way over there, trapped in Rome. Furthermore, although I ask him, beg him, to show me some of the other parts of the film, so I can see what kind of context this footage is in, he will not tell me or show me this. In fact he even tells me that he doesn't want me to know anything about the film other than what I see and what music I write.

Because if I do see other parts, or know anything more about the movie than I already know, that could very easily spoil the music that he wants me to write.

Let me say this: in all the days and in all the films for which I have written musical scores, nobody, not one single person, has ever treated me like Antonioni did. Never. Everybody else always showed me anything I wanted to see and answered any questions I asked in the belief that the more I knew about the movie the better I would understand what kind of a score they wanted.

This Antonioni creature is not normal. He is a sadist. He's got me trapped.

And furthermore I feel very strongly about this jerk, and MGM, and Mike Curb who kept calling me up and asking me for progress reports, and anybody else connected in any way with that horrible movie. They all played a really dirty trick on me.

Really dirty.

I felt that my intelligence was insulted. That, *qua* musician, I was being treated quite rudely and wrongly and unethically. I thought that this was an insult to my mind, my reality, my commitments, and everything that I was, and everything that I stood for.

And I was mad as hell.

How can I get revenge on this jerk, Antonioni, and still get paid? I mean *revenge*. Let me say it again.

REVENGE.

Because in my whole life, both before and after this incident, I have never been insulted to this extent.

Never.

Of course now that I am older and wiser, I see that I should have told him how I felt and went home.

But I was younger and meaner and stronger and quicker and much, much more confident of myself.

Revenge. Yes. But how?

I decided to play along with Ant until I saw an opportunity to "get" him.

As it turned out, I didn't have to think about revenge.

Not for one minute.

Fate or God or Providence took care of the whole thing.

And in more ways than one.

Anyway, Ant takes me into this little "bistro." I think that that's what you call it.

It's not a real restaurant. It's more like a snack bar. Only they serve drinks there. Ant has a drink. But not me. I want to keep my cool and my own counsel because I am dealing with an insane pervert who has played a really dirty trick on me.

Probably knowingly, too.

So anyway, we are in this thing called a bistro and I am playing it cool and I want to come out ahead, so I say:

"Gosh, Mr. Antonioni, that sure is a beautiful sequence you just showed me. I've never seen anything like it. It must have taken real courage for you to get that footage. I really must say that I admire you. Very few directors would have the guts to film anything like that. Gosh. It was really beautiful."

And now

THE RETURN OF BELA LUGOSI

"Yes, John, it is a very beautiful sequence."

"Yes, indeed," I say.

"Yes, indeed," he says, "it is very beautiful in the desert. Yes. But, John, there is something that I want you to understand before you begin writing the score for that very beautiful scene."

"Yes," I say, "certainly, just tell me. I want to understand it the way you do."

"Of course, Johnny, you are a good boy."

"I try, Mr. Antonioni," I say, lying.

"You see, Johnny," he goes on, "it is certainly true that the desert is a most beautiful place. Indeed, this is quite true. Very beautiful. But, Johnny, I want you, in your music, to bring out something else about the desert. Because you see, Johnny, the desert, while it is very beautiful, is a place of

DEATH."

"Uh oh," I thought to myself. "Here it comes." I knew something bad was gonna happen.

"Yes, Johnny," he goes on, "the desert is a place where there is no water, no plants except for the cactus. The snakes are all poisonous rattlesnakes. Gila monsters. You can't stay alive out there for very long can you, Johnny?"

I wonder, "What the hell is he using the Socratic method for?" The fact is, I spend a lot of time in the desert researching the habits of desert tortoises (*Gopherus agazizi*) and not indulging in group sex for Christ's sakes. And actually I can stay alive out in the desert for quite some time but that is only because studying the desert is my hobby. I love the desert. But I don't let him know that. He's the guy with all the shekels.

"No sir, Mr. Antonioni," I say, "a person can't stay alive out there very long. It's too hot and there's no humidity. There's bones all over the place of animals who died out there. I guess they got lost or something. You know."

"You are so right, John. So terribly right. The desert means death. Death. Death."

"Right," I say. "Death, death..." and pretty soon we are both sitting there chanting, "Death, death, death..." together. Real fun.

"Yes, John," he goes on, "that is perfectly true. The desert means and is a place of much death, death, death. Absolutely right.

"Ah, but Johnny, there is something else in my film besides death. It is a place of young love. John, it is a place of young love, love, love."

"Yes, of course. I understand," I say to this nutcase, "it is also a place of young love, love, love, love. No doubt about it."

"And so, John. It is a place of death and young love, John, isn't it?"

"Boy it sure is, Mr. Antonioni. Love and Death."

"Right, Johnny, you've got it now, love and death and love and death, love, death, love death, love death..." (and now we are chanting love-death together) "...love death love death love death."

And he abruptly goes out the door into the sunshine of sanity where he does not belong and leaves me to face the lunacy alone.

And as he departs, he is chanting, of course,

LOVE DEATH LOVE DEATH LOVE DEATH.

Then a pleasant, young, obsequious English-speaking Italian guy comes up to me and says,

"Good morning, Mr. Fahey. My name is Carlos" (well, something like that) "and I've been assigned to you to be your assistant. What is the first thing you would like me to do?"

"Let's go out and score some drugs. This is gonna be a tough job. This guy Antonioni is obviously a nut."

"Yes, that is true. We all know that here. But the foreign press gives him such accolades and rich people lay so much money on him because they think that he is such a genius that he keeps on getting these gigs making movies that don't make any sense to us Italians, but there's nothing we can do."

"Well look, Carlos," I say, "I never heard of the guy before and I'm an American and I say he's nuts. I am in complete agreement with you.

"You know what he wants me to do?" I ask.

"No," says Carlos.

"He wants me to write some music that at the same time is love death love death love death love death love death love death...."

"Yes," says Carlos, "that sounds like something Antonioni would try to pull. That certainly *is* Antonioni. I'm very sorry you had to find out this way."

"Find out what?"

"Find out about his insanity only after you have come all this way and are, more or less, trapped. Or perhaps you only feel trapped. I don't know."

"Yes, Carlos," I said, "you hit the nail on the head. I'm not really trapped. But I sure feel trapped. And I have to stay because of the wife and her relatives. I have to stay and make a bunch of shekels or they will be mad at me."

"Ah, life is so sad," says Carlos, "life is so sad."

You know this is the first sane person I have met since this whole damn thing started.

He understands.

Nobody else does.

"Yes," he says, "life is so sad. I know so myself. I have to keep working for this madman because I too have a wife and a lot of relatives. I know just what you mean."

"Well, how do *you* keep from going insane working for this madman, Carlos?"

"My sanity is only an illusion," he says. "I understand your predicament exactly. And so I also know what kind of drugs you need and where to get them. You see, the drugs *are* my so-called sanity. Come and I will take you to the place of the drug salesman. Also I won't let you get screwed either, because I know what's happening around here, man. Do not fear."

So we go out to a doctor and explain to him that I am working for this insane man Antonioni and I just want something like Carlos takes here so that I won't go insane like Antonioni is.

The Doctor is most understanding and obliging and gives me some prescriptions that he says will keep me from going nuts.

And to some extent, or perhaps even to a greater extent, I think they worked.

Anyway, I am expecting the imminent arrival of Wife.

This was the arrangement Wife and manager had made.

Wife, all Wife, is a terrible pain in the tail when you're on the road.

All musicians know this.

No Wife knows this.

They always think traveling around and working your tail off playing guitar on some stage somewhere is easy work.

And staying up until the wee hours of the morning in smoke-infested, noisy, loud, smelly, crowded joints is easy work.

And they think that waiting around and doing nothing in between sets is easy work.

But sitting around doing nothing is the hardest work there is.

So anytime I take Wife along, it invariably and irretrievably and without fail happens that I get exhausted and can't play very well.

And no Wife understands this.

Even Jan, who was the best of my wives, didn't understand it completely.

She understood it some, but not all.

But the fact that she understood it at all speaks very well for her.

None of the other Wife understood it all.

Anyway, Wife is coming and when she gets to Rome, where I am, she will make me take her to art galleries and the Coliseum and the Lyceum and the Vatican and all kinds of horrible places to *do*. So that the whole time she is there I will be exhausted.

OK, so I know what is going to happen.

So I don't let it happen.

For two or three days, I stayed in the studio which Antonioni had reserved for me.

I told Carlos to go to the zoo.

That I needed three days alone to outline what we were going to do.

But that, of course, is not what I did.

No.

What I did was this: I played and improvised and worked out on the guitar for many, many hours. I had the guitar fixed so the low A string was where the B string should be and vice versa. And I put it at random tuning. It was harmonically in tune but was scordatura, i.e., detuned. That way I would get a unique sound.

And furthermore nobody would ever be able to figure out how I did it.

And I played and played and played until I came up with a

reasonable facsimile of some desert young-death-love music.

I mean, it was mostly desert.

Ominous sounding.

That was because I spent so much time in the desert.

It is ominous out there.

You have to be careful.

I knew that.

And I knew that if you were very cautious and careful you could stay out there alive for a long, long time.

But nevertheless there is something ominous out there in the desert.

Something ominous behind every rock, every cactus, every rattle-snake, every deserted motor bike, every stack of camel bones and horse bones and rabbit bones and cattle bones.

Something out there wants your respect.

And it had mine.

So then I told Carlos to get a recording session together the next day and let's do some recording.

But it had to be a closed session.

I didn't want anybody to know how I did what I did.

And I didn't want Antonioni to know that I was recording so early.

I didn't even let Carlos be there.

What I mean by "so early" is this. My wife was coming, and once she got there I probably could not compose or play any good music because as good as she was in re this respect, she would nevertheless make me go to museums and observatories and zoological gardens and garden gardens and the Spanish steps and places like that and, as a result, I would be too exhausted and couldn't compose any good music for anything.

But, you see, in addition to front money and money I would be paid on completion and acceptance, I was being paid by the day.

And it was an enormous sum.

And so my manager Gene told me to keep up and work—or pretend to work—as many days as possible. And Gene also thought that Antonioni would accept anything I turned in even if it was twelve-tone music or music *à la* random or "Found Object" music or new wave music or no wave music or even punk music, except of course that that did not yet exist.

Because Antonioni, while mad, spun, insane, etc., did have a great deal of respect for my music. And Gene had done some research, you see, and apparently Antonioni just didn't understand music at all, not music of any kind, so no matter what I handed in it would be accepted. And it was true, and to Antonioni's credit, that he never bothered me at the studio once.

He gave me complete freedom.

I must say that for him even though he was about to do something terrible and he had already done something awful using MGM's muscle to get me over there.

But actually I was having a pretty good time.

And this was the case but only because Carlos helped me set up casuals for several musicians, and when they got there gave them music paper and on the music paper it said something like

THIS IS A PHONY JOB. JUST PLAY ANYTHING AT ALL. BUT PLEASE DON'T LET IT EVER COME TOGETHER. NEVER PLEASE PLAY WITH ANYBODY ELSE. JUST MAKE NOISE.

And so that's what we did for several days.

The musicians enjoyed it.

Carlos enjoyed it.

I enjoyed it.

And that way we racked up hours and hours of pay.

Just to make sure it looked like we were actually doing something, we recorded some of it.

But before we started doing any of this nonsense, I had a closed session of just me and an engineer.

And with my detuned guitar, I made three takes of Antonioni gangbang, young-love obscenity music out in the desert.

I mean, really now, what else can you call it? He paid these people to gang up in the desert and do the hoobala boobala.

Well, my wife arrived and, just like I knew would happen, I was exhausted all the time.

I put my foot down though when it came to visiting the Kremlin, I mean the Vatican.

So for a few more days we had the musicians come in and play whatever they felt like as long as it didn't cohere.

And then one day Carlos said to me:

"John, Mr. Antonioni is getting worried about the film music. I think it's about the right time to come up with something. And I am saying this to you, John, as a friend and a fellow enemy of Mr. Antonioni's. What I mean, John, is that it's been great and it's been fun having these parties, but John, as your friend, and I mean that, we must come up with something quick."

"I've already got it."

"You've already got it?"

"Yes, Carlos, when I first recorded with just my guitar, the third take was just what I think the Big Ant wants. I have listened to it again and again and it's really good. And I am quite certain Big Ant will accept it and be very pleased. Because it is really very good. I had a copy of the third take made, see, and I've heard it time and time again and it's great."

"Well, John, in that case, and I don't mean to imply that I don't trust you or your judgment, could we listen to it right now?"

"Sure, let's do just that."

And that's what we did.

We listened to it several times.

At first all that Carlos would say was that, yes, it was very good, but he wasn't sure about it. But after he heard it three or four times, he looked at me with slow and prolonged astonishment and said:

"You know, John," he said, "I believe you are absolutely right. That is exactly what Mr. Antonioni wants."

"And," I said, "if he doesn't like it—well, I really couldn't do any better. That *is* the best I can do. So let's call him up and play it for him."

So we made an appointment with the big man and you know

what? He said exactly the same thing.

"That is exactly what I wanted, John. Exactly. I congratulate you. I am very pleased. For a while I was worried but I have heard several of your records and I really thought down deep the whole time that you could do it, and I was right, you did do it, and I thank you, John, I thank you. Would you care to have dinner with me tonight? I know a nice place where we can talk quietly, and the food is excellent."

So of course, I said:

"Sure, Mr. Antonioni. Nice of you to suggest it. I'd like to do that very much."

So I spent the remainder of the afternoon with Jan, my wife, looking at some old, broken-down ruins and old statues and paintings and all that stuff.

You know what I mean.

And that evening another goddamned limo and chauffeur came and picked me up and took me to this nice restaurant that did indeed have excellent cuisine.

Yes.

But that was not all that happened.

Not by a long shot.

We were of course drinking wine during the dinner.

But neither one of us had very much.

You couldn't say that what happened happened because of the wine.

It would have happened without any alcohol anyway no matter what.

Now you see, like I told you before, I didn't know very much about the film scene in Italy.

I didn't know that Michelangelo Antonioni was a Communist and that he hated the United States.

No, I didn't know that.

And I didn't know that this stupid skin flick was his attempt at making a hate film about the United States.

No, I didn't know that.

How in the hell could I know things like that? I am not and never have been a culture vulture.

And I am not and have never been a politico.

Anyway, so we sit down in this really great and very expensive café where you don't even make choices about what you are going to eat and drink. The waiter does all that for you. And so you don't have to make all kindsa difficult decisions.

And it is one of those places where there are many courses.

And Antonioni begins the conversation by telling me how much he likes my score.

And I am being polite and always calling him "Mr. Antonioni."

Out of phony respect because I didn't have any respect for this guy who I knew was underneath it all a madman.

And we are talking and talking, and he says something in a very casual manner, almost like a throwaway sentence.

"Yes, John, you simply couldn't have any idea how much I hate the United States."

"Oh really, why?"

"Because all the people are all so materialistic and dull and stupid and pretentious."

"They are?" I reply. "Gosh, I know lots of people who aren't like that."

"You're still young and impressionable and believe in the lies they tell you and each other."

"What lies?"

"Oh, about how wonderful America is. How free everybody is. Free. Yes, John, everybody in the USA thinks they are free. But of course it is all a lie. All a mirage."

"Pardon, Mr. Antonioni, but I don't understand."

"Oh, perhaps not now, but as you grow up you will begin to understand about the United States and you will learn to hate it, too."

"Oh, I don't know about that. Fact is, even though there are lots of things wrong with the United States, I love the United States. That's why I live there. I really wouldn't want to live anywhere else."

"Well, that will change, John, as you get older and more mature.

Then you, like I, will also hate that terribly decadent country—that power-mad country, that self-righteous country—the United States.

"Yes, you will."

I was really getting mad.

"Look, Mr. Antonioni," I said, "if you were a visitor in my country I wouldn't tell you how I hated Italy even if I did. It's not a very polite thing to do."

"Who cares about politeness in the face of truth?" he asked.

"What truth?" I asked.

"The United States is a hellhole in the world."

"Damn it," I said, "it is not."

"It is so. It's the worst, most evil place on the globe."

And so this back-and-forth stuff went on for about ten minutes.

And finally, one or the other of us said:

"Oh yeah? You wanna fight about it?"

And we were both so mad that we both got up and started hitting at each other.

And I decked him.

Then I got a cab and went back to the hotel where my wife and I were staying.

I told her about it.

She was horrified that I would do such a thing.

I still can't understand why she was so horrified. We flew home the next day.

Was I ever glad to get home.

Wow.

But you know what this jerk Antonioni did?

He took out all of the music I had done for him and which he had told me was very great and just what he wanted—he took it out and had a Jerry Garcia-ism machine do some music for it in place of mine.

But frankly I didn't care very much because I got paid anyway.

And when the movie came out I could see that it was one of the worst movies ever made.

And it was.

Just that. So bad, in fact, that it is listed in a really funny book, *The Fifty Worst Films of All Time*. And my name is in that book, too. And you know why? Ant accidentally left about two minutes of my music in the final production.

And that's that.

Except for one thing.

If it ever happens to you that a great big powerful giant or organization calls you up and asks you to do something you don't want to do then don't do it because if you do you will get into trouble. OK?

And that is no joke.

Watch out.

Oh, yes, the name of the "film": *Zabriskie Point*.

I went to see it when it came out.

This was Michelangelo Antonioni's brilliant and insightful exposé in story form, of what the "relevant" people in the USA were doing.

HAR HAR HAR HAR HAR HAR HAR HAR HAR HAR

Did he ever miss the boat! Maybe he did OK on England in *Blow Up*, but *Zabriskie Point* blew up. What a dumbass film! I told you, it is included in a book called *The Fifty Worst Films of All Time*! Har, har, har, har, har!

Volk Festivals

There once was a time when universities and other institutions used to make exist a thing called a folk festival. This was in the days when there were still some

VOLK

around. They got their culture through oral transmission. Talk talk talk. Sing sing sing. Etc.

Now of course everybody gets their culture through TV sets and computers and sometimes books and shows, like concerts, but mostly through TV sets.

Now things have become normalized and everybody thinks the same thing. So now, or at least pretty soon, there won't be any wars any more, or pestilence or floods or poverty or not much of anything, because there won't be any disagreement about anything because everybody will be in agreement about everything.

Then, and then only, will we be able to know that everything is cool and forever will be cool.

Just give it a few more years and it'll all happen.

Now, some people don't like this harmony and prefer dissonance.

They even go around collecting dissonance, disagreement, disenfranchisement, disunity, discord, dismemberment, disfiguration, disintegration, and on and on and on and on.

And they put this stuff that they find in computers now. They used to use 3×5 cards.

And if it is audible they record it on tape recorders or whatever.

And some people actually like this oddball stuff and pay lots of money to make libraries and preserve this junk for the future.

I have had people tell me that.

These people are called, now get this,

> VOLKLORISTS.

Can you imagine that?

Let me tell you what one of these

> VOLKLORISTS

>> told me.

This is what he said.

He said it is and has always been thought that the next authority below religion, the next-down repository of wisdom, is the folksoul. The folkmobile.

"See," he said, "these volks are unencumbered by modern mass media. They make up their own stuff for themselves and for collective parties and social organizations like the church and places like that."

And he went on to say that these volks have in their literature and music and poetry and lyrics and paintings and sculptures and games and customs and all that stuff—he went on to say that these people, I don't know where the hell these people exist anymore, but he went on to say that there is great profundity and wisdom in the collective unconscious of these volks.

"Next to religion," he said, "of course."

And all kinds of people believe that, he told me.

So I said well then show me one.

So he showed me some lyrics to some stupid old country dance song and some things he called proverbs which were usually self-contradictory and didn't make any sense, and he took out a record player or something and played me some

> VOLKMUSIC

and on and on and on and on and on.

Wow!

I got away from him as quickly as I could.

You know, he might *have* something.

Wow!

And then one year, I can't remember which year, a funny coincidence happened. I got a telephone call from some booking agent and he told me he wanted me to go to this thing called

THE BUFFALO VOLK FESTIVAL

and he wanted me to play my guitar in and at it.

The pay was great.

So I said I would go anyway, even though I am no Volk.

I needed the money.

So anyway it was either in 1964 or 1974 because they did it twice and paid me to play the guitar at both of them and I went and I did.

But I can't remember at which one which stuff happened because it's been a very long time and both of them were pretty terrible and awful things happened to me at both of them, and to other people too, like we all got very tired and exhausted and it is very hard to remember anything that happened at a time when you were tired or exhausted.

You know what I mean?

I just can't remember which year. They were terribly disorganized and got us all exhausted and wouldn't let us go to sleep at normal hours, and I just can't remember which was which. But I can remember some things that happened at one of the shows.

I arrived at Buffalo by way of Amtrak almost on time and somebody came and picked me up and took me right to the headquarters where they give you a schedule and a button and a map and a little spending money and stuff like that.

And then they either take you to someplace else, like a motel or a hotel, or they tell you "get lost."

Well, I decided not to do either one. No, after I secured my guitars in the lockup room, where I later had a great deal of trouble getting them out and stuff, I decided to take a seat near the entrance to the headquarters. I might see somebody I knew or I might meet somebody I didn't know.

You can never tell.

The first thing I noticed was a twenty to twenty-five-year-old skinny, blonde kid, clutching a Bible to his chest. As if it might fly away while he was answering questions from a bunch of toxic-looking, too-plainly-dressed young women.

They all had this glazed look in their eyes and this dim smile on their faces as they looked up admiringly at this creep with the Bible. The smile said: "I know something you don't know."

See, what it looked like was this: They worshipped him. He worshipped the Bible. And the Bible book was getting strangled to death.

You know what I mean?

Now this guy might have been a pimp. And these chicks might have been hookers, but I don't think so. I mean there were lots of those people around, but I don't know, these people seemed very strange and out of place and they were afraid of everybody else, and so that's why they hung out together so close and held on to that Bible.

Hold on to that Bible, man. Hold on.

You know what I mean.

Then I saw one of my favorite entertainers come in, Bryan Bowers. This guy builds his own autoharps and is frequently billed as the greatest autoharp player in the world. He has a really great voice and plays an excellent autoharp sound.

Of course he's no stupid hillbilly or volk or whatever. He just puts people on, like, pretends. You know?

But they don't care. They can't tell the difference. And there aren't any folk around anyway, so who cares?

I paid my respects to him after he got his packet of schedules and maps. Then a youngish fat chick turned up and said:

"Hi Bryan, I'm your chauffeur. I'm going to take you to a quiet place where you can tune up your autoharps and relax."

"Great," he said.

"Yeah, it's in the contract. We had better get over there pretty soon," said Fatso. She yelled at the chick at the desk, "Hey Bev, what's the address I'm supposed to take Bryan to?"

"587 Eglioclastic Street. You know where it is?"

"No, but I can find it."

Har, har, har, har, har. Famous last words. "I can find it." Har, har, har. Poor Bryan.

So off they went.

Then I saw these old black guys come in named Martin, Bogan, and Armstrong.

This was the Armstrong of "Blind Bluie Hooey."

I had read about them. They weren't volk either. But nobody cared.

It was just a gig.

You know.

These guys had been playing white parties around Chicago for twenty years. Or more.

Their music had no Negro content left in it. They had been playing white swing-band music with guitars, mandolins, and violins. Their show was not exceptional.

A gig's a gig.

You know.

The leader, Martin, played fiddle quite well, although he only knew one lick. But he could play it in any key so it didn't matter. He wore a black beret hat symbolizing some kind of experience in a revolutionary war.

But he was secretive and covert about that. Nobody ever found out what that hat was all about.

He never told anybody.

Bogan came up to me and sat down across from me. Smiling brilliantly and beatifically, he said, "Here, now, I want to sing you this song."

So then he sang "My Gal Sal."

This guy knew orchestral-guitar style chords up and down and all over the neck like Les Paul.

Of course, it didn't make any difference. It was still "My Gal Sal."

And although the fingers of his left hand went all over the place and everything, it didn't sound very different to me.

And it was still just

MY GAL SAL.

And that was OK. I like

MY GAL SAL.

Of course it has nothing to do with folk music, but then neither did anything else and nobody cared and that was OK. A gig's a gig.

Know what I mean?

Later in life I saw Bola Sete do the same fingers-everywhere routine, but it was different because Bola liked to let some of the strings sound open, i.e., not fretted, while all the others were fretted.

It sounded a lot better that way because Bola Sete's method permitted lots of the overtones to sound.

With the finish of "My Gal Sal," Bogan asked me,

"Did you like that song?"

"Yes, Ted, very much."

"Well, we have to serenade everybody we can before the show. Both the entertainers and the audience too. That's our *thing*."

He meant "shtick," of course, but he didn't know that that was what he meant.

"So long," he said. "I'll see you later," and he was off.

Nice guy. I liked him.

And I liked "My Gal Sal," too.

Let me tell you what they did. As soon as they all had their buttons and everything they went outside and split up and individually or in pairs began approaching groups of students and individuals.

All the students acted the same way. They looked at these guys as if they had escaped from a nut factory.

There was very little if any understanding or commensuration between the two groups.

The students looked dumbfounded.

Well, that's the way I felt when Bogan sang to me.

What the hell?

* * *

Well then I thought I would go to the Holiday Inn on Delaware Street and take a nap before dinner and the evening's performance.

Suddenly I saw a very nervous and upset Bryan Bowers and his driver come back inside, both exhausted.

Zelda, the driver, yelled, "Hey, I couldn't find Bryan's practice area."

"Oh, well, there's plenty of time. You don't go on Bryan until ten. Why don't you go to your hotel and rest up a bit?" She called Zelda.

"No, no, please, not Zelda. I can't take it anymore. Please, please just call me a cab."

"But don't you want to hang around and meet all your brother musicians?"

"No, no. Please, just call me a cab."

He was almost in tears.

"Well, OK, if that's the way you want it, but I don't see why."

"Please just call me a cab, please. I've got to rest. Please, no more driving around."

I saw why. Things like that catch you once in a while. It pays to be anxiety-ridden on days you have to play. You are surrounded by the enemy.

I know.

I took in what I had to see until I couldn't stand it anymore and then I ordered a cab, too.

"Don't you want to get to know everybody?"

"Uh, no, not right now," I said obsequiously, and secretly and covertly.

"Later," I said, smiling phony. "I just gotta rest awhile so I can play good tonight."

When I got to the motel I rented a car so I would be safer from the enemy.

That night there was only one dressing room for everybody. I practiced some.

Bogan came over again and insisted upon singing and playing "My Gal Sal" to me.

And you know, it wasn't so bad. I was beginning to remember this old song and I kind of liked it.

Yeah, kind of little nice things happen on the road sometimes.

You usually don't notice them at the time.

But they do happen.

That is a nice song

> Well, they called her invidious Sal.
> She was nobody's one kind of gal.
> Oh they say she lived in Love Canal
> Where everything went so afoul.
>
> Never on the level,
> A student of the Devil
> My gal Sal.

Or something like that.

Eventually my turn came and I walked onto the stage. People clapped and yelled and I sat down and talked with them for a while, making jokes whenever I could. Then I started playing.

This was a great PA system. The audience could hear well, and I could hear myself which is even more important.

You can't imagine how important.

Because how can you tell if you are in tune or if you are in rhythm if you can't hear what in the hell you're doing?

So anyway I'm about five minutes into the first song, whatever it was. And something happened and all of a sudden the speakers went dead. I couldn't hear anything. Nobody could hear anything.

Of course it wasn't folk music, anyway. I'm no folk. But a gig's a gig. Right.

So I announce to those few who can hear me a story I always tell when a string breaks or when the PA goes out or when a bomb drops or there is a fight or somebody goes crazy and takes his clothes off and they have to carry him out or whatever. And this is the story I told and it is a true story.

BIG JOE, "THE DRILL," WILLIAMS.

I always wondered why they called Big Joe Williams "The Drill."

I always wondered.

Well, anyway, one time I was at the Club 47 in Boston, and I was watching and listening to Big Joe Williams, who I suppose you could actually consider a

REAL VOLK

and he was singing and playing along and he broke a string. So what does he do? This is what he did. He reached into his guitar case and pulled out a new string and a small hand drill.

That's what I said, a drill.

So he took the drill and drilled a new hole into the guitar near the bridge. Then he put the string into the new hole, tuned it up, and looked at us as if he was going to conspire with us and tell us the meaning of life which is what we were all looking for anyway, and he looked at us and he says:

"That's a trick I learned in Mississippi, ha, ha, ha."

And then he went ahead and sang and played some more.

And his guitar sounded the same as it did before.

Just the same. But I don't want to go into that because that is a different story and a side issue, and I'll tell you about that some other time.

So anyway after his set, which was so-so, I went up and looked at his guitar. It was full of holes, I mean *full* of holes. There were so many holes, in fact, that I wondered what the hell kept it from exploding.

You know, I wondered what the hell kept it together.

And that was the story I told, and it is a true story.

But nobody laughed because nobody could hear me. And those people who did just looked puzzled.

The sound was still dead, so I tried to make humorous small talk with the audience.

Suddenly the great sound was back. Oh boy, I thought, the torture is over for the evening.

I mean, that is what I thought. That isn't what was the case, but that is what I thought.

I was still young and impressionable.

And then the sound went off again. And it came on and went off again.

"Look, sound man, you are the worst sound man I ever saw. You're killing my set. Is this your idea of fun, fuckhead?"

"Hey man, did you call me 'fuckhead'?"

"Damn right, fuckhead."

"Take it back."

"Nuts. Maybe if you fix the goddamn sound system and stop dangling me I'll stop calling you 'fuckhead,' fuckhead."

I was really mad, you see.

Wouldn't you have been embarrassed and frustrated and mad, too?

"Stop calling me 'fuckhead,'" he said.

"Drop dead twice fuckhead. I'll call you fuckhead the rest of my life, and I'll tell all of my friends and all of your friends to call you 'fuckhead' too, you stupid fuckhead."

"OK," I heard him yell, "I'll show you who's a fuckhead," and I see this moderate-sized fuckhead start approaching me from the rear of the auditorium.

SHOWDOWN AT OK CORRAL.

So I started moving guitars and equipment around so we would have plenty of room to fight without breaking anything unnecessarily. I was so mad, and I was ready to kill this parasite.

Nobody should pay this fuckhead any money to pretend he's a sound man when he's no damn good at being a sound man at all.

You know what I mean?

I mean it felt like he was trying to drive me crazy and everything. Torture me.

He was halfway up when the sound came all the way on.

"You better keep it on or I'll kill you," I yelled at him because he was halfway up the aisle towards me.

I was so upset that my hands were shaking. I was breathing far too heavily, but after three or four songs I was back to normal and the set ended on a high plane of vibrationary presence. The audience was screaming and stomping.

Thank God. I don't know how to fight very well. I am pretty strong and I suppose I could.

And so there's some good examples of how much fun it is to be a musician and go out on the road and work at various places.

And I know lots of other stories and I'll tell you about them too.

But not just now.

Maybe later.

Oh well, you know what I always say to myself when this kind of thing happens, I say it to myself, and I say:

> *As you wander on through life,*
> *Whatever may be your goal,*
> *Keep your eye upon the doughnut,*
> *And not upon the hole.*

That's what they used to write on bathroom walls before they started writing

> *Kilroy was here.*

And you know it's not such bad advice either, if you can do it.

You know what I mean?

It's a hell of a lot better than

> *Kilroy was here.*

FISH

I met Booker (Bukka) White in 1964 in the course of music biz.

Booker was one of the best blues singers that ever lived.

He played all over the South and made many, many blues records between 1928 and 1936.

He was very popular among black people and his records sold like hotcakes.

He was born in Houston, Mississippi, somewhere around 1915. He wasn't sure himself which year he was born in.

He had lived all over the Southland.

But when I met him he was living in Memphis and doing manual labor.

Carrying newly manufactured tanks around.

To be honest I never understood what kind of tanks these were.

Or what they were used for.

Booker was a very gregarious man.

Everywhere he went he talked to everybody he could.

He seemed to enjoy every conversation he had.

And he had a genuine affection for every person he met.

Nevertheless considering the great differences between us like our age, race, and section of the country which we were from—I am from Maryland—it was unlikely that we would become good friends.

But we did become good friends.

Very good friends.

We were both crazy about trains. We spent hours watching trains. All over the South and Southwest.

Booker knew all about trains and had been riding freights for forty years or so.

Booker taught me how to ride freight cars.

And we had lots of adventures all over the South.

We went fishing a lot. Especially in the sloughs and bayous around Memphis, Tennessee.

We usually didn't catch anything at all.

But we drank a lot of whiskey and had a lot of fun.

One day in the summer, Booker and I were out fishing in some shallow slough along Horn Lake.

We were fishing for mudcats and snapping turtles.

Booker's old black landlady, Velma, knew how to prepare and cook these Southern delicacies.

She had made me the first snapping turtle stew I ever had. And it was really very good.

So there we were, Booker and I, underneath the hot summer sun on the shore of Horn Lake.

It is a very large but fairly shallow lake.

So we didn't expect to catch anything very big.

We were surrounded by giant cypress trees with their knees in the water. Giant turkey vultures were perched in the limbs of these trees.

Crows and ravens, too.

And there were blacksnakes slithering around in the trees, trying to catch and eat the baby birds in songbirds' nests, like robins and starlings and sparrows.

Sometimes these big blacksnakes fell out of the trees and scared everybody to death.

Just for a second or two.

The snakes never got hurt that way. After they landed, they just wiggled away into the bushes and eventually climbed up the Spanish moss and vines into the trees again.

There were cottonmouths around, but that day I didn't see any.

There was a whole world up there.

Because of the Spanish moss.

It was everywhere.

Booker and I were being eaten alive by the mosquitoes out there until we broke open the whiskey.

The odor of whiskey repels mosquitoes.

At least that's what Booker told me. And it seemed to work.

For a while.

Malaria had returned to the Mississippi Valley.

It was 1966. I was in my twenties and Booker was in his fifties.

Booker was as strong as an ox.

He was a giant of a man.

He looked like an enormous bullfrog.

I saw him pick up an old Ford V-8 motor once out in a car junk-yard when we were looking for parts.

All by himself.

So we were out there fishing and fishing.

Nothing was biting, and it was hot.

After a few hours we got low on whiskey.

So Booker took my '55 Chevy back to town to get some more whiskey.

I was alone.

But I was used to being alone a lot.

Nothing new to me.

I was kind of a loner anyway.

So I wasn't particularly afraid of anything that day.

Nothing ever happened on these fishing trips anyway except that we drank a lot of whiskey.

And had a lot of fun.

That was all.

I wasn't expecting anything to happen.

It never did.

And for a long time after Booker left, that is what did happen.

Nothing.

Nothing at all.

I was just standing there waiting for nothing to happen.

Then, all of a sudden, there was an explosion out in the water where my bait, a half of a bass fish, rested on the bottom.

And I got a fast and enormous pull on my pole. It was so strong it almost pulled me and my pole into the water.

But the water around there was only five or six feet deep at most. What in the world could be out there so big in only five or six feet of water?

Some unknown monster took the bait and was trying to pull the bait and the pole and myself into the briny water.

This wasn't supposed to happen.

I was no real sportsman. I wasn't interested in being a sportsman or being sportsmanlike.

Being sportsmanlike means you give the fish a big chance to get away.

I wasn't interested in that. I always used two-hundred pound test fishing line and a big saltwater reel.

I only wanted to catch a big fish. If I caught a small fish I just threw it back.

I wanted to catch a big catfish like I had seen photographs of in various sportsman magazines.

Even though I was not really a sportsman.

I had seen pictures of catfish that weighed eighty or ninety pounds or more that were caught in the lakes created by the TVA systems in Tennessee.

That was what I wanted.

But this? This was no catfish. Or turtle.

I could hardly hold the pole. I used the star drag, but it didn't help.

Something unnatural had come along and taken my bait. Some unknown monster-fish that must have been in the slough since the beginning of time.

And nobody knew about it.

Maybe it was a coelacanth.

A giant living fossil.

There wasn't enough oxygen in that water to support anything bigger than a small bass.

Was there?

It was terribly hot out. And humid. And there was no shade.

I was already dripping sweat when the water broke.

And then the mosquitoes started biting me again. They smelled the salt in the sweat. That's what attracts them to the blood. They wanted blood. My blood.

They were after my blood.

I couldn't reach over to the whiskey bottle, because if I did I would have had to let go of my pole. And if I did that the damned fish would take my pole and reel and line.

The buzzards were excited. They were making a lot of noise. And flapping their wings.

But not flying.

They had seen this sort of thing before. They had seen everything. Buzzards have been around a long, long time.

Buzzards would always be around a long, long time.

And they know more than I did.

I fought the thing for five minutes. I fought it for ten. What the hell was going on?

It didn't make any sense. What kind of fish was this that was as big as me and maybe bigger and lives in a little bend of a slough where the water is shallow? And nobody knew it was out there.

A lost muskellunge?

After fifteen minutes, my muscles were getting tired. They hurt. And my eyes were full of sweat. I was blind. I wanted to cut the line but I couldn't lay the pole down to get the knife out of the tackle box.

I'd lose my pole.

So I had to stand there and fight.

And ache, and turn into blood and water, and ache.

The sun wouldn't quit. The issue was no longer clear to me at all: Who had gotten caught here, me or the fish-thing?

Then I began to hear music.

I heard a Highland bagpipe band. I knew I was hallucinating but I couldn't stop the music.

And I couldn't stop the sun.

And the awesome humidity spread out all around Memphis. It came from the nearby Mississippi River and I was in the middle of the great midday wetness.

Maybe this awful damned fish or whatever it was came in during a flood from the great river and got stranded in Horn Lake.

But now I was stranded, too.

And the thing kept bearing down and trying to swim straight ahead, away from me. He, it, whatever it was, wouldn't give up. The damned thing was so big that it left a wake as big as a small outboard motorboat.

Now I was hearing an entire symphony orchestra playing "Mars, the Bringer of War" from *The Planets* by Gustav Holst.

Angry, strife-like music.

Bang, bang, bang, bang, bang. In 11/4 time.

Insane.

The whole thing.

And then I started getting nauseated. Funny pictures took shape in my head.

Now I was seeing from above—like I was coming down in an airplane—parts of my hometown in Maryland where a person is safe.

In the middle Atlantic states things, nature, people, what have you, do not get out of hand like this secret, unknown monstrosity.

I saw parks, schoolyards, playgrounds. Old friends and enemies.

I saw an old girlfriend walking down Ethan Allen Avenue, trying to look tough. Her name was Dorothy. She was trying to look carefree. Trying to look like she wasn't concerned about anything. Sufficient unto herself. Not thinking about what her father had done to her.

And then later me. And then all kinds of men.

Why was I seeing this? What the hell was going on?

I didn't understand.

Twenty-five minutes. Thirty. Three-quarters of an hour. Completely blind now. But I fought on. There was no way to stop.

Wasn't I fishing with a friend when this thing I was doing started? Oh yeah, I was with Booker. But he had gone back into town to get some more whiskey. Why didn't he come back?

Maybe Booker could tell me what to do.

I ached everywhere. And I was getting more and more nauseated.

There I saw in my head or in the water—I wasn't sure which, and it didn't matter—I saw Georgie and Gene Wahlstrom walking down the street.

But they weren't walking like normal, healthy people.

No, they were walking like snails and slugs because they weren't getting the right food and nutrition. Their father drank up all the food money. So they always creeped along, shoulders down. They couldn't walk upright.

I had always looked down on them. Made fun of them. Oh yeah, I used to be mean.

I remembered how I had laughed at them when their father got sick and couldn't work anymore.

They got poorer and poorer. Why did I act that way back then? They couldn't help it. Was I still so mean?

Where was Booker? Why didn't he come back and get me out of all this trouble? Musta had some trouble with my car.

"Christ," I wondered, "what am I going to do? This fish, this heat, and these awful memories could kill me."

Then I started retching into the water. Over and over again. Even when nothing came up.

Why the hell wouldn't it stop? But I couldn't let go of the pole or of the insult-to-nature fish or whatever it was. I couldn't let go.

Then I saw myself laughing at this other girl I knew when she told me she was pregnant.

She was only fourteen. I might have been the father. But so could a lot of other guys.

Why was I laughing at her maliciously? Why was I so mean?

Wow, I used to be a real motherfucker. Why?

I stopped retching. Now I couldn't even feel my muscles. I was just a head floating in the air. Having bad memories. Fighting an insane, unnatural, unknown obscenity. Bigger than I was.

But then I really got scared. I was back in my baby crib when I was three or four and it was late at night and dark. I saw my father walking towards me. Naked. But I saw my father walking towards me with his penis and balls exposed and a horrible grin on his face and some mean, mean laughing.

"Now I'm gonna getcha you little bastard. I've been waiting for this. Kid, are you ever gonna be sorry someday. It won't bother you now, but someday you'll start having bad dreams, but they'll all be symbolic and you won't understand. And you'll start to think you're going to go crazy. And you will go crazy in time. Yes, you will. Just like me. Just like they did to me in Mount St. Charles.

"But I fooled them all. Now I'm a big wheel in the US Public Health Service. Personnel Administration. I fooled them all. If they only knew what I was gonna do ta you, whoo-hoo!"

Then I got sick and started retching again. Nothing came up. Just retching.

My thoughts were the same color as the water.

He was playing with himself. He had a gruesome grin on his face.

Then he started playing with me.

And he was giggling like a madman.

"Your mother doesn't love ya, kid. If she does love you, where is she? How come she isn't here with you?" he taunted me.

"But don't worry, kid. I love you. See how I take care of ya, kid? Forget about your mother. I love ya, kid."

I got even sicker. Everything was too big. The fish, the sun, the heat, the memories.

At first I enjoyed the things my father did to me. The games we played. At first.

But later I hated them.

And then I remembered one time when my father took me up in

my grandmother's sewing room. I was five. He was punishing me because I told on him so that maybe the others in the family would make him stop. But they didn't believe. And they told him what I had said.

"Now I'm gonna getcha you little bastard." He was giggling. "I've been waiting for this. Kid, are you ever gonna be sorry. 'Cause today I'm gonna kill ya."

He made a noose out of the sash pull hanging down from the ceiling. He made it very slowly and looped end around end. And while he did this he told me what it was like to die by hanging. How I would gag and gasp for breath but wouldn't die because he wouldn't let me die by breaking my neck. Oh no. That would be too easy and too quick. He wanted me to strangle and strangle for a long time.

And then finally he had an actual noose right there in front of my face. And he slipped it around my neck and started pulling it tight and tighter and tighter. I didn't even feel it at the time. I had to keep this one thought going through my mind:

"He's not crazy. He's just mean. He won't kill me because if he kills me the police will come and take him away and lock him up. He won't kill me. He's just pretending. He won't kill me. He's just pretending, he...."

And then he said he'd changed his mind. He'd do it a different way. He'd use grandpa's pistol. Yeah. That was they way to do it.

But first he laid me on the floor, and he took off his shoes and socks and rubbed his feet in my face. He really got a bang out of that. Just for a few minutes. And telling me, "It won't come off, you know. Never come off. But you won't be alive anyway, so don't worry about it."

Why was I having all these terrible memories?

Were they real?

Oh yes, they were real.

But I wasn't in control of them. Who was? God? Was there really a God? Nature? What the hell is nature? Were these grotesque recollections part of nature? Like the vultures?

But I didn't have much time to reflect upon these things because

I kept being assailed by the thing in the water, the memories, the heat, the wet, the sun....

Then he carried me into my grandfather's room and got his .45 out of the drawer and held it up to my temple and said, "All I have to do is pull the trigger and it'll all be over. Think I oughta do that? Whatdaya think, kiddo? Whatdaya think?"

But I couldn't talk. My voice wouldn't work. All I could do was shake my head back and forth. Back and forth. "Don't do it. I know you won't do it because you don't wanna get locked up. You're too smart for that. Aren't you? Aren't you?"

But inside I wasn't absolutely certain, and my voice and the terror were frozen inside of me.

"Well," he said finally, "I guess I'll letcha go this one time, kiddo. This one time. But if you ever tell anybody again, I will blow your stupid head off. And I'm not joking, kiddo. So don't ever tell anybody again. Understand?"

I still couldn't talk. So I shook my head up and down, up and down, up and down.

And then I remembered that in the seventh grade I got kicked out of school for attacking a girl classmate of mine. I knew it was wrong. I knew it was evil. But it wasn't fair. After all, I was just doing what my father did to me all the time. Nothing unusual. What was all the fuss about? Oh, I knew. I knew. I was wrong and my father was wrong, too.

Very much in the wrong.

Evil.

But I couldn't tell anybody or he might come and get me and kill me.

Or torture me again.

In my grandmother's sewing room.

And I remembered what my mother said to me when she found out I had been kicked out of school because I had attacked this young girl.

"How could you do this to me?" she said at me.

"To me," she had said.

And I had thought, "To you? What about me, Mom? Where have you been all these years when my father was doing the same awful things to me? I wish you knew what he did to *me*. My father was right. You never really did love me, Mom. Never. You told me you did but you never did really love me. You never did really love me. You never loved me, Mom. And so you know what, Mom? I hate you. Yes, I really hate you. Oh, I love you, too. Sure. Of course I do. But I hate you, Mom. I hate you. Because you never loved me, Mom. Never...."

"Jawn," somebody calls from far away. And somebody's hand claps me on my shoulder and holds me tightly. It is Booker.

"You OK, Jawn?" he asks, knowing I'm not OK. Booker can tell. He's a very sensitive man.

I am so far away I don't even know who it is at first, or for that matter where I am or what I am doing.

Booker has returned with more whiskey. And he can tell something is wrong.

"Jawn," he said, "come out of it. Whatsa matter? It's me, Booker. Your friend Booker."

"Oh, hi Booker," I mumble. "I'm sorry but I was fighting with some great big monster fish for about two hours, and I got sick, and I guess the fish broke the line and got away."

"Jawn," he says, and he slams the whiskey bottle in my hand. "You take a couple big drinks o' this whiskey. Booker got the Coca-Cola, too. Now drink."

I try to pour down a big drink, but it comes back up right away.

"Jawn," Booker says, "sip a little of the coke first," and I do. The coke stays down. "Now take a small drink of this here Ol' Grand-dad." And I do.

Then, just after I feel the warmth but not the burn, he raises my hand with the Coke in it. Just in time I swig it. Then I wait a few minutes so my head gets clear, and I try a bigger whiskey drink and coke drink, separate, and both stay down.

"Now," says Booker, "take two big gulps of whiskey, and then drink the coke. Booker know what's goin' on, Jawn. Booker'll fix everything up fine, Jawn. Booker your friend, Jawn."

"Yes Booker, I know you're my friend. I got sick because the fish was too big. It wasn't natural. No fish oughta be that big. I'm sorry, Booker. It was so hot and everything that I got all mixed up. The fish wore me out and I guess it got away."

"Jawn," Booker bursts out in laughter. "Jawn, that fish didn't get away. You done landed it. Look!"

I looked down and there was a giant fish the kind of which I had never seen before. About twelve feet long and three feet at the girth.

But I had no recollection of landing it. I must have been on automatic.

"Yes Jawn," Booker says laughing and shaking all over, "you done landed a great big ol' alligator gar fish, and you didn't even know it. Ha ha ha. No wonder you got sick. First time Booker see one o' those things, Booker get a little sick, too. That fish ain't no natural creature. Look at the eye. Mean. I mean, *mean*."

And pointing down at the water, he says, "You done caught a great big ol' alligator gar fish. First time Booker saw one of those things, Booker didn't feel so good either. But you done landed it Jawn. You done landed it. That big gar didn't get away. Take another big drink, Jawn. Booker got a whole fifth here. Enough for both of us."

So I take another drink of Old Grand-dad and then some Coke.

The whiskey and Booker's warm hand on my shoulder is bringing me back from—from what shall I call it? My reverie? I still feel nauseated. I didn't want to have those goddamn memories. I don't tell Booker about them. Although now I realize I could have and Booker would have listened and understood and wouldn't look down on me. I could trust Booker to help me.

"Take one more drink, Jawn. Booker know what's comin' down. Booker get you out of this. Goddamn monster-fish. Shouldn't a been in these waters. Somethin' wrong. Maybe he got trapped here in a flood. Too goddamn big, Jawn."

"That's what I mean, Booker. It's too big. It made me sick."

"Sho' Jawn. Booker understand. First time I saw an alligator gar I damn near threw up. They ain't natural anything get that big. It's ten feet long and three feet at the girth.

"Not one of God's creations like you and me. I understand, Jawn. You be OK."

And you know, Booker did understand. He really did. I don't believe anybody else could do what he did next. He spoke and he said just the right words.

"Have another drink, Jawn. I'm afraid of those things, too. But I know something you don't know, Jawn. Ha ha."

He's cheering me up slowly. What a *Mensch* Booker is. No hurry. And he just explained my problem. What I feel which I hadn't noticed:

FEAR.

Now I notice I'm shaking. But he's right. I'm afraid of the damn thing. Especially when I look down on it. It's big enough to eat Booker and me—both of us.

And now that I recognize fear, I don't feel sick anymore.

I am very much afraid of it. But so is Booker. And if Booker, a local, a rustic, a product of local mud and water, something poetic and profound, I haven't quite got it—if Booker knows all about local atrocities like this goddamn alligator gar fish then.... And once he was a murderer? Well, maybe. But he's my friend and I can trust him and if *Booker* is afraid of the damned thing, then it's OK for me to be afraid.

Booker walks down to the water and stabs the fish with a big gaff and pulls it out. But he keeps looking at me to see if I'm alright.

"Thanks, Booker," I say. "That's what it was made me sick. Fear. I was afraid of the damn thing. I didn't know there were any kind of fish like that around."

"They only be in the South, Jawn. I don't think any live up where you come from. And I don't think there be any out West in California.

"Booker understand. Some say they ain't afraid of alligator gar fish. Bullshit. You look at that thing. It's big and mean. Swallow both of us. Them people say they ain't afraid tellin' lies. Booker know. This be Booker's home. You my guest. Booker treat you right, Jawn, and not let anything happen to you. You can trust Booker. Have another drink, Jawn. You done had a bad time, man."

So I have one.

And I begin to feel OK.

It was like I had been away somewhere else for awhile and now I had come back to myself.

That is exactly what happened.

But now I was OK.

But the fish was still gasping. It wasn't dead yet.

And I wouldn't feel really OK until the damned thing was dead and I knew it was dead.

"Now I'm gonna kill it, Jawn. Then we be safe."

Booker pulled out a .45 from somewhere. I had never seen it before, and I had no idea where he had kept it hidden.

I never did find that out.

He shot the gar a few times in the head.

But it didn't die. It kept gasping.

"Maybe you need silver bullets, Booker," I said jokingly, but actually the fact that those three or four bullets in its head hadn't killed it made me a little bit—maybe more than a little bit—uneasy.

"Maybe so, Jawn," he said, "but this be all Booker got."

He loaded five new bullets into the chamber and fired those into the thing's head, too.

Finally it stopped gasping and wiggling its tail.

We be OK now, Jawn," said Booker. "That gar's dead. Real dead."

Then Booker got out a great big machete knife and started cutting the thing's head off.

Giant head. It took Booker about ten minutes to complete this task.

Ten minutes and several swigs of whiskey.

Finally the head came off. It was dripping blood all over Booker and all over the ground.

"Get rid of it, Booker. It's all wrong," I said.

"OK, Jawn. Now watch the crows," Booker said, and he wound up with the fish head in his hand like he was a baseball pitcher and he threw it way down the lake shore as far as he could.

But the birds in those cypress trees weren't crows. They were huge turkey vultures. And they all jumped into the air at the same time. And they all caught the hot airflows which were rising from the sun-heated lake, and they flew around and around and up and down. They hardly flapped their wings at all. They soared around and around in circles like they didn't know where they wanted to go. But they knew what they were doing. This was nothing to them. This was something old as time. Black, very black carrion crows with unspeakably ugly, red, turkey-like cartilage hanging from their beaks.

Oh yes. They knew what they were doing. They knew where they were going.

Eventually they all landed down the lake by the chopped-off head. And they strode up to it like kings and queens. No reason to hurry. They were the masters of this situation. They had no competitors. This was nothing new to them.

Nature knew what was going on. Nature had everything wrapped up in some great system whereby everything came clean at the end.

Very clean.

I looked down, and I saw Booker sawing off the thing's tail.

I wondered why he was doing that. And I wondered why he had cut the thing's head off, too.

So I asked him about it.

And this is what he said: "Now Jawn, Booker got a big surprise for you. You go and take the car and go to Booker's landlady and ask her for a tarpaulin and then you come back here."

"Well, OK Booker, but . . . ."

"Now Jawn," Booker insisted, "you just go and do what I say and you'll find out what Booker's talking about."

So got in my Chevy and drove all the way across Memphis in the hot wet until I came to Booker's rooming house.

When I got there I parked it and went to the front door and rang the bell.

Velma, the old black landlady, came to the screen door and looked out at me.

"Why, hello there," she said almost as though she were singing. "You Booker's new friend. Come in. How you doin'?"

"Just fine ma'am. A little hot, but...."

I went in and she got me some lemonade.

"Is Booker alright, boy?" she asked.

"Oh, yes ma'am, Booker's alright. See we caught this great big fish, and Booker sent me back to get a tarpaulin from you."

"Oh," she said. "Booker musta caught a very big fish."

"*I* caught the fish, ma'am. It's a great big alligator gar fish. I never saw one before."

"I see," she said. "Well I reckon there's going to be some good eatin' around here."

"People eat those things?" I asked.

"Why they sure do," she said. "I have to soak it a couple of days, but then we'll have great big gar steaks. Deeelicious. You *will* come and eat some with us, won't you?"

"Well," I said, "I'll come, but I don't know if I'll be able to eat any of that thing because it scared me to death."

"Well you'd better come. Either you eat it or it eat you. Ha ha. And besides, you hurt Booker's feelings if you don't come."

I took the tarpaulin back to Booker, and we wrapped the carcass up in it. We tried not to get blood on us, but we did anyway.

We drove it back to the rooming house, and a few days later I sat down to supper with Booker and Velma and a few others. I couldn't believe that a fish that big and that ugly could taste so good.

But it did.

And those days, at night, I slept quite well.

I did have a lot of dreams, but that was OK.
I still slept well.
A lot of the dreams were about my father.
And Booker.
And the fish.
And the vultures.
And, funny thing: They were not entirely all bad dreams.
No, not at all.
And that surprised me.
But that's the way it was.

SKIP JAMES

It is the mid-sixties. Berkeley, California.

My family exploded, I am ten thousand miles from home. Trying to find a niche. A place to fit into. Some good friends. Maybe even a girlfriend.

I do not know yet that you cannot find these in Berkeley. Berkeley is the worst possible place in the world to meet people who will love you and appreciate you.

Friendship does not exist here.

Because Berkeley people regard the expression of emotion "bad form." You must never show love or hate or even affection.

Mellow. You can—in fact you must—always project mellow. Even though it is purely an affectation, even though it is not an emotion, it is not even real, you must always show forth mellow and nothing else.

Berkeley people are cursed by this imprisonment in mellow. But they do not know it.

And the last thing they want is for someone to tell them so.

Mellow is of course a cover-up. A disguise for what Berkeley people really are: individualists ranged roughly in pretend, obnoxious social welfare movements which make a lot of noise but never achieve any goals.

But I do not know this yet. I am young and stupid and naïve.

While I am trying to figure it all out, I am distracted by a sudden fad about the singing and playing of various retired country blues singers. Unprecedented national attention is thrown capriciously at dusky remnants. Forgotten itinerants, tenant farmers, and criminals emerge from unhappy cotton and cornfields, and bayous full of alligators and cottonmouths.

Although it is never articulated around Berkeley, the sentiment that these guys have something important to tell us is obligatory and omnipresent.

That is because Berkeley people are not aware that they have emotions.

They know that emotions exist because they have read about these curious oddities. But since they cannot locate them in themselves, they assume that they exist elsewhere. And where better than in the bosoms of country blues singers, who they have noted exhibit a wide range of affect, mostly incomprehensible to themselves, the Berkeley-ites.

After all, these primitives are the repositories of the Folk-soul, the collective unconscious.

Big Karl, the official psychiatrist of the Third Reich and inventor of so many words whose prefix is *Rassen*, said so.

Eschewing emotions, Berkeley-ites never read Siggie. Too dangerous.

Therefore let these strange effusions and emanations of *Geist* emanate from forgotten black entertainers. That way feeling will always be alien to Berkeley-ites.

Jesse Fuller, who has been in the area for decades, is suddenly discovered. So is K. C. Douglas. What strange behavior. Expressing emotions.

Wow!

Probably the good Bishop feared that he did not exist because he could not feel.

Rhetoric is in your path everywhere you go in Berkeley. In the streets, sidewalks, byways, freeway entrances, exits, formats, door-mats, posters....

Peace, love, freedom, equality, Be Here Now, Power to the People, buzzwords never ending.

It looks to me like all this experimentalism and noise is jejune, joyless, vulgar, insensitive, uncaring, unfeeling—folks getting carried away in the moment, in the noise and excitement of the rally.

I must be wrong of course because so many well-educated, well-off citizens, cream of the intelligentsia—they couldn't all be wrong.

Could they?

Impossible.

But one thing I notice quite clearly and am quite certain about.

None of these people are happy.

None.

Oh, they can spout Marx at me all day long, and Engels and Bertie, and Voltaire and Rousseau, and Vienna *Kreis*, and Boolean algebra and B. F. Skinner, and even though they are engaged in a continuous orgy, nobody is happy.

Lots of instinctual exploration and explosion. Sure. And lots of
SYPHILIS.

Preposterous glorification of sexual promiscuity, violence, political radicalism, and activist narcotic obfuscation.

Nobody seems to notice that this revolution is old hat. Nothing new about it.

They read history books but do not perceive similarities between past uprisings and present ones.

Is all this ignorant behavior spontaneous?

Hype stalks the streets of B-town. These kids are pretty easy. Naïve marks. Hypeman walks down Telegraph Avenue spewing propaganda and sales pitches and buzzwords and slogans, and the people are too stupid to notice what he is and what he is doing....

And they think that *I* am naïve.

The new Madison Avenue sales category is called
THE NEW AGE.

All of it is for sale. If you want to fit in and belong and buy the right clothes and listen to the right records just buy
THE NEW AGE CATALOGUE.

It's for sale too, at a high price, but all the info you need is in this book.

All things "New Age" are for sale.

Even the old blues singers are for sale. Records and videos of them are for sale. Archaics are paid enormous sums of money to rave and bang on stage.

Whitey perceives, incorrectly, that these eternally young rustics are presently well-known and popular in their own *Heimats*. Right now. Celebrities for decades now.

But Whitey does not know what's going on in these isolated communities. He never goes to the inner city. He never visits coal miners in Appalachia.

Poor Whitey just doesn't know what's going on. These old folks are considered archaic and useless in their own communities.

Go watch Jesse Fuller play Oakland. All the kids make fun of him. I've seen it.

Whitey of Berkeley learned all he knows from the Communist folksong book and the people who put it out and their cronies. Leadbelly (who actually was a great singer), Pete Seeger (who on occasion is a slightly good singer), Alan Lomax, the Silber Brothers. These are the people who wrote these supposedly informative books.

These poor idealists had a perfect right to speak and sing and write and attack middle-class society, and all the other things they did.

Absolutely. Their rights are guaranteed in the Constitution of the United States.

The HUAC, misguided, and probably acting unconstitution-ally itself, elevated and popularized these lefties. Gave them more power.

But they never had much power.

A matchstick dropped in a snowdrift.

The totality of their combined effect on American culture was null.

Maybe it was fun for some folks, but...nothing.

And here in Berkeley they and their henchmen accost me every day as I try to walk up Telegraph Avenue to get an education.

Noise. Just noise.

I'm going to step out of the scene now into that eucalyptus grove over there and smoke my pipe. The memory of those days has exhausted me.

I've got to reflect. Make sure I'm on the right course. You know what I mean.

There is something about guitars—maybe something magical—when played right which evokes past, mysterious, barely conscious sentiments, both individual and universal. The road to the unconscious past.

Guitar is a caller. It brings forth emotions you didn't know you had. It is a very personal instrument.

One hears a guitar in the distance on the way home from work on an October day. The shadows lengthen and occupy the territory as one is stroked by pleasant and familiar odors, especially burning leaves and pork cooking and exhaust fumes from various automated vehicles.

And there are other faint odors which one cannot quite identify. Friendly cats abound on the Landscape within the Encompassing. Man's best friend follows one out of curiosity. The cotton and woolen clothes one wears subliminally connect one with Nature, Soil, Blood, Iron, *Volk* alive and gone to Valhalla, dead Nazis and the great *Uhr. Rasseninerung* and stirrings of the ancient and eternal perceptions and connections with the One, the All, overcome one.

Yes, one knows as one inhales a lungful of pipe smoke—just like our Aryan ancestors did—that everything is truly

ONE.

There have never been two. Just one. And you and I are part of the One. We have met many times before, you and I, only you do not recall these meetings and renewals.

But you will.

Oh yes.

We are one, the same thing, just like everything else. And it has always been that way.

And YOU are part of it, my dear brothers and sisters. You *are* the waterfall which you think you only perceive. You *are* the dry brown leaves burning in the many funeral pyres which line the ox path we are traversing through these eucalyptus trees.

There are no enemy *Uhr*-wolves here. We are the wolves. There are no saber-toothed tigers waiting to spring on us. We are the saber-toothed tigers. Everything now in reverie is

EINHEIT.

This was the Führer's true message which he wanted to bring to us all. But the enemy who did not wish to believe that everyone is one wore him out, exhausted him, until the Führer himself forgot that everything is one, that he himself was part of the One, and so he went mad and went out and started raping and pillaging and killing and murdering and electrocuting and slashing and shoot bang stab slice and....

Oh sorry, I got carried away.

We should all mourn the Führer's loss of true wisdom and pray that it be returned to him in Valhalla.

I was talking about, uhhhhh, oh yes, the wonderful guitar playing of some of these ancient rustics. Yes, of course, but here again we are caught up in reverie.

Aren't we?

Is not guitar playing the same as smoking a pipe? Both are personal and bring about reverie and consciousness of *Einheit* with the One. Guitars are the royal roads to the retrieval of racial and dimly perceived, but nevertheless known, timeless feeling-recollections so essential to the unity, I mean *Einheit*, of the race and the Landscape.

Yes, I hold these moments of reverie to be the *Uhrsache*—the real cement that binds mankind together, the real behind the scenes of

GOETHE-GEFÜHL.

Well, there it is. I didn't mean to but I just gave you a complete explanation of "longing," i.e., *Sehnsucht*, that would even please Oswald Spengler, the late, great historian.

Are you sure you don't understand what I am talking about?

Are you certain?

Reflect for a moment or two. You might discover something wonderful that you didn't know you had—the earliest "blues singers" to record were Bessie Smith, Mamie Smith, Clara Smith and others who sang double-entendre songs, some of which were pretty funny. But their accompanists were black and white, and the arrangements were done by whites. Sometimes subsidized by whites like John Hammond. They were slow and similar and boring. Bessie Smith's records all stated under her name

COMEDIENNE WITH ORCHESTRA.

Country, or uneducated, blues singers, such as Blind Lemon Jefferson, Papa Charlie Jackson, and Blind Blake did not read music. But they accompanied themselves with complex, hot virtuoso guitar playing. And that guitar playing was what attracted us young white kids.

Great stuff to listen to and learn to play if you could.

This first fad of fat women blues singers only lasted a few years and was then replaced by another fad of insane sounding, screaming, guitar-banging blues singers like Blind Lemon Jefferson and Charley Patton. Then this fad was replaced by a taste for slick urban entertainers like Leroy Carr and Roosevelt Sykes.

I knew Sykes personally. He was a great man.

This fad was soon replaced by interest in jazz and bop and other kinds of music.

Musical forms are ephemeral.

The sixties arrive with a whimper and these fossils suddenly find themselves in capricious demand by Whitey. Only by Whitey.

Why?

In retrospect it is clear that the sixties were not an age of analysis and insight. Just the opposite, in fact.

For any glitch or break in the smooth flat life, any waywardity in the dyna-cushion and dyna-flow and dyna-flex ride to the rainbow bridge to the beyond, the edge of the Encompassing to the Elysian Fields of Valhalla, attention was directed outward. The Berkeley oligarchy enforced this outwardness by beaming Evil Thought Rays into our craniums.

Like "wow," man.

Much was kept from us by B-town's Ostrogoths, but nevertheless they did not manage to annihilate the desire in me to know why this revival of interest in blues songs, blues men, blues motions, crossroads, broomdusting, blues records, and so on—why did this rapture happen in the sixties? Why not some other decade? Was it a child of the times or was it a non sequitur?

Thinking back we will recall that interest in folk singers, black ones included, was not alien to mainstream, liberal, hippie, upscale appetites among white suburbanites in the '40s and '50s. Leadbelly, Big Bill, Brownie and Sonny were around. Blind Gary Davis, K. C. Douglas, Elizabeth Cotton, Jesse Fuller were playing shows for white folks.

But none of them were virtuosos. Some were very good, but none were great entertainers.

None were spellbinding, hypnotizing, mesmerizing, captivating, desensitizing.

No. Not one.

But then in 1960-something, Mississippi John Hurt was rediscovered by one Thomas Hoskins, AKA "Fang." Hurt was a spellbinding virtuoso and there was something mysterious which came through in his singing and playing. Something you couldn't quite put your finger on. Something barely stated. An enigmatic echo of the previous century's zeitgeist and *Zeitgefühl*.

Hurt drew great audiences and made many records not because of ideological reasons or agreements but because he was a truly great guitarist. Vocally, he sometimes went off-pitch. But that was incredible, intricate guitar playing....

There is no mistaking a genius who comes along.

Other brilliants turned up like Reverend Robert Wilkins.

When great musicians started to show up, even mid-cult and middlebrow ears brought up on Marx started to perk up.

Previously, lefty politicians were actually bored with most of their ethnic frontmen performers.

Now suddenly they found themselves enchanted by the *music*—

much to their own surprise and embarrassment.

These lefty leaders played guitars or banjos and sang at parties and political meetings in Unitarian churches in an attempt to get everybody into a group and make them sing horrible repetitious, togetherness, *Einheit*-commie and commie-symp songs.

I saw a lot of it in Berkeley. And in Washington, D.C., my home, friends of mine and I went to parties given by the children of the officials who lived at the Red Embassy.

These kids invariably had expensive Martin guitars. None of us could afford such instruments. We sat in these song circles and sang along with everybody else until the togetherness started creeping in, at which point we started singing off-key, and to the wrong rhythm, insulting these foreign creeps, threatening fights with them which never materialized.

This was great fun.

Now according to Marx, as I'm sure you know, music is worthless because it cannot help the revolution.

Add revolutionary words like Petie did, and others, and suddenly the music is considered valuable, even though most of it was pretty bad, aesthetically speaking.

Suddenly the Movement found it was losing members, losing interest, not making converts.

Where were the missing? What had happened, bigwigs like Petie wondered.

Eventually they discovered that those not present at party meetings were somewhere listening to John Hurt or somebody like him.

But what could a Marxist high-IQ shepherd do when some ethnic moved into the land of virtuosity?

This wasn't supposed to happen, you see.

Hell's bells, Karl M. said so, didn't he?

Said what?

Said that ethnics could never approach virtuosity.

Well, he didn't actually say so, but he assumed it along with his political opposites and everybody else in European High-Art culture.

And so his disciples assumed it, too.

Pete Seeger was one of the greatest five-string banjo players I ever heard. He was on a par with Uncle Dave Macon.

But he counted his proficiency to be of no worth other than as accompaniment to his political and togetherness songs. He didn't notice that many were listening to the banjo more than the words.

False modesty.

The amusing truth is that many of these politicos got so carried away by the great beauty of harsh ominousness expressed coherently and frequently in the new music.

Many musical-political ombudsmen found themselves losing interest in politics and gaining interest in folk guitar music.

Clearly, Marx had missed something. The *Volk* do, on occasion, come up with wonderful creations.

And waiting for them were the brokers and Madison Avenue Krell-like beings. The product changed from Marx to business and in some cases to greedy thought-control media mongers who heard the neat, previously unknown music, too.

Rather than use it as a tool of political ideology, these guys used it as a tool of financial teleology.

Inevitably they played favorites, and not only over-falsified it and exploited it, but overexposed it.

Too much too soon.

Entrepreneurs made fortunes fast and then moved on to other fields to pick the daisies and sell them to the farmer.

Overall this was an improvement. Where racketeering was not involved or the skimming was slight, backwoodsmen and farm workers with some talent were actually treated with sufficient respect such that they made some money at least for a while. And in many cases for a long while.

John Lee Hooker is a good example. From the very beginning he had a sharp lawyer manage all his financial affairs and music biz. Not just the dough but the connections.

Hooker worked for some real carnivores, too.

But his contracts were methodically and carefully managed by his lawyer, his publishing was protected, none of his songs got stolen, his royalties were collected with great care.

Hooker had made money from the very beginning and is still making lots of dough.

Most hicks weren't as sharp or as lucky as Hooker, but many, many hicks under the able and experienced leadership of such people as Manny Greenhill and others made out fine. A hell of a lot better than their Marxist protectors. Outwardly paternalistic, inwardly selfish and greedy.

"Underground," "folk" this and that, "hippie," and "folknik" were marketing terms.

This sales pitch and thought-control captured the entire populace.

All of these "expressions" of alternative living or the folk soul or whatever—all could be bought. The prices were very high.

Hippie didn't know all this.

Hippie didn't know much about anything.

Worse, Hippie didn't know that he didn't know much about anything.

And nobody told him.

But Hippie did have one or two things: money and a bunch of pretensions.

All Hippie was pretense.

It seems as though I was the only person who noticed this perversity.

In previous days, hippies were simply called criminals or bums.

But now they had some money.

Why?

Because they were criminals.

That is why they had money.

They and their Madison Avenue bosses were always telling me that I should celebrate.

"Celebrate what?" I asked.

But they couldn't answer me.

They told me to make love not war. They told me that Black is beautiful.

Madison Avenue.

The new hookers wore different clothing. Lots of flowers. Called themselves and their pimps "flower children."

Hookers and pimps have to be fashion-conscious. Part of their trade.

And so hookers and other criminals were glorified. Automatically made part of

THE MOVEMENT.

"Love-ins." Everybody said they loved me.

Sure.

Even convicted murderers were glorified. Provided they could play guitar.

In order to be a great retired country blues singer participating in the, har, har, "revival" and simultaneously representing and interpreting the *Volk*-soul, you have to have at least one conviction for murder—Son House, Texas Alexander, Hambone Willie Newburn, Booker (Bukka) White, Robert Pete Williams, Lightnin' Hopkins, Leadbelly. . . .

Or you could be a murderer but escape prosecution and persecution for venting such normal aggressive emotions—Skip James, Blind Joe Reynolds. Finally, if you couldn't achieve one or both of these it was OK if you *got* murdered—Blind Lemon Jefferson, Robert Johnson, Sonny Boy Williamson.

All retired blues singers, including the ones who could hardly play and sing anymore, or never could in the first place, brought scores of people, looking for their "roots."

White folks are root-hungry, too.

The typical ticket or record buyer could not tell one blues singer from another. But then did it really matter?

You see, there was this expectation of revelation from the collective unconscious and/or the folk-soul. Gnostic teaching—maybe even initiation—into the mysteries of the universe, internal and external, from a perfect or almost perfect master, who had seen and done all, who had put it all together in a great big pot, and boiled it until it was broken down into its simplest elements, the non-essential or phony parts, the extraneous, the put-ons, the advertising all filtered out until there was nothing left except essence of noble savage reality soup.

In concert this reality would emanate forth in the music or noise and in the talk-talk in the steam of the evening's reality soup blues singer.

Whitey had a commitment to the NEGRO and felt obligated to yell and clap and scream his head off. But you know, while he was at it, why not get a little something back, you know, what the hell? A little wisdom from the alphabet—I mean reality—soup.

It didn't matter if the show was an aesthetic disaster. Aesthetics weren't the issue. Hell, they were nothing but value judgements, anyway. Everybody knew that. Especially in Berkeley.

No, the commitments were to Negro and to gnosis. I mean, man, that's what you did to help support Black Power. You went and listened to a sick geriatric try to perform *something*.

Ofttimes it was hard to tell what it was this guy *did* exactly, or tried to do, or intended to do. But that didn't matter.

Everybody went home from these shows with clear consciences in re black poverty so near, so clear down the road in Oakland.

And why fight the pricks if you caught a glimpse of the eternal inside-outside? Wisdom.

Suffering produces wisdom.

Doesn't it?

And you can catch that fish without going through the prelims. Just be here then. Osmosis.

But, oh, was it funny when the blacks learned what the game was and started bringing you "wisdom" intentionally.

But before I go on, I think it might be a good idea to rest here by this balustrade and have a bit of pipe smoke. *So* many ideas are being put forward—let us spend a little time in meditation and allow them to digest by reflecting and *Sehnsucht*.

Yes, a pipe smoke is in order.

Because surely it is the experiences in reverie that are identical and recur throughout all Aryan history. WE know that all is one. Yes, we know that.

But in reverie we also know that all is peace. Strife is illusion. *Maya*.

These bodies, these names, these corpses, these accidents are for computer techs to count.

But here, now, with my pipe, in the still-rural, on a cold fall afternoon as one walks home from work at the dog oil factory or the involuntary organ donors program, here now, I am one with the race. I am one with the soil. I am one with the all, with the

GREAT BEAT.

Past, present, and future. I am one with my pipe and with my pipe smoke.

This reverie, this revelation of Being, is what abides and unites.

We all "know" this, but we forget.

Ah, yes, I'm supposed to tell you about Skip James.

Sorry.

Contrary to everyone's expectations, not only was James not a member of the collective unconscious, he had never heard of it previous to his rediscovery by me.

And he wanted nothing to do with it. Nor was he an archetype. Or an emanation of the Hero with a Thousand Faces, har, har, har, or a *Satguru*, or avatar, or bodhisattva.

No.

James was a pimp. He was a pimp for many years. He was also a bootlegger, a gambler, a robber, and a killer. He performed "significant acts of criminality, ones that he recognized as crimes. The crimes would involve...naked aggression or duplicity: armed robbery or theft." This is a quote from Stephen Calt's most excellent book, *I'd Rather Be the Devil*.

Calt is mincing words here. James told both of us about murders he had committed.

I think it is a shame to permit a man like Skip James who had so many talents such as being a pimp and a killer to only display one section of his creativity, i.e., his music. Limitations should not have been placed on such a multifaceted renaissance man like James.

But singing and playing were all that his contracts allowed for.

John Hurt, by contrast, was a simpler soul. He was never into crime. He was a religious man.

A very religious man. And he was content with being a farmer.

And he was a gentleman.

Finally springtime comes and it is time for me to make my annual journey through the Southland looking for Skip James and other decadent blue singers. But mainly for James.

So now once again I went searching the South for blues singers. I already had turned up Booker (Bukka) White in 1964.

Booker was a convicted murderer like many others, but he had given up crime long ago and now enjoyed respectable socializing with the Negro middle class of his neighborhood.

Booker was gregarious to a fault. He loved people. He loved to talk to others. It didn't matter who. Black, white, cat, he didn't care. Booker was an orator. An entertainer.

Perhaps all the time.

His neighbors loved him and the people he worked with at the tank factory loved him.

He became a close friend of mine.

We had lots of adventures together.

On all of these trips I asked everyone I met about blues singers. Many people remembered Charley Patton, who with one mysterious "Rube Lacey" (who we later turned up), shared the title of best blues singer in the Delta.

A few people recalled Son House, Booker, Blind Lemon Jefferson, Leroy Carr, and others.

Nobody I talked to had ever heard of Skip James.

He was a cipher.

But why was I so interested in Skip James? What was so distinctive and wonderful about his records?

Well, that is a heavy issue. Let me have one more Spenglerian pipe smoke here in the declining afternoon, looking longingly, ingesting....

I notice that as I regard the flowers at eventide as, one after the other, they close in the setting sun. And strange is the feeling that then presses in upon one—a feeling of enigmatic fear in the presence of this blind dreamlike earth-bound existence, not unlike
THE BLUES.

The dumb forest—the silent meadow, this bush, that twig—do not stir themselves.

Only the Spider, he moves whither he will. This means that it will be the characteristic task of the 21st century to get rid of the existing systemic ideation of superficial causality—whose roots reach back into the Baroque period—and to put in its place a pure physiognomic. The two concepts, Goethe's form-fulfillment and Darwin's evolution, are in as complete opposition as destiny to causality.

We should always bear that in mind.

Ah, that was a good one. Back to James.

Dick Spottswood, an *Uhr*-collector, played me several of James's 1931 recordings in 1955. James was Spottswood's favorite blues singer.

James sang and accompanied himself on both piano and guitar.

One at a time.

I never heard anybody sing and play guitar in such a sad, sadistic, and discomforting manner.

James played guitar in a clandestine tuning. I searched and searched my guitar neck but I could not find these furtive sounds.

I was envious.

I decided then and there in 1955 that I must find this James and learn his secrets.

James was the Sphinx.

I suspected that James was from the state of Mississippi. My "evidence" was meager. It consisted of one item.

James sang this stanza:

> *Hitch up my pony, saddle up my black mare,*
> *Gonna find me a rider in this world somewhere.*

Others recorded this entendre, if that's what it is.

All were Mississippians.

James was such a prehistoric impossibility that engineers and others who produced and manufactured recordings got the title wrong on the record that contains these words:

> *If you haven't any hay, get on down the road.*

He actually sang:

> *Put your habit in your hand, get on down the road.*

I know this because when I FINALLY did find James he told me so.

"Habit" is ancient for clothing. The religious still use the term.

James's recordings were grief-stricken. I wondered how he and the engineers got through the sessions without hospitalization.

Later James will be hospitalized and have a short tryst with Ishtar on the great sacrificial altar in the great pyramid of Cheops. And what will befall James in Washington, D.C., General will be his worst excursion ever. Ishtar always demands a sacrifice from her worshipers. Always. And this decree will affect James's music.

James's style was so aggressively melancholy, so desperate and wretched, and full of gloom that we librarians reasoned that James's life must have been unbearable.

Just underneath the great sadness in James's music we hear anger. Disguised and hardly noticeable. We see through the camouflage a lot of hatred.

We collectors also reasoned thus: If James managed to survive with his unprecedented moroseness and didn't go insane or kill himself, then James must be the strongest person in the Universe. James must apprehend

THE PURPOSE OF LIFE.

After all,

THE PURPOSE OF LIFE

is external, outside, the goal of an expedition, a search, a trek, a

TRIP.

Isn't it?

James must be a sage. Omniscient, all-knowing.

He is the Sphinx at the

CROSSROADS.

Holy Grail man.

James's profoundly disturbing and obscene expressions of melancholy had affected our reason.

In rare moments of clarity we recognized our predicament. And the conclusions we came to were preposterous. We knew that. But they wouldn't go away any more than we could take James's records out back and burn them.

Our conjectures became suspicions, puzzles, arcane obsessions.

Pyramids along the Mississippi River.

Castration Mountain, tall, purple-veined, far away in the East, center of the chain.

THE MOUNTAINS OF PROJECTION

AMID THE

FIELDS OF DECEPTION

Many explorers drawn by orientophilia and the eternal search for the missing female penis had set out for these snow-covered upthrusts. But none had ever returned.

I wanted to go. Because if I saw the real thing—i.e., the genuine projections themselves, pristine—then in the future I might be able to spot spurious, furtive projections.

Was I brave enough, fool enough to go?

Well, fool enough. Definitely.

Prototypical ultimate investigation into the nature of reality.

Necessity. I had to go so I could stop playing those accursed records.

Answer the questions and destroy my obsession with them.

But they all told me—all the Berkeley-ites, and all the -ites from everywhere else—smoke some dope. You'll feel better. Hide. Repress, exercise, fuck, keep busy.

The giant Spider can't get you if you keep busy. It's not that far to the end of the road.

Just keep busy.

See, all these unique and extravagant and esoteric practices are all here in B-town, man. All under the same tent, all wearing the same hat, price of admission is no exit, man. Phenomenology, man. Husserl, Heidegger, man. *Krishnamurti*, man. Fillmore, man, Grace Slick, man.

The Grateful Dead, man, Jerry Garcia, man....

Those mountains you talk about—they aren't even real, man. You'll never get to them because they aren't there.

Can you see them? I can't.

"Yes," I replied, "I can see them everywhere I go."

"Oh go fuck yourself with a file, Fahey. You're trying to dive deep when there isn't any deep water around. I'm going over to see Country Joe, man, you comin' or not?"

"Ah no, man, the suffering is bad enough right here. See ya around."

"You're just plain crazy, Fahey, just plain crazy. What's within anyway? Everything is outside. The inside is empty. Nobody home.

"What you are saying implies duality. Try some ginseng. Mysteries are in the out.

"Somewhere else. Not here. What you're looking for isn't here. It doesn't exist. There's nobody, nothing inside. Trungpa says so. Just emptiness.

"Emptiness.

"STOP BEING SO

EMOTIONAL EMOTIONAL

EMOTIONAL.

"Not here."

"But look," I tell them, "the imagery is unnerving. Dissertations on death. His symbols 'mean' things, damn it."

I feel those same things myself. They are familiar. But I don't know what they are or what they are about. Nobody wants to help me think about them. Remember them.

Everybody wants me not to feel those feelings, not to know where those feelings are coming from.

And why? Nobody wants you to know why.

What happened?

Something happened, I tell you. Happened to me. I am not talking about a lit class.

I'm talking about me.

What happened? Won't somebody help me find out why I have these feelings? Where they originated?

"You're always trying to make trouble, Fahey. Shut up. Forget about those feelings. Don't rock the boat. Those feelings aren't real anyway."

What the hell do you mean? If I feel a feeling it is real. Don't tell me it isn't real.

I know it's real. I feel it. But I don't know what it is.

And look—cypress trees. Always cypress trees. Only cypress trees.

Big deal. He was just trying to make some bucks. He didn't mean it. Just a gig, man.

But quicksand pulling you under? Vultures in the cypress limbs. Blacksnakes crawling through the Spanish moss.

Oh hell, Fahey, that's not even in the text.

I don't care. I'm not a fundamentalist. Furthermore there are alligators in the cottonmouth water. Stay out of the water, Skip.

If you can, can, can, can, can, har, har, har.

Yes, pulling him under. Some monster. James just can't stay land-side much longer. What is the monster? If only James could figure it out....

Aqueous devils all around. Contemplation of final among bleak trees.

James: "I am very weary, seasick. I hate it."

He's talking about sex.

You know what? I'm the same way. Is there actually any other way to be? If there is, I don't know it.

There is never the leer in James's voice that is heard in so many blues singers. Smirking double-entendres are not for James.

> *Little cow and calf is gonna die.*

> *If I go to Louisiana, they'll hang me sure.*

> *And if she gets unruly,*
> *take my 22-20, I'll cut her half in two.*

I BELIEVE I'M GONNA DIE.

James's lyrics are sadistic and masochistic. Chop. Cut. Die. Kill.

James, the king of the sadistic and masochistic blues. Cruelty everywhere.

WOW WOW WOW WOW WOW WOW WOW WOW

James would "rather be the devil then to be that woman's man." He would "rather be dead, buried in some cypress grove, than to have a woman, man, I can't control."

> *I love my cherry-ball better than I love myself.*

* * *

In 1965, the very reliable Blues Grapevine informed me that Ishmon Bracey, another prime blues artist, had turned up in Jackson, Mississippi. Bracey had recorded for the same company as James at about the same time.

Bracey's manner of singing was and remains the meanest sounding, most dangerous and hate-filled blues singing that ever existed, more so than even Skip James's vocals.

If records could kill. . . .

Bracey was completely overlooked by the "blues revival." Why? I do not understand. He was as good as the best of them.

Because I was seeking out mean, sadistic, aggressive, hateful, and maybe even dangerous expressions and expressers of music most cruel. Because the search was urgent and of utmost importance. Because I had to find them, locate them, understand them (maybe not master them), but at least have some knowledge of their origins. Because of all this, I was so desperate that I thought nothing of jumping in my car and driving all the way across the country just to ask this new guy, Bracey, if he knew anything about James.

I set about organizing one more trip. I asked two friends, Henry Vestine and Bill Barth, to go a-collecting with me.

So off we go into the wild blue Delta.

James the Sphinx is waiting over the next hill. Through the next rainstorm. The next state.

Somewhere out there, man.

Trip.

Unnoticed, dimly lit, there is an ambush ahead in the frontier wilderness of forest and people.

The ambush is called "reality."

Destination unknown we merrily chase wraiths and specters.

Land of the time-warp.

People still believe in antebellum, sunny Southland.

Autochthons faithful to this archaic, antediluvian dream.

The Delta—The South.

Capitalize, baby.

ANNOUNCEMENT: Here we are. Three young whiteboys from suburbanland, mid-cult land, lukewarm land, incorporeal land.

Stalk that myth. Safari in jungleland.

Alligators. Alligator gar fish. Alligator snapping turtles.

In swamps which issue strange-colored rising gasses. Farell pastel-green against sky painted shades of red. Not of *this* solar system. Surreal silent firmament of the maybe-God above and over the flat, flat, flatland, where you can see all the way to the sun setting blood-red directly—right there—in front of you. Miles and miles away on the horizon, see, overcome by the great round burn, site of the end-place where the land stops and falls over the edge and dies asphyxiated.

We are the drawn-lovers of these hues and impossibilities.

This is no place to smoke a pipe.

Yes, here we are.

Way down in Egyptland.

Henry Vestine, ace modern blues guitarist. Member of Frank Zappa's group, the Mothers of Invention.

In the future Vestine will play with the Canned Heat Blues Band. Jimi Hendrix will learn much from Henry. And in the future (1997), Henry will die. And when Henry goes down, a legend will fall.

Bill Barth's goals are a bit hazy. A bit of mystery. Especially to himself.

He is guitar player and maven of successful, comfortable itinerancy.

Me? I am looking for the secret of a savage expression.

That is what each one of us thinks.

We are mixed up as to the outside and the inside.

Which is which? How do you tell a projection from a real thing?

Is my hunch that Skip James is the Sphinx correct?

Can one see the mountains of projection and fields of denial from the state of Mississippi?

And, why, right in the middle of those ever-so-courteous looking hills is there the Great Castration Mountain? And what has it got to do with us?

We are the dreamers and lovers of this Faulkneresque, Freudian fantasy.

We search for artifacts of long-dead civilizations.

There is, of course, one small problem. Many locals are not aware of the fact that they live in the gone-dead past.

And for that reason, I ask you, are they in fact living in antiquity?

Maybe this dream is more than a dream.

Out of our element. No question about that. We are occidental Egyptologists searching for remnants of Pyramidland.

Just after nightfall we cross the river, which is known here as just that: "The River."

Nobody calls it the Mississippi River. Just "The River."

Exhausted, we park in the middle of a swamp, not knowing.

Unaware that we are in the breeding grounds of the alligator snapping turtle and the alligator gar fish but, even worse, the alligator mosquito.

Har, har, har.

We awake with the sun, surrounded by alligator men harvesting cotton. These Negroes are green.

Don't they read the travel books? Don't they know they are supposed to be black and picturesque?

It is then that we discover the alligator mosquito bites. Just for the record I count the wounds on the top of my left hand and wrist.

Twenty-two.

No joke.

Not dissuaded by mere loss of blood, we trek onward in our youthful search for the inside outside.

Let us pass into Jackson.

Not far from the elephant compound we spy a rickshaw boy and flag him over. We tell the coolie what we want and he paddles us through the mud to a Rexall drugstore with a sign in the window:

EATS

across the street.

We wait for the green light while a herd of camels pass by.

While we are waiting for our alligator chicken eggs and bacon I contemplate the alligator phone book.

"You know, I ought to look in the phone book for Bracey. I'm sure he's in there. Why not? Alligators live a long time."

Surveying the jungle terrain with my binoculars, I see the directory in the distance hanging innocently from the side of a native hut.

Unfortunately, I am not used to the many pie-dogs in the street. I'm a bit fearful of them. But I ask myself, did Frank Buck, the

BRING 'EM BACK ALIVE GUY

ever worry about pie-dogs?

Hell no. So I put on my macho and walk nonchalantly through them and the wild pigs until I reach the mud hut there in Egyptland, go down Moses.

"Bracey, Alligator Ishmon, Reverend," the book says with an address and phone number.

Of course he's in the book. I knew it all the time. I just didn't know that I knew it.

Repression.

"Sure, it's me. I used to make blues records for Paramount and Victor. Come on over."

Yes, we are in a strange and alien place. Why everywhere you go you can pick up a phone book listing all the simians in the state.

My friend and great blues singer Booker (Bukka) White wrote a song called

STRANGE PLACE BLUES.

Yes. That is where we are. City of

STRANGE PLACE BLUES.

Lots and lots of blues bards live right here in Jackson, Mississippi,

Africa. Sure, use the telephone. Oh, the pharaohs? Right up the road. Keep to the left. You can't miss their temples.

But watch out for the Ishtar temple. You know what they do to you in there. Don't fool around with prostitutes. You never know. Never.

Come to Mississippi and see the pyramids. And the dinosaurs, too. We have Brontosaurus, Pterodactyls, and man-eating plants. Still quite abundant here.

But watch out for Ishtar. You know what....

Lions and tigers and cannibals line the jungle paths. Yes, cannibals just like in Tennessee Williams. Why hell, while you're here why not visit Tennessee? It's right up the road.

Most of the cannibals have been Christianized. They won't bother you.

Most of them.

And so to Ishmon Bracey's house we go. I'll tell you the show blow by blow.

Bracey is bitter. At disconsolation he is not a quitter.

He's been dissatisfied for years. His personality is in arrears. Looks at us with leers.

No tears.

Bracey makes extravagant claims. He is into one-upsmanship games.

For Bracey, humility is an impossibility.

Tells us tales that with lies is fraught. All other blues singers he has taught.

He big man. Greatest in the lan'.

With lesser figures, Bracey does not flirt. He has even taught Mississippi John Hurt.

Bracey the truth does bend. Louis Armstrong is his good friend.

Armstrong and Count Basie have both asked Bracey to get his guitar and with them go afar, and do the rounds, and make great sounds, on the road. This is the bull that Bracey did unload.

As I said before, a blues singer who sounds so mean, had never been seen.

That's the way it is, at blues Bracey is a whiz.

But a jazz player he could never be. He simply cannot play in that key.

You see?

Although in re other matters with truth Bracey has been quite free, in re James he *does* have the key.

For thirty dollars dough, seeds of truth Bracey will sow.

So we gave him the bread and he said:

BENTONIA. GO!

Shortly thereafter Ishmon Bracey, one of the greatest blues singers ever, dies and is buried with no "revival." Buried in the land of obscurity.

The Brahmins feed him to the sacred gators in the Orpheus temple while everybody chants, "Hare Krishna, Hare Krishna, Krishna, Krishna, Hare, Hare, Hare Rama, Hare Rama, Rama, Rama, Hare, Hare." The Maha Mantra. Bracey will go to the Krishna Loca and never sing the twelve-bar blues again.

What we are doing is surrounded by and described by only one word: lunacy. This chase is thoroughly difficult because we do not even comprehend what we are looking for.

We might find it and yet not know it for what it is.

And there is danger lurking all around us. Something big, growing bigger, surrounds us.

We are in the action-vortex of the civil rights storm.

Everywhere we go and talk to, or ask questions of, or look at, or even think about black people, there are eyes watching us.

Whitey's eyes. And behind them white brains thinking suspicious thoughts.

We are expected to do something destructive and dangerous that will bring about the downfall of antebellum. Even though we are wearing Louisiana license plates, white eyes are peeking, keeping track, counting, locating, following, surveying. The hunters are being hunted. Whitey thinks we are going to help give the vote to blacks. That is what all those brain-eyes perceive. We are the enemy. Out to destroy civilization.

We couldn't possibly be looking for old blues singers and records. Nobody does that.

Not even crazy people.

Therefore we are liars, intruders, troublemakers.

Ishtar is watching. She knows where it's at, man.

Several times in the next few days we will be accosted by police, guns drawn and pointing because:

WHAT ARE YOU BOYS DOING FOOLING AROUND WITH OUR NIGRAS? DON'T YOU BOYS KNOW YOU CAN GET IN TROUBLE FOR FOOLING AROUND WITH OUR NIGRAS?

Our feelings of fear are not groundless.

That very summer three busybodies will be put in the sod.

Found dead long later, their killers will not spend a day in jail.

Faulkner/Weltyland folks are not joking around.

And so in addition to our feelings of absurdity, alienness, confusion about the inside-outside, resurrected castration complexes, lostness, add fright comma constant.

Yes, we get to Bentonia unharmed. And we find some of James's relatives who try to help us but really can't. Even relatives of James find him hard to pin down.

An aged uncle relative of James tells us with authority that James lives in a town or city near Tunica, Mississippi. The first letter of the name of this town is, he thinks, a "D." Dunirk, Dubbs, Detritus, Dundee, Dalks, Denton, maybe Demeter or Day, but he's really not sure, it may be that the name of the town begins with an "M." I mean, you know they are so similar sometimes it is hard to tell them apart.

But of one thing he is certain. The end of the rainbow is near Tunica. Not in Tunica.

But near Tunica.

So off we go towards Tunica.

About twenty miles from Tunica, near Dubbs, we stop at a gas station.

I engage the young black gas pumper in conversation leading up to the person of my quest. I have been doing this for years to no avail. Always, these miscellaneous impromptu inquiries draw complete blanks.

"Skip James? No, 'fraid not. Nevuh heard that name. Sorry."

But now and finally, something very interesting happens. This young attendant is not familiar with the name. No, but:

"I don't know if this is the right guy you looking for, but one night I was over at Benny Simmons's barbershop in Dubbs and this crazy, drunk old man came over and started yelling and screaming at us. He was out of his mind, you know. But one of the things he raved about was that he used to be a famous and great blues singer and that he played guitar and piano. Said he made all kinds of records in Wisconsin. Kept yelling at us saying he was a genius. But he was drunk out of his mind."

Yes, finally the key words, or at least some of them:

CRAZY GENIUS GUITAR *AND* PIANO WISCONSIN.

It had to be James. In his peculiar mad and obnoxious manner, James certainly was a genius.

When we finally find James, which is about to happen, we also discover that James is a creep. We are all of one opinion. A creep.

I offer the kid some money, but he won't take it. But he gives us directions to Benny Simmons's barbershop.

And as I start up the car I have a mysterious vision. Far away I finally, actually see Castration Mountain, clearer and nearer than I have ever seen it before. Right in the middle of beautiful blue Mountains of Projection upthrust amid the famous fields of self-deception.

And there at the foot of Mount Castration is the temple of
ISHTAR,
beckoning and shining like the North Star in the bright morning.

And it whispers to me somehow across the great distance
              I HAVE A SURPRISE FOR YOU.

Benny Simmons points right next door.

"There."

On the front porch of an old shack sits an old lady with a look of transfiguration. Yes of course, James's wife would have to be a mystic, a saint. Sure.

In days to come we discover it is very, very bad, poisonous transfiguration. The worst I have ever tasted. I try to swallow it and I can't.

"Yassuh," she said, "this is the house but he ain't here. He in the hospital."

The sun is about to set but I ask her:

"Well, look, Mrs. James, would you like to go over there? If you show us the way we'll drive you there."

"Let's go."

This was James's "plantation wife," name of Mabel.

Off we go to the Tunica County Hospital. A black nurse takes us to the black ward.

Nurse: "How you feelin' Mr. James? There's some boys here want to talk with you about some music. Is that alright?"

The silent figure in semi-dark nods his head up and down. Not much, but just enough.

He says nothing. He stares at us the way he would examine some butterflies just before he sticks the specimens to the pasteboard with needles.

He gives us no expression of emotion whatsoever except for a slight but not significant curiosity. As though we are mental patients. Crazy as hell, but safely tranquilized.

Mildly interesting. Just before he sends us off to electro-shock therapy.

After a great while: "You fellas hear one of my old records?"

Me: "Yes, sir. We've heard several of them. They're great."

He: "Yes, that's true."

Me: "Uh, err, eh, we were wondering if you might be interested in resuming your career as a musician and making some new records up North? Play some concerts? That sorta thing."

"Hmmmmmmm," he barely uttered. "Well, that might be a good idea. Might be. But right now Skip is awful tired. Sleep on it. Meet me at the house in the morning. We can talk about it then."

And you know what he did then? With a slight wave of his hand he dismissed us.

He dismissed us!!!

Morning is the end of idealism. James has no guitar. Bill Barth goes to the car and gets his. James fools around with the chordophone awhile. Tuned in standard tuning. He does know standard a little. But not much.

Slowly, confidently, he changes the tuning. He's going back towards a—no, it can't be.

He's headed for open D minor. Primarily a theoretical tuning which nobody in his right mind uses.

But there it is.

And he knows chord shapes in it. Chords nobody else on this planet knows. Beautiful, terribly intense, hitherto-unknown chord positions. He sings and plays "Cherry Ball Blues," "Illinois Blues," and "Hard-Time Killing Floor Blues." A few others.

James is a little rusty but that is all.

And he shows me how to make the chords. Great Sphinx chords. I could never have found them.

Then, abruptly, he shoves the guitar into me.

"Show me."

I have it all.

The Sphinx is very original. Astounding even when out of practice.

But what about the riddle?

What is the riddle? To whom is the riddle addressed?

To James, not me.

He will find out later at the Mountain when he courts Ishtar.

We hang around a few days discussing the pros and cons of James resuming his musical career.

Things start to get boring. Nobody is going anywhere. There is no motion.

I begin to appraise the situation. What have I got? What have I learned? What is it worth?

I apprehend despair. What are those Sphinx chords worth? What is James's gnosis worth?

What is James worth? What am I worth? What is everything worth?

Nothing. Less than nothing.

Some trip!

I had played a trick on myself. I expected to find something interesting and enlightening.

Something of great value.

But instead all I found was this obnoxious, bitter, hateful old creep.

James had cancer. Cancer of the genitalia. And in Washington, D.C., General Hospital James had an operation.

Everything had to be removed.

And it was removed.

James had to give up his Sphinxhood.

He finally made it to those mountains I told you about.

He continued to sing a little. James the tenor became a counter-tenor.

James became a frightful figure who inspired fear and loathing everywhere he went.

Not because of anything external or physical or corporeal.

No. It was his attitude towards his music. Towards his audience. Towards himself.

Towards everything.

246 I Skip James

He made no attempt to hide his disgust and disdain for the people he met, the music that they played and liked, and for his gigs.

Everybody noticed it. James's connection with the collective unconscious was broken.

He didn't have anything to teach anybody anymore.

As a result of his attitude, attendance at his shows was always minimal.

James was a horror show. Not a pretend horror show, like in a movie. A real horror show.

And so he faded away.

And one day he died.

I was the guy who rediscovered Skip James. I wanted to tell you about this part of his life and about the lives of other people including myself.

For the rest of it, you should read Stephen Calt's book, *I'd Rather Be the Devil*.

I don't want to duplicate Calt.

Read Steve's book. It's very interesting and he's got it all right. It's just that he didn't tell you my part in the great hunt. He didn't tell you the new riddle of the Sphinx. He didn't tell you the answer to the riddle. He didn't tell you about Ishtar.

He didn't tell you about the significance of Skip James—or the lack of it—in the lives of other people.

No, he didn't tell you about those things.

But I did.

Thank you for hearing me out.

I am

John Fahey.

THE CENTER OF INTEREST WILL NOT HOLD

I. **How Bluegrass Music Destroyed My Life**

One day in 1954 or '55, I was listening to radio station WARL, Arlington, Virginia. This station blanketed Washington, D.C., as well as suburban Maryland and Virginia.

Now it has different call letters.

When I first started listening to this station there was an afternoon show called "Town and Country Time." The DJ played country-western records. Emphasis on western and electric.

Eddy Arnold, Webb Pierce.

People like that. No bluegrass. None.

I was still an innocent. I didn't know about bluegrass music.

Yet.

I liked Webb Pierce a lot.

And Hank Snow.

I was still reasonably happy.

Even though I was unhappy.

I hadn't heard any bluegrass music yet.

I was loved. I had friends. I was one of the crowd.

All of us united all day long. When we weren't separated by artificial things like school.

That sorta stuff.

We were all terribly lonely. And we were all excessively social. We were aggressively social. We were compulsively social.

Yes.

There was nothing we could do about it.

Because almost all of us had "family problems."

And there was nothing we could do about it.

Divorces, mainly divorces.

But some of our parents were criminals. They got locked up sometimes, and we didn't see them for a long time. Didn't have anybody to counsel us. To understand us. To commiserate with us. To give advice, to

HELP US.

Some parents were sick or out of work. Things like that.

But mostly divorces.

Yes.

When we got together—us kids, we were all in our teens—when we got together and managed to get away from the adults, what we did was we got together and talked about the hillbilly hit parade we heard on WARL.

Some of us sang and played on guitars.

Anyway, radio station WARL and that show were very important to us. It is hard now for me to believe just how important that show really was to us.

You see, next to each other, WARL was the only thing we had that kept us from going nuts from loneliness and pain caused by our

PARENTS.

Or step-parents or relatives or whatever they were.

There was a lot of incest going on.

Know what I mean?

All of us were severely unhappy because of lack of attention and love from our elders.

I mean, you know, you call sex with them love?

I'm not joking. *My* parents were in the early stages of this long-suffering disease.

I mean divorce.

Not incest.

We all knew about that.

That was tolerable as long as you didn't talk.

But divorce?

That was much worse.

Much.

I felt lousy all the time.

So you might say that me and the other kids were "thrown" together (Heidegger).

WE needed each other. And a connecting link.

WARL was that connection.

Glue.

That's how important it was.

I'm perfectly serious.

And you could say that the reason we took the music and the personas so seriously—the reason why we discussed the virtues of this or that record—was to feel something good. Rather than the despair we felt as a result of the stupid and reckless activities of mom and dad. The lack of attention they paid to us.

WARL helped us escape the terrible sadness.

That's how it was.

Pretty bad, all things considered.

Anyway, one day the format changed.

WARL hired a new guy named Don Owens. AND the programming changed.

On the *morning show* we now heard country music.

Yes.

That's what they called it back then.

Prior to the advent of Don Owens, the morning show DJ played white popular music.

And white popular music was running out of steam. It was dying and taking a very long slow time to expire.

In the forties popular music was great. But it ran out of life.

In the early fifties.

It was inane and insipid.

Ridiculous.

BIPPITY BOPPITY BOO

Know what I mean?

Cute.

Kitsch.

Krap.

Worse even than "easy listening music."

And even now, a lot of people don't understand why punk and industrial and noise and alternative and noise and grunge and Sonic Youth and Throbbing Gristle and the German Shepherds and....

Sorry. I got carried away.

You know.

Anyway, WARL wasn't the only station that changed. WGAY changed. WTOP changed.

WRL changed. WOL Changed. WMAL changed. WDON changed.

WWDC changed.

WQQW changed its call letters to WGMS. Ha.

Washington's Good Music Station.

Good music.

Shostakovich, Prokofiev, Stravinsky, Rimsky-Korsakov, Ipolatov-Ivanov, Khachaturian, Gliere, Glazunov, Kalinikov, Tchaikovsky, Rachminov, Mussorgsky, Kabalevsky, Borodin, Qui, Gliere, Scriabin....

And on and on and on and on and on and on and on....

Russians. All Russians.

This radio station was Communist.

Everybody knew it.

What the hell could you do?

All these stations started playing rock and roll music by black people.

We didn't know that they were black.

No joke.

We assumed that these guys were white. Crazy as hell but white.

Boy, what a shock we all had when we discovered reality.

Most of us were prejudiced against black people and black music.

We learned it all from our parents.

And not just our parents.

One day WARL DJ Mike Honey Cut put on an obviously black record, played it for about forty-five seconds, then took it off abruptly and said

NO, NO. WE DON'T PLAY THAT KIND OF MUSIC ON THIS RADIO STATION.

What the hell did he do that for?

Honey Cut didn't know anything about country music.

All he knew about was popular music.

So Don Owens did the selection.

So all day long we heard music chosen by Don Owens.

I know all this because my father was a friend of Honey Cut's and helped him out a lot.

Mike had a big problem with alcohol. A big Jones.

He was a great talker.

But nothing about music. Nothing.

Now, thinking back, I wonder who programmed the anti-black-music episode.

Neither Don Owens nor Mike Honey Cut

CUT CUT CUT

were like that.

BOOM BOOM BOOM.

No.

Owens did an interesting and very perverse thing.

He changed the music. But he did it slowly and gradually.

So you didn't notice.

Until well after the fact.

Know what I mean?

SNEAKY GRADUALISM HEH HEH HEH

He started playing more and more bluegrass and other acoustic country music.

In fact he started each show with a Bill Monroe record.

He played Molly O'Day a lot. Grandpa Jones. Carl Story. Jimmy Murphy. Wilma Lee and Stoney Cooper. Flatt and Scruggs. Jim Eans.

People like that.

But we didn't notice.

And gradually Webb Pierce, Eddy Arnold, even Ernest Tubb disappeared.

He liked Hank Snow. But electricians other than Snow and Hank Williams simply disappeared.

It was as though they had never existed.

And by the time us kids noticed the change, Owens had gotten us used to, familiar with the bluegrass and acoustic sound. And the high, tenor voices of folks like the Stanley Brothers and Reno and Smiley and people like that.

But I didn't care about the change. I hardly noticed it.

Until one day Owens did this crazy thing which I could in no way have anticipated.

It was a dirty trick on me and on others, but I didn't know it at the time.

Hell, it changed my life.

Permanently.

Isn't it weird how somebody like a DJ who you don't even know and have never ever seen can do some apparently trivial thing—at least that's what you think at the time—and it changes your entire life for the rest of your life?

Wow.

Yes, Owens and another guy ruined my life.

I'll get around to the other guy in a minute.

Just wait.

Owens: "Well, friends, this is a very old record and it has a lot of scratches on it and it's hard to hear but it's such a good record that I'm gonna play it anyway. Bill Monroe and the Bluegrass Boys doing Jimmie Rodgers's

BLUE YODEL NUMBER SEVEN."

Christ.

You're not safe anywhere.

Not from bluegrass music.

No.

Then I heard this horrible, crazy sound. And I felt this insane, mad feeling. Neither of which was I in any manner acquainted. It was the bluesiest and most obnoxious thing I had ever heard. It was an attack of revolutionary terrorism on my nervous system through aesthetics.

It was blacker than the blackest black record I had ever heard. It reached out and grabbed and it has never let go of me.

I went limp. I almost fell off the sofa. My mouth fell open. My eyes widened and expanded. I found myself hyperventilating. When it was over I tried to get up and go and get a paper bag to restore the correct balance of power between oxygen and carbon monoxide. I screamed for help but nobody was around and nobody came. I was drenched with sweat. It was like I had woken up to a new and thrilling and exciting horror movie.

Nothing has ever been the same since then.

You see, I had gone insane.

And I didn't even know about it.

Wow.

I had to hear that record again. It was madness and I knew it would get me in trouble and it did get me in trouble but I couldn't help it I was out of control.

So I went to the record store in Silver Spring, Maryland, the name of which I forget. It was at the intersection of Georgia Avenue and Colesville Road.

Right around the corner from the Silver Theatre.

I asked the man behind the counter about that record. He was a "nice guy." He looked it up in some great big yellow catalogue and actually found it.

But it was out of print. And there wasn't one on the shelf.

"Sorry kid, I don't have one and I can't get you one."

"But I've got to hear it again. I've got to."

"Listen kid," he went on, "that record is no good. In fact it is evil. It caused a lot of trouble while it was around. Women left their husbands. Husbands left their wives. Children ran away from home and were never seen again. There were sunspots on the moon. Revolutions started, massacres happened, suicides and alcoholism went sky-high, wars started, monsters were seen on the Edge, it was bad, kid. It was bad. Maybe it would be better for you if you didn't hear it again. I mean I just feel like I gotta tell ya that, kid. It's dangerous for anybody your age to get interested in things like that."

"I don't care," I said, "it must be fate."

"Fate schmate. I gave you a warning. But if ya don't take it the only thing I can do is tell ya this. You gotta find a record collector. Chances are a record collector would know about it."

"You know any of those guys you are talking about?" I asked.

"No, I don't hang out with weirdos like that. But they're around. And I'll pray for ya kid. I'll pray for ya."

"Thanks a hell of a lot. I may need it."

"Oh, you're gonna need it alright."

I was more than heartbroken. I was thoroughly confused because I didn't understand this new and rebellious emotion I had heard. I had to get in touch with it again. I had to.

Yes, it had woken me up.

But it had also turned me into a monster.

But I didn't know it yet.

Anger. I was beginning to experience revolutionary terrorist anger. And I didn't even know the name of it.

Yes, bluegrass music made me into a monster. Filled my head with unecological and un-PC concepts and thoughts and desires and reaction formations and obsessions and sex mania and deviousness and Oedipus complexes and inferior complexes and incorporealities and alligators and snapping turtles.

No longer pure transcendence (Hegel-Kierkegaard).

But, having a lot of curiosity about life and death because of what my father had done to me, I had to investigate the thing.

You know.

But was I ever stupid.

But I didn't know that yet because I was stupid.

But now that I'm not stupid I know now that then I was very stupid.

Very.

So I sat down and started "thinking" (Freud).

And planning.

And making commitments (Kierkegaard).

And so this is what I did, har, har, har, har, har.

I could always find an angle.

So what I did was this. For a week or two I asked everybody I knew if they knew someone who was a

RECORD COLLECTOR.

And I wondered, what kind of records does a record collector collect? All kinds, like classical and pop and race? New and old? I didn't know. I had never heard of a

RECORD COLLECTOR

before.

Now, it so happened that I knew this umpy-frumpy intellectual chick named Kris who spent a lot of time reading books and stuff. She might have been passably good-looking but she wasn't because she went around all the time with kind of a startled, freaked-out look on her face. She wasn't one of the crowd. There was something wrong with her.

She wore strange and unusual clothes that didn't make any sense. She wore glasses and she didn't even know how to wear lipstick.

I mean, she could have been a slight turn-on but....

And, for some unfortuitous circumstances which I can't remember, I ran into her one day soon after. I asked her if she knew anybody who was a

RECORD COLLECTOR.

And my god she did, in fact.

"Really? Who is it? How can I find this guy? Is it a guy?"

"Yes. It's a guy named Dick Spottswood. He goes to the same church I go to."

"No shit," I said. "What church do you go to?"

"The Unitarian church, a little down on Sixteenth Street. He comes to the Liberal Religious Youth Fellowship every Sunday night."

"What the hell is that? I never heard of…what did you call it?"

"Liberal Religious Youth Fellowship," she repeated.

"Great, but what is it? What is a 'Liberal Religious Youth Fellowship'…."

"Oh, it's just a meeting of kids who go to the Unitarian church. See John," she went on, "Unitarians believe in liberalism. In everything."

"Why the hell do they do that? You mean they actually sit around and think about things in a liberal manner? Or do they think about things that are liberal? Maybe they do both? What d'ya mean by 'liberal' anyway?"

"Well, see John, these really neat people like Pete Seeger come and we all get together and sing songs with him about strikes and labor battles and stuff like that. It's lotsa fun. Unity."

"Oh," I said, "I see." Not seeing.

"Will you take me to this thing you go to? I've got to find a record collector because I heard this record on the radio and I went to the record store but the guy who works there told me the record was outta print, see. He said I had to find a
RECORD COLLECTOR."

"What record?" she asked me.

"Oh well, see," I had to explain to her because I knew she wouldn't know about things like radios and hillbilly music, much less danger-ous music like bluegrass, and I didn't want to upset her because I didn't think she could take too much, so I said a little deviously:

"Well, see Kris, sometimes," I had said "sometimes" because I didn't want her to know too much about what I did because she might get upset and go crazy or something, "I listen to this hillbilly radio station on the radio and the other day they played a record by

Bill Monroe called 'Blue Yodel Number Seven.' I mean, it was kinda strange, ya know? I wanna hear it again so that I can capitulate it and understand it. You know, encompass it."

"Oh, I see," maybe seeing, but I doubt it, she said, "yes, I have heard that name Bill Monroe. Who is he?"

"What d'ya mean, 'Who is he?' He's the guy on the record, Kris," and I put my arm around her shoulders and smiled at her, so she wouldn't freak out or anything.

"I don't know who in the hell the guy is," I continued. "How could I know that? I don't collect records. I'm not spun. I gotta move around a lot, ya know?"

"Yes I know," she said, and I believe she was knowing because she had been moving around with her mother because her father had split and all that.

It can happen to anybody. Even to ozmatroid girls like her.

You're not safe anymore. Nobody is.

"Well, why don't you come to the Liberal Religious Youth Fellowship meeting and meet Dick? I'll bet he has that record, if anybody does. I saw his collection once. It is enormous. He has everything. Thousands of records."

"Thousands of records. Is that what a record collector does? He has thousands of the damn things? Not just a few, ya know, like the really good ones? How the hell can he move about? He'll get caught in claustrophobia. And where the hell does he keep them all?"

"In his room," she said, there in the midst of time.

"You mean in his bedroom?" I asked. Now I was getting upset and I kind of blew it because I yelled at her:

"What the hell were you doing in this guy's bedroom?"

"I wasn't doing anything," she said, "I was just visiting him with some other kids from Liberal Religious Youth."

"Whaddaya mean you weren't doing anything in this guy's bedroom? If you were in this guy's bedroom obviously you were doing something for Christ's sake. There's no way you can be somewhere and not doing anything because if you are somewhere you have to be doing something because if you're not somewhere and you're not doing something then you're dead. Right?"

"Well, I mean, we weren't doing anything wrong or bad, we were just listening to records from his record collection."

"Sure, and then you get into each other's bed and get liberal? Don't you. That's what it's all about, isn't it? Because if that isn't it, it doesn't make any sense. Does it?"

"John, we don't get into each other's beds and get liberal in the Liberal Religious Youth. And, besides, what if we do sometimes? It's just a segue to a mature relationship. What's wrong with that?"

She called me "John." I hated that. My first name. Why didn't she call me "Fahey" like the regular kids did?

And furthermore she didn't make any sense in what she was saying. She was caught in self-deception or something like that.

But I wasn't.

Not me.

"What the hell is a mature relationship? What is all this stuff you're talking about? Why are you getting all upset and using words that don't make sense, Kris?

"What in the hell is wrong with you today?"

"There's nothing wrong with *me* today, John. I feel fine."

She was smiling at me.

But she was also looking very nervous, so I started rubbing her deltoid muscles. So she would calm down.

She liked that. She said:

"Mmmmmmmmmmmmm."

"He played us some strange hillbilly records with banjos and things. Some people named Flatt and Snuggs or something like that."

"Banjos? I don't like banjos," I said. "I hate banjos.

"This song I heard didn't have any stupid banjos on it. I don't wanna hear any stupid banjos. Those things are dangerous."

Then she started quivering and shaking all over. So I took both of her hands and held them and pulled her towards me a little bit.

"Hey, calm down Kris, they won't get you. I'll take care of them.

There aren't any around here anyway. Don't worry about things. I'll take care of things."

"What things?" she asked.

"Banjos, Kris. Calm down. I won't let 'em hurt you."

Sometimes I had to talk to her like she was a little kid or something. She was very impressionable. She had phobias and things like that, I think.

"How could a banjo hurt me, John?" she asked.

"Damnit, Kris, stop calling me 'John.' I hate it. What is the matter with you? You're always doing strange things I can't understand like going in some guy's bedroom and being liberal and stuff like that. Just calm down, the banjos can't hurt you. You got it right. Everything is OK. Relax. There won't be any banjos."

"I'm not afraid of banjos," she said matter-of-factly.

"Of course you're not, Kris. Nothing to fear. Big John is here. Ha ha. Just calm down and I'll take care of things."

"I like banjos. There's nothing wrong with banjos," she said in a confused manner.

"Of course there isn't, Kris. There's nothing wrong with banjos. You're absolutely right."

This chick had a split personality or something. She thought banjos were OK. I felt sorry for her. So I hugged her a little bit and kissed her on the cheek.

She liked that but then she started sneezing and coughing and lost her breath. She was coming down with shock or something. God knows why. People like that—you never know. She had three box turtles. That was cool. But she kept them in her basement and I don't think she ever fed them. She just didn't know anything. Didn't have any common sense. So I said:

"Kris, maybe I oughta take you home now. I think you're coming down with a cold or something."

"Oh no, really John, I'm OK. There's no need for. . . ."

Now sometimes with an inferior specimen like this you have to be a little rough because they don't always seem to know what the hell's going on. You know? So this time I pretended to threaten her. I had to.

"What is this 'John' shit? I just told you about that for Christ's sake. Get the hell in the car or I'll beat the shit outta you. You're going back home. You're not safe on the streets."

Now she started shaking and getting faint. Her face got white because of lack of blood. Too bad about her. I don't know what ever happened to her. Probably ended up in a nut factory or something.

"Yes John. OK. Don't get upset. I'll go with you."

"Me upset? What is this? You're the one who's upset. Get the...."

But she was already complying with my requests.

Now, at this time, I didn't have a '55 Chevy with a 283 cubic inch V-8 engine. All I had was a stupid black '51 Dodge 6. So I was still a nobody.

But she got in, nevertheless. So I took her home.

"See ya Sunday afternoon about five," I said as she got out.

"OK, John. Take it easy. See ya."

And that was that.

Sunday rolled around and I went over to her location and honked my horn.

She came out to the car without her coat on. Ya know. She couldn't help it.

"Don't you wanna come in the house for a few minutes and get warm or something? Before we go?"

She seemed for some strange reason to be begging me.

"Hell no," I replied. "Stop messing around. Go get your coat and let's get going. There's a heater in the car," I said. "You know that."

So she got her coat.

Eventually she got in the car. All the way to the other side of town she kept talking about justice and labor unions and social equality and *Volk* music and liberalism. Mostly about liberalism.

Talk talk talk talk.

But I humored her and I pretended I understood what she was

talking about. I went even farther than that and pretended that she knew what she was talking about. What the hell did this rich broad know about labor and all that stuff? What did she care about it? She would just end up being a schoolteacher or something stupid like that. A librarian. Or in a loony bin, maybe.

Eventually we got to the location of the Unitarian church and the Liberal Religious Youth. Despite all the talking, we got there.

So anyway she took me up to where there was this great big room. It was full of rich kids sitting around and talking about labor and politics and *Volk* music and liberalism and on and on and on and on.

Talk talk talk talk.

Wow!

After a while this other rich kid showed up. Kind of fruity. He talked like he was some college professor. Full of wisdom, ya know? Yeah, full of warmth and wisdom. Full of—he didn't fool me.

But he was a

RECORD COLLECTOR.

I pretended that I knew what he was talking about until he felt at ease with me. You had to humor these rich brats always going around and talking about crazy things like liberalism, communism, and fags like Pete Seeger. Pedophiles. Type II. This creep Seeger was an old man at the time. And he was no goddamn *Volk*. He was just after some young chicks like all the rest of his commie friends. On false pretensions, I went to see him once with this same sick chick. He was a catastrophe. And nobody was onto him and his game with kids.

Nobody except me.

What he did was he got all of these kids into singing this stupid kind of political music. Everybody was singing together. Ya know. It didn't make any sense. These people were really dense. Incorporeal. They didn't have any incarnation. But they didn't know it.

There wasn't anything I could do to help them. They didn't want to be helped.

And why should I help out a bunch of rich kids anyway? They looked down on me anyway and didn't want me to help them. They didn't understand anything about anything. Every one of them was spun.

I was from the wrong side of the tracks, ya know?

Condensation. No combustion. All smoke and no fire. Nothing I could do for these unfortunate specimens.

Spottswood was wearing clothes and fruit boots. He couldn't help it. He didn't understand.

And he didn't know that I was onto him, too.

But that was OK. I wanted to hear that record.

Ya know?

"Nice to meet you, Dick," I said without showing any condensation towards him although, in fact, that's the way I felt. And with justification.

"Say, I heard you were a

RECORD COLLECTOR.

I never met anybody like you before. Tell me, what does a

RECORD COLLECTOR

do?"

"Oh, I go door to door in colored sections mostly. I ask the *volks* if they have any old records and then when they do I give them some money. Then I take them home and listen to them and play them for other people and stuff like that."

"What the hell do you do that for, Dick," I asked him. "Dontcha have anything better to do? I mean don't you like to go out with girls or shoot pool or something normal?

"I mean you'd have to spend a lot of time all alone in your room with those records taking over and everything. Listening and listening. You could get sick that way."

"Oh no," he replied. "I have"—he always pronounced his As like *ah*, wow—"lots of friends. They come over and we spend lots of time listening to old records all the time. And we have lots of fun."

"Oh," I said. "They have the same problems, too. Hell, you all could get sick. Don't you care about that? You all could spread a bunch of diseases all over the place. Make a lot of people sick, ya know? What the hell d'ya want to do that for? I mean listen, Dick," I said. I was trying to help these eggheads out so they wouldn't get in trouble.

Ya know?

"You gotta get outside a lot and get plenty of fresh air and sunshine and stuff like that. If you don't you guys'll all get sick with typhoid or something and then everybody will get sick. Dontcha know that?"

"Oh no, John," he went on in a condensationing manner. "We all go to doctors and things. We take very good care of our health."

He spoke of health like it was a collective thing or something.

Weird.

I figured he was the ringleader. And I was right. And he was dangerous to the other rich kids. But not to me, heh heh, I thought to myself.

Little did I know that this creep would have a dangerous influence on my life. Little did I suspect that this jerk would influence me into byways of life that were in no way healthy.

Like sitting around inside in some goddamn room listening to old records.

And playing the guitar!

The guitar!

What a pervert. I would have grown up to be a normal human being if I hadn't have met this perverted monster Dick Spottswood. Yeah.

Because you see, as it turned out, Dick Spottswood was not only a

RECORD COLLECTOR,

no, not only that, but even worse, he had a copy of Bill Monroe singing "Blue Yodel Number Seven" by Jimmie Rodgers. I went over to his location lots of times and listened to this strange, seductive, angry, hate-filled bluegrass—or rather proto-bluegrass music lotsa times. And he played me records by all kinds of other great, destructive musicians. White ones, black ones, Chinese ones, Japanese ones, Hawaiian ones, Indonesian ones, Mexican ones, German ones, Cajun ones, but mostly American ones. I'll have to admit that. Nevertheless, he and Don Owens ruined my life.

Maybe someday if I make some more money I'll go back to D.C. and seek vengeance on these jerks.

Well, that will be kind of hard. Don Owens was planted a long, long time ago. And of course eventually Dick Spottswood got sick just like I told him he would. But so did I. It was all his fault.

Oh well, what the hell can you do when you're young and impressionable and some creep like

DICK SPOTTSWOOD

comes along? A guy who is a

RECORD COLLECTOR.

Not really very much, I am afraid. Not much.

It's not fair because I even tried to help the guy out a lot. I taught him how to smoke for example. I mean, that's very important when you're young and impressionable and just coming up. Cigarettes can help you in that they prevent you from feeling all kinds of socially unacceptable emotions and stuff.

Of course, you don't want to smoke too many of them or you might get lung cancer or something. I mean, I taught him all of that stuff.

Bluegrass music and blues are full of anger and fear and anxiety and trembling and hostility and propaganda and...well, mostly aggressively angry sentiments and stuff. I mean I was too young to understand that. What the hell could I do? Of course, now we all know better but back then.... He taught me that bluegrass is just sad music. It isn't. It is: unhappy music. Discontented music. Nihilist music. Atheistic music. Terrorist music. Godless music. Irresponsible music. Uncanny music. Sensual music. Unbridled music. Troubled music. Distressful music. Harassing music. Agitating music. Panic music. Demoralizing music. Tormenting music. Instrumental music. Shocking music. Browbeating music. Unfriendly music. Outlaw music. Gloomy music. Heartaching music. Lamentable music. Desolation music. Pagan music. Death music. Electric Chair music. Castrating music. Sadistic music. Nazi music.

And bluegrass music gives you liberal ideas, perverse cravings, makes you horny, angry, antisocial, neurotic, criminal, reptilian, sociopathic, lonely, unhappy, un-PC,

EVIL.

Know what I mean?

So because of Dick Spottswood and Don Owens and Bill Monroe, I became a professional guitar player and composer.

What the hell kind of a gig is that?

I could've been a contender.

So let me tell you something. It could be of use to you.

If you're ever somewhere and you hear some maniac playing minor thirds on a mandolin against an E-major chord on guitar— run. It's bad ecology, man.

Go find somebody who has records of people playing major thirds on a piano or something.

That's not a dangerous instrument.

Not like the mandolin.

No.

Never.

Mandolins and banjos are evil. I was right all the time.

Bluegrass music is the music of

PAN.

II. Adventures on the Edge

I was fifteen or sixteen years old. Dick Spottswood was teaching me how to find old pre-WWII records. His method was to canvass old sections of the South. We used to go door to door and ask whoever answered if they had any old records. Then we'd buy them. If they'd sell them. We found a lot of old records that way. We usually canvassed black sections because we found not only jazz and blues records but lots of hillbilly records, too. Blind Willie Johnson and Jimmie Rodgers. Charley Patton and Carter Family records. That old music was the kind of music we liked the best—except of course for the newly emerging bluegrass music of Bill Monroe, Jim Eans, the Stanley Brothers, etc.

Spottswood had carefully taught me how "collective improv-isation," "the solo," "hot" syncopation, and five-string banjo music were preserved. At that time they existed only in bluegrass.

Aside from bluegrass, river boat music had disappeared from the face of the earth.

That day in the summer of one of the middle-fifties we had been working local areas in suburban Maryland. Just north of the D.C. line. We had found Louis Armstrong and King Oliver records—old ones from the twenties—in a black home right beside the Takoma Park Library in Maryland. Nearby, we found a copy of "God Moves on the Water" by Blind Willie Johnson. Johnson's version of the story of the sinking of the *Titanic*.

Wow!

But we hadn't found any bluegrass records that day even though it was not unusual to find them in Negro homes. The closest we had come was a Carter Family Victor scroll, "When My Roses Bloom in Dixieland" backed with "No Telephone in Heaven."

That was on Ritchie Avenue East.

After that I drove us over to Sligo Mill Road. This is an old gravel road right on top of the section called "Hell's Bottom." The racial makeup here was mixed.

New Hampshire Avenue, north of the District line, had been built in 1939. It was a short imitation of the Robert Moses-type freeways which were built in New York state. And it served the same purpose. It enabled white urban dwellers to escape the downtown, expanding slums which were mostly black. It paralleled Sligo Mill Road. It was made of concrete and it had four lanes. So all the traffic was on New Hampshire Avenue. Not on dusty little Sligo Mill Road. There was no longer any mill on Sligo Creek. So the old gravel road existed for the sole purpose of serving the transportation needs of just a few, very poor people that lived along it.

It was a time warp and we were in it.

I was driving my '55 Chevy 283 V-8 slowly down the sandy road when we saw a tall, light-skinned black man walking towards us. I stopped the car and asked him out the window if he had any old Victrola records he would like to sell us.

No he didn't, but just as we were about to take off he saw my old Martin "New Yorker" guitar lying in the back seat. I had bought it from Joe Bussard for twenty dollars and a Bill Monroe record of two Jimmy Rodgers songs, "Blue Yodel Number Seven" and "Mule Skinner Blues." A fantastic record. A record that had a devastating effect on my life.

"Oh," said the black, "please let me play your guitar. I'll be real careful with it."

Mentor Spottswood encouraged me to pull over and see what the guy could do.

I handed him my guitar and he thanked me. Then he knelt down in the sandy road on one knee and started playing a really primitive, raucous twelve-bar blues song in E.

Five minutes later he was still playing the same song. Talk about hot syncopation. Soon Spottswood and I were sitting beside him on the roadside.

After about ten minutes the guy stopped abruptly.

"How you like that?" he asked triumphantly.

We were a bit astounded and told him so.

"Know anything else?" asked Spottswood.

"Oh, yes," he replied. "I know lots of songs."

Then he broke into the song written by Emmett Miller but made famous by Hank Williams.

> I've got a feeling called the blu-uu-uuuuuuues,
> Since my baby said good-bye…

Spottswood and I were both somewhat surprised at the selection of songs. Musical miscegenation. We looked at each other dumb-

founded, there in the midst of time. We were sitting on top of Hell's
Bottom, listening to a black man singing a country-western song,
yodel and all. And the next song he played was an instrumental
arrangement—a very good one—of Kitty Wells's "One by One."
Another country-western song.

What would he play next? Some flamenco? A raga?

No. Even better than that, he sang us "Little Brown Hand" a
bluegrass coon song. A light happy song, probably the last coon song
ever written. Jim Eans had written and recorded this one:

> Down in Carolina,
> Morning glories hanging 'round the door,
> Lives the prettiest little coon gal I ever did see,
> She'll be mine for now and evermore.
>
> Now, honey, more than once I caught your big eyes a-roaming,
> Just to give me your little brown hand.
> If you'll be my missus, I'll give you love and kisses,
> Honey, want to be your man.

Spottswood, a rich kid from Northwest D.C., and hyperliberal,
civil rights commie symp, egghead, atheistic Unitarian, sexually
perverted consciousness and self-righteousness oozing out of his
brain—Spottswood was flabbergasted. I was surprised, but then you
see I was born and raised out there. I knew you could never predict
what was coming down along the Prince Georges County Line.
The Edge.

There was always something happening. And it was usually pretty
interesting.

But Spottswood and I also thought it was funny. We knew the guy
had heard the song over radio station WARL, Arlington, Virginia,
on maven DJ Don Owen's show. This station blanketed the greater
and lesser Washington, D.C., area. But the last thing we expected
was to find a black guy singing it. Not only that, he had a copy of the
record. Not only that—and worst of all—he wouldn't sell it to us.

And he had lots of other records, many of them bluegrass.

Spottswood asked him what he thought about the song. He said he liked it a lot and thought it was a great song. Hell, that's why he sang it for us.

"Don't you find it a bit condescending?" asked Spottswood.

"What in the world are you talking about, man? Condescendin'? Who's condescendin' who?"

"Uh," Spottswood rejoined, "the word 'coon.' What about that?"

I was laughing a little.

Then the guy looked at me, and he said, "This your guitar, isn't it?"

"Yes," I answered.

"Mind if I play it a little longer?" he asked.

"You can play it all afternoon if you want."

"Thanks, you nice boys. Both of you, but," he said, looking at me, "yo friend a little strange, though. He OK, but he got funny ideas 'bout music."

Then he broke into one of the Blue Yodels. He had learned it from a Gene Autry record. Not a Jimmie Rodgers record. Later he showed us the record. But he wouldn't sell that to us either. Maddening.

A few years later when I met Jim Eans we discussed many things including "Little Brown Hand." Eans, from Martinsville, Virginia, is a nice guy. He doesn't hate black folks.

He said that he had written it sometime before the civil rights movement and wasn't trying to poke fun at blacks. He saw it the way our new black friend saw it—a bright, happy, picturesque love song but with, Eans granted, a not entirely kind tradition behind it.

"Williams my name, Elmer," he said. Spottswood and I told him our names and we shook hands.

We spent the rest of the afternoon in this bucolic, aesthetic pursuit, trading songs. We were making good—and sometimes funny—music and laughing a lot.

When the sun started to drop, Williams told us he had to go but for us to come back any time. He and all his friends all played music and most of them sang. There would be a crab feast Friday night.

"Bring some soft-shells and some wine," he told us. "We have lots of fun.

"And don't fo'get your guitar, Jawn," he told me. "I show you some more songs."

And he was off, walking up the road into the sun, along the old gravel road until he disappeared around a corner.

We went to lots of parties on Sligo Mill Road and we always had a lot of fun. It soon became apparent that I was the best guitar player. I was frequently asked to back one of the guys who could sing.

There were never any women.

Elmer and his brothers and friends liked all kinds of different music but the kind they liked the most were blues and pop country songs by Hank Williams. Hank Williams had died a few years previous but, before he died, I saw him do a show.

Elmer Williams really admired Hank Williams. He knew Hank was dead. When he found out I had seen him, he got really excited and made me tell him all about it.

About the second time Spottswood and I visited Elmer Williams, one of his brothers, Arthur, came out of the woods with a mandolin. We played a few songs and sang. This guy Arthur was really quite good.

All the Williams brothers and in fact all the people in Takoma Park who played guitar or banjo or mandolin claimed they had learned to play from "Mister" Williams. Elmer told me his father's main instrument was fiddle. Sometimes we got Mister Williams to come downstairs or outside and join in the festivities.

But rarely.

Anyway, we tried first to sing and play some old religious songs because they were slow and easy. Songs like the "Will the Circle Be Unbroken," "Take Your Stand," and even "In the Garden." But we had trouble with that one because of all the chords.

After a few practice sessions, we were not half bad. A mixed-race bluegrass band. We played blues and spirituals, too. We only had one public performance and that was for some folklore society around D.C. and they didn't like us much because we weren't PC.

But that's another story.

Anyway, Spottswood, me, and Elmer and Arthur Williams got together at least once a week and worked out. It was a lot of fun.

One time Elmer said to me, "You know this young white girl 'bout your age, Connie?"

"Oh yeah, I know who she is, but she's older than me. She won't pay any attention to me. She has a Gibson guitar and plays and sings pretty good."

"That the one," said Elmer. "She know more Hank Williams songs than I know. She good. She hear you play guitar and she talk to you, all right."

We were in the middle of a party with about thirty people around us.

"Yes," Williams went on, "she talk to you all right. In fact, she be *all over you*, she hear you play guitar, ha, ha, ha."

Everybody else was laughing, too.

But then he said, "Yes and she know all about Hank Williams, too. *All* about him."

He said this cryptically.

But nobody laughed at that one.

It sounded like Williams knew something I didn't know but I didn't pry. I didn't want to find out something that would create a barrier between Elmer Williams and his brothers and their friends and I. Still, I wondered, what was the connection between Elmer Williams and Connie?

III. Dance

In those days, I worked for Enough-Nose angel courier service. Just part-time. E-N gave me extra money to make sure my '55 Chevy, 283 cubic inches V-8, was always ready and always fast.

Their gigs were always short and sweet—and fast. But you had to be ready to go on instant notice, twenty-four hours a day. The pay was great. And you met interesting people. And angels. Anyway, one night our mixed-race bluegrass and blues band was about halfway finished playing when Elmer had an inspiration. Where it came from, I don't know.

"Say, Jawn, let's go ovah to Ritchie Avenue. You know, Jawn, *Ritchie Avenue.*"

The emphasis on "Ritchie" was his way of saying, politely, that he wanted to go over to the other colored section. He didn't want to embarrass me by mentioning race. Or himself. Or anybody else.

I wasn't touchy and he knew that. But there were lots of other people around. You never know.

One section of Ritchie Avenue branched off into an egg-shaped cul-de-sac which you couldn't see from the main road, Piney Branch Road. The people who designed and built Takoma Park did this on purpose. You could live there a long time and never know that any splibs lived there.

It was a very dark but still warm, late evening. Not a soul could we see.

There was only one streetlight in the egg. Elmer told me to park underneath it and turn my engine off.

I did.

Then he took my guitar and went and sat on the right front fender. He started quietly playing that same twelve-bar blues in E which he had played for me the day I met him.

I got out and sat on my trunk, just a little afraid. I didn't know the rules of this game.

Williams was playing slowly and as he did so doors began to open. In the secret houses. Men and women, young and old, began to take tentative gyrations. All danced alone. All danced differently.

Nobody paid any attention to us: dancer, spectator, black, white, musician. This was the original "twist." But it was very slow. Chaos was potentially everywhere, everybody was doing a different "step." But then everybody was in their own "space," as we say nowadays. And nobody "violated" anybody else's space.

You know what I mean.

The music got a little faster. A few more people came out and joined the "dance."

After about fifteen minutes, a few white folks came out of the woods from their settlement below and across Sligo Creek. They lumbered up the hill and found their own territories. "Ethan Allen Avenue" Connie, the beautiful black-haired and big boned girl emerged from Piney Branch Road. She wore a Blue and White Northwestern High School jacket just like she always did. "Northwestern Wildcats" was sewn in an arc above the embroidered face of a wildcat.

Connie? Center of my fantasies and fascination? How in the hell did she know about this? Had she been here before? Elmer had indicated he knew who she was. But that was all. Connie of the big F-hole Gibson guitar. She sang Hank Williams songs, mostly. Just like Elmer Williams had told me. I knew that, but. . . .

She waved at Elmer. Boy was I getting an education. Elmer didn't see her because he was so wrapped up in his Arthur Crudup imitation.

The music got a little faster. The rockers followed along.

Connie found her *place* and started making small, short, tentative motions. I looked at her obliquely. She saw me but ignored me. As usual.

"Nevertheless," I thought, "if this is one of her secret pleasures, she will gain some small respect for me. Seeing me in the same forbidden location, the site of the *Unheimlich* secret 'dance.'"

Nobody said a word. They just sort of jumped around once in a while. Dancing to the rhythm of my guitar—played by Elmer. Nobody knowing anything, nobody speaking, nobody thinking about what was going on. Everything was simply happening.

It was very quiet out there. Secret and thoroughly mysterious. Like a dream, almost.

Finally the cat people came out. Just a few. But they leaped and soared above everybody. Over each other, over my car they flew. There in the virtual silence of the forest primeval, the old Negro homes, a barely audible acoustic guitar sound—lost, abandoned, in the midst of time.

A non-event. A something which no one spoke of at the time. And no one would speak of in the future.

It was inconceivable and virtually occult.

I had heard of but never seen any cat people. How can I explain about them? They were ordinary human beings. Perfectly ordinary. Except they were all kind of thin—ascetic starvers. But they could leap enormous distances slowly and gracefully. It looked as if once they jumped high enough they could diminish the effect of gravity and soar slowly for short distances. I just say it because it looked that way.

I had never seen the section they lived in but I was told that they were very poor people. They were poorer than anyone else who lived along the Prince Georges County Line—the Edge, as it was called. Maybe they were nonconformists? Perhaps they were inbred? Rumors. Nothing but rumors.

But they never hurt anybody. Never bothered anybody.

Practically nobody knew them or was ever seen with them. But once in a while you would see this very old cat person smoking a pipe with Mr. Jarboe on his back porch. And I heard they knew some few of the other, older residents along the Edge.

The kids all said they were part cat. I'll leave it at that.

Uh, but of course they did wear rather strange clothes, even for that part of the country. They all wore cat masks, the main point of which was the inclusion of whiskers and great big ears. Their clothing from top to bottom was wrapped red and white cloth. From neck to ankles.

They wore mittens, too.

They were all skinny. You never saw them in the daytime.

And nobody knew exactly where in the woods they lived. And maybe they moved around a bit all the time.

About twice a year the churches took up collections for them because they had some disease or were without food.

Suddenly, I felt Williams looking at me. I stood up without looking over at him or thinking about it. Then I was walking towards him. When I got to him he pushed the guitar in my hands.

"You play."

I would have been scared, but I was slightly mesmerized along with the others. Besides, I could play that song note-for-note just like Williams did.

So I played a while. Nothing changed. Everybody kept dancing.

But after about an hour, some of the people started disappearing into their houses or into the woods. Connie had simply evaporated. Too bad. I wanted to offer her a ride home and let her know I was on the inside of things. The same inside she was inside.

I was *more* than "OK." Ha. She would remember.

Wouldn't she?

Williams was in the car, the show was over. Everybody felt and knew it was over.

But I couldn't tell you how.

The fog had gotten thicker, but that wasn't it.

So I drove my car slowly and carefully back to the Williams place.

Not one word had been spoken or sung the whole time we were in the Ritchie Hollow.

Nobody—black, white, or cat—asked me who I was or said anything to Williams. We could have been locals or we could have been from Mississippi.

Or from Mars. It wouldn't have made any difference.

All the rules had been suspended. None of the usual stuff had any significance.

For that matter, as far as I could tell, nobody regarded what had happened as particularly important.

Nobody except me. And how much did I think....

What did I think?

Well, not much, I guess. Not very much had happened.

Too bad these somethings that weren't very important didn't happen more often.

Just some music. Some dancing. Some unusual intermingling.

Yeah. Too bad.

IV. Fog

One time in 1953 me and my friends went to see Hank Williams play on the Potomac River excursion boat. It went from D.C. to Marshall Hall—Maryland—amusement park. These evening idylls were produced by some guy named Connie B. Gay.

What a name!

These boats didn't have paddlewheels anymore. But that was OK. There were lots of girls.

Who cares about paddlewheels anyway except people who are in love with the past?

None of the other writers believe that Hank Williams played this gig. I'm not going to get rhetorical and argue about it. I was there. If you don't believe me, tough.

It could, of course, have been an impostor. Fred Rose or somebody. It could have been Ira Stamphill.

After riding South for a while and looking at all the girls, the show started.

First, Jimmy Dean and his Texas Wildcats came out and did a nice, reasonably entertaining, polite, urbane, phony country music show. I can't remember what the hell they played. They always played the same things anyway. When I went to see Webb Pierce or Kitty Wells or when I went to see the same producer put on Bob Wills's last show—in the city—the Texas Wildcats warmed up and played the same damn thing every time.

In the same order, too.

After an interval of about fifteen or twenty minutes Hank swaggered and stumbled onto the stage with his band. He appeared drunk. Not only did he appear drunk, he was drunk. He talked drunk. Walked drunk. Everything he did was drunk.

Except his singing and guitar playing. Those things were not drunk at all.

First thing Williams did was curse and swear at us.

"Why dontcha all go home?" he yelled into the mike. "I hate every damned one of ya."

And what did we, the audience, do? We all yelled and screamed and applauded.

I mean I didn't start it, but I got caught up in it. You know?

"I ain't gonna sing any songs tonight. There ain't gonna be no show. I feel like hell. Yeah, why don't ya'll go straight to hell.

"Drop dead. Leave me alone."

"Aw, come on, Hank. Just sing us one song. Just one," somebody yelled.

"Nah, I don't feel so good."

"Come on, Hank," everybody yelled. "Just one."

"Oh well, hell," he said, "I guess I can give you one song. But just one. That's all."

"Hoooooooorayyyyyy."

And then he started playing, not singing, "My Bucket's Got a Hole in It," a twelve-bar blues in E.

And he played it and played it over and over again. For about ten minutes. Then he started singing. But when he did sing he only sang a few verses and then he came to an abrupt halt. It was so incredibly surprising and intense that it was frightening. After he stopped there was a silence for a long time. We were all hypnotized.

And while we were still clapping and yelling he started singing some other song and his band joined in.

He didn't sound like the guy on the records. He was ten times as good as that.

He never missed a beat or a note or a single nuance—not anything.

The band knew him much better than we did. When he started singing, they started playing without any indication from Hank as to what song he was going to sing or what key it was in.

Yeah. They knew him real well.

And he sang and played song after song. Hardly paid attention to us or the band. And when he was through, he was through. That was it. He just walked off stage, and on his way out he yelled:

"That's enough for now. Maybe I'll see y'all later. Maybe."

No amount of hand clapping and screaming brought him back out.

Everybody was happy. Very happy. Ecstatic, in fact.

Even I was, and I was no fan of Hank Williams.

At some point in the show he sang "Alone and Forsaken" and while he did that many of us almost died of grief and fright.

"Alone and Forsaken" is the greatest song of despair ever written.

But he never played my favorite of his songs, "The Singing Waterfall."

Now, I watched him carefully. I wasn't far from him. And I want to say that I don't believe the corporate lie, i.e., that he was twenty-nine years old. He was supposed to be twenty-nine that night, right? He died when he was twenty-nine. Right?

But I didn't see a twenty-nine-year-old man that night. Maybe thirty-nine. Maybe even forty-nine. But never twenty-nine.

Take a look at those photographs again. You'll see what I mean.

And listen to the sentiments expressed in a lot of his songs. Longing for death. Longing for the next world. Fascination and expectation of imminent death. This world is impossible to understand. He is sick and tired of it and wants out. World-weary. He wants out.

Those are not the sentiments of a twenty-nine-year-old man.

Pessimism, despair, yes. The hope and expectations everybody still has at twenty-nine? Never.

Hank sees nothing but trouble down the pike. He's had it.

But that night he was devastating.

He was a great songwriter. Everybody thought so. Of course, now we know that Fred Rose and Ira P. Stamphill wrote many of the songs, but surely "Hank" wrote some of them.

He even wrote a book about how to write good country-western songs. I read it. Damn good book.

"Alone and Forsaken" is the most distressing desolation song I have ever heard. It's even in a minor key.

We met in the Springtime...

By the fifth word you know it's all over and you know more in those five words—and you feel more—than it takes most song writers five stanzas or more to say. That leaves him the rest of the song to tell how he feels. But as usual there is no self-awareness, no mention of the cause of the breakup. No insight into the other's feelings and motives. These events that happen to Hank come uncaused, from out of the blue. They are complete mysteries to Hank and to us.

Life is uncannily unbearable. We've all been there. What's the point in trying to figure things out? Life on earth is incomprehensible. Why bother?

He does manage to pull an incredible *coup de grâce* in this song. An entirely new sentiment. Even though he's living in the desert and life is hell without her and he hears wild dogs and senses the coming of the Apocalypse, he sang,

Oh where has she gone to, where can she be
She may be forsaken by another like me.

Hank is worried about her!

This sentiment I have never heard anyone else sing.

The left-alone lover is always mad and sad, encompassed by self-pity. Never concern for the other.

Hank and his doubles came into the big-time Nashville Music Biz scene by writing songs for Molly O'Day. *I* think that Nose and Stamphill wrote the pop songs like "Setting the Woods on Fire,"

"Hey, Good Lookin'," etc. And I think he wrote the religious songs and "The Singing Waterfall," and, of course, "I've Got a Mansion Just Over the Hilltop." Other Williams fans think it's the other way around.

I believe the real Hank wrote "I Don't Care if Tomorrow Never Comes" and "When the Pale Horse and His Rider Go By."

I suppose he wrote "I Saw the Light," and I hope he did.

I don't like "Jambalaya" or "Hey, Good Lookin'." White trash kitsch!

The guy I saw that night was a magnet for demons.

Molly O'Day's band had an incredible sound. All acoustic instruments. (I know there were a few recordings with one or more electric instrument, so what?) Dobro, fiddle, flat-top guitar, and mandolin. Great instrumentalists and side vocalists. In fact if you listen closely, Molly is the weakest singer in the group.

Sometimes she plays a banjo.

Molly quit recording because she came to believe that music is a gift of God and shouldn't be sold. And of course she had to stop singing sinful tunes like "Poor Ellen Smith."

Then Hank was recorded on the Sterling label. Despite the enormous amount of money Hank fans will pay for these records, they aren't all that rare and must have sold quite well.

MGM bought the masters and issued them on their own label and then continued to record Hank.

He was brought to the Grand Ole Opry and brought the house down many times.

And now with the publicity of being a big hit on the "opera" and with the presumably better distribution of MGM Records, Williams suddenly found himself rolling in dough.

All his life he had suffered from a very painful disease, "open spine." And he had always been a drinker and hellraiser. He had a terrible neurosis. He had lived hard and showed his many years.

And now add an incredibly intense ongoing pace and schedule—it was all too much for him. He started taking pain pills and downers and washing them down with more and more booze.

He was frequently semi-comatose, and he started making no-shows. More and more no-shows.

Club owners and booking agents were afraid to book him.

He found himself in a vicious circle. The more no-shows he made and the more he didn't get bookings the worse he felt so he drank and took dope for that reason, too. And that in turn caused more no-shows and around and around and around. See how it works?

Ira and Nose and his wife did all they could for him.

Nothing.

So one day he accidentally woke up sober and saw that his career was in shambles and disintegrating more and more. So what did he do? He called up his friend Claude Boone and asked him if he, Hank, could come out and stay with him in his home in the forest and the two of them read the Bible a lot and ask the Lord to help him kick all this stuff.

Put his career back together again.

Boone personally didn't care much about Hank's career but he liked Hank and was always ready to help out a backslider. I mean he was willing to put in a lot of time with Hank and the Lord for Hank. And he did. He, Boone, told me all about it. He was Carl Storey's bass player for many years. Carl Storey's big shtick was gospel. I liked and still like Storey a lot.

About '59 or '60, Storey came to New River Ranch, Rising Sun, Maryland, on a sunny Sunday.

I talked with Boone and he told me all about it.

He even knew about the river boat show.

Boone had had a hit called "Burglar Man," but he was suspicious of city life and glamor and saw music biz, and especially music biz in re Williams, as a dangerous occasion of sin. He personally avoided it now except to play with Carl. That was safe because Carl was gradually changing his show and de-emphasizing secular songs. Pretty soon it would be a purely religious enterprise. Boone encouraged Carl in this respect.

In re Hank though, he tried to talk him out of music biz alto-gether. Hank was too well-loved for his secular stuff.

If Hank was on the road he would have to sing the sinful tunes. Not that Hank avoided gospel songs. He always sang several at each of his shows. Not just one. Several.

But it didn't work and Boone saw that.

But Hank was old and he was thoroughly mated to raising hell on the road, if not at home. Boone came to realize Hank wouldn't give up the road, but still he spent a lot of time praying with and for Hank and reading the Bible and meditating on the parables and beatitudes with Hank. How could he refuse him? That man was really in trouble.

And Hank? Hank loved reading the Bible with Claude. Hank loved Jesus and God very much.

This was no show with Hank. He was really into Christ and Christianity.

And they even fasted together out there.

The only thing that would have saved Hank's sanity—and his life, as it turns out—was for Hank to quit the road and live off royalties. But he said he couldn't do that. Something about big money debts.

And, let's be honest, Hank loved to raise hell.

Please, please, do not think that I am in anyway putting Hank Williams down. While I am telling you the truth I am also thor-oughly in sympathy with the man. I'm not joking. I've made my money off music biz for many years and I have the same problems with the exception of the spinal problem. But I've got pain in other parts. Lots of pain. I know what it's like.

Hank was no longer in control of himself. I wonder if he ever really was in control. I think maybe it just looked that way and when he was younger it looked better—his raising hell—and didn't hurt him so much or show so much.

But I don't want to argue about that. I just don't want you look-ing down on Hank. You, me, and Hank are not really very different people, even if it looks that way.

The pressure is a hell of a lot different. That and the disease—that's the only difference.

Anyway, all of this action with Claude Boone and God and the woods and the Bible—it was too late. That's the title of one of Hank's songs. "Too Late—Too Late." Humpty Hank couldn't be put back together again. Not at thirty-nine or forty-nine years. Never.

No mortar left. He should have quit but he couldn't.

He had let himself be booked and he had to go.

Hank didn't have any illusions about what was going to happen. Hank saw disaster down the road.

And as it turned out I got to see his last performance. Of course I couldn't have known that at the time—but I tell you in all seriousness Hank was Apocalyptic that night on the Potomac River. He was dynamite.

It's entirely possible that I saw the best show he ever gave.

Anyway, after the down-river show was over the river boat stopped at Marshall Hall amusement park and dropped anchor for a couple of hours.

My friends and I knew we couldn't get backstage and see Hank. We were too young. Later in life I became a maven at this and met all kinds of musicians and other kinds of artists.

So we walked ashore and went looking for girls.

V. The Singing Waterfall

At some point I saw a girl in the distance waving at me and flagging me to come over to her.

It looked like big-boned, beautiful, black-haired Gibson guitar-playing Connie. So I moved out towards her but somewhere along the way I got engulfed by a cloud of fog.

I couldn't tell where I was for a while. I walked and walked, but just more fog.

Finally the fog began to lift and I was able to see that the scene had shifted and I was back on Ritchie Avenue, not far from my home.

It was, as before, very dark in the Negro cul-de-sac. There was a lot of smoke all over the landscape such that I could hardly see. There had been a big crab feast in the unpaved street. We used giant trash cans to cook the crabs and to keep us warm. That's where the smoke came from. Everybody had gone to sleep. The fires were burning out slowly and that made very thick smoke and lots of it.

And as the flames and smoke dwindled I could see that the strange cat people were still out. They were leaping over the trash cans, gracefully silent, to and fro, to and fro, through the smoke from the fires, silently leaping through the smoke, to and fro, the smoke from the fires burning silently, virtually flying back and forth flew the cat people, back and forth, to and fro, to and fro, on and on up and down over and across, down and under, under and over across and over, to and fro, down and over, and then I heard someone walking towards me from out of the forest. I wasn't surprised. Remember, I worked for Enough-Nose angel courier service. Things like this happened to me all the time. See, I am a mystic. That's another reason I could do that work so well. I wasn't afraid of death. However....

"Who's that? I can't quite see you."

"It's just Hank. Hank Williams."

"I work with Acuff-Rose and Stamphill. You got a message for me to deliver?"

"Well," he said, stepping out into the light, "yes, but it's a heavy message. A little more than your average run. I want you to help someone for me."

"Sure, Hank, no problem. I'll take the gig."

"Wait a minute, son," he said, putting a hand on my shoulder, "you don't know who the recipient is yet.

"It's Connie," he said.

"Oh, that's tough, Hank. I gotta tell you something. She doesn't pay any attention to me. It's like I'm invisible to her."

"Not since she heard you play the guitar that night, son. Not any more."

"Oh you mean she was still here when I took over for Elmer?"

"Yes and she was very impressed. I was, too, by the way."

"Uh...."

"You still wondering about the connection between her and Elmer? Don't worry, son. It's not what you thought. She didn't climb all over *him* or anything. My daughter is not stupid and neither is Elmer. There was a time around here, not so long ago, when Elmer would have gotten lynched for hanging around her, teaching her guitar, and he knows it."

"Uh...your daughter? Uh...."

"OK, well," said Hank, "Connie is my natural daughter. Elmer Williams is a natural child of Emmett Miller. Mixed. Connie knows all this. But the Connie-Elmer Williams connection is purely musical.

"They teach each other Hank Williams songs or, if you will, songs by and attributed to me by Ira or Fred. That part you know about. But it's OK if you tell them. I don't care. Oh, and *my* real father's name is Emmett Miller, too."

"Wow. What a story. OK, I think I got it right except for one thing. *What* are you?"

"Oh, I am an angel, son. Always have been. Mostly earthbound these days, but the bigwigs in Sinspiration work me pretty hard, too. Wait till you graduate!"

"Wow."

"I run a lot of errands for the biggies at Sinspiration and the Moody Bible Institute, but I've got a lot of loose ends to tie up down here. I left some incomplete processes around and created some strange configurations. But I have permission to clean them up.

"And that's why I'm here tonight and that's why you're here.

"I'll tell you about that shortly, but you know what I've been doing all day?" he asked me.

"No."

"I've been up in West Virginia practicing my death tonight.

"But of course there's no such thing as death to us believers. Are you a believer, son? Have you been saved?"

"Oh, yes, Hank. When I was twelve, a traveling widget salesman came by and since he couldn't sell us any widgets he talked me and my parents into performing

THE GREAT OUR LADY OF SORROWS KALI PUJA.

"So we were all baptized into the dharma just like you.

"But," I said, a little confused, "if you were in West Virginia all day, who was that guy on stage on the river boat? You don't have omnipresence, do you?"

"Oh that, yes, I see. No, I haven't reached omnipresence, yet. Well, tonight it was either Ira or Fred. I don't really know. My booking agent handles all that stuff. They're both cousins anyway. We can all impersonate each other so well that you can't tell the difference."

"But, Hank, surely there must be a central personality. Either that or you're all three of you schizophrenics—or worse."

"Oh, we made up a persona for the public. We just used split-off parts of each one of us. Spare parts. They're not really so bad. And to create a loony musician, why that's all you need, boy—spare parts.

"As for the core personality, we're all three just different aspects of God. Nothing unusual."

"I see," I said. "Well, tell me this, Hank. Who wrote 'The Singing Waterfall'? That's my favorite of 'your' songs."

"Oh well, son, I have good news. *I* wrote that one. Really, I did. It was me. Oh, by the way, I forgot to tell you—I'm also your guardian angel. I'll be around a lot, especially after you and—well, be patient, you'll find out more about that later."

"About what?"

"When you hear me laughing late at night—then you'll remember—and you'll understand, too."

To and fro, the cat people were still leaping back and forth silently above us through the light blue haze. The fires were still slightly burning. Back and forth, to and fro, to and fro, ever so silently, secretly there in the middle of Takoma Park forest where nobody could see.

"Let's get back to Connie," he said.

"Fine," I said. "There's something I wanted to ask you about."

"Shoot."

"OK, does Connie know that you are her father?"

"Oh yes, Jawn, she certainly does. We're very good friends now. I settled a big estate on her when she was born. I visit her sometimes. I'm *her* guardian angel, too. And who do you think bought her that big Gibson box she's got? You haven't heard her sing 'Singing Waterfall' yet. When you do, you, son, will melt."

"OK," I said, "what did you want to ask me about Connie?"

"I want you to deliver her from the gossip."

"Oh, that. I heard about it. I don't believe it. And if it is true I would still be on her side."

"It's been going on for months and Connie is not aware of it. Nobody will talk to her at school anymore and she's very, very lonely and sad."

"I heard she threw a party at her house and got drunk. She passed out on her bed. Some guys came in and gang-banged her. She never noticed it. Yeah, I heard it. I don't believe it. I'll help her if she'll let me, but...."

"You really mean that, son?" Hank asked.

"Yes," and I bowed my head in resignation. "I'm in love with her. I'll do anything to help her if I can."

"Oh you can, you can. She'll take to you if you'll help her and remember—she heard you play guitar and she liked it. She liked it a lot."

"So what do I do?"

"Well, Jawn, tomorrow you better be with her in the afternoon and evening because that's when she's going to find out about it. A little after noon."

"OK, I'll go over there, but what can I do for her, Hank?"

"Listen, son, when the news hits her she's going to need somebody around that she can trust. She's not going to care how old you are or whether you can play the guitar or not. This is serious stuff."

"Yeah, it is."

"Connie always trusted everybody. She has a good heart. This is going to break her. I want you to go over there and take care of her, stay with her, listen to her, play shrink, and maybe even fight for her. All you really have to do is be there for her and listen to her. That will probably get her over the grief and anger. But one thing, though . . . ."

"Yes?"

"Please do encourage her to fight. Fight for herself. You both go find the ringleader and beat her and her friends up. They started this gossip just because they're jealous of her. But one thing, though. If you're in love with her, don't rush her after the fight. These things take time to get over."

The cat people were gone now. The fires were out. We were completely alone.

"OK, Hank," I said, "I'll do it. The best I can, anyway."

Then suddenly I was back at Marshall Hall with my friends.

"Where you been, Fahey? You disappeared," said one of my friends.

My brain was still on the other side of the river with Hank and Connie on Ritchie Avenue.

"Don't ask me. You wouldn't believe me anyway." So that's all I said.

The river boat returned to Washington and one of Hank's country cousins cursed out the audience and then sang more of "Hank's" hits. I couldn't tell the difference, and neither could anyone else.

Hell, for all I know I might've been talking with Stamphill or Nose or Emmett Miller for that matter.

But tomorrow I would help Connie—if only she'd let me.

VI. High Noon Connie

Next day, high noon. I felt like Gary Cooper. I knocked on Connie's screen door. It was very hot out there on Ethan Allen Avenue where the concrete turns to asphalt.

Eventually Connie came to the door. She was crying continuously and held a box of Kleenex tissues in her hand.

"What do *you* want?" she asked. "Listen, I've had enough trouble today to last a lifetime. I feel like I'm going to die and I wish I could, so...."

"I know all about it, Connie. Your father told me."

"My father! *You* don't know who my father is. Nobody knows except me."

"I know who he is. He told me. I just saw him last night. He sends his love."

"Oh sure. Last night you talked to him, eh? Well, OK, if you know his name what is it?"

"He wrote 'The Singing Waterfall' and taught it to you."

"Ohmygod," she said. "How in the...."

"I saw him last night. He's an angel now and he came to visit me and he told me everything. And he told me to come and see you through this. Take care of you. I said I would. I am on your side no matter what. Can I come in now? I'm your friend. I won't hurt you."

She unlocked the screen door and let me pass by, and we both sat down on the sofa.

"Do you believe the gossip, Johnny?" Well! She did know my name.

"No, Connie, I don't believe it, but if I did it wouldn't matter to me. I'd still feel the same way about you."

"What way?" But before I could answer her she threw herself and her tears all against me and started wailing.

So I just sat there and held her and kind of rocked her back and forth gently and hummed "The Singing Waterfall," and she cried and she cried and cried and....

We remained that way a long time, and she cried and cried but after a while she began to slow down, just tears coming out.

She sighed. "Oh, what am I going to do?" she asked. "Would you like some lemonade—or iced tea? It's very hot and I've been climbing all over you and crying on you."

So we had some iced tea. Then we cried some more and she clung to me like the I was the Rock of Gibraltar. Much later, her parents came home from work.

She introduced me and then she asked me if I would like to stay for dinner.

Then her parents noticed that her face was all red and that she had been crying.

She explained that some people had been gossiping about her and that none of it was true and that I had come over to help her clear things up.

During dinner her mother asked me if I lived nearby.

"Right around the corner in those apartments on New Hampshire Avenue, right on the east edge of the Edge. I work at Martin's Esso."

This was a big deal because we were the only place in the county that was open all night long. We—I—was an institution. The cops rendezvoused there and hung out there.

After dinner, Connie asked me if I would really help her stop the gossip, and I said I would.

And I did.

The very next day we took the long, frightful walk through Evil Montgomery County and found the ringleader girl and Connie beat the hell out of her. She never talked about Connie again. Then we found the others, and I helped her beat them up, too.

And the talk stopped altogether at once.

And when the battle—the external battle—was over we walked the long walk back to her house and sat down on the sofa again.

"It's all over," she said. "How can I ever repay you, Johnny?"

"Don't worry about it. You don't have to pay me back. Forget it.

"Just play me 'The Singing Waterfall,'" I said.

"OK."

And she sang:

> There's a singing waterfall in the mountains far away,
> That's where I long to be at the close of every day.

That's where my sweetheart's sleeping, beneath the cold, cold clay,
And I often sit and wonder why the Lord took him away.

We met there every evening, as the sun was setting low,
And listened to the water, as it whispered soft and low,
But since he's gone to Heaven, I miss him most of all.
Tonight my darling's sleeping by the singing waterfall.

Last night as I lay sleeping, I heard my loved one call,
And then I went to meet him by the singing waterfall.
He took me in his arms, just like he used to do,
And then I heard him whisper, "We'll meet beyond the blue."

In the ensuing months, the weather cooled off and we hung out a lot together. She sang me "The Singing Waterfall" a few more times. And each time I did melt, just like Hank said I would. We took things slowly. There was no need to rush and her father had cautioned me not to rush. I didn't make much money working at Martin's Esso so when the time came and we got married, I moved in with her. Her parents liked me and we got along just fine. Couldn't be happier. But you know sometimes at night I wake up, we wake up, and the air and the trees are still and it's not raining—but we hear some almost musical sounding water splashing around somewhere in the distance. And we hear somebody laughing up a storm.

Laughing and laughing just to let us know he's there.

I mean, I think that's why he's laughing.

Don't you?